For the Warped Spacers,

the group who was there from the very beginning . . .

and who still make me look my best

THE BONE LABYRINTH

A Σ SIGMA FORCE NOVEL

JAMES ROLLINS

WILLIAM MORROW
An Imprint of HarperCollins *Publishers*

This is a work of fiction. Names, characters, places, and incidents are products of the author's imagination or are used fictitiously and are not to be construed as real. Any resemblance to actual events, locales, organizations, or persons, living or dead, is entirely coincidental.

HarperCollins books may be purchased for educational, business, or sales promotional use. For information, please e-mail the Special Markets Department at SPsales@harpercollins.com.

Map provided and drawn by Steve Prey. All rights reserved. Used by permission of Steve Prey.

FIRST EDITION

Library of Congress Cataloging-in-Publication Data has been applied for.

ISBN 978-0-06-238164-4 (hardcover)
ISBN 978-0-06-240948-5 (international edition)
ISBN 978-0-06-240950-8 (international edition)

15 16 17 18 19   DIX/RRD   10 9 8 7 6 5 4 3 2 1

ACKNOWLEDGMENTS

So many folks have their fingerprints all over this book. I appreciate all their help, criticism, and encouragement. First, I must thank my first readers, my first editors, and some of my best friends: Sally Anne Barnes, Chris Crowe, Lee Garrett, Jane O'Riva, Denny Grayson, Leonard Little, Scott Smith, Judy Prey, Caroline Williams, Christian Riley, Tod Todd, Chris Smith, and Amy Rogers. And as always, a special thanks to Steve Prey for the great maps . . . and to Cherei McCarter for all the cool tidbits that pop in my e-mail box! To David Sylvian for accomplishing everything and anything asked of him and for making sure I put my best digital foot forward at all times! To everyone at HarperCollins for always having my back, especially Michael Morrison, Liate Stehlik, Danielle Bartlett, Kaitlyn Kennedy, Josh Marwell, Lynn Grady, Richard Aquan, Tom Egner, Shawn Nicholls, and Ana Maria Allessi. Last, of course, a special acknowledgment to the people instrumental to all levels of production: my editor, Lyssa Keusch, and her colleague Rebecca Lucash; and my agents, Russ Galen and Danny Baror (along with his daughter Heather Baror). And as always, I must stress that any and all errors of fact or detail in this book fall squarely on my own shoulders; hopefully there are not too many.

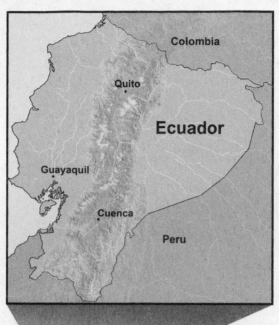

NOTES FROM THE HISTORICAL RECORD

Two historical figures play prominent roles in this book: a pair of priests who lived centuries apart but who were tied together by fate.

During the seventeenth century, Father Athanasius Kircher was known as the Leonardo da Vinci of the Jesuit Order. Like his namesake, the priest was a master of a hundred disciplines. He studied medicine, geology, and Egyptology, and engineered intricate automatons, including a magnetic clock (a reconstruction of which can be found at the Green Library in Stanford University). This Renaissance man and his work would eventually influence figures throughout the ages, from Descartes to Newton, from Jules Verne to Edgar Allan Poe.

But also one other.

Father Carlos Crespi was born centuries later in 1891. Inspired by Kircher's work, Crespi became a monk of many talents himself. He was a botanist, an anthropologist, a historian, and a musician. He eventually settled as a missionary in a small town in Ecuador, where he served for fifty years. It was there that a vast cache of ancient gold artifacts came into his possession, delivered to him by the Shuar natives of the region. Stories claimed the objects came from a cavern system that spanned the breadth of South America, one rumored to hold a lost library of ancient metal plates and crystal books. The relics bore strange depictions and were inscribed with indecipherable hieroglyphics.

Some archaeologists believed these artifacts were fakes; others came to trust the priest's story of the objects' origins. Either way, in 1962, a mysterious fire destroyed the museum that housed most of these artifacts, and the Ecuadorian government locked away the few that remained.

So how much of Father Crespi's story was true and how much was pure fabrication? No one knows. Still, no one questions that this devout monk *believed* his story, or that the vast cache *existed*.

In fact, in 1976, a British military and scientific team sought to find this lost subterranean library, only to end up in the wrong cavern system. Oddly, this expedition was headed by an American—none other than Neil Armstrong, the first man to walk on the moon.

What drew out such this solitary and reclusive American hero, one who seldom gave interviews? The answer connects to an even greater mystery, one that threatens the very foundation of our place in this world.

NOTES FROM THE SCIENTIFIC RECORD

A fundamental mystery tied to our origins—to what makes us *human*—can be summarized by a single question: *Why are we so smart?*

The evolution of human intelligence still puzzles scientists and philosophers. Yes, it's possible to trace the growth of our brains from earlier hominins through the emergence of *Homo sapiens* some 200,000 years ago. But what remains unknown is *why* our species suddenly and inexplicably had a burst of intelligence 50,000 years ago.

Anthropologists refer to this moment in time as the Great Leap Forward. It appears in the fossil record as a sudden explosion of art, music, even advancements in weaponry. Anatomically, nothing had changed in the sizes of our brains to explain this leap of ingenuity, yet something fundamental must have occurred to cause that abrupt spike in intelligence and consciousness. Theories abound, attributing this event to climate change, to genetic mutations, even to alterations in diet and nutrition.

Even more disconcerting is that for the past 10,000 years our brains have been *shrinking* in size—by a full 15 percent as of today. What does this new change mean? What does it portend for our future? The answer may lie in solving the mystery of that Great Leap Forward. But as of yet, no firm conclusion has come to the forefront to explain this pivotal development in human history.

Until now.

And with the revelations found within these pages, a more disturbing question arises: Are we at the cusp of a second Great Leap Forward? Or are we doomed to fall backward once again?

Intelligence is an accident of evolution, and not necessarily an advantage.

—ISAAC ASIMOV

The measure of *intelligence* is the ability to change.

—ALBERT EINSTEIN

THE BONE LABYRINTH

Autumn, 38,000 B.C.
Southern Alps

"Run, child!"

Fires lit the woods behind them. For the past day, the flames had chased K'ruk and his daughter higher into the snowy mountains. But it was not the choking smoke or searing heat that K'ruk feared most. He searched behind him, seeking to catch a glimpse of the hunters, those who had set the forest afire in pursuit of the pair, but he saw no sign of the enemy.

Still, he heard the howling of wolves in the distance, great beasts that bowed to the will of those hunters. The pack sounded closer now, only a valley away.

He glanced worriedly toward the sun as it sat near the horizon. The ruddy glow in the sky reminded him of the promise of warmth that lay in that direction, of their home caves tunneled under green hills and black rock, where water still flowed and the deer and bison roamed thickly in the woods of the lower slopes.

He imagined those home fires blazing bright, spitted meat dripping fat into the sizzling flames, the clan gathering together before settling in for the night. He longed for that old life, but he knew that path was no longer open to him—and especially not for his daughter.

A sharp cry of pain drew his attention forward. Onka had slipped on a moss-slick rock and fallen hard. She was normally surefooted, but they had been in flight for three long days.

He hurried to her and pulled her up, her young face shining with fear and sweat. He stopped long enough to cup her cheek. In her small features, he saw whispers of her mother, a clan healer who had died shortly after Onka was born. He curled a finger in his daughter's fiery hair.

So like your mother's . . .

But he also saw more in Onka's features, those aspects that branded her as different. Her nose was thinner than any of K'ruk's clan, even for a girl of only nine winters. Her brow was also straighter, less heavy. He stared into her blue eyes, as bright as a summer sky. That shine and those features marked her as a blended spirit, someone who walked halfway between K'ruk's people and those who had come recently from the south with their thinner limbs and quicker tongues.

Such special children were said to be omens, proving by their births how the two tribes—new and old—could live together in peace. Perhaps not in the same caves, but they could at least share the same hunting grounds. And as the two tribes grew closer, more were born like Onka. These children were revered. They looked at the world with different eyes, becoming great shamans, healers, or hunters.

Then two days ago, a clansman from a neighboring valley had arrived. He had been wounded unto death, but he still had enough breath to warn of a mighty enemy, a blight spreading across the mountains. This mysterious clan came in large numbers, hunting for such special ones as Onka. No tribes were allowed to harbor such children. Those that did were slaughtered.

Upon hearing of this, K'ruk knew he could not jeopardize his clan, nor would he allow Onka to be taken. So he had fled with his daughter, but someone must have alerted the enemy about their flight.

About Onka.

I will not let them have you.

He took her hand and set a harder pace, but before long, Onka was stumbling more than walking, limping on her injured ankle. He picked her up as they crested a ridge and stared down into the forest below. A creek cut along the bottom, promising a place to drink.

"We can rest there," he said, pointing. "But only for a short—"

A branch snapped off to the left. Dropping into a wary crouch, he lowered Onka and raised his stone-tipped spear. A slender shape appeared from behind a deadfall, cloaked and booted in reindeer leather. Their gazes met. Even without a word spoken, K'ruk knew this other was like Onka, one born of mixed spirits. But from his clothing and from the way he tied his shaggy hair with a leather cord, it was clear he was not of K'ruk's clan but from those slender-limbed tribes who came later to these mountains.

Another howl rose behind them, sounding even closer.

The stranger cocked his ear, listening; then a hand rose and beckoned. Words were spoken, but K'ruk did not understand them. Finally, the stranger simply waved his arm, pointed toward the creek, and set off down the wooded slope.

K'ruk considered whether to follow, but another baying of the enemy's wolves set him off after the stranger. He fled, carrying Onka to keep up with the man's agile passage. Reaching the creek, they discovered others waiting for them there, a group of ten or twelve, some younger than Onka, others hunchbacked elders. They bore markings from several clans.

Still, the group shared one common feature.

They were all of mixed spirits.

The stranger came forward and dropped to a knee before Onka. A finger touched her brow and ran along her cheekbone, plainly recognizing Onka as one of a similar kind.

His daughter in turn reached and touched a marking on the stranger's forehead: a pebbling of scars in a strange pointed shape.

Onka's fingertip ran over those bumps as if finding hidden meaning there. The other grinned, seeming to sense the child's understanding.

The stranger straightened and laid a palm upon his own chest. "Teron," he said.

K'ruk knew this must be his name, but the stranger spoke rapidly after that, waving to one of the elders who leaned heavily upon a thick gnarled staff.

The old man came forward and spoke in K'ruk's people's tongue. "Teron says the girl may join us. We are heading through a high pass that Teron knows, one that is yet free of ice, but only for another few days. If we can make it ahead of the enemy, we can break the hunters from our trail."

"Until those snows thaw again," K'ruk added worriedly.

"That won't be for many moons. We will have vanished by then, our trail long cold."

A fresh howling of wolves in the distance reminded them that the trail was far from cold at the moment.

The elder recognized this, too. "We must go now before they fall upon us."

"And you will take my daughter?" He pushed Onka toward Teron.

Teron reached and gripped K'ruk by the shoulder, squeezing a promise with his strong fingers.

"She is welcome," the elder assured him. "We will protect her. But on this long trek, we could use your strong back and sharp spear."

K'ruk took a step away and gripped the shaft of his weapon more firmly. "The enemy comes too swiftly. I will use my last breaths to turn them from your trail or hold them off long enough for you and the others to reach the pass."

Onka's gaze met his, already teary-eyed with understanding. "Papa . . ."

His chest ached as he spoke. "This is your clan now, Onka. They will see you to better lands, where you will be safe and where you will grow into the strong woman I know you can be."

Onka broke free of Teron's grip and leaped at K'ruk, wrapping her thin arms around his neck.

With grief choking him as much as his daughter's arms, he pulled Onka free and passed her to Teron, who hugged her from behind. K'ruk leaned and touched his forehead to Onka's brow, saying good-bye, knowing he would never see his daughter again.

He then stood, turned, and strode away from the creek, heading up the slope toward the howling of wolves—but all he heard were the plaintive cries of Onka behind him.

Live well, my child.

He climbed more swiftly, determined to keep her safe. Once he reached the ridgeline, he sped toward the baying of the hunters' beasts. Their cries had grown more raucous, rising from the next valley over.

He ran now, loping in great strides.

He reached the next crest as the sun sank away, filling the valley below with shadows. Slowing, he descended more cautiously, warily, especially as the wolves had gone silent now. He ducked low, sliding from shadow to shadow, staying downwind of the pack, careful of each step so as not to snap a branch.

At last he could spy the bottom of the valley, noting the stirring of darkness below. The wolves. One of the beasts shifted fully into view, revealing a shape unlike any wolf. Its mane was heavily matted. Scars marked its massive bulk. Lips rippled back to reveal long, yellowed fangs.

Though his heart pounded in his throat, K'ruk remained crouched, waiting for the masters of those monstrous beasts to show themselves.

Finally, taller shadows folded out of the trees. The largest stepped into view and revealed the true face of the enemy for the first time.

K'ruk went cold at the sight, terror icing through him.

No, it cannot be . . .

Still, he tightened his grip on his spear and glanced over his shoulder.

Run, Onka. Run and never stop.

Spring 1669
Rome, Papal States

Nicolas Steno marched the young emissary through the depths of the museum of the Collegio Romano. The stranger was heavily cloaked, his boots muddy, all a plain testament to both his urgency and secrecy.

The German messenger had been dispatched by Leopold I, the Holy Roman Emperor to the north. The package he carried was intended for Nicolas's dear friend, Father Athanasius Kircher, the creator of this museum.

The emissary gaped at the many curiosities of nature found here, at the Egyptian obelisks, at the mechanical wonders that ticked and hummed, all crowned overhead by soaring domes decorated with astronomical details. The young man's gaze caught upon a boulder of amber, lit behind by candlelight, revealing the preserved body of a lizard inside.

"Don't tarry," Nicolas warned and drew the messenger onward.

Nicolas knew every corner of this place, every bound volume, mostly works by the master of this museum. Nicolas had spent the better part of a year here, sent by his own benefactor, the Grand Duke of Tuscany, to study the museum's contents in order to construct his own cabinet of curiosities back at the duke's palazzo in Florence.

At last he reached a tall oak door and pounded a fist on it.

A voice responded. "Enter."

He hauled the door open and ushered the emissary into a small study, lit by the coals of a dying fire. "I'm sorry to disturb you, Reverend Father."

The German messenger immediately dropped to one knee before the wide desk, bowing his head.

A long sigh rose from the figure bent amid the piles of books atop the desk. He held a quill in hand, the tip poised over a large parchment. "Come to rifle through my collection yet again, dear Nicolas? I should tell you that I've taken to numbering the books shelved here."

Nicolas smiled. "I promise to return my copy of *Mundus Subterraneus* once I've fully refuted many of your claims found therein."

"Is that so? I hear you're putting the final flourishes upon your own work concerning the subterranean mysteries of rock and crystal."

He bowed his head in acknowledgment. "Indeed. But before I present it, I would humbly welcome a similar searing analysis from one such as yourself."

After Nicolas had arrived here a year ago, the two had spent many long nights in deep discourse concerning all manner of science, theology, and philosophy. Though Kircher was thirty-seven years his elder and deserved respect, the priest appreciated anyone willing to challenge him. In fact, upon their first meeting, the pair had argued vigorously concerning a paper Nicolas had published two years previously, declaring that glossopetrae or "tongue stones" found embedded in rocks were actually the teeth of ancient sharks. Father Kircher held a similar interest in bones and pieces of the past locked in stratified stone. They had hotly debated the origin of such mysteries. It was in such a crucible of scientific inquiry that the two had become each other's admirers, colleagues, and most of all, friends.

Father Kircher's gaze settled upon the emissary, still on bended knee before his overloaded desk. "And who is your companion?"

"He comes with a package from Leopold I. It would seem the emperor has remembered enough of his Jesuit education to send something of import to your doorstep. Leopold appealed to the Grand Duke to have me present this man to you with some urgency, under a cloak of dire secrecy."

Father Kircher lowered his quill. "Intriguing."

They both knew the current emperor had an interest in science and the natural world, instilled in him by the Jesuit scholars who had tutored the man in his youth. Emperor Leopold himself had been headed into the church until the death of his older brother to the pox placed the pious scholar on that cold northern throne.

Father Kircher waved to the messenger. "Enough of this foolish posturing, my good man. Stand and deliver what you've traveled so far to present."

The emissary rose up and pulled back the cowl of his hood, revealing the face of a young man who could not be more than twenty years. From a satchel, he retrieved a thick letter, plainly sealed with the emperor's sigil. He stepped forward and placed it upon the desk, then quickly stepped back.

Kircher glanced toward Nicolas, who merely shrugged, equally in the dark about the particulars of this matter.

Kircher retrieved a knife and slit through the seal to open the package. A small object rolled out and toppled to the desktop. It was a bone, frosted with crystalline rock. Pinching his brow, Kircher pulled out and unfolded a parchment included with the artifact. Even from steps away, Nicolas saw it was a detailed map of eastern Europe. Father Kircher studied it for a breath.

"I don't understand the meaning of all of this," Kircher said. "This map and this bit of old bone. They come with no letter of explanation."

The emissary finally spoke, his Italian thickly accented. "The emperor chose me to deliver the other half of this message, words I was sworn to set to memory and reveal only to you, Reverend Father."

"And what are those words?"

"The emperor knows of your interest in the ancient past, in those secrets buried in the bowels of the earth, and requests your aid in investigating what was revealed at the site marked on the map."

"And what might be found there?" Nicolas asked. "More bones, such as this?"

He stepped closer and studied the ossified sliver, the crusts of whitish rock. He sensed the great antiquity of what lay upon the desk.

"Bones and much more," the messenger concurred.

"And who do these bones belong to?" Kircher asked. "Whose grave do they mark?"

The young man answered, his words shocking. Then, before either man could respond, the messenger swiftly drew out a dagger and sliced his own throat from ear to ear. Blood poured forth as the man choked and collapsed first to his knees, then to the floor.

Nicolas rushed to the young man's aid, cursing at such brutal necessity. It seemed those final words were meant only for Father Kircher and himself, and once dispatched, were never to be spoken again.

Father Kircher rounded his desk and dropped to a knee, taking the young man's hand between his palms, but his question was for Nicolas. "Could it be true?"

Nicolas swallowed, dismayed by the last message spoken through those bloody lips.

The bones . . . they belong to Adam and Eve.

FIRST

BLOOD AND SHADOWS

1

We shouldn't be here.

A trickle of superstitious dread stopped Roland Novak on a switch-back of the trail. He raised his hand against the morning sun and stared at the craggy mountaintop ahead. Black clouds stacked in the distance.

According to Croatian folktales—stories he had heard as a child—during stormy nights, witches and fairies would gather atop the summit of Klek Mountain, where their screams would be heard all the way to the neighboring city of Ogulin. It was a peak haunted by tales of the unwary or the unlucky meeting horrible fates.

For centuries, such legends had kept the peak fairly unmolested. But in the past few decades that had changed when the crag's towering cliffs drew an ever-increasing number of local rock climbers. Still, this was not why Roland and the others risked scaling the northern side of the mountain this morning.

"It's not much farther," Alex Wrightson promised. "Best we be in and out before the storm hits."

The British geologist led the foursome, looking as solidly built as these peaks, though he had to be close to seventy years old. He wore khaki hiking shorts despite the chill, revealing strong, wiry legs. His snow-white hair, fuller than Roland's own receding blond hairline, was tucked under a climbing helmet.

"That's the third time he's claimed that," Lena Crandall mumbled under her breath to Roland. A fine sheen of perspiration from the hour-long climb made her cheeks glow, but she didn't seem winded. Then again, she was in her midtwenties, and from the well-worn boots on her feet, he figured she must do a fair amount of hiking herself.

She stared at the skies, studying the towering wall of dark clouds. "Luckily I was able to get here a day early," she said. "Once that storm breaks, these mountains will be swamped for who knows how long."

In acknowledgment of that threat, the group set a harder pace up the unmarked trail. Lena unzipped her thermal expedition jacket and adjusted an old backpack higher on her shoulders. It bore the logo for Emory University, her alma mater in Atlanta, Georgia. Roland knew little else about this American, except that she was a geneticist who had been called away from a fellowship at the Max Planck Institute for Evolutionary Anthropology in Leipzig, Germany. And like Roland, she was equally in the dark about the reason behind this sudden summons by the British geologist and his partner, a French paleontologist.

As they climbed, Dr. Dayne Arnaud spoke in low whispers with Wrightson, and though Roland could not make out the paleontologist's words, especially with the man's thick French accent, the researcher plainly sounded irritated. So far neither of the men had shared any more details concerning the group's destination or what they had discovered here.

Roland forced himself to be patient. He had grown up in Zagreb, the capital of Croatia, but he knew all the stories surrounding this peak of the Dinaric Alps. Its summit bore an uncanny resemblance to a giant lying on its back. It was said to be the body of the giant Klek, who battled the god Volos and was turned to stone for his affront. Before being petrified, the giant swore that he would one day break free from his slumber and exact revenge upon the world.

Roland felt a flicker of superstitious unease.

Because that giant had been rumbling of late.

This region was prone to earthquakes, a fact that possibly gave rise to this legend of a slumbering giant. Then last month a strong quake registering 5.2 on the Richter scale had shaken the region, even cracking the bell tower of a medieval church in the nearby city of Ogulin.

Roland suspected that quake was tied to whatever had been discovered by the geologist and paleontologist. His suspicions proved true
when the party circled past a craggy shoulder of the mountain and into
a dense patch of pines. Ahead, a massive chunk of rock had broken from
the cliff face and shattered into the forest, knocking down trees and
smashing through the landscape, like the stomping of the mighty Klek
himself.

Wrightson spoke as they followed a path through the maze of boulders and shattered trunks. "A local bird watcher stumbled upon the destruction here after last month's quake. He was hiking early enough in the
morning to see steam rising from between a few boulders, hinting at the
possibility of a cavern system below."

"And you believe the recent earthquake cracked this system open?"
Lena asked.

"Indeed." Wrightson waved an arm. "Not a particularly surprising
outcome. This whole range is made up mostly of karst, a form of limestone. All the rainfall and abundant springs have made this region a
geological playground, full of marvels. Underground rivers, sinkholes,
caves—you name it."

Roland stared at Arnaud. "But it was *more* than just an old cave you
found here."

Wrightson glanced back, his eyes glinting with amused excitement.
"Best we don't ruin the surprise. Isn't that right, Dr. Arnaud?"

The paleontologist grumbled sourly, a match to the scowl that seemed
permanently etched on his features. While Wrightson was gregarious and
outgoing, the Frenchman was his dark shadow, ever grim and mean-
spirited. The researcher was only a few years older than Roland, who
was thirty-two, but Arnaud's attitude made him seem far older. Roland
suspected much of Arnaud's attitude rose from his annoyance at both his
and the American's inclusion here today. Roland knew how some scientists
could become very territorial about their work.

"Ah, here we are!" Wrightson declared, stepping forward to the top of
a ladder that protruded from a nondescript hole in the ground.

Focused on the goal, Roland missed the figure standing in the shadow of a boulder until the large man stepped into the sunlight. He had a rifle resting on his shoulder. Though the guard was dressed in civilian clothes, his stiff stance, the sharp creases in his clothes, and the steely glint in his eyes all suggested a military background. Even his black hair was shaved to stubble, looking more like a peaked skullcap.

He spoke rapidly to Arnaud in French.

Roland didn't speak the language, but from the attitude, the guard plainly was not subservient to the paleontologist, more a colleague on equal footing. The guard pointed toward the darkening skies, seeming to be arguing about whether to allow them to go below. Finally he cursed, stepped to a generator, and yanked on a cord, setting the engine to rumbling.

"That would be Commandant Henri Gerard," Wrightson introduced. "He's with the Chasseurs Alpins, the elite French mountain infantry. He and his men have been keeping anyone from trespassing here."

Roland glanced around, trying to spot any other soldiers, but he failed.

"A sad but necessary precaution, I'm afraid," Wrightson continued. "After the birder discovered this possible entrance, he contacted a caving club to investigate. Lucky for us, the club's members adhere to a strict and secretive code of conduct. When they discovered the importance of what lay below, they preserved what they found and reached out to their French comrades, those who oversaw the preservation of such famous caves as Chauvet and Lascaux."

With a background in art history, Roland understood the significance of mentioning those two caves. The sites were famous for their Paleolithic cave art, paintings done by the oldest ancestors of modern man.

He stared toward the opening, suspecting now what must lie below.

Lena also understood. "Did you find cave artwork down there?"

Wrightson lifted one eyebrow. "Oh, we found so much more." His gaze settled on Roland. "It's why we contacted the Vatican, Father Novak . . . why you were summoned from the Croatian Catholic University in Zagreb to join us."

Roland peered down into the tunnel. As thunder rumbled in the distance, dread drew him to touch the white Roman collar at his neck.

Arnaud spoke in his heavily accented voice, his disdain ringing clear. "Father Novak, you are here to witness and verify the miracle we've found."

11:15 A.M.

Lena climbed down the ladder, following Wrightson and Arnaud. A power cable paralleled their path, leading from the generator above toward the faint glow of lights below. Like the others, she wore a caving helmet with its own lamp. Her heart pounded in her ears, from excitement but also from a touch of claustrophobia.

She spent most of her time locked up in some genetics lab, her eyes fixed to a microscope or reading code off a computer monitor. Whenever she had free time, she escaped into any wild places afforded her. Lately that was mainly the ribbons of parklands running alongside the rivers that crisscrossed Leipzig. She missed the wooded acres that surrounded her former research station outside of Atlanta. She also missed her twin sister—a geneticist like her—who continued working on their joint project in the States, while she did ancillary work here in Europe, which meant spending sixteen to eighteen hours a day building ancient code from bits of decaying bone or teeth.

If this cave was truly some lost Paleolithic site, rich in fossilized remains and artifacts, she could guess her role here: to carefully collect samples for analysis back at her lab. The Max Planck Institute was well respected for its ability to sift through old bones for fragments of DNA and reconstruct those ancient sequences.

Lena stared between her boots as she scaled the ladder, wondering what she might discover below. She wished her sister Maria were here to share this moment.

A slight gasp sounded above her as Father Novak slipped slightly on the ladder, but he quickly caught himself. She frowned a bit, wondering yet again why the priest had been enlisted here. En route from Zagreb, she had engaged the man in conversation, learning that he taught medieval history at the university, a strange background for someone exploring a prehistoric cave.

She finally reached the base of the ladder, and Wrightson helped her down and pointed for her to follow Arnaud, who crouched and continued along a tunnel. She ducked her head under the low roof, but she still kept bumping the top of her helmet and bobbling the beam of her lamp. The air here was actually warmer than that of the chilly morning above, but it was heavy with moisture—the limestone walls damp to the touch, the ground slippery with wet silt.

After a bit of traversing, Arnaud finally straightened ahead of her. She joined him, stretching a kink in her back as she stood—then froze at the sight before her.

A cave opened ahead of them, fanged with stalactites and stalagmites. The walls ran with drapes of flowstone, while the ceiling was festooned with elaborate chandeliers of spiraling snow-white crystals, ranging from twisting tiny straws to antler-like horns.

"A spectacular showcase of helictites," Wrightson said, noting her attention as he stood. "Those types of speleothems grow from capillary forces pushing water through microscopic cracks. Takes about a century to grow a few centimeters."

"Amazing," she whispered, afraid even her very breath might disturb the fragile-looking displays.

Arnaud spoke more sternly. "Take care from here. Walk only on the ladders we've laid out as bridges across the cavern floor. What's preserved underfoot is as important as what hangs overhead."

The paleontologist continued to lead the way, stepping along a thin trestle of steel treads that led deeper into the cavern. A handful of light panels, powered from the generator above, dotted their path. Lena noted objects strewn across the floor, frosted over and glued in place by calcite deposits. Through the crystals, she could make out the shapes of animal skulls and leg bones.

"There's a treasure house of prehistoric life preserved down here,"

Arnaud said, some of his earlier sourness fading to wonder. He nodded to one such object. "There's the intact hind leg of *Coelodonta antiquitatis*."

"The woolly rhinoceros," Lena said.

Arnaud glanced at her, a flicker of respect showing, along with an insulting amount of surprise. "That's correct."

She pointed to an artifact resting on the plinth of a broken stalagmite: a skull fused to rock by runnels of calcite. "If I'm not mistaken, that's from *Ursus spelaeus*."

"The notorious cave bear," Arnaud conceded grudgingly, which earned a chuckle from Wrightson.

Lena hid a smile. *Two could play at this game.*

"Clearly from its position," Arnaud continued, "it was likely used as a totem. You can see the black stain of an old fire pit resting in front of it. The flames likely cast the shadow of the beast's skull across the far wall."

Lena pictured such a sight, trying to imagine what that display would have evoked in the spirits of the ancient people who had made this cavern their home.

The paleontologist continued, identifying other rare treasures as they traversed to the far side of the cavern: horns of a saiga antelope, the skull of a bison, a pile of mammoth tusks, even the complete remains of a golden eagle. Dotted throughout were smaller black smudges, likely marking individual home hearths.

Finally they crossed out of the smaller cave and into a vast chamber that dwarfed the first. The ceiling arched several stories above them. A double-decker bus could easily have turned around in the large space.

"The main show," Wrightson announced, taking the lead now, heading across more of the makeshift steel steps.

Lena needed no one to point out the wonders of this cavern. Across the walls, massive petroglyphs decorated the chamber's lower half, depicting all manner of life, a snapshot of the natural world. Some were drawn in what appeared to be charcoal; others were scraped into the black rock to reveal the lighter shades beneath. Several had brighter hues incorporated into them, imbued with ancient pigments.

But what struck Lena the most was their sheer beauty. These were no simple stick figures or crude renderings, but works of true artistry. The horses' manes seemed to whip and flow. Bison were drawn with a flurry of legs, as if caught in motion. Herds of deer flung their antlers high, as if trying to ensnare the eagles flying overhead. All around, lions and leopards sped through the mass, either hunting or fleeing themselves. To one side, a single mighty cave bear reared up on its hind legs, towering over all.

Lena had trouble keeping her boots on the treads as she tried to look in all directions at once. "Spectacular. I wish my sister could see this, too."

"All of this puts those scribblings in Lascaux to shame, does it not?" Wrightson said with a large grin. "But that's not all."

"What do you mean?" Father Novak asked.

"Should we show them what's hidden in plain sight?" Wrightson asked Arnaud.

The Frenchman shrugged.

Wrightson drew their attention away from the walls to the room's center. A wide black stain, spreading two meters across the floor, marked the site of what must have once been a large bonfire. A tripod of lighting panels rested there.

The geologist dropped to a knee beside a panel of switches wired into the power cable. "If you'll be so kind as to douse your helmet lamps."

After they had all obeyed, he flipped a switch, and all of the light panels extinguished. Darkness dropped heavily over them.

"Now to be transported forty thousand years into the past," Wrightson intoned, sounding like a circus ringmaster.

The snap of a thrown switch popped and light flared anew, coming solely from the trio of panels in the room's center, but it was still bright enough to dazzle and blind, especially as the lighting flickered and strobed.

To mimic a bonfire, she realized.

At first she did not understand the point of such a display, but a gasp rose from Father Novak. She followed the priest's gaze back to the walls. Giant shadows now danced across the walls, rising far taller than the swirl of petrogylphs below. The shadows were cast upon the walls from a circle of stalagmites rising from the floor. Only now did Lena note how they had been carved and sculpted, drilled and shaped, all to create the shadowy army on the wall.

The silhouettes were clearly human in shape, but some bore curled horns and others lofted spears in the air. The flickering light also added to the sense of motion in the animals below, making them look panicked. The lone cave bear faced one of those figures; only a shadowy spear now pierced the side of the mighty beast. Its former bellow of rage now appeared more like a frozen moment of torment.

Lena turned in a slow circle, entranced by the images, an innate terror seeping into her bones. Even Father Novak crossed himself protectively.

"Enough of this foolishness," Arnaud snapped.

Wrightson obeyed, and the rest of the lights flared to life.

Lena took a deep breath, inhaling the earthy scent of the air, feeling the steel tread under her boots, grounding herself back into the present. "Im . . . impressive," she managed to eke out. "But what do you think it means? Was it some representation of a hunt, some accounting of the tribe's skill at tracking and taking down prey?"

No one answered for a moment until Father Novak spoke.

"It felt like a warning," the priest said. He gave a small shake of his head, as if unsure how to put into words how he felt.

Lena understood. The display here did not look like the celebration of a tribe's skill with spear and club. It felt like an affront, something brutal and threatening.

"Such mysteries are not yours to solve," Arnaud said, drawing them forward yet again. "That is not why we've brought you on site."

The Frenchman led the way toward the room's far side, where an archway led out of the painted cavern. As they passed one of the carved stalagmites, Lena wanted to stop and examine it, to see how these ancient people managed such an illusion of shape and motion, but Arnaud kept them moving quickly.

There were no more light panels beyond the main chamber. Past the arch in the cave was only darkness. Lena clicked her helmet lamp back on.

A spear of light pierced the shadows, revealing a short tunnel that ended at a crumbling wall.

Arnaud led them up the slight incline toward the passageway's end.

"It's been bricked up," Father Novak said, clearly as surprised as she was.

"This isn't the handiwork of any Paleolithic people," Lena said. She ran her hands over the bricks mortared in place. "But it is old."

Wrightson stepped forward, bending down to shine his light into a man-sized hole that had been broken through the wall. "Past this obstruction, the passageway continues another fifty yards, then ends in an old tunnel collapse. I believe this passageway was the original entrance into the cavern system. Someone plainly bricked it up to keep everyone out. Then some old quake centuries ago sealed it even more thoroughly."

Lena peered through the hole with him. "Apparently what one quake sealed, another opened up."

"Precisely. Buried secrets have a stubborn habit of returning to light."

"What's beyond this wall?" Father Novak asked.

"The very mysteries that drew us to summon you two here." Wrightson leaned back and waved an encouraging arm toward the hole.

Beyond curious, Lena crawled through first, following the beam of her helmet lamp. The wall was two feet thick. On the far side, a small chamber opened, bricked on all sides, forming what felt like a small chapel.

Father Novak joined her, shining his light across a ceiling supported by a crisscrossing of double arches. "I recognize this architecture," he said, sounding shaken up. "Such Gothic brickwork was typical of the Middle Ages."

Lena barely heard him, her attention drawn to an alcove in the wall to one side. It had been hewn out of the natural rock. Inside, a skeleton lay in a shallow niche in the floor, the bony arms crossed on the chest, all surrounded by a perfect circle of rocks. Within that ring, smaller bones— ribs, carpal and tarsal bones, tiny phalanges—had been artfully placed around the body, forming a complicated and purposeful design.

"Could this be the grave of one of those men who sealed the tunnel long ago?" Novak asked.

"From the pelvic shape, it was a male." Lena leaned closer, moving her lamp from toe to head, wishing for better lighting. "But look at the skull, at the heavy brows. If I'm not mistaken, these are the remains of *Homo neanderthalensis*."

"A Neanderthal?"

She nodded.

Novak glanced to her. "I've heard such remains had been discovered elsewhere in Croatia."

"You're correct. Up in the Vindija cave."

Lena began to understand why she had been summoned here. It was the Max Planck Institute that had performed the DNA analysis on those remains at Vindija. The discovery helped the institute build the first complete Neanderthal genome.

"But I thought Neanderthals were not cave painters?" Novak asked, glancing in the direction of the main cavern.

"That's debatable," she answered. "There is the El Castillo cave in Spain. The chambers there are full of art: handprints, animal drawings, and abstract designs. Dating suggests that some of that artwork might have been done by Neanderthals. But that's still up in the air, and you're right in regards to the level of sophistication found here. The most beautiful petroglyphs—like those found in France at Lascaux and Chauvet—were all done by early man. No one has ever found any cave paintings of this complexity and skill done by a tribe of Neanderthals."

Possibly until now.

Arnaud spoke behind them, coming into the chapel with Wrightson. "It is why we sought the help of you and your fellow geneticists, Dr. Crandall. To discover if the cave dwellers here were indeed Neanderthals. And if so, to perhaps discover what made them so different, such fervent artists."

Lena shone her light toward the back of the gravesite, toward one last piece of art, a petroglyph made of palm prints arranged in the shape of a star. The large prints were a reddish brown under her light, reminding her of dried blood.

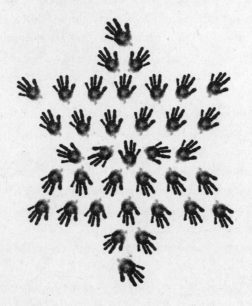

She pulled out her cell phone and took a few shots of the gravesite, then returned her attention to the body in the shallow depression, wondering if those prints were made by the Neanderthal man resting here. She also remembered the terrifying shadows flickering on the wall, along with Novak's conviction.

It felt like a warning.

Wrightson cleared his throat. "Which brings us next to the mystery . . . this one intended for our Father Novak."

11:52 A.M.

Upon hearing his name, Roland pulled his attention away from the remains in the grave. *Is it not mystery enough why someone had entombed the remains of a Neanderthal inside what plainly felt like a medieval chapel?*

"One last step, my good man," Wrightson said, and pointed to another hole broken through a section of the bricked back wall. According to the geologist's earlier description, this way led toward where the tunnel once continued to the surface.

Intrigued, Roland crawled through and stood up in the far tunnel. He shone his light ahead but saw nothing of particular note—except for a parallel set of scrapes in the floor that gouged deeply through the layers of calcite.

Wrightson joined him, scowling at the damage himself. "Looks like something heavy was dragged out of here. Likely taken by whoever blocked up this tunnel and sealed it."

"And you believe I might help solve that mystery?" Roland asked.

"I don't know if you can, but there is one matter where I believe you can be of assistance."

Wrightson took him by the shoulders and turned him back toward the wall behind him. Only now did he see a metal plate bolted to the wall, like a grave marker.

"Something's written on it," Wrightson said, bringing his light closer. "In Latin."

Roland squinted. Age and corrosion had obscured some of the etched letters, but it was clearly Latin. He could make out a few snatches, including the last line and the signature of the person who had left this message.

"*Reverende Pater in Christo*, Athanasius Kircher," he read aloud, then translated this in turn. "The Reverend Father in Christ, Athanasius Kircher."

Roland glanced with shock toward Wrightson. "I . . . I know this man. I did my dissertation on this priest and his work."

"A fact of which I'm well aware. It's why the Vatican assigned you here." Wrightson nodded toward the plate. "And the rest of the message?"

Roland shook his head. "I can make out bits and pieces. With time and the proper solvents, I might be able to restore it. But the longest line I can discern right now translates roughly as *Let none pass this way, lest they bear the wrath of God Himself.*"

"A little late for that, I'd say," Wrightson mumbled.

Roland ignored him and studied the marker.

Here was yet another warning.

In the distance, a loud rumble of thunder echoed down to them. The storm had finally struck the mountains.

"Time to go," Wrightson said, and led him back through the chapel, gathering their other two teammates along the way. When they reached the main chamber, the geologist pointed ahead. "We should get topside before—"

An explosive crack of thunder rang out, cutting him off. Then the cavern's many lamps suddenly extinguished, leaving them with only their helmet lamps for illumination. From out of the deeper darkness ahead, a distant screaming reached them.

But this time, it wasn't the cries of witches out of ancient folklore.

A faint spatter of gunfire echoed to them.

Arnaud grabbed Roland's arm. "We're under attack!"

2

Terror wakes him.

The pounding in his ears drives him to move. He rolls from his bed as an image flashes before his eyes, a face . . .

Mother.

He rushes across his dark room to the window and slaps his palms, then his fists against the thick glass. Pressure builds in his chest until it can be held no longer. He roars his frustration.

Finally light flares overhead, and a face appears beyond the glass, staring back at him. It is not the one he wants.

He places a thumb to his chin, repeating the motion over and over.

Mother, mother, mother . . .

6:22 A.M.

An abrupt knock on the door woke Maria in her office. Fueled by a vague sense of panic, she jerked up to an elbow. Her heart pounded in her throat. An open book, resting on her bosom, toppled to the floor. It took her a half breath to remember where she was—though no more than that, since she had spent many nights at work.

Calming herself, she glanced to the computer monitor on the neighboring desk. The screen scrolled with data from the latest genetic assay. She had fallen asleep while waiting for it to compile.

Damn . . . still processing.

"Y-yes?" she managed to croak out.

"Dr. Crandall," a voice called through her office door. "I'm sorry to disturb you, but there's a bit of a ruckus with Baako. I thought you should know."

She sat quickly, recognizing the nasal twang of the animal husbandry student from Emory University.

"Okay, Jack, I'll be right there."

She climbed to her feet, took a swig of stale Diet Coke from the can on her desk to wash away her morning dry mouth, and headed into the hall.

The student on duty, Jack Russo, paced beside her.

"What happened?" she asked, trying to keep any accusation out of her voice, but her maternal instincts made her words harsher than she intended.

"Don't know. I was cleaning some empty pens nearby when he just went off."

She reached the door that led down to Baako's domicile. Below, he had his own dedicated playroom, bedroom, and classroom, separate from much of the rest of the facility. During the day, under supervision, he also had a fair amount of free run of the hundred wooded acres that made up the field station of the Yerkes National Primate Research Center. The main facility was located at Emory University in Atlanta thirty miles away.

That was still too close for her tastes. She preferred the autonomy she had out here in Lawrenceville. Her project was mostly independent of the rest of the research station, financed through a DARPA grant provided under the auspices of a new White House initiative, called BRAIN, short for Brain Research Through Advancing Innovative Neurotechnologies.

With a dual PhD in genomics and behavioral science from Columbia University, Maria had been handpicked—along with her sister Lena—for this unique project: an exploration into the evolution of human intelligence. The project had additional funding through the Max Planck Institute for Evolutionary Anthropology in Germany, where her twin sister was currently overseeing parallel research on the latest in genomics.

Maria reached the lowermost door and waved her keycard across the electronic reader to gain access. She rushed through, trailed by Jack. The student stood a head taller than her and wore a pair of oversize khaki work overalls with the Emory University badge on the shoulder. He kept rubbing nervously at his scrubby blond goatee, a match to his unkempt long hair, which was tied back with a bandanna in a typically collegiate hipster manner.

"It's okay," Maria tried to reassure the worried student as she entered the foyer to her research suite. "Why don't you go fetch Tango? That always helps."

"Will do." Jack looked relieved to rush off through a side door.

Maria crossed to a wide window of three-inch-thick safety glass. It opened a view into a room scattered with boxes in a rainbow of primary colors, each bearing a letter of the alphabet. They looked like a tumble of child's toy blocks, except each was a foot in diameter and made of thick plastic. The far wall was covered in an erasable whiteboard with slats holding an array of markers. The only piece of furniture was a wide table with a set of chairs.

It was the classroom for a unique student.

That pupil paced before the window, knuckle-walking on his left arm while making vague signs with his right, as if mumbling to himself. He was plainly agitated.

"Baako," Maria called to him, placing her palm against the glass. "It's all right. I'm here."

He hooted at her and moved in her direction.

She crossed to the entry, used her keycard to unlock the main door, and passed into the small cage on the far side. She unlatched the cage gate and joined him inside the classroom.

Baako hurried toward her, shambling upright. When he reached her, he hooked a warm, furry arm around her waist and pressed his heavy brow against her belly, plainly wanting to be reassured.

She sat down on the floor, urging him to do the same, while studying him, reading his body language.

Baako was a three-year-old western lowland gorilla, an immature male weighing a hundred and fifty pounds and standing over four feet high. While he was powerful, there remained a gangly nature to his limbs and body. As he settled to his bottom in front of her, his large eyes, the color of dark caramel, stared at her, crinkling at the corner with clear distress. His furry black brows remained pinched with worry. His lips were stretched taut, almost a wince, showing a hint of his white teeth.

Having raised him since he was born, Maria knew every detail about Baako—everything from his behavior to minute details of his physiology. Complete MRIs were done quarterly to keep an exacting record of his bodily growth, concentrating on the anatomy of his skull and the conformation of his brain.

As she held him, she ran her fingers over the bony sagittal crest that ran along the midline of his cranium. It was less prominent than would be expected for a gorilla at this age. Even his mandibular and maxillary bones were less pronounced, creating a flatter muzzle than typical for a primate.

"Now what's wrong, my handsome boy?" she asked in soft, reassuring tones.

He raised his fists to either side, then opened his hands and drove his splayed fingers across his torso, palms toward his chest.

[*Afraid*]

Responding with both voice and sign, she pointed to him, repeated his gesture, and finished by opening her palms upward with a slight shrug. "You afraid of what?"

He flicked his thumb on his chin, his other fingers splayed open.

[*Mother*]

Maria knew Baako considered her his mother, which in many ways she was. While she might not have given birth to him, she had fostered him and raised him as if he were her own child. Additionally, even from a biological standpoint, Baako was technically hers. Baako was not wholly a western lowland gorilla. His unique genome had been engineered in her fertility lab, with the resulting embryo carried to term by a surrogate female gorilla.

"I'm fine," she told Baako, emphasizing this by giving him a squeeze. "You can see that."

Baako wiggled free and shook his head.

He repeated the sign for mother, then followed it by cupping his chin with his right hand and dropping it firmly to his left hand, which was clenched in a fist with the index finger pointed toward her.

[*Mother-Sister*]

Maria nodded, understanding better now.

He's worried about Lena.

Baako had two mothers: Maria and her sister Lena. Baako considered them both to be equally his maternal caretakers. At first they thought Baako might have been confused because the two sisters were identical twins, but it was quickly evident that he had no trouble telling them apart, unlike some of their colleagues at the field station.

Baako repeated his first sign, over and over again.

[*Afraid, afraid, afraid . . .*]

"You don't have to worry, Baako. We talked about this. Lena might not be here right now, but she'll be back. She is okay."

She signed the letters O and K.

Again he gave a shake of his head and repeated the gesture for afraid.

She returned to her earlier question, signing more emphatically to pry out the particular source of his anxiety. "Why are you afraid?"

6:38 A.M.

He sinks more heavily to his rear and stares at his open palms. He clenches and unclenches his fingers, struggling to think how to make himself clear. Finally he places his fingertips to his brow, then turns his palm toward her.

[Don't know]

He crosses his left arm over his chest and jabs his right thumb twice toward his face, striking his right wrist against his left.

[Danger]

She frowns, then stares into the other room, toward the nest of blankets

*atop his bed. She touches her forehead with an index finger, then lifts it away
and flexes it twice while speaking.*

"It was just a dream, Baako."

He huffs out a breath.

"You know about dreams, Baako. We talked about them before."

He shakes his head, then imitates her gesture.

[Not dream]

6:40 A.M.

Maria read the certainty in Baako's expression. He clearly believed that
Lena was in danger. It suddenly reminded her of her own inexplicable
anxiety upon waking on her office sofa earlier.

Should I be worried?

While growing up with an identical sister, she had read about the
unique bond that could develop between twins, how some pairs seemed
to have a sense of each other even across vast distances. Likewise, animals
were also said to share a similar preternatural ability, like dogs moving to
the door several minutes before the unexpected arrival of their master. But
as a scientist, she put little weight upon such reports, preferring empirical
data to anecdotal accounts.

Still . . .

Maybe I should call Lena.

If nothing else, her voice on the phone should reassure Baako.

And me, too.

She glanced to her watch, wondering what time it was in Croatia. She
and Lena spoke almost every day, either by phone or over a videoconfer-
ence call. They compared notes, shared stories, often talking for hours on
end, trying their best to preserve their close bond across such a distance.
She knew it wasn't unusual for twins to maintain such a lifelong intimate
relationship, but she and her sister had been forged even closer by hardship
and heartbreak.

She closed her eyes, remembering the small apartment where they
grew up in Albany, New York.

The door to their bedroom creaked open. "Where are my two kittens?"

Maria huddled more tightly against Lena under the blanket of the twin bed. Already nine years old, she had her own bed, but she and her sister always slept together until their mother came home. Though they never knew their father, sometimes Lena would take down a photo album. They would stare at his face and make up stories of where he went, why he left them when they were babies. Sometimes he was the hero of those stories, sometimes the villain.

"Do I hear purring under those blankets?"

Lena giggled, which set Maria off, too.

The blanket was peeled away, bringing with it the fresh scent of peach soap. Their mother always washed her hands after coming home.

"There are my kittens," she said, sinking to the bed, plainly tired after working two jobs: at the liquor store around the corner at night and at the crosstown Costco during the day. She hugged them both deeply, then gently encouraged Maria off to her own bed.

Maria and Lena spent most of the day alone in the apartment. Babysitters cost too much. But they were taught to come straight home from school, then lock themselves up tight. Neither of them minded—at least not much. They had each other for company, playing games or watching cartoons.

Once Maria was nestled in her own bed, her mother kissed her forehead. "Back to sleep, my little kitten."

Maria tried to meow, but ended up yawning instead, drifting back to sleep before her mother even closed the door.

A loud tapping drew Maria back to the present.

She turned to the observation window. Jack waved to her, lifting the end of a leash in his other hand.

She cleared her throat and called to him, "C'mon in!"

She tried to compose herself, to push aside her misgivings about Lena. Still, the memory reminded her how quickly life could change, how love could vanish in a moment. While they were in their sophomore year at college, there had been a midnight call to their dorm room. A robbery had left their mother dead on the linoleum floor of the liquor store.

From then on, it had been just the two of them.

Another sharp pang of anxiety rattled through her.

Lena, you'd better be okay.

As Jack headed toward the door, Baako hooted, bouncing on his hind legs, growing excited—not so much at Jack's arrival as at who usually accompanied the student at the end of that leash.

Still, Maria saw that the student was trailed by another man, someone far less welcome. The bald head of the field station's director appeared behind the window. Word of the early-morning commotion must have drawn Dr. Trask from his offices across the station's campus.

Maria straightened, girding herself for the confrontation to come. Jack entered first, then pushed through the cage door and unhooked the leash from his charge.

Baako huffed in excitement as the Queensland Heeler pup bounded across the distance and slammed into Baako. The pair rolled across the floor. Tango was a ten-month-old Queensland, a teenager like Baako, with speckled gray fur and a black mask. Half a year ago, Baako had picked him out of a group of young pups. The two had since become best buddies.

Dr. Leonard Trask scowled as he entered. "I heard there was a problem with your test subject."

"Nothing that couldn't be handled." Maria pointed to the joyous greeting. "As you can see."

Trask crossed his arms, ignoring the pair. "You read the board's recommendations for your subject as it grows more mature. Safeguards should be in place already."

"Like locking him in a cage when he's not under direct supervision."

"It's for the subject's safety as much as for those working here." Trask waved to Jack. "What if it had broken through the window and gotten loose?"

"He's not strong enough—"

"Not yet." Trask cut her off. "It would be better to get the subject accustomed to being caged at this pliable age rather than later."

She refused to back down. "I've forwarded the board reams of reports on how such confinement of primates can retard mental growth. Primates are intelligent creatures. They're self-aware, able to comprehend past and future, able to think abstractly. For such creatures, isolation and confinement can inhibit healthy psychological development, which in turn can lead to stress-induced disorders, if not full-blown psychosis. That's the greater occupational safety issue."

"The board took in your concerns and made their judgments. You have forty-five days to implement the new restrictions."

She knew the board was little more than a group who rubber-stamped Trask's will. Before she could argue further, Trask turned his back on her and headed out. She let him leave, knowing this harassment was born of professional jealousy. The amount of grant money flowing into her project dwarfed the rest of the research studies currently under way at the center, and as a consequence sucked up a lot of the resources here, including space.

She had heard Trask wanted to expand his own program involving transplant research, using chimpanzees as test subjects. She had read his grant proposals and found them lacking. Not only did they repeat work already performed elsewhere, but they were unnecessarily cruel.

All the more reason to hold my ground here.

She returned her study to Baako, who cradled Tango in his lap. He had grown quiet during their argument, plainly sensing the tension, perhaps even understanding that he was at the center of this dispute. She glanced around the suite of rooms that made up his domicile, trying to imagine confining him at night.

But is this space any less of a cage already?

A familiar twinge of guilt flared through her. She sensed that much of the rancor she directed at Trask was the result of her own inner conflict concerning the ethical nature of her own work. She certainly did her best to minimize any stress to Baako. She refused to allow anything invasive to be done to him, nothing beyond blood draws and scans. Additionally, she tried to keep him exercised, stimulated, and entertained.

Still, is it right?

Many countries had research bans on the great apes: New Zealand, the Netherlands, the UK, Sweden. The United States had no such restrictions in place. This unique study could be performed only in a primate center such as this one.

Baako huffed softly at her, perhaps picking up on her distress. He hugged his fists to his chest, trying to reassure her with this sign.

She smiled. "I love you, too."

Baako pointed to Tango and repeated the gesture.

"Yes, and I love Tango, too."

Satisfied, Baako rolled to his legs, snatched an old blanket, and began a tug-of-war game with Tango.

With Baako's earlier fears mollified for the moment, Maria headed out with a firm goal in mind.

To call Lena.

3

Lena lay flat on her belly on the mud-slick rock. Beside her, Father Roland Novak kept to her shoulder, breathing heavily. Both of them hid in a horizontal crack off the main cavern. The opening to their hiding place was low to the floor, offering only a knee-high view beyond where they lay.

In the pitch-darkness, she strained for some clue as to what was happening outside. Thunder rumbled as the threatening storm broke over the mountains. Behind her, she heard the telltale roaring of water, echoing up from some subterranean river. She swore the noise had grown louder since the two of them had crawled in here. She pictured that stream surging with floodwaters draining from the higher elevations.

Or maybe it only sounded louder in the darkness.

As she waited, all her senses had sharpened to a razor's edge. The coppery taste of terror filled her mouth. Her heart hammered against her ribs, against the rock floor under her chest.

"What is going on up there?" she whispered breathlessly.

The question was rhetorical, but Father Novak answered it. "Maybe the attackers are gone. With Arnaud and Wrightson turning themselves in, maybe they left."

She prayed the two older men were still alive.

Shortly after the outbreak of gunfire, a bullhorn-amplified voice had echoed from the cavern entrance, demanding that the paleontologist and geologist show themselves. Apparently the attackers had successfully ambushed the French infantry team above and now held the mountaintop. The final command echoed in her head.

If you both want to live, come out now!

The order was blasted in English and French.

Upon hearing that, Wrightson had made a hasty decision. "The bastards are only demanding we show ourselves." Wrightson faced Roland and Lena. "But not you two. Whoever planned this attack must not know we took you two down here. You weren't originally scheduled to be here for another day—until the storm accelerated matters. So stay here, stay hidden."

While such subterfuge was risky, it was the best hope for all of them. With any luck, Roland and Lena could raise the alarm once it was safe to make an escape. With little other choice, she and Roland had crawled into this crack while the two older men headed up to face their fate. Afterward, Lena remained tense, expecting to hear a burst of gunfire as the two scientists were executed.

"Someone's coming," Father Novak hissed, reaching over to clutch her fingers.

Alerted by the priest, she noted a soft glow rising from the neighboring cave that led up to the surface. A knot of dark figures, all in black combat gear and wearing helmets, burst into the larger cavern. The beams of their flashlights bobbled as they rushed headlong across the space, ignoring the carefully laid-out bridge of ladders, trampling through this perfectly preserved collection of prehistoric bones and skulls. The team headed directly to the other side and vanished into the far tunnel that led to the strange burial site hidden inside a bricked-up chapel.

"What is going on?" Father Novak whispered.

Through her terror, a twinge of anger flared. She knew looting and grave robbing still plagued archaeological digs. Someone clearly had gotten wind of the discovery here, and they were grabbing what they could before anyone was the wiser.

Scuffling noises, along with the sharper retorts of broken stone, echoed from the far tunnel. Minutes later, Novak squeezed her hand harder.

"Here they come again," he warned.

The team reappeared, retreating just as carelessly through the cavern, but now two of the men carried a long case between them. It looked like a plastic coffin. Lena could guess what that box held. She pictured the Neanderthal remains carefully interred within that Gothic chapel. Such a perfectly preserved and intact skeleton could fetch a tidy sum on the black market. Still, the men ignored the other valuable artifacts underfoot, crushing hundreds of thousands of dollars of relics under their boots.

Why are they—?

A muffled boom made her gasp. Smoke and rock dust coughed out of the tunnel the team had just evacuated. Lena stared in stunned disbelief.

They must've blown up the chapel.

But why?

The looters vanished out of the cavern, taking their lights with them. As darkness returned, Father Novak began crawling out of the hiding place.

"We should wait," Lena warned, snatching at his coat sleeve. "Make sure they're gone for good."

He glanced back at her. "They didn't look like they were returning, but you're right. We should remain hidden in these caverns for a bit longer. In the meantime, I intend to see what's left in the wake of their destruction."

He shoved free and clicked on his flashlight, muffling the light with the fingers of his other hand.

Lena followed him out, recognizing the wisdom of the priest's assessment and embarrassingly fearful of being left in the darkness by herself. She took a few shaky steps, but her terror quickly ebbed now that she was moving and had a goal, something to focus her attention on.

Novak led with his light.

As she tagged along behind him, she cast anxious glances over her shoulder, watching for any sign of the thieves returning. Once they reached the smoky mouth of the tunnel, she asked, "What does it matter if anything's left here?"

"Dr. Wrightson summoned me here personally to solve the historical mystery that's been hidden here for centuries. I won't let his and Arnaud's sacrifice be in vain."

Lena bit back a twinge of guilt. She pictured Wrightson and Arnaud vanishing into the darkness. She had also been called here to solve a mystery.

In her case, a *scientific* one.

Before entering the tunnel, she took a final look at the carved stalagmites and the impressive swaths of cave art. Father Novak was right.

They might as well learn as much as they could.

Before it was too late.

1:16 P.M.

As the only member of the Roman Catholic Church present, Roland was determined to bear witness to the desecration of this small chapel, a chapel whose construction had apparently been overseen and sanctified centuries ago by Father Athanasius Kircher. As he headed into the tunnel with his flashlight, questions swirled in his mind.

Why did the reverend father sanctify this place centuries ago? Why was it kept hidden—and more important, why was it looted and desecrated just now?

Hoping for answers ahead, he followed his beam through the churning rock dust and residual smoke. At last he reached the cratered remains of the Gothic chapel. The stone walls were now a pile of rubble. It looked like most of the debris had been blasted in such a manner as to completely bury the grave site with its strange petroglyphs and carefully laid-out bones.

The American geneticist—Lena—coughed behind him, doing her best to suppress the noise with a fist pressed to her lips. "Looks like they were covering their tracks, obscuring evidence of their theft here."

"But you took photos earlier, yes?"

"Damned straight, I did." The note of righteous indignation in her voice tweaked a smile out of him. "Sorry, Father. I didn't mean to—"

"It's all right. I'm *damned* glad you took those pictures, too. And please call me Roland. I think we're beyond formalities here."

She joined him at the edge of the blast site. "I don't think we're going to salvage anything here."

"Don't be so sure."

Roland carefully stepped and climbed through the worst of the desecration, hoping the thieves were so focused on their goal that they failed to examine the far wall of the chapel, especially the side facing the old entrance to this cavern system.

Before he could cross through the rubble, Lena called behind him. "Father . . . Roland, come see this."

He turned to see her shining her helmet lamp toward the cavern wall opposite the ancient gravesite. The blast had collapsed a section of bricks there, revealing what appeared to be another alcove hidden on that side. He joined her and added his light, shining it into the space once sealed by the chapel's brick wall on this side.

He gasped at the sight. On the back wall of the alcove was another large star-shaped petroglyph. Again made of palm prints. "It's just like the one across the way."

"Not exactly," Lena said.

"What do you mean?"

She pulled out her cell phone and pointed it into the space. "The prints are smaller and more numerous, and note all the pinkie marks of these palms . . . they're bent askew, like the artist's finger was broken and healed crooked. Definitely someone different made this petroglyph. And from the size of the prints, maybe a female."

As Lena snapped a series of pictures, Roland glanced back to the pile of rocks covering the opposite grave. "Maybe that other man was this woman's mate."

"Maybe, but we'll never know." Lena angled her light to the bottom of the alcove. "There are no bones here."

At least not any longer.

Roland turned and worked his way to the far side of the rubble. He dropped to a knee and studied the twin set of scrape marks gouged in the floor that he had noted earlier. The centuries-old trail headed away from the chapel and toward the former entrance.

Maybe today's thieves were not the only ones to steal something from here.

He straightened and returned his attention to the toppled section of the back wall of the chapel. He overturned loose bricks, examining each, a silent prayer on his lips.

"What're you looking for?" Lena asked.

Before he could answer, his beam glinted off a piece of metal poking from under a stone. He flipped the brick over, sighing with relief.

"This," he said, running his thumb over the name inscribed at the bottom of the metal plate bolted to the brick. It was the small grave marker that he had examined before.

Lena joined him, staring over his shoulder.

"Written here," he explained, "might be some clue to solving these mysteries. Though the surface is heavily corroded, given time, I think I can—"

Another boom rocked through the cavern, echoing from a distance away. Roland grabbed Lena's arm.

"What is it?" she asked.

Fearing the answer, he hurried with her down the tunnel to the main cavern. The beam of his light picked up a fresh wash of smoke and dust coming from the far passageway that led to the smaller cave and the surface.

"No . . ." Lena moaned, clearly understanding what this meant.

The thieves must not have been satisfied with merely blowing up the chapel. They also intended to seal up the entrance to this cavern, further masking their crime.

"What are we going to do?" Lena asked.

As he started to answer, a deep rumbling shook the floor underfoot. A large chandelier-like chunk of fragile helictites broke from the roof and shattered onto the stone, scattering snow-white pieces to the toes of his boot.

Lena clutched his elbow, waiting for the shaking to stop.

Roland remembered how a 5.2-magnitude earthquake had broken off a shoulder of the stone giant that was Klek Mountain and revealed this ancient cavern system at its heart. The sudden storm and the weight of all that flowing water must have put additional strain on the fault lines underlying the mountain, triggering an aftershock—or maybe even the concussions from the recent blasts contributed to the new quake.

Either way, they were in deep trouble.

He held his breath until the tremors finally faded and the ground stopped shaking.

"It's all right," Roland whispered, trying to reassure his companion as much as himself.

"Look!" Lena pointed toward the crack where the two of them had hidden earlier.

From the mouth of that crevice, water now gushed forth.

The quake must have altered the hydrology of the mountain, shifting the veins and arteries of the giant Klek, turning that storm surge toward this open pocket. From other smaller cracks and crevices, more water flowed.

Lena stared up at him, her face stricken, looking to him for some hope, some plan.

He had neither.

4

The phone rang at a most inopportune moment.

Commander Gray Pierce stood naked before a steaming tub in the hotel bathroom. From the window of his suite, he could look out upon the majestic and historic tree-lined Champs-Élysées of Paris. Still, the view closer at hand was far superior.

From the mists of the lavender-scented water, a sleek leg hung over the lip of the tub. A layer of bubbles did little to mask the figure luxuriating within the bath. She was all long limbs and sweeping curves. As she shifted, a fall of damp hair, as black as a raven's wing, fell away to reveal emerald-green eyes.

Irritation at the interruption shone there.

"You could ignore it," she said, stretching that leg high, before lowering it slowly into the bubbles, stealing away the sight.

He was tempted to follow her suggestion, but the ringing did not rise from the hotel phone; it was from Gray's cell on the bedside table. The unique ringtone identified the caller: his boss, Painter Crowe, the director of Sigma.

Gray sighed. "He wouldn't call unless it was urgent."

"When is it not?" she murmured, sinking fully underwater, then rising again. The surface of her face steamed as water sluiced along her wide cheekbones and down her delicate neck.

It took all his strength to turn away from the tub. "I'm sorry, Seichan."

He headed into the bedroom and fetched his phone. For the past three days, he and Seichan had been enjoying the delights of Paris—or at least what could be viewed through the windows or ordered from room service. After being apart from each other for three weeks, they had found themselves seldom venturing far from their suite at the Hôtel Fouquet's Barrière.

Seichan had flown to Paris directly from Hong Kong, where she had been overseeing the construction of a women's shelter. He had come from the other direction, from D.C. He was taking a brief vacation—not only from the demands of Sigma, but also from managing his father, who suffered from Alzheimer's. His father at least seemed more stable of late, so Gray had felt confident enough to leave for a short spell. While he was gone, a daytime nurse and Gray's younger brother split his father's caretaking duties.

Still, as he picked up the phone, he felt a twinge of foreboding, expecting this call to be about his father. Day in and day out, that fear sat in his gut like a chunk of granite: hard, cold, and immovable. A part of him was always girded, waiting for the other shoe to drop.

He clutched the phone to his ear as the scrambled connection to Sigma headquarters was made. He caught a glimpse of himself in a mirror above the dresser, reading the anxiety in the hard set of his jaw. Impatient at even this small delay, he swept damp hair from his eyes and rubbed the dark stubble over his cheeks.

C'mon . . .

Finally the connection was made, and the director immediately spoke. "Commander Pierce, I'm glad I could reach you. I apologize for interrupting your vacation, but it's important."

"What's wrong?" he said, his fear spiking sharper.

"We have a problem. About twenty minutes ago, I fielded an emergency call from General Metcalf."

Gray sank to the bed, letting go some of his fear. This wasn't about his father. "Go on."

"It seems French intelligence received a frantic SOS dispatched from one of their units in Croatia."

"Croatia?"

"In the mountains out there. A French alpine military team was acting as a security force for some archaeological dig. From the sound of it, the team was ambushed. So far, attempts to reestablish communication have failed."

Gray didn't see how this involved Sigma, but if Metcalf had called Painter, then something significant must be up. General Gregory Metcalf was the head of DARPA—the Defense Advanced Research Projects Agency—and Painter's immediate superior. Sigma Force operated under the aegis of DARPA and was composed of former Special Forces soldiers who had been retrained in various scientific disciplines, which allowed for covert teams to be tasked against specific threats to U.S. or global security.

"I don't understand," Gray said. "This sounds more like a matter for the French military. How does this involve Sigma?"

"Because DARPA has some skin in the game. The team being protected by that French unit was an international group, including an American geneticist, Dr. Lena Crandall. Her current project is partially funded by DARPA. It's why General Metcalf called us, to get someone from Sigma out there to investigate."

And as I'm practically in the neighborhood already . . .

"Kat is arranging to have a jet readied for you," Painter continued. "She can get your boots on the ground in those mountains in under two hours."

Kat—Captain Kathryn Bryant—was Sigma's chief intelligence analyst, serving as Painter's right hand. She and her husband were also Gray's best friends.

"What about Seichan?" Gray asked.

"Kat assumed she would be coming, too."

Movement drew Gray's attention to the bathroom door. Seichan leaned against the doorframe, wrapped only in a wet towel that hid very little.

"Where are we going?" she asked, plainly guessing the general gist of the conversation.

Gray smiled at her powers of perception, a skill surely honed from her years as an assassin for hire. Even now, there remained layers of mystery to her. Still, while several countries maintained a bounty on her for past crimes, there was no one he wanted more by his side.

And not just for her talents with a gun.

He took in the sight of her body, the sultry mocha of her bare skin. Even motionless, her limbs exuded equal parts grace and power.

"Looks like our vacation will have to be cut short," he warned.

She shrugged, letting the towel fall from her torso. "I was getting tired of Paris anyway."

She turned, baring the full curve of her backside.

That's one view I'll never get tired of.

Painter interrupted. "As a precaution, I'll also be extending the investigation stateside."

Gray drew his attention back to the phone. "What do you mean?"

"Dr. Crandall's project is based out of Emory University. I'm dispatching a team to Atlanta to interview the project's co-researcher, Dr. Crandall's sister."

"Her sister?"

"Her twin, actually. Dr. Maria Crandall. Seems the project is a family affair."

"What were the two working on?"

"Much of it's classified. Even Metcalf didn't know all the specifics at this early stage. All I know is that the project involved the search for the origin of human intelligence."

The origin of human intelligence?

Intrigued, Gray wanted to know more, but he suspected Painter was holding back until he could get a full accounting of that project. "Who are you sending to Atlanta?"

"That's the thing . . . I need someone who's fluent in American Sign Language."

Gray frowned. He didn't understand why such a skill was necessary, but surely if this was an investigation into human intelligence, Painter would send Sigma's best and brightest.

"So who's going?" Gray asked again.

Painter only sighed.

7:55 a.m. EDT

"I thought she was pregnant," Joe Kowalski said, picturing the furious expression on the new security guard who manned the desk upstairs. Sullenly, he exited the elevator into the heart of Sigma command with Monk Kokkalis at his side.

"Still, you never ask a woman when she's due," Monk said. "Never. Not even if you're sure she's carrying triplets."

Kowalski scowled. "It's the damned uniform, that big black belt. I swore she was almost due."

"You're lucky she didn't shoot you."

Maybe she should have . . .

He stared at the ceiling of the hallway as he strode alongside Monk. Sigma Command was buried beneath the Smithsonian Castle, occupying a warren of World War II–era bomb shelters. Moments ago, returning from a morning jog along the National Mall, he had tried to be a good neighbor, to show some interest in the new addition to the staff above. Of course, it hadn't hurt that the woman was cute with full lips.

"Talk about burning a bridge," Monk scolded.

Kowalski growled his irritation. He didn't need to be reminded about his sorry track record with women of late. "Drop it already."

Monk shrugged and ran a palm over his bald scalp, possibly sensing he had taken the joke one step too far. He stood a head shorter than Kowalski and would certainly win no beauty contests. Then again, Kowalski knew his own charms were few and far between. More than one woman had compared him to a shaved ape—and they were probably being generous.

Ahead, a slender form, dressed in crisp navy blues, appeared from the doorway that led into Sigma's communication nest. "There you two are," Kat said, drawing alongside them. "I was just headed over to the director's office."

"So what's this sudden summons about?" Monk asked, slipping his hand into his wife's fingers as they continued down the hallway.

Kowalski noted the simple gesture of affection, so effortless and easy. A bitter flare of envy burned through him, along with a flicker of hope.

If this guy could win the heart of such a woman . . .

Then again, Monk made up for his looks in countless ways. He was a former Green Beret, with the scars to prove it, and now served as Sigma's medical forensic expert. Many enemies misjudged his brutish exterior, underestimating his skills and sharp mind.

Director Crowe had once told Kowalski that Sigma got its name from the Greek letter Σ, the mathematical symbol for *the sum of*, because Sigma Force was the union of the best of man's abilities—the joining of brain and brawn. That certainly fit the description of Monk Kokkalis.

Kowalski caught his own reflection in the glass of a closed door, staring at his lumbering form, his thick neck, his crooked nose.

So what the hell am I doing here?

During his time in the navy, he had climbed no higher than the rank of seaman. Even at Sigma, his "scientific" training centered on how to blow things up—not that he didn't enjoy that. But he knew down deep that when it came to balancing brain and brawn, in his case, those scales were tipped far to one side.

Kat spoke ahead of him. "I'll let Painter explain the reason for calling you both down here. We're just getting a handle on the details ourselves."

Kowalski followed the pair down the hall to the director's office. He and Monk had been ordered to return to Sigma as they rounded the Lincoln Memorial during their morning jog. Both still wore sweat pants and hoodies.

Kat led her husband through the director's open door first, leaving Kowalski to tag behind. They found Painter Crowe at his usual station in his office, seated behind a desk stacked with files. He held up a palm toward them as he finished up a call. Behind his shoulders, the three remaining walls of his office glowed with large flat-screens, displaying various maps, news feeds, and aerial footage of some mountains. Though Sigma's headquarters were buried underground, the monitors served as the director's windows to the world at large.

Painter finished his call and slipped the Bluetooth receiver from his ear. He stood up. "Thank you both for coming. It seems a case has arisen that suits your unique set of talents."

The director continued, explaining about an ambush of a French military team in the Croatian mountains. He elaborated with topographical maps and live satellite images on his monitors, finally briefing them about a group of scientists who were being guarded by that French unit. The researchers' faces flashed on the various monitors: a British geologist, a French paleontologist, and some historian from the Vatican. The last photo was of a young woman wearing a white lab smock. She was smiling at the camera, showing perfect teeth, suntanned skin, and a dash of freckles across both cheeks. Her long, dark blond hair was efficiently tied back.

Kowalski sighed out a soft whistle of appreciation.

Painter ignored his reaction. "Dr. Lena Crandall. A geneticist from Emory University. She was overseeing a project funded by DARPA."

"What was she working on?" Monk asked.

Kowalski didn't care. He continued to stare at the photo.

"That's what I want you both to answer for me," Painter said. "Kat's arranged to have you two fly down to Atlanta this morning and interview Dr. Crandall's sister, to find out how their research at Emory connects to an archaeological dig in Croatia. There are pieces of this puzzle that still are missing."

"What about the research team in Croatia?" Monk asked.

"Gray and Seichan are on their way to investigate that right now." Painter glanced for confirmation from Kat, who nodded. "I want the particulars about this research project by the time they land."

Monk cracked the knuckles of one hand as he studied the various screens, taking it all in, clearly readying himself for the mission.

Painter placed a palm on Monk's shoulder. "With your background in medicine and genetics, I thought you'd be best suited to communicate with Dr. Maria Crandall regarding her research. You'll also be joined by a liaison from the National Science Foundation, a scientist who has oversight on the funding of the project."

Painter then faced Kowalski. "And you . . ."

Kowalski frowned, unable to imagine how he could contribute beyond acting as a bodyguard.

"You're best suited to communicate with Dr. Crandall's test subject, the cornerstone and culmination of her research."

"And why's that?" Kowalski asked.

"Because you're fluent in sign language."

Kowalski furrowed his brows, surprised the director knew this detail about his past, but when it came to background searches, Sigma was thorough. So of course Sigma would know about his family background, about how he had been raised in the South Bronx, literally on the wrong side of the tracks. His grandparents had emigrated from Poland during the war. His father eventually started a small deli, but drank away most of the profits on the weekends. Kowalski had one sibling, a kid sister, Anne, who was born with Goldenhar syndrome, a birth defect that left her with a twisted back and severe hearing loss. After their mother was killed by a drunk driver, his father took this tragedy as a reason to drink even more heavily, leaving most of Anne's care to fall upon Kowalski's own young shoulders.

He took a deep breath, shying from those hard memories of the agony his sister suffered, both physical and emotional, before dying at only eleven years old. He found his fingers reaching to a pocket, to the cigar stashed there. He fingered the cellophane wrapper, wanting suddenly to smoke.

"I'm pretty rusty at it," he mumbled.

"That's not what I heard," Painter said. "I heard you sometimes volunteer, working with at-risk deaf children at Georgetown Hospital."

Monk glanced at him, lifting his eyebrows in surprise.

Kowalski silently cursed Sigma's prying. "So who exactly am I supposed to be interrogating over there?"

Painter crossed his arms. "I think I'll let you meet him in person be-

fore answering that. If we're going to win over Dr. Crandall's full cooperation, such fluency with her test subject may prove beneficial."

Whatever . . .

Kowalski turned away, not bothering to hide his irritation.

"What about the other sister, the one in Croatia?" Monk asked behind
him. "You've still heard no further word about the fate of that research
team?"

Painter's tone grew graver. "Nothing. The only news from the region
is that they're suffering through a series of small earthquakes. It's left the
whole mountain range rattling with aftershocks."

Kat added, "And it's likely only to get worse."

5

Shivering in the dark, Lena crouched on a lip of rock. Her helmet lamp shone across the black surface of the growing lake that filled the bottom of the cavern.

We need to get out of here . . .

In the past twenty minutes, the floodwaters had erased all evidence of the prehistoric encampment that once occupied this subterranean world, swamping over the calcite-crusted bones and the charred sites of old home fires. All that remained were the tops of stalagmites protruding from the lake and the cave paintings along the walls—only now those painted herds of deer and bison looked like they were drowning.

Despite her own terror, she mourned the destruction.

At her side, Father Novak shoved his cell phone back into his pack. He shook his head, having no better luck getting a signal than she had a moment ago. She had tried to reach her sister in the States, but she could get no service this far underground.

"We should wade over to the next cave, to where we climbed down here," he suggested. "See if there's any way out. After all of these aftershocks, maybe something knocked loose, reopened what the thieves blasted closed."

He didn't sound hopeful, but Lena nodded, wanting to do something—if nothing else, to keep moving. She hiked her pack higher on her shoulder and slipped off the lip of rock into the dark lake. The icy water immediately filled her boots and soaked her pants to midthigh. Gritting her teeth, she took a few steps and continued on.

"Careful," she warned. "It's pretty slippery."

The priest followed her, gasping loudly as he waded in. "Slippery? Should've warned me about how cold it is."

She couldn't help but grin, appreciating his attempt to lighten the mood. Together they crossed the large cavern and headed toward the tunnel that ran to the neighboring smaller cave. She prayed there was some escape in that direction.

As they neared the tunnel mouth, a low rumble rose around her, rippling the surface of the lake.

"Another aftershock," Roland said, stopping with her.

They waited together, holding their breaths, expecting the worst, but like the half-dozen previous quakes, this one quickly subsided. Still, she splashed more quickly to the tunnel's mouth and shone her light down its throat.

"It's half flooded in there," she said.

"Better than *fully* flooded."

"That's true."

She ducked beneath the low roof and headed along the tunnel. She breathed hard, doing her best to hold her claustrophobia at bay. She was not normally prone to anxiety in tight places, but with the weight of the mountain overhead and the need to bend over and bring her nose close to the flow of dark water, she could hear her heart pounding in her ears.

Luckily, the tunnel climbed at a slight angle, and by the time she reached its end, the water was only ankle-deep. Still, she was already soaked and had a hard time keeping her teeth from chattering, a reaction only partly due to the cold.

Roland fared no better, shivering as he faced a tumble of broken rock along the base of the far wall. He craned upward, pointing his beam toward the ceiling. She joined her light to his. Together they scanned the roof for any sign of the old entrance, but it had been thoroughly blasted away. Only a few streams of water trickled down from up there, draining through the boulders from the storm-swept mountaintop.

Roland clenched a fist and mumbled under his breath. His words were in Croatian, and though she couldn't understand him, they sounded more like a curse than any prayer to God.

"It'll be okay," she offered uselessly. "We'll wait out the storm. Surely someone will come looking for us. If we hear anything, we can scream and shout. Once they know we're down here, they can dig us free."

Roland studied the water, which had already climbed to midcalf. He didn't state the obvious, which she appreciated. If the flooding didn't kill them, the cold and exposure surely would.

He nodded. "So then we wait and—"

A low groan cut him off, rising from the shadows to the left. She swung in that direction. From behind a thick folded curtain of flowstone, a dark figure fell into view. Roland pushed Lena behind him, likely fearing this was one of the thieves.

The man, on his hands and knees, rolled to the side of a hip and raised a hand against the blinding glare of their two helmet lamps.

"Père Novak . . . Docteur Crandall . . ." he croaked out, a French accent thick on his tongue. *"C'est vous?"*

Lena centered her beam, discovering a familiar face, one half covered in blood. Though she had glimpsed the man only briefly, she recognized the leader of the French infantry unit.

So did Roland.

The priest rushed forward. "Commandant Gerard!"

The soldier looked relieved and dragged a rifle from behind the flowstone curtain. Its solidness seemed to help center him. He faced them both. *"Qu'est-ce qui s'est passé?"* he asked hoarsely, then tried again in English. "Wh-what has happened?"

Lena joined Roland as the priest checked the soldier's head wound. A scalp laceration continued to bleed slowly. She suspected his injury must have happened during the explosion.

"How . . . how did you end up down here?" Lena asked.

Gerard stared toward the blasted remains of the old entrance, then spoke slowly, hesitantly, still dazed. "When we were attacked, I rushed down here to protect you all. That was our highest priority."

She understood. *To keep the civilians in his charge safe.*

"But the enemy was too fast," Gerard explained. "I barely had time to hide when they came down in force on my heels. I heard them call for Wrightson and Arnaud to show themselves. When you two did not appear with the other men, I suspected they had hidden you. To protect you, *n'est-ce pas?*"

She nodded at his assessment.

"There were too many for me to risk an assault to free the professors. Any attempt would've gotten them both killed. So I waited, hoping to rescue you two, then raise an alarm when it was safe."

"We had a similar plan," Lena admitted.

The soldier frowned at the roof. "I was about to move when . . ." He shook his head. "I do not remember."

"The thieves blew up the entrance," Lena explained. "You must have been knocked out."

Gerard gained his feet unsteadily, keeping one hand on the wall and shouldering his rifle with the other. He stared down at the water splashing over his legs.

"The caverns are flooding," Roland warned. "We should try to get as high as possible."

The soldier ignored him, stepping away. He unclipped a small flashlight from his belt and shone it down the throat of the tunnel to the neighboring cavern. A few yards down the passageway, water now fully flooded the tunnel.

Lena joined him. "I think Roland . . . Father Novak is right. We should climb higher on these walls, try to stay above the rising tide."

Gerard shook his head. "Any rescue team will take too long to reach us here."

"Then what would you have us do?" Roland asked.

Gerard led them back to the curtain of flowstone and pointed behind it. Lena peered into the space and discovered that the soldier's hiding place was the mouth of another tunnel. It opened four feet above the flooded floor.

But where did it lead?

She turned to find Gerard pulling out a hand-drawn map from his pocket. He shook it open and splayed it on the wall. It appeared to be a detailed sketch of this cavern system.

"We are here," he said, stabbing a thick finger on a spot on the map. "According to Wrightson's geological study of the surrounding area, this set of caves connects to a series of tunnels and caverns that run deeper and farther through the mountains. Possibly as far as Đula's Abyss."

Gerard turned to Roland, but the priest wore a doubtful expression.

"What is he talking about?" Lena asked.

"You came through the city of Ogulin to get here, yes?" Roland asked.

She nodded, remembering the quaint medieval village with its stone castle and old homes.

"The town sits atop Croatia's longest caving system, over twenty kilometers of caverns, passageways, and subterranean lakes. In the center of town is one of the openings into that system."

"In the middle of town?" she asked.

Roland explained, "The River Dobra flows out of the neighboring mountains and carves a deep gorge that runs halfway through Ogulin. In the town's center, it drops through an abyss, where it vanishes underground and becomes a subterranean river. That point is called Đula's Abyss. Legends surround that place, telling of a young girl named Đula who threw herself into its depths to avoid marrying an old and cruel nobleman."

Lena turned to the French soldier. "And you think this set of caverns might lead to that abyss and a way out of here."

"Wrightson believed it might," Gerard said. "But it's never been fully explored."

"How far away is that town?"

Roland answered, "About seven kilometers as the crow flies."

That's over four miles.

She felt a sinking despair.

"I have ropes, climbing gear, and extra batteries in my pack," Gerard offered.

Trying to stave off panic, she stared down at the rising water. "What if the rest of that cavern system is equally flooded?"

"Je ne sais pas," Gerard said with a shrug. "I do not know, but *here* it is definitely flooding."

Roland turned to her. "What do you want to do? If you wish to remain, I will stay with you."

Lena flashed her light toward the mouth of the tunnel, pondering the unknowns that lay out in that darkness. But the French soldier was right. Better to head off into the unknown than stay here, where death was almost certain.

She straightened her back and faced the two men.

"Then let's go."

4:04 P.M.

Gray clutched a handgrip near his shoulder as the helicopter jostled roughly through the storm. Rain swept in heavy sheets across the window canopy, threatening the ability of the craft's wipers to maintain visibility. Though sunset was still a couple of hours away, a heavy cloak of black clouds hugged the mountaintops and turned day into night.

Next to Gray, the pilot struggled with his controls as the rotors chopped savagely through the harsh weather. Winds continually buffeted the small craft, seeming to come from all directions at once as they fought higher into the Alps. Finally they cleared a mountain pass and a scatter of lights appeared in the next valley.

"Ogulin!" the pilot yelled through his radio, swiping beads of sweat from his brow. "That's as far as I can take you in this storm. Reports say the weather is even worse in the mountains beyond."

Gray turned to Seichan, who lounged in the rear cabin, seemingly unperturbed by their turbulent ascent into these mountains. She shrugged, accepting this change of plans just as readily.

Half an hour ago, the two had landed in Zagreb, the capital of Croatia, where a local pilot and helicopter had been waiting for them. The hop to the coordinates of the missing French unit should have taken only fifteen minutes, but the storm had doubled that flight time and now threatened to pummel them back to the ground.

Gray faced around, preparing to browbeat the pilot into continuing onward, not wanting to lose any more time. The longer they delayed, the more likely they'd lose any trace of the research team and their guards. But as he stared at the black skies, at the crackles of lightning forking over the mountaintops, he sank back into his seat.

"Take us down," he conceded.

The pilot nodded, blowing out a sigh of relief, and lowered the craft toward the lights scattered across the bowl of the valley.

"I can land in a field at the edge of town," the man said, pointing. "I'll radio for a car to meet us. Once the worst of the storm blows out, we can try again. But it'll likely be morning at the earliest. I can arrange a hotel in the meantime."

Gray barely heard him, already adjusting the timetable in his head, seeking alternatives. "How long would it take to reach the site on foot?"

The pilot cast him a skeptical look. "You can take a car to the village of Bjelsko. It's only six kilometers away. From there, it's a hike of forty minutes. But that's in good weather. In this storm, through those dense woods, with the trails washed away, it could take hours, and you could just as easily get lost. Better to wait out the storm."

As if to punctuate this recommendation, a hard gust pounded the helicopter, jolting it to the side. The pilot returned his full attention to landing his craft in the field.

Gray reached into his pocket and retrieved his phone. He used his thumbprint to decrypt its contents and reviewed the mission files loaded there. He had reviewed everything thoroughly en route to Zagreb and knew what he wanted to find. He brought up a photo of a man in his midfifties with salt-and-pepper hair, decked out in a climbing harness, standing at the edge of a gorge.

Twisting around, he showed the picture to Seichan. "Fredrik Horvat, head of the local mountaineering society. It was his group that first entered the caves up in the mountains and kept it secret until a research team could be put together to secure the site."

Seichan leaned forward. "And he lives in this little town?"

"He does. And I expect he knows these mountains better than anyone. If he can guide us there . . ."

Seichan sat straighter. "Then we wouldn't have to wait until morning."

"I have his address."

The pilot quickly landed the helicopter in a wide field. Shortly thereafter, the twin beams of a sedan pierced the gloom and sped along the neighboring road toward their position. Gray and Seichan exited the aircraft and hunched in their jackets against the wind-whipped sheets of rain. As soon as the sedan arrived, they climbed into the backseat.

Once the car started moving, Gray gave the driver—a young man named Dag—the name and address of the local mountaineer.

"Ah, Fredrik . . . I know him," Dag said in halting English, smiling brightly, showing a wide gap in his front teeth. "This is a small place. He is crazy man. Crawling through all those caves. Me, I want open air. More the better."

"I tried phoning him," Gray said. "No answer."

"He maybe at the pub. At Hotel Frankopan. He lives nearby. Lots of people go to the pub during storms. Good to drink brandy when the *vještice*—witches—howl." Thunder boomed, loud enough to shake the windows of the sedan. Dag ducked slightly from the din, then straightened and made the sign of the cross with one arm. "Maybe best not to talk about those *vještice* right now."

As they headed toward the center of town, Gray repeatedly tried to raise the mountaineer on his cell, but he had no better luck reaching the man. Gray was left with little other choice.

"We'll try the pub first," he told Dag, then turned to Seichan. "If we fail to find Fredrik there, someone at the hotel might know another guide."

"That is, if they're not all afraid of those witches," Seichan added, leaning her head back and closing her eyes.

As they entered the town, Gray studied the passing landscape. It was a quaint fairy-tale village of narrow streets, small wooded parks, and homes roofed in red tiles. All around, the town's sixteenth-century origin revealed itself: from an old stately church with a tall steeple to the remains of an ancient fort atop a nearby hill. They finally stopped below the thick walls of a stone castle, each corner flanked by massive round towers. Its battlements overlooked a deep river gorge, likely the same one pictured in the photo of Fredrik.

"Frankopan Castle," Dag said as he parked the car at the curb. He drew their attention to the neighboring whitewashed building that abutted the Gothic castle. "And that is Hotel Frankopan. The pub is just inside. I will show you and ask about Fredrik."

Normally Gray would have preferred to maintain a low profile, but they'd already lost enough time detouring here and still had a long slog ahead of them.

"*Hvala*," Gray said, thanking the man in his native tongue, which raised another wide smile from Dag.

"Come then. Perhaps we drink a brandy, too. To keep the *vještice* away."

Gray had no objection. If Dag could put him in front of Fredrik quickly enough, he would buy the kid a whole bottle.

Dag led them quickly through the rain and up the steps to the main entrance of the hotel. Inside, the lobby was equally whitewashed but warmed by wooden furniture that looked like antiques. They passed by the front desk, earning a curious look from the receptionist, but Dag waved to her.

"*Zdravo*, Brigita!"

She nodded back, but her curiosity hardened into wariness.

"It seems everyone knows everyone in this town," Gray said.

"Also who doesn't belong here," Seichan added ominously.

Gray glanced to Seichan. Her easy stroll changed imperceptibly, something anyone would easily miss. But Gray noted the slight narrowing of her eyes, how each step was taken with a measure more care.

"What's wrong?" he whispered as they headed toward the murmur of a crowded bar.

"Did you see her reaction to us? It was hardly welcoming. I'm guessing we're not the first strangers to appear here recently. Whoever they were, they certainly left a sour impression on that woman."

Gray glanced back to find the receptionist still glaring at them with her arms firmly crossed.

"I think you may be right," he said. "Makes me wonder. Whoever ambushed the French team likely had to come through this town. Maybe they even stayed here. It's worth checking out and making a few discreet inquiries."

"And maybe they're still here, trapped in this village by this storm as we are." Seichan cocked an eyebrow toward him. "Could we be that lucky?"

A spat of gunfire erupted ahead them, accompanied by screaming.

It seems we are.

4:24 P.M.

Roland slid on his backside down a muddy slant of rock into the next cavern. Braking with his heels, he ground to a stop, and Commandant Gerard helped him to his feet. Roland joined Lena, who leaned an arm on a wall, her head slightly ducked from the low ceiling.

"How much farther, do you think?" she asked, gasping slightly after the two hours of climbing, crawling, and shimmying through this subterranean world.

Gerard had his map out again, splayed against a wall. They had already traversed beyond the British geologist's cursory survey. They were literally in uncharted territory. The commandant had his compass out and marked on his map with a wax pencil, recording their progress to keep them from getting even more lost.

"It can't be much farther," Roland said, though in truth he had no idea.

"Listen," Lena said, straightening.

Roland tried to obey, quieting his ragged breath. Even Gerard lowered his map and cocked his head. Then he heard it: a distant rumbling, like thunder underground.

"A river," Gerard said.

Up until now, their path had avoided the worst of the flooding. So far they had had to skirt and wade through only a few pools along the way. Even those had appeared to be permanent features of this world, not born of the recent storm.

He offered a silent prayer that the river was passable.

"Let's go," Gerard ordered dourly.

They set off through the low cavern, led by the beams of their lamps. As they continued, the roof rose higher and higher. Its surface grew ever more festooned with fanciful horns of white helictites, interrupted by a protrusion of thick stalactites. All the while, the thunder of the river grew in volume, echoing across the vast space, drowning away their occasional whispers, leaving only the pounding of their hearts as accompaniment.

"Roland." Lena grasped his elbow and pointed. "Look. There's another petroglyph."

He licked his dry lips, beyond really caring about such ancient paintings. Over the past hours, they had come across occasional bits of art, single depictions of various animals: a bison, a bear, an antelope, even a lonely spotted leopard. It seemed the artists who decorated the main cavern had also explored deeper into this system, leaving behind these prehistoric markers.

"This one's not an animal," Lena said, stepping toward the wall to the right, drawing him with her.

She shone her lamp upon the vast figure standing tall across the surface of the stone. Painted in shades of white, it climbed two stories tall. From the prominent bosom, it appeared to be the giant ghostly representation of a woman. Her eyes, painted in circles of crimson, seemed to be staring down at them. Upon her brow, blue dots formed the shape of a six-pointed star, very much like those symbols found in the graves.

"Do you think this could be a depiction of the Neanderthal woman whose bones were removed from that other cavern?" Lena asked.

Stolen by Father Kircher centuries ago.

"This is the first painting of a *person* we've seen down here," Lena added, glancing back at him. "All the other petroglyphs were animals."

Except for the shadow images cast by the carved stalagmites, he added silently, *depicting some great enemy of these people.*

"And look at this," she said.

She dropped the beam of her lamp, centering it between the white ankles of the petroglyph, where the dark mouth of a low tunnel opened. He moved closer, shining his own light inside, revealing that the tunnel was actually an arched doorway leading into a side cave.

"Leave it," Gerard warned them both. "We don't have time to waste exploring."

The thunderous rumble of rushing waters amplified his warning.

Still . . .

Lena made the decision for them both. She ducked and crawled on her hands and knees across the threshold. As curious as she, Roland followed, ignoring the mumbled complaint from the French soldier.

The next chamber was small, no more than five meters across. Here there were no bones on the floor, just flat rock with a charred spot in the center that marked some ancient hearth. Lena stood and slowly turned, splashing her light across the walls. She let out a small gasp of surprise.

Instead of paintings, the cave walls had been carved into rows of niches. Each cubby held sculpted figures, all animals—a veritable stone menagerie. In one niche, a small mammoth raised a curled trunk. Another held a lion, with the beast reared up on its hind legs. Roland added his light, revealing sculptures of wolves, bears, and bison, along with all manner of deer and antelope. The higher shelves held birds of every feather, from hunting hawks to waterfowl.

If there was any question as to this collection's age, the crusts and runnels of calcite that caked everything in place removed any doubt of its prehistoric origin. It would have taken millennia to accrue this much buildup.

"These must be tribal totems," Lena said, reaching toward the figure of a hunched leopard, then lowering her arm. "If these were carved by Neanderthals, it would change our fundamental understanding of them."

Roland nodded and stepped over to the largest of the cubbies. It lay directly across from the cave opening. Small markings drew his attention. A single palm print flanked each side of the niche, again painted in blood-red.

Lena joined him. "This one on the left has the same crooked pinkie, like we saw in the older ransacked grave." She hovered a finger over the image to the right. "And this one . . . I bet it would match the collection of palm prints above the bones of the Neanderthal male."

He glanced to her, furrowing his brow. "Signs of the same two figures again."

"Clearly they were important to this tribe. Maybe leaders. Or, judging from this collection of totems, perhaps revered shamans."

He shifted his light to illuminate the depths of the dark niche. Unlike the others, this cubby held no stone figure. Instead, something lay on the bottom, wrapped tightly.

He reached for it.

"Careful," Lena warned, but she didn't attempt further to dissuade him.

He took out the object, seeing that it was folded in layers of stiff cloth. Flakes of old wax crumbled from his fingertips. "This isn't from prehistoric times."

She pressed closer. "What is it?"

He licked his lips and peeled away the layers of old cloth, shedding more wax. Finally he revealed a leather-bound book inside. Its surface was embossed with a symbol, a design of convoluted loops forming a pattern.

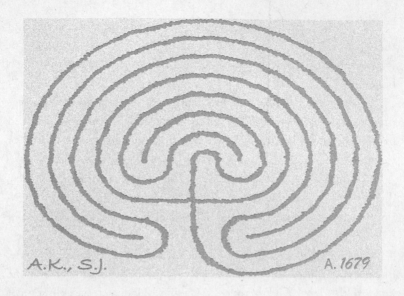

A.K., S.J.   A. 1679

"It almost looks like a cross-section of a brain," Lena said, awed.

He smiled. She was a geneticist, so of course that was what she saw. "I think it's a labyrinth," he corrected her. "Such mazes have been carved and painted since man first started to produce art."

"But what does it mean?"

"I don't know. But look at the initials along the bottom."

At his shoulder, she read them aloud. "A.K . . . and S.J."

He let some of his own reverence show in his voice. "Athanasius Kircher . . . the Society of Jesus."

His hands trembled as he realized he was holding a book that once belonged to the Jesuit father whose history was the center of his life's work. Unable to resist, he gently used a finger to pull back the cover. Something fell free and struck the cavern floor with a metallic clang.

Lena bent down and retrieved it. "It's a key."

She held it up to the light. It was as long as his palm, with an intricate head showing a cherub surmounted by an arch of skulls.

He could not help but picture the skull and bones stolen from the grave in the other cavern. *What did this all mean?*

He turned to the book for answers, but the pages between the leather covers had not fared the passage of time as well. Over the centuries, moisture must have seeped through the layers of waxed cloth, turning the paper to a wad of pulp. The impression of the key still remained, but whatever had once been written here had been obliterated long ago by time and dampness.

"We must go!" Gerard ordered them, his tone brooking no argument.

Lena dawdled long enough to search within the cubby, probing with her fingertips. "I can feel broken pieces of calcite, like something was once embedded here but was broken free and taken."

Roland looked to the rows of totems, equally glued in place by the seeping of calcite over the millennia. "Kircher must have taken whatever lay in this place of prominence, leaving this book behind, perhaps as some clue to what he found, to where he took it."

He looked down at the sorry state of the old journal.

"Maybe something could be recovered," Lena offered. "If we can get the book into the hands of an expert restorer . . ."

He doubted anything could be salvaged, but he nodded and waved toward the exit. "Before that can happen, we need to escape these damnable tunnels."

They rejoined Gerard. Roland immediately understood the Frenchman's demand to get moving. Out here in the main cavern, the thunderous rumble of rushing water echoed much louder now.

Lena glanced at him, the fear raw in her face.

They were out of time.

4:48 P.M.

The gunfire echoed from the bar ahead.

A clog of people burst through the doorway at the end of the hall and rushed toward Gray and Seichan. Gray grabbed Dag and shoved him back toward the hotel lobby.

"Go call the police."

As the stampede swept past them, Gray flattened against the wall. He slipped a black SIG Sauer from a shoulder holster under his wet jacket. Against the opposite wall, Seichan drew forth a long tactical dagger in one hand and held her own pistol in the other. Once the way was clear, the two set off toward the bar, keeping low and to either side of the hallway.

Before they could reach the door, footsteps pounded up behind Gray. Dag had returned, huffing, his eyes wide on the weapon in Gray's hand.

Gray shoved the kid hard against the wall. Seichan scowled, dropping to a knee, keeping a bead on the bar's door. The gunfire had ended inside, but yelling still rang out, sounding like demands shouted in Croatian. It appeared the assailants—whoever they were—had hostages in there.

What the hell is going on?

Dag had the answer. "I heard from the others," he gasped out, still wide-eyed with terror. "Bunch of *razbojnici* . . . bandits burst into the pub.

THE BONE LABYRINTH   69

Demanded that Fredrik show himself. They fire at the roof. Shoot one man in the leg."

Gray glanced at Dag, then to Seichan. So the gunmen must be after the same mountaineer. *This attack must be connected to the assault in the mountains.* Was someone cleaning house here, covering up their tracks, making sure anyone in town with knowledge of that secret site was eliminated?

"And Fredrik?" Gray asked.

Dag pointed to the bar.

"So he's still in there."

The young man nodded. "In the bathroom at the back. Only his friend knows he is there, I think."

"Is there a window? A way to climb out?"

"Window, yes. But too small."

So the guy is trapped in there.

Gray doubted Fredrik's hiding place would remain secret for very much longer. He eyed Seichan, knowing she had heard everything. She nodded, already understanding what he needed. This wasn't their first dance together. She dashed to his side and grabbed Dag by the collar.

"You're coming with me," she said coldly.

As she dragged him down the hall, Gray rushed to the doorway of the pub and hid to one side of the opening. From low to the ground, he took a fast glance into the bar, then slid back out of sight. With a snapshot fixed in his head, he assessed the threat: four armed men, wearing knit masks, all with pistols, no assault weapons. Two guarded a trio of patrons stuck in a red-cushioned booth. Another loomed over a man clenched in a ball on the floor. Blood seeped across the polished wood floor. The fourth maintained a wary watch, but luckily the mahogany bar had helped screen Gray's low peek into the room.

Gray had also noted one other detail: one of the patrons in the booth had been pointing toward the back of the bar, likely toward the restrooms.

Time was up.

As if on cue, fresh gunfire erupted, accompanied by the shatter of glass. The noise rose from the rear of the pub, from the one of the restrooms. It was his signal to move. He rolled across the threshold, keeping somewhat shielded by the bar. The four gunmen had all turned toward the bathrooms, responding to the gunfire by aiming their weapons back there.

Gray squeezed off two rounds, both head shots. As the pair of men dropped, he aimed for the leg of the third, taking out his knee and sending him crashing next to the patron on the ground, who had been similarly wounded.

Karma's a bitch.

The fourth gunman, the one farthest to the back, lunged for the only shelter available. He charged through the door into the women's restroom, likely believing the gunshots came from his target, Fredrik, in the other bathroom. The attacker must have hoped the women's restroom had a window through which he could make his escape.

But Gray remembered Dag's earlier words.

Window, yes. But too small.

A single gunshot rang out from there, again accompanied by a shatter of glass.

The fleeing assailant came falling back into the bar, crashing to his side, the back of his skull a cratered ruin.

Wanting answers, Gray quickly closed on the only man still alive on the floor, the one he had shot in the leg, but before he could reach him, the masked man raised a pistol to his own head—and fired. The blast was loud, drowning out Gray's own curse.

Biting back his disappointment, Gray hurried to the men's room and barged inside. He found Fredrik huddled in one of the stalls, his face ashen, his lanky salt-and-pepper hair disheveled. Despite the man's raw fear, he glared at Gray, ready to face what was to come.

A voice rose from the shattered window on the far wall. "Fredrik!" Standing in the rain outside, Dag leaned his face near the broken glass, speaking rapidly in Croatian, his voice full of reassurance.

Gray also sought to calm the man, attempting the little bit of Croatian he had memorized en route here. "*Zovem se* Gray," he introduced himself, holstering his pistol and lifting his palms.

Seichan pushed Dag aside and called to him through the window. "Everything's clear out here."

Gray pictured Seichan hightailing it around the hotel's exterior and shooting through this window, creating the initial distraction. She must have also heard that last gunman crash into the neighboring bathroom, and from her position outside, eliminated that threat, too.

Fredrik gained his composure, revealing his fluency in English. "Wh-what is going on?"

Gray waved to the door. "Let's discuss this somewhere more private. We can't trust that these four didn't have companions nearby."

Fredrik needed little convincing to vacate the restroom. Gray led him through the pub and out a side exit of the hotel, avoiding the lobby. He met Seichan and Dag back out on the streets. They hurried to the parked BMW and climbed inside.

Before he could urge Dag to get moving, Gray's satellite phone vibrated in his pocket. He answered it, immediately recognizing Kat's voice.

"Gray, we've just picked up a ping off Dr. Crandall's cell phone. It's weak and intermittent. Not enough to connect a call, but we were able to roughly triangulate its location—but it makes no sense."

"Where is it coming from?"

"I'll transmit the GPS location to you."

He lowered the phone and studied a map that appeared on his screen. The village was laid out in the shape of a horseshoe, as its streets and homes hugged around a deep river gorge which split halfway through the place, ending at a deep chasm that the neighboring castle overlooked.

A blinking dot marked the location of the detected ping on the map.

Frowning, Gray raised his head and stared toward the dark chasm at the end of the street. The signal seemed to come from down there.

That can't be good.

6

Why aren't you answering?

Maria lowered her phone, pressing it nervously between her palms as she sat at the desk in her office. For the past two hours, she had repeatedly attempted to contact her sister, without success. Each unanswered call cranked her anxiety up another notch.

She had already reached out to her liaison at DARPA and learned that there was some trouble at the archaeological site in Croatia, but the details remained sketchy. She was instructed to sit tight and to keep trying to raise Lena. In the meantime, an investigative team was en route to Georgia from D.C.—both to interview her about the details of her research and to provide her with additional information about the current status of events out there.

She glanced at her phone to check the time.

They should be arriving at any moment.

She took in a deep breath, trying to stay calm, but unable to forget Baako's anxiety this morning. She pictured him signing repeatedly: splaying his fingers and driving his open palm across his chest over and over again.

Afraid, afraid, afraid . . .

"So am I," she whispered to the empty room.

She pictured Lena's face. Her sister was only minutes older than her, but Lena had always taken on more of a maternal role in their relationship, assuming the mantle of those extra minutes of maturity. It was Lena who microwaved their dinner while their mother was at work. She made sure Maria finished her schoolwork before watching television. Such responsibilities had left Lena more serious, more cautious, while Maria had always been the more carefree of the two, bolder at facing new challenges.

But I'm not feeling bold now, only worried.

After another failed attempt to reach Lena, she heard low voices on the other side of the door. A firm knock sounded. She opened the door and found Leonard Trask standing there. Behind the director of the Yerkes National Primate Research Center stood two strangers and a woman she knew well, Amy Wu. Amy worked for the National Science Foundation and was one of the project managers for the White House's BRAIN initiative. The woman had personally helped arrange the funding for Lena and Maria's research. In addition, the three—all the same age, all women in a male-dominated profession—had developed a friendship over the years.

Amy pushed past Trask and gave Maria a firm hug. She smelled of a soft honeysuckle perfume. Her dark hair, trimmed in a boyish cut, tickled her ear. She pulled back to stare into Maria's eyes.

"How are you holding up?" she asked, her concern genuine.

Maria appreciated the gesture, but at the moment, she wanted news about her sister. "Have you heard anything?"

Amy glanced to the two men who accompanied her; the pair looked like bouncers at a biker bar. They wore suits, but the muscular bulk beneath their clothing was unmistakable. From their shaved heads and stiff demeanor, she guessed they were military. The shorter of the two men nodded at her, offering her a small smile that was reassuring.

Amy made introductions. "These two men are from DARPA. This is Monk Kokkalis. And his partner, Joseph Kowalski."

"Joe," the other man corrected as he stepped inside, having to duck his head slightly to enter. He studied the room, his face hard, his manner guarded.

Trask began to follow them inside, but Amy held up a hand and stopped him at the threshold. "I'm afraid this conversation has become a matter of national security. I'm sure you understand, Leonard."

Amy shut the door in his face, but not before Trask cast a scathing look at Maria.

She knew she'd pay for that later, but for now, nothing else mattered but finding out about Lena. Maria didn't have to inquire further. As soon as the door was closed, Amy spoke.

"I know you're concerned about Lena. And we'll be as honest and forthcoming as we can be, but many variables are up in the air. We're still trying to discover exactly what happened up in those mountains."

"What do you know so far?"

"Only that the site was under some form of attack and that we've lost communication with the French military team who were running security."

Maria looked down at the cell still in her hand. Each word felt like a blow to the gut. She found herself dropping heavily into her office chair. "And Lena?"

"Let's not fear the worst. Like I said, we've failed to make any contact. Right now there's a fierce storm raging in those mountains, and the region has been hit by a series of small quakes. DARPA has dispatched a team to search the area, and hopefully we'll have additional news soon. But we do have one hopeful sign."

Amy turned to Monk Kokkalis.

He cleared his throat and explained. "As you can imagine, we've been continually attempting to make contact, and just a few minutes ago, while we were on our way here from the airport, we learned that our communication team was able to get a ping off Lena's cell phone. It was weak, but detected well *away* from the coordinates of the dig site."

Amy took Maria's hand. "Which suggests your sister is on the move, possibly heading out of the mountains."

Maria felt tears welling, both from relief and a residual measure of fear. "But you don't know if she's alone or not? Maybe kidnapped or injured?"

"That's right," Monk admitted. "But I know the man who was sent out there. He'll find her."

Maria heard the firm certainty in his deep voice and wanted to believe him.

He continued, "If this assault was more than just some group trying to raid the dig site, the best hope for your sister and the rest of the research team is to discover what might have motivated the attack. That's why we're here. To gather as much intelligence about the nature of your research as we can."

"I'll answer anything I can. But I don't see how our research would motivate any attack."

"It may not have," Monk admitted, "but we're trying to cover all leads."

She swallowed hard. "What do you want to know?"

"I've been debriefed on the big talking points of your research." He nodded to Amy. "But I wanted to hear from you personally, if you'll bear with me."

Maria nodded.

"I understand that the purpose of your research is to explore the origins of human intelligence. Could you elaborate about your methodology and the hypothesis you are pursuing?"

She sighed loudly, not knowing where to begin or even if this military guy would understand, but she straightened in her chair, wanting to cooperate. "My sister and I have been investigating a moment in mankind's history known as the Great Leap Forward. That point in cognitive development, some fifty thousand years ago, when there was an inexplicable burst of art and innovation."

Monk nodded. "The Big Bang of human consciousness."

She stared harder at him, realizing maybe there was more behind that pugilist exterior. In the glint of his eyes, she read both amusement and a sharp intelligence.

Okay, then let's step this up a notch.

"Modern man first appeared on the scene some two hundred thousand years ago," Maria explained. "Back then, our rise from our hominin ancestors happened rapidly. According to recent research done by a trio of geneticists at the University of Chicago, this sudden appearance of *Homo sapiens* is attributable to the rapid mutation of *only* seventeen brain-building genes. A scant few, really. But from those few changes, there was a cascade effect—a snowballing, if you will—that resulted in hundreds of changes to thousands of genes in a relatively short period of time."

Monk furrowed his brow in thought. "And this snowballing gave rise to our modern brain, what set us apart from the chimpanzees and earlier hominins?"

"And also gave us most of our uniquely human traits. Our cognition, our self-awareness, our consciousness." She stared at the attentive faces around her, glad to keep talking, anything to distract from her fears about Lena. "Which then brings us back to the Great Leap Forward. Prior to the leap, mankind had basically stagnated for a hundred and fifty thousand years. Yes, we were certainly chipping away at crude stone tools, but during this time, we created no art, we didn't adorn our bodies with jewelry, and we didn't bury our dead with any rituals."

"And after?" Monk asked.

"A sudden burst. We graduated from stone tools to bone, we developed new tanning techniques, we were heating pigments to create new colors, we were transporting shells to make jewelry. Suddenly we were wearing necklaces and bracelets and burying loved ones with grave goods: food, tools, and other offerings. And most dramatic of all, we began producing magnificent works of art, decorating cave walls with pigmented representations of the natural world. Here was the moment when modern man was truly born."

A gruff voice spoke from behind the others, rising from Monk's glum-faced companion. "What caused all of that?"

"That remains a mystery," she answered. "It is what my sister and I are exploring. Our brains certainly didn't change in size. We know from the fossil record that we had the same-sized brainpan both before and after this Great Leap. So with no gross anatomical explanation for this advancement, theories abound as to the exact *cause* of this uptick in ingenuity. Some say it might have been the introduction of a better diet, one richer in omega fatty acids, which helped us think better. Others attributed it to climate change, when environmental pressures forced us to step up our game. And another camp believes it was because early man was beginning to migrate out of Africa during that time, exposing our brains to new stimuli and requiring ingenuity to survive."

"And your theory?" Monk asked.

She pointed to her diploma on the wall. "I'm a geneticist. If the brain didn't grossly enlarge, then possibly the source of this change could be found at the genetic level. Remember, it was only a handful of genetic mutations that gave rise to modern man in the first place, so could something equally unique have happened fifty thousand years ago that altered our genome, something significant enough to spark this Great Leap Forward?"

"Like what?" Kowalski asked.

Monk answered, his face thoughtful, "Like the introduction of new genes, from a new species."

She nodded. "It was around that same time that *Homo sapiens* encountered the Neanderthal tribes and began interbreeding. Are you familiar with the term *heterosis*?"

Kowalski shrugged, but Monk simply crossed his arms. She suspected he knew what she meant. In fact, he was likely several steps ahead of her but was letting her take the lead.

"Heterosis is also called hybrid vigor," she explained. "It's a biological phenomenon when the mating between two different species produces an offspring—or hybrid—who displays traits that are stronger than either parent alone."

"And your hypothesis," Monk said, "is that the interbreeding of Neanderthal and early man produced offspring who were smarter, resulting in this uptick in ingenuity."

"It's what Lena and I were exploring. Two to three percent of modern man's genome is made up of Neanderthal genes—with the exception of most African populations, who never interbred with Neanderthals. Additionally, we don't each carry the *same* bit of Neanderthal DNA. If you add those disparate parts together, the total contributes to about *twenty* percent of all our genes. Certainly enough to significantly alter the path of mankind. Geneticists have already determined that some of those stretches of Neanderthal DNA likely helped our migrating ancestors adjust to the northern climates of Europe, giving us more body hair and less pigmented skin, for example."

"But as I understand it, there's no indication that it enhanced intelligence in any way?" Monk asked.

"That's correct. And my sister and I are disinclined to believe that there's such a direct correlation."

Monk frowned. "Why?"

"Because the African population of ancient man also participated in this Great Leap Forward, while having *no* Neanderthal DNA. Which raises the *second* mystery concerning this turning point in history. This change was not an *isolated* phenomenon, but one that occurred almost simultaneously throughout the scattered populations and tribes of the world. Spreading across Europe, Asia, and the African continent."

"And how do you interpret that?"

"Our hypothesis is this Great Leap Forward was due to a mix of genetics *and* social engineering. We believe this global change was indeed *first* sparked by interbreeding, resulting in the sudden appearance of those vigorous hybrids I mentioned—unique individuals who thought and acted differently. They in turn inspired rapid social changes—in art, in rituals, in weapon design—skills that were then taught and spread globally through migration. We know from genetics that the migration patterns of early man were not one way. Not just *out* of Africa, but some populations—including those carrying Neanderthal genetic markers—also returned *to* Africa."

"Let me see if I'm understanding this correctly," Monk said. "Your hypothesis is that interbreeding triggered an intuitive leap forward in a scattering of unique individuals. Then their new way of thinking and knowledge were spread wide and far."

"Exactly. And it's not just our theory, but one we extrapolated from a paper published in 2013 by an Oxford University philosopher, Nick Bostrom. He wrote that it would take only a handful of super-enhanced individuals—those with a superior intelligence—to change the world through their creativity and discoveries, innovations that could be shared globally. He was writing about the future in that paper, but his theories are just as applicable to the past, to explain mankind's Great Leap Forward fifty thousand years ago."

"Super-enhanced individuals?" Monk asked. "Like your theoretical hybrids?"

"Possibly. It's what my sister and I are exploring: what it meant to be that first generation following the union between *Homo neanderthalensis* and *Homo sapiens*. To be fifty percent Neanderthal and fifty percent modern man. The truest hybrid. We know that the number of Neanderthal genes quickly diluted out of our genome, eventually winding down to just that two or three percent, too scant to have any stimulating effect on our intellect today." She glanced around the room. "But what if we could reverse that biological clock and re-create that true hybrid today?"

"And that's what you and your sister were working toward?" The man sounded equal parts horrified and astounded.

"Not only working toward, we accomplished it." Maria stood up. "Would you like to meet him?"

11:35 A.M.

You've got to be goddamn kidding me . . .

Kowalski stared beyond the glass into what appeared to be a preschool classroom, but one that was clearly built for a very strange student. Ropes were strung from the ceiling. A tire swing hung limply in the corner. Big plastic toy blocks were scattered everywhere.

Amidst the clutter, a small furry figure faced them, leaning on the knuckles of one arm, his flat nose sniffing at the strangers behind the glass.

"His name's Baako," Maria introduced.

"He's a gorilla," Kowalski said, unable to keep the disdain from his voice, and not really wanting to. He had had some bad experiences with apes in the past.

No wonder Painter kept this under his hat.

"He's a western lowland gorilla," Maria explained. "A three-year-old immature male."

Equally dumbfounded, Monk stared into the space. "This is your hybrid?"

Amy Wu, the National Science Foundation researcher, answered. "We certainly couldn't authorize this study using human embryos. Not without raising a firestorm of protests. While altering the DNA of humans for experimental purposes is not illegal per se, it is frowned upon. Especially in the realms of creating human hybrids."

"Not to mention the moral and ethical implications," Maria added. "It's why we opted to use the gorilla as a model. The entire genome of *Homo neanderthalensis* was sequenced six years ago. Using that information and the latest gene-editing techniques, we were able to re-create the Neanderthal genome from scratch. We then used that engineered sample to fertilize the ovum of a gorilla to produce a viable hybrid embryo, which we carried to term using a female gorilla as a surrogate."

Maria must have misinterpreted the disgust on Kowalski's face for disbelief and tried to explain how such a monster could have been created. "Scientists have been producing human-animal hybrids for years. Back in 2003, a group of Chinese scientists successfully fused human cells with rabbit eggs, producing growing embryos. The very next year, the Mayo Clinic here in the States announced they had produced pigs with human blood running through their veins. Since then, there have been mice grown with livers, even brains, that are made up of human cells, along with many similar projects involving other species: cats, sheep, cows, et cetera."

Amy Wu supported her, motioning to the window and the furry subject of this discussion. "I suspect this fellow is only the first step toward more ambitious endeavors in the near future."

"So for your research purposes," Monk said, "I'm guessing you started with a gorilla because of the species's close proximity to humans."

"That's right," Amy said with a nod.

Monk stared through the window. "But why not choose a chimpanzee instead? Aren't they supposed to be even closer to us genetically?"

"Yes and no," Maria answered. "While chimps share more than ninety-eight percent of the same genes as us versus a gorilla's ninety-six percent, for our study it was more about quality than quantity. When it comes to those sequences involving sensory perception, hearing, and more important, brain development, the gorilla's genome is significantly closer to ours than that of a chimpanzee's."

"This also bears out from past communication studies with chimps versus gorillas," Amy added. "Washoe and Nim are probably two of the best known sign-language-speaking chimpanzees, but their vocabulary topped off at about two hundred signs, whereas Koko the gorilla learned closer to a thousand."

Kowalski stared down at his own hands, remembering this was why Painter had sent him. "So why's signing so important?" he asked.

Maria gave him a small smile, which made his face heat up. She had the same bright blue eyes and the same dash of sun freckles across her cheeks as the photo he had seen earlier of her twin sister; only Maria's white-blond hair had been cut into an asymmetrical bob, worn longer over her right ear. On that same side, a thumb-sized tattoo on her neck—of a double helix of DNA—peeked above the lab coat's collar whenever she turned her head.

"Language skills are a good barometer for intelligence and ingenuity," she explained, drawing back his focus. "And after decades of ape language research, we have a ready-made baseline against which we can compare Baako's intellectual development."

She placed her palm on the window. "But more important, we're talking about the conception of a unique soul, unlike any on this planet. So of course we would want a method of communication, a way to better understand such a creation." She faced them all again. "Come and meet him and you'll understand."

Maria led them toward a door and waved a keycard over an electronic lock.

Kowalski reluctantly trailed the others, knowing he had little choice.

Seems this is my place in Sigma—to be the guy who talks to apes.

As he passed through the door, he found himself standing in a tall cage. Maria unlatched the barred door ahead of them, but only after the outer door had sealed and relocked, plainly a safety feature. Kowalski kept to the back of the group as they crossed into the makeshift classroom. The enclosed space was too hot and humid for his tastes, and though it didn't smell like a barn, as he had expected, there was still a distinctly musky odor.

Maria moved ahead of the group, holding out an arm. "Baako, come over and say hello."

The young gorilla straightened, standing on his two legs, but he stayed put, still wary.

Kowalski eyed him in turn. Standing upright, the gorilla rose only as high as Kowalski's stomach, but he still looked powerful. Curious, Kowalski searched that furry body for any evidence of the creature's hybrid nature, but he didn't know all that much about gorillas to recognize any real difference.

"It's okay," Maria encouraged softly.

Baako hesitated for a moment. Then with a soft hoot, he dropped to the knuckles of one arm and bounded over to her and took her hand.

"That's a good boy." She turned to the group. "Best you let him come to you."

Amy Wu lowered to a knee. "Hey, Baako, do you remember me? We use to play tickling games."

The gorilla half hid behind Maria's legs.

"It's been over six months since you were last here," Maria said, placing a palm atop the gorilla's head. "I doubt he remembers."

Baako made another soft grunt, almost as if disagreeing. He let go of his caretaker's hand and lifted both arms toward his ribs and wiggled his fingers. It didn't take someone fluent in sign language to interpret this gesture.

[*Tickle*]

Amy laughed. "That's right!"

Baako came forward, his head and shoulders bowed shyly. He crossed to the scientist and gave her a one-armed hug. Amy proceeded to tickle him under the ribs, earning a brief chuffing that sounded like hoarse laughter. But even to Kowalski, it was like the guy was going through the motions, patronizing the scientist's efforts. Especially as Baako's gaze never left the two men in the room.

Monk tried next. "How about a little love this way?" he asked, also dropping to one knee and holding out both arms.

Baako grunted, looking ill at ease.

"He's a nice man," Maria said, signing her assurance by sliding her right palm over her left.

[*Nice*]

"Say hello," she encouraged.

Baako came forward, plainly reluctant, but from the pinch of his eyes, he was also curious. He sniffed the air as he approached. Once near enough, he motioned with his right hand, waving from his brow.

[*Hello*]

He then cupped his hand before his chest and swept it down. Then his fingers flashed through various letters.

[*I am Baako*]

Those dark eyes stared up at Monk, who looked bewildered.

Kowalski nudged his partner. "The guy's telling you his name."

Maria glanced to Kowalski, her eyebrows lifting. "You're right."

Kowalski pointed to Monk, then spelled his partner's name.

[*His name is Monk*]

Baako bobbed his head, clearly understanding, and closed the distance. He took Monk's hand in his own, squeezing it. Then he leaned over and sniffed his partner's other hand, cocking his head and hooting quietly.

"It's a prosthetic," Monk explained both to Baako and to Maria, who came over.

"Really," Maria said. "I couldn't tell."

Kowalski was not surprised. The prosthetic hand was an amazing bit of hardware, and not just due to its lifelike match. It had been engineered by DARPA to function with amazing dexterity, and this was the latest model, built to respond to a neural implant in Monk's brain, allowing him to control his artificial hand not only via the titanium contacts that linked the nerves in his wrist to the prosthesis, but also by his very thoughts.

Monk demonstrated another unique feature of his new hand. He reached over and detached the prosthesis from his wrist, freeing it from the metal cuff wired to the stump of his arm. He let Baako hold the hand.

The gorilla flipped it over and examined it from every angle. Monk was even able to wiggle those fingers, the motion achieved via a wireless command. Baako's brows climbed higher at this demonstration. Even Maria gasped slightly at the sight. Baako lifted the prosthesis to his mouth and gently bit at one of the fingers.

Kowalski cringed, doubting the DARPA engineers would appreciate such abuse to their technological marvel. Monk must have felt the same way and stepped forward.

Maria held him back, eyeing Baako with amusement. "Don't worry," she explained. "He's only trying to tickle you. It's the way gorillas sometimes do that, by biting softly at fingers or bellies."

Monk laughed—but it was less because of the tickling and more likely amazement. "I can actually feel what he's trying to do."

"Amazing." Maria pinched her eyes and stared anew at the prosthesis. "I had read that DARPA was testing artificial limbs with sensory inputs, but I never imagined they were so far along."

Monk shrugged. "Just consider me one of DARPA's guinea pigs."

Finally Baako offered the hand back.

Monk accepted it. "Thanks, little guy."

The gorilla turned to the last member of the party and eyed both of Kowalski's arms.

Kowalski raised his hands. "Don't get any ideas. These are both real." He finished by clamping the fingers of one hand over the other.

[*No biting*]

Baako chuffed loudly, followed by an offended grunt of protest.

Maria smiled, her eyes twinkling toward Kowalski. "You sign well. I'm impressed."

Feeling awkward at her attention, he spiraled two fingers in the air and landed them on the back of his other hand.

[*Of course I do*]

Baako was less awed. The gorilla refused to draw closer and dropped heavily to his haunches. He then flicked his fingers in Kowalski's direction, then pointed at him.

[*Don't like you*]

Kowalski scowled back at the ape.

Feeling's mutual, bud.

11:48 A.M.

Baako sees how the man stands, smells the sourness to his body, reads the small tics of disdain on his face. He knows the man does not like him and doesn't understand why. Confusion leads to hurt—also to anger.

His mother comes over, her lips hard, ready to scold. She gestures.

[He is nice man, too]

Baako doesn't know how to explain, to argue, so he crosses his arms, refusing to talk.

Man doesn't like me, so I don't like him.

Plus his mother had praised the way this man talked with his hands. He saw how she smiled at him. She should only like the way Baako talks.

Not this man.

She points to the door at the back and motions firmly. "Go to your room, Baako."

He grunts, voicing some of his hurt and frustration.

She points her two fingers again to his bedroom door.

[Go]

He huffs and obeys, pushing up. He heads away, walking on both arms, burning with chagrin. Before he leaves the room, he casts one last glare in the man's direction. He doesn't sign it, but he thinks it.

You go away.

11:49 A.M.

"He's tired," Maria explained, hoping she hadn't been too hard on the little guy, but firmness was necessary at times.

"Don't worry," Monk said with a grin. "Kowalski has that effect on a lot of people. It takes time for him to grow on you."

His partner frowned but didn't protest otherwise.

Maria felt sorry and tried to reassure the big fellow. "Baako didn't sleep well last night. He had some nightmares about Lena."

Amy stepped closer. "Is that right?"

Maria heard the interest in her voice and tried to dissuade it. "It was just a coincidence." She glanced away. She certainly wasn't going to talk about waking with similar misgivings about her sister.

"Speaking of Lena," Monk said, "what exactly was your sister doing in Europe?"

Maria was happy to turn the discussion in this direction. "We were granted a fellowship by the Max Planck Institute for Evolutionary Anthropology in Leipzig, Germany. It's the predominant research institute when it comes to hominin studies. The fellowship allowed for one of us to work in a program whose goal was to build a more accurate model of genetic variability in the Neanderthal species, along with developing new retrieval methods for collecting DNA from old bone fossils."

"And why did Lena end up going instead of you?" Monk asked.

"While we both have an interest in genetics, my research leans more toward a *macro* understanding of DNA. The end results, you might say. Whereas Lena concentrated at the *micro* level, fixing her studies on gene-editing and -splicing. So it seemed more important that she take on this German fellowship."

Stabbed by guilt, Maria hugged her arms around herself, regretting that decision now. Here she was safely in the States while Lena faced who knew what dangers out there.

"We thought this fellowship was important," she continued. "I can count on one hand the number of Neanderthal fossils that offer decent recoverable DNA. Good sources are few and far between. With better samples, more accurate collection techniques, and a comprehensive understanding of the variability of genes among the different Neanderthal tribes, Lena and I hoped to discern what made the Neanderthal species unique from us and how a hybridization of those traits could have helped trigger the Great Leap Forward. There was so much to gain."

She pictured Lena's face.

And now so much to lose.

"Do you know who she's working with over there?" Monk asked.

She gave a shake of her head. "There was a whole team. I have their names on my computer upstairs, but they're all experts in various fields, studying other hominins who contributed to our genome."

Kowalski cleared his throat. "So we have more than just Neanderthal genes in us?"

She nodded. "That's right. Another hominin species, the Denisovans, were contemporaries of *Homo sapiens* and Neanderthals. They also interbred with us, leaving behind their genes in our gene pool."

Kowalski grunted. "Sounds like that *pool* was getting pretty damn polluted."

"On the contrary, those Denisovan genes helped our species survive. For example, the gene EPAS1 activates when oxygen levels are low in the atmosphere to produce more hemoglobin. A variant of this gene is found in the Tibetan people and allows them to survive at extreme altitudes, where oxygen is extremely low, like high in the Himalayas. Data shows this variant came from the Denisovans."

"So is that everybody?" Kowalski asked, scoffing a bit. "Or were there other cavemen who joined this prehistoric orgy?"

Maria glanced to Amy. She knew this question was of particular interest to her friend.

Amy spoke up. "Genetic analysis of bone fossils from both Neanderthals and Denisovans suggest there was a *third* species who also interbred with us, a hominin who so far remains unknown and, as of yet, undiscovered and unclassified."

"Proving yet again," Maria added, "that if it weren't for those matings, we wouldn't be who we are today. All of this supports our theory of hybrid vigor and that the interbreeding of man and hominin species gave us the genetic variability to allow us to spread across Europe and eventually around the world. These borrowed genes were what allowed our species to survive to the modern day."

"And that's what you're studying with Baako," Monk asked. "Analyzing those unique traits that might have contributed to the Great Leap Forward."

"Exactly. And while Baako is still young, we've already noted some remarkable progress in his cognitive abilities. He's learning at a rate three-fold faster than any ape studied in the past. And the anatomy of his brain is also significantly different, showing an increase in surface folding of the cortex and a larger volume of gray matter making up his cerebrum, all of which we've documented through a series of MRIs."

"I wouldn't mind seeing those," Monk admitted. "It sounds fascinating."

"They're filed on my office computer. I can show you where—"

A whimpering cut her off. The noise was quiet, easily dismissed, but with a mother's keen sense of a child in distress, she stopped and turned toward the neighboring bedroom. Baako hunched in the shadows of the threshold and circled his chest with his fist.

[*I'm sorry . . .*]

Amy touched her arm. "I can take the others over to your office and help them review the pertinent reports. In the meantime, it looks like someone is trying to make amends."

Maria's heart ached at seeing Baako so wounded and distressed.

"And I need to report in with D.C., too," Monk added, stepping away. "Hopefully I'll also have an update from Croatia for you shortly."

"Thank you."

Monk pointed to his partner. "I'll leave this big guy with you. Something tells me he's part of the problem here and may be part of the solution."

"What did I do?" Kowalski asked.

Monk ignored him. "Once we're done in your office, I'll phone Kowalski and let you know."

Maria nodded. She suspected all of this was an excuse for Amy and Monk to compare notes with a measure of privacy. She glanced at Kowalski as the other two left. Apparently this one's contribution regarding scientific matters was not wanted. They were leaving him to babysit her instead.

She wasn't sure who should be the more offended.

Still, she was too tired to protest, and she wanted to soothe Baako anyway. But before she headed over to him, she pulled out her cell phone and hit redial. She called up the last number—Lena's number—and waited for the connection to be made. She expected the usual discordant beep, followed by an automated voice telling her the call failed.

Instead, a shiver of static screeched, then died away into a voice.

"—ria!" The answer was both frantic and shocked. "Can you hear—?"

Those words cut off as the connection dropped again. A CALL FAILED message flared on the screen.

Still, Maria yelled into the phone. "Lena!"

7

No, no, no . . .

Lena clutched her phone and tried to reconnect the call. She breathed hard as attempt after attempt failed. Gerard and Roland stared at her. Roland had tried his phone, but he had no better luck.

"It was her," Lena swore. "My sister."

The trio stood vigil on a shelf of rock overlooking a subterranean lake that filled a massive cavern before them. It stretched at least a hundred yards across and twice as long. To the far right, a large river roared in from a tunnel, flowing heavily into the lake, slowly flooding the place. The reason it hadn't already completely flooded lay to the left. There, the black surface of the lake churned with a large whirlpool, marking the cavern's drainage point. She pictured that water flowing into the deeper levels of this system, washing everything into the roots of these mountains.

And we may be next.

"That must be the River Dobra," Roland said, studying the thunderous flow of water. "The river runs into the village of Ogulin, then vanishes underground at Đula's Abyss."

"Father Novak must be right," Gerard said. "We must be near that gorge if your phone got signal, even for a moment."

Lena lowered her cell, giving up. "We're so close."

She stared toward the fierce deluge.

Yet so far.

"If only we could swim against that current . . ." Roland said.

No one bothered to entertain this hope. If they jumped in, they'd be sucked down that whirlpool before they even got near the headwaters of that river.

Tears of frustration welled, blurring her sight. She swiped angrily at her eyes, refusing to accept defeat. Then water splashed over the toes of her boots. She looked down. The lake had risen to the height of their rocky perch.

Gerard pointed behind them. "We'll have to go back."

"To where?" Roland asked, sounding forlorn. "The caverns are flooding just as much behind us."

"There must be higher ground somewhere," the French soldier said firmly. "Somewhere we can wait out this storm."

No one argued, but they all knew such a plan was futile.

Lena lifted her phone and hugged it to her chest, wishing she could regain that connection. Not that she held out any hope that reaching Maria would save her.

But at least I'd get to say good-bye.

6:11 P.M.

From the bottom of the deep gorge, Gray looked up at the stone battlements of Frankopan Castle far above. Rain splashed in his face while lightning forked along the bottom of the black storm clouds.

Gray concentrated closer at hand. A rope hung from a balcony that protruded over the cliff at street level. He watched the thin, muscular form of Fredrik Horvat slide down the line on a rappelling harness. The mountaineer quickly landed beside him on a rocky bank of the flooded river. Behind them, a steel U-shaped dock protruded into the water, sheltering a Zodiac pontoon boat.

As Fredrik freed himself from the rope and shed his gear, Gray tried once again to dissuade the mountaineer from this course of action. "I can do this myself," he said. "I know boats."

"But you don't know this river or the caverns that swallow it away." Fredrik clapped him on the shoulder. "I've been leading tours into the depths of Đula's Abyss for the past two decades. I know every twist and turn, every rock and boulder. If you hope to find your friend, then you will need me."

Despite the bravado and confidence in the man's voice, Gray noted how his dark eyes shone with glassy fear. This local might know the river and the neighboring caverns, but traversing that course now, in the middle of this storm, nothing was predictable. The currents would be treacherous, and any landmarks would likely be flooded or washed away.

Still, Fredrik pointed to the pontoon boat. "Get aboard. This river isn't going to get any less wild."

Gray glanced one last time toward the balcony. Seichan leaned over the rail, staring down, with the young man Dag at her side. She was not happy to be abandoned, but there was no reason to risk any more lives than necessary in this attempt. Besides, Gray didn't trust that whoever had tried to take out Fredrik wouldn't return to finish the job. If so, he needed someone to watch his back.

He lifted an arm toward Seichan, but she simply pushed away from the rail, still plainly angry.

Gray turned and climbed into the boat. Even tied down, the boat jerked and bobbed in the strong current, like a rodeo bull in a bucking chute. He shifted to the bow of the craft while Fredrik chucked loose the lines and hopped to the outboard engine at the stern.

"Hold tight!" the man called out and yanked on the engine's cord.

Gray grabbed a rubber handgrip as the engine roared throatily to life, but the noise was nothing compared to the thundering rumble of the storm-flooded river.

The Zodiac burst out of the dock and into the current. The flow immediately tore at the craft, spinning it crazily before Fredrik could wrestle the boat in the correct direction. The steep walls of the gorge soon swept past to either side. Ahead, the river vanished down the gaping maw of a tunnel.

"Here we go!" Fredrik shouted.

6:15 P.M.

Seichan watched the boat fishtail for a breath in the current—then whisk away into the tunnel. Her fingers clutched hard to the iron rail of the fence that separated a parkland trail from a precipitous drop into the gorge.

I should be down there.

After Fredrik had told them about the Zodiac, she and Gray had devised this plan from the safe confines of the BMW. Still, they had hesitated at proceeding. To search those flooded caverns via the river would be treacherous, and while Sigma command had picked up the ping of the missing geneticist's phone, there was no guarantee the woman was alive. The scientist could have been killed in the tunnels and her body—or just her cell phone—washed out of the higher mountains to this valley.

Then ten minutes ago, they'd received word from D.C. of a brief connection, a snatch of conversation between the two sisters.

It seemed the woman still lived, trapped down below.

Even upon learning this, Seichan had tried to play devil's advocate, debating the reasons *not* to attempt a rescue. What would it serve for Gray to put himself—and the mountaineer, for that matter—in harm's way to save one woman? As far as anyone knew, this whole attack was nothing more than thieves raiding an archaeological site. To risk losing a skilled Sigma operative for the sake of one person seemed reckless. A more conservative approach—such as waiting out this storm—seemed the wiser course.

In the end, her words had fallen on deaf ears.

She had expected no other outcome.

The wet clapping of footsteps drew her attention back around. Dag came running down a tree-lined path. He had gone off to scout the situation back at the hotel, to get a handle on how local law enforcement was responding to the raid at the pub.

"What did you learn?" she asked, noting the flashing lights of emergency vehicles through the park's foliage.

"It's chaos at the moment. No one really knows who—"

A loud boom silenced him, causing him to duck slightly. She immediately knew this was no crack of thunder. She turned to the west and watched a sooty fireball climb into the dark skies.

She pictured the soaked fields in that direction—and the abandoned helicopter that sat parked out there.

Even Dag guessed the source of that fiery blast, his voice hushed. "Someone took out your ride."

Closer at hand, sirens wailed louder in the wake of the explosion. Shouts echoed across the park from the direction of the hotel. Moments later, the blaze of lights fled away, heading to the west, toward the outlying fields.

Seichan breathed through her nose, then slipped her SIG Sauer from her shoulder holster.

Dag eyed her. "What are you doing?"

She ignored him and turned back toward the gorge.

She suspected someone blew up that helicopter—not only to trap her and Gray here but also to draw off local law enforcement, to turn attention to the west.

Away from here.

She kept her senses sharpened, listening for any approach through the park's trees, but it was a whining noise echoing up from below that drew her attention. A trio of small lights raced downriver toward her position. Jet Skis. They all bore the logo for a local marina, and from the prominent headlamp affixed to each vessel, they must be used for exploring this subterranean world, similar to Fredrik's Zodiac.

Only these passengers weren't joyriding tourists.

Each watercraft carried two men, both wearing helmets. She spotted the telltale shadows of rifles over their shoulders.

The enemy must've also gotten word that there was a survivor of their attack.

She aimed for the lead watercraft as it approached, using the fence rail to steady her arm. From her high vantage, she squeezed off three shots. The first round took out the man seated in the back. His body went jackknifing into the river. The second shot ricocheted off the steering assembly, behind which the driver hunched. As she hoped, the vehicle wobbled. It exposed her target for a second, allowing her third round to strike his shoulder. The impact spun the driver out of his seat and into the water. The abandoned Jet Ski careened and crashed into the steel dock below.

One down . . .

She adjusted her aim toward the next target, but the enemy had quickly recognized the threat. The two remaining watercraft slalomed across the current, cutting back and forth, moving swiftly and unpredictably. She fired, emptying her weapon, but all her shots went wild.

Then the two vehicles escaped out of sight, swallowed up by the tunnel.

She banged the butt of her gun on the fence rail, cursing this reckless plan—and the man who was foolhardy enough to attempt it.

Damn you, Gray . . .

6:21 P.M.

Maybe this was a mistake.

Gray crouched low near the boat's bow—both to help Fredrik see past his shoulders and to keep his head from hitting any low-hanging stalactites. By now the flooded river had swollen to the point it almost filled the massive tunnel. Stalactites hung from the roof, looking like limestone fangs cutting into the current. And those teeth could just as readily rip the Zodiac's pontoons to shreds.

"Keep the light pointed straight ahead!" Fredrik warned.

Gray obeyed, clamping harder on the handle of a lamp at the bow of the boat. It was all he could do to help.

The current churned high up the walls with every slightest turn. Riptides and eddies spun into side caverns. And these natural formations were not the only hazards. Dead logs raced alongside them, spinning and cracking against boulders or walls.

And all the while, the roof pushed lower and lower.

Fredrik expertly fought this mad current, earning Gray's deep respect.

The Zodiac's engine whined and growled as the mountaineer spent most of the time with the propellers running in reverse, braking against this flow as best he could.

"Hang on tight!" Fredrik called.

Gray immediately spotted the danger. The tunnel veered sharply to the left. The river thrashed high around that corner, roiling with white water. It looked fierce enough to chew them up.

A change in the engine's timbre drew Gray's attention back to the stern. Fredrik had switched out of reverse and now throttled the engine up. Gray understood. They needed *speed* if they were going to make it past here.

Gray swung back around as the Zodiac shot toward the maelstrom. The boat now ran with the current rather than fighting it. Once at the turn, the engine roared even louder as Fredrik goosed the boat to an even swifter flight. The boat banked high at the corner, tilting up on one pontoon, nearly vertical.

Gray held his breath, but then they shot out of the rapids and into smoother water.

He sagged with relief.

"End of the line!" Fredrik called out and pointed.

Directly ahead, the beam of their lamp vanished into a vast cavern, one half flooded by a wide lake.

Fredrick slowed their approach, plainly cautious. "This may be tricky," he warned.

"Why?"

His answer was a single word. "Charybdis."

Gray frowned, recognizing the reference. According to Homer's *Odyssey*, Charybdis was the name of a monstrous whirlpool that sucked down unwary sailors and their ships.

That did not sound promising.

6:24 P.M.

Roland stopped suddenly, one leg slipping as he swung back around. Water flowed underfoot, streaming down from where they had abandoned their ledge alongside the lake. The trio had set off away from the flooded cavern, descending back the way they had come, pursued by the ever-growing deluge that spilled out from that overflowing lake.

Gerard led them, searching for any side path that might lead to higher ground, some way to escape the flooded roots of these mountains.

"Wait!" Roland said.

Lena halted, her face exhausted. Her helmet's headlamp flickered as the batteries began to fade. "What is it?"

"Listen."

Gerard growled. "We don't have time—"

"Just goddamn listen," he swore. He would beg God's forgiveness later for cursing, but right now he needed to get the others' attention, to cut through the despair, cold, and fatigue.

His effort worked. Lena cocked her head; then her eyes grew wide. "Is that a motor?"

Echoing from the lake behind them, cutting faintly through the roar of the water was a new note, a higher-pitched whining.

"It's an engine!" Gerard confirmed. He pointed. "Go! Go back!"

Roland needed no such encouragement. He splashed upstream, stumbling a few times, half crawling near the end. By the time he returned to the lakeside ledge, the water was ankle-deep. It was hard not to be washed back the way they had come. Gerard helped Lena join him.

He silently thanked God for His mercy.

Out on the dark lake, a bright star shone.

A boat!

"Hold tight!" a voice echoed from there. "We'll be right over!"

From behind the craft, a new pair of lights burst forth, shooting out from the tunnel.

Roland choked out a sob of relief and waved an arm.

It seemed a whole fleet had come to rescue them.

6:27 P.M.

Gray swung around as lights flared behind him, accompanied by the sharp growl of engines. A pair of Jet Skis flew into the cavern.

What the hell . . .

Blinded by their lights, he could not tell who manned the vehicles, but he had a bad feeling about it. This was confirmed a moment later when gunshots rang out—but he was already moving, responding to his gut reaction. He yanked his SIG Sauer from its shoulder holster and fired back while lunging toward the stern.

He drove Fredrik to the floor of the Zodiac.

Gray's rounds shattered the lone headlamp of the lead Jet Ski. Before the light died, he spotted shadowy masked figures aboard the watercraft: a driver and a rifleman behind him. Under Gray's barrage, the craft angled away.

The second Jet Ski swung in the opposite direction, its bright headlamp turning it into a star shooting across the dark lake.

They're trying to flank us.

Gray grit his teeth. If their Zodiac got pinned down between the two Jet Skis, they were doomed. Aboard the boat, he had the only weapon and could defend only one side at a time. He needed help.

Firing one-armed at the brightly lit craft, Gray pointed with his other hand.

"Fredrik! Stay low, but keep us ahead of those two!"

The mountaineer proved to be made of strong mettle. He rolled to the engine and gunned it. The Zodiac sped forward, trying to outrun the two Jet Skis.

Gray dove low to the starboard pontoon and continued to fire at the brighter craft, but the driver of the other Jet Ski—the one with the broken headlamp—had regained his composure. Rifle blasts rose from that direction. Rounds pelted the pontoon on that side. The whistle of escaping air announced a new threat.

Even if he and Fredrik avoided getting shot, the Zodiac might not survive.

Gray returned his attention to that dark Jet Ski. He had to get that bastard to back off. He raised his weapon—but fresh gunfire came from a new direction. Muzzle flashes flared among the trio of lights at the edge of the cavern.

Someone over there has a gun, someone who must have encountered these masked assailants before.

The dark Jet Ski swung around to face this new threat, firing toward the cavern wall. Two of the lights vanished, dropping out of sight. Rifle blasts continued to echo from over there. Gray knew whoever had come to his defense was too exposed and could not hold out for long.

Still, the brave effort offered him a breath to deal with the other watercraft.

Gray twisted back around. By now the brightly lit Jet Ski had caught up with them and rode alongside their boat. He cursed the smaller watercraft's speed and nimbleness. He aimed carefully. By his count, he was down to two rounds and had to make them count.

"Hold on!" Fredrik yelled.

Before he could object, Fredrik cut the engine. The boat slowed, then jerked hard as Fredrik kicked the propellers into reverse.

Out on the lake, Gray's target raced ahead, then swung across their bow with a rooster tail of water spraying high.

Damn it . . .

Gray's worst fear had come to pass.

Their Zodiac was now pinned between the two Jet Skis—one in front, one in back. As if giving up, Fredrik continued to chug them in reverse.

"What are you doing?" Gray called out.

Behind him, the gun battle along the cavern wall had ended. Whoever had tried to help them had either been killed or driven into hiding. Free now, the dark Jet Ski sped toward them, a hawk falling upon a wounded prey.

Gray turned to Fredrik, but the man was grinning savagely.

A scream rose from beyond the bow, from the direction of the brightly glowing Jet Ski. Gray peered over the pontoon. The enemy's craft spun within a deep depression in the lake, sucked into the maw of a large whirl-pool. Its tidal forces proved too fierce for the small engine.

As Gray watched, the Jet Ski capsized and was dragged down into the depths, along with its two passengers. The beam of its headlamp glowed out of the depths for another breath—then was gone.

Gray now understood Fredrik's maneuver. He had led the enemy straight down the throat of the monster Charybdis.

But there was still one other threat.

Gray turned and aimed toward the remaining Jet Ski, taking advantage of its driver's momentary shock. But before Gray could fire, a new volley of gun blasts erupted from the cavern wall.

Aboard the Jet Ski, the rifleman seated in the back toppled sideways, splashing heavily into the lake.

That takes care of one . . .

Gray cradled his SIG Sauer between his palms and squeezed his trigger two times.

The faceplate of the driver's helmet shattered, and his head jerked back twice from the double tap of slugs. Then his body fell limply over his controls. Left unguided, the Jet Ski flew past the Zodiac and into the heart of Charybdis, where moments later it joined its companion in the watery grave.

"Turn us around!" Gray twisted and pointed to the cluster of lights along the cavern wall. "Let's get them and get the hell out of here!"

Fredrik studied the deflated section of pontoon, then turned to the river flooding through the tunnel. "That's if we can."

6:33 P.M.

Lena huddled in the middle of the boat. Her ears still rang from all the gunfire. She tried not to stare as Roland bandaged a deep laceration on Gerard's upper arm. The French soldier had stripped off his jacket after hopping aboard the idling boat. The wound was not from a gunshot, but from a shard of blasted rock that had grazed him.

"If it hadn't been for your support, we wouldn't have made it," their rescuer told Gerard, motioning to the rifle. "That was some good shooting."

He had introduced himself as Commander Gray Pierce, a military adjunct of DARPA, if she understood him correctly. But she was beyond caring *who* rescued her, as long as they helped her escape this subterranean hellhole.

Gerard reached over and tugged his weapon closer. "I owed them . . . for my men."

Gray nodded, his face stern, plainly understanding the loyalty of a unit.

The boat's pilot—a local named Fredrik—throttled the engine up. He wore a worried expression that kept her heart thudding heavily in her chest. As they sped across the lake, she shifted farther away from the sagging section of pontoon. By the time they neared the mouth of the river tunnel, they were flying over the water, going frighteningly fast.

"Need as much speed as possible!" the pilot hollered. "River's a lot higher! So everyone stay low! It's going to be a tight squeeze!"

Lena took him at his word and ducked until her helmet was even with the pontoon. Still, she spied ahead, refusing to look away.

If I'm going to die here, I'm doing it with my eyes open.

The Zodiac reached the headwaters of the river and shot into that torrent at breakneck speed. Momentum carried them through the mouth and into the tunnel, where the roaring amplified to a deafening din. The Zodiac vibrated and shook, bobbling in the current, quickly slowing under the river's assault.

She knew what lay behind them if they lost this fight, picturing the swirl of that massive whirlpool. But what lay ahead looked no better.

Ten yards away, the river thrashed around a turn, churning with white water.

Fredrik aimed for the inside edge of the curve, where the river was less turbulent. He wrestled the boat forward as their progress slowed to a desperate crawl. He cursed in Croatian, hunkered low, forcing them forward inch by inch around the turn.

Lena stared up at the wall of raging waters that banked along the outer edge of the curve. *Oh, God, oh, God . . .*

Then they were suddenly through, past the corner. The river still flowed heavily against them, trying to drive them back into that turn, but the current was not as wild.

Still, a new danger presented itself.

"Can we get through there?" Roland called out.

"We'll have to," Fredrik answered.

From here, the storm-flooded river filled the tunnel, rising to within a yard of the roof. To make matters worse, rocky pillars jutted down from above—*stalactites*, she realized.

The pilot had to throttle back some of his speed to help guide the boat through that jagged maze.

If we got hung up on one of those . . .

But there were other dangers lurking *under* the water. A ripping sound drew her attention to the floor. A sharp spear of rock pierced the bottom of the Zodiac, tearing a hole.

Fredrik jostled them free, but the damage was done. Water surged into the boat, swamping them.

"Use your helmets to bail!" Gray ordered. "Quickly."

She yanked on her chin strap and tore off her headgear. Roland and Gerard did the same. They began a war with the river, scooping as fast as they could.

But even she knew it was useless.

Despite the scream of its overtaxed engine, the waterlogged Zodiac began to drift backward. She saw Gray share a look with Fredrik. The pilot gave a small shake of his head.

Then a new noise rose in volume—a familiar noise—coming from ahead of them.

The telltale throaty whine of a Jet Ski was unmistakable, echoing off the stone walls. A dark shape shot into view, led by a brilliant beam of light. The shadowy driver was ducked low, avoiding the roof, sweeping swiftly toward them.

It seemed the enemy was not done with them.

Swearing loudly, Gerard raised his rifle—but Gray pushed the barrel away.

"Don't shoot."

6:46 P.M.

Seichan closed in on the foundering boat.

She searched beyond it for any sign of pursuit, any sign of the two other Jet Skis. After watching the pair of enemy craft vanish into the tunnel earlier, she had scaled down the rope from the balcony to the dock, to where the abandoned third vehicle had crashed. Thankfully, the keys were still in the ignition and not tethered to the driver she had shot.

She now raced forward aboard the commandeered Jet Ski toward the Zodiac. Once there, she skidded her craft sideways and around, drawing alongside the boat. She took stock of the situation in one glance: the water filling the boat, the sunken pontoon, the screaming engine that seemed to be doing little good.

"Throw me a rope!" she ordered.

Confused faces stared back at her, but at least Gray understood.

He tossed her a mooring line. She caught it and wrapped it around a tow hook behind her seat. Gray twisted the other end of the rope in his gloved hands and braced his legs against the pontoons at the boat's bow.

She gave him a nod and sped upriver. Once the line snapped taut behind her, she added the horsepower of her Jet Ski to the engines of the Zodiac. At first they made no progress.

C'mon, you piece of—

Then slowly the two vessels started to fight the current together. The tethered pair began a painstaking slog upriver, grappling for each hard-won yard. Finally, after what seemed like an hour, the world brightened ahead.

They'd reached the tunnel's end. Once free, she lifted her face to the pelting rain, while lightning crackled overhead. She was never happier to be out in foul weather. She dragged the Zodiac back to its riverside dock, and after some maneuvering, got everyone off-loaded.

She then hopped off the Jet Ski—and into Gray's arms.

He hugged her hard. "I thought I ordered you to stay here," he whispered in her ear.

She leaned back, frowning at him. "And leave you all the fun?"

7:12 P.M.

Gray waited at the curb with the others. They huddled under a bower of trees that lined a small park. The dark bulk of Frankopan Castle shadowed the street. He wanted to be out of this damned village as quickly as possible. He didn't know who the enemy was, but they were clearly paramilitary. This was no grab-and-snatch raid by thieves, but a well-orchestrated attack.

And I've had enough with running blind.

The rumble of an engine drew his attention to the street. A BMW shot wildly around the corner and braked hard to the curb. Dag sat behind the wheel, but it wasn't the same sedan he had driven earlier. It was an SUV, a late-model X5.

"Time to go," Dag said through the rolled-down window. "Roads are open for now, but between the police still hunting for those pub raiders and the storm over the mountain passes, best to be out of here quickly." He reached through the window and slapped the side of the vehicle. "Borrowed this from a friend. Might need four-wheel drive to get us over the mountains to Zagreb."

"You're staying here," Gray said, yanking open the driver's door.

Dag pulled it back shut. "Do you know these roads? Who knows what's washed out up there?" He patted his chest. "I know all the ways up and over these mountains."

Fredrik offered some advice. "Kid's right. You'll want someone who knows the terrain."

Gray looked questioningly at the mountaineer.

The man lifted both palms. "No offense, but I think I'm done playing tour guide for you all."

Gray couldn't fault him and nodded.

"Besides," Fredrik said, "I'll get Commandant Gerard the medical attention he needs."

Gray glanced to the Frenchman. The soldier had also declined accompanying them, committed instead to staying and discovering the fate of his men. Gray had understood, knowing he would choose the same if matters were reversed. Gerard offered one promise, though: to share any knowledge he gained from his search—about the enemy or about the two kidnapped professors. Gray had given the soldier a secure number to call.

With matters settled, Gray got everyone off the street and into the waiting SUV. He took the front passenger seat, leaving the back to Seichan, Lena Crandall, and Father Novak. The plan was to head to Zagreb, where they would regroup.

After Gray said his good-byes to the other two men, they set off out of town.

Lena leaned forward from the backseat. She clutched a cell phone in her hand. Gray had already taken out the battery, fearful that the enemy might use it to locate her again.

"When is it okay to call my sister?"

"Not yet," he warned. "For now, it's better to let the enemy believe you're dead."

She leaned back, looking dissatisfied with his answer and worried about her twin.

He tried to reassure her. "Your sister is safe where she is."

Lena sighed. "That's true, I suppose."

8

Maria sat at the small table inside Baako's classroom. She stared down at the cell phone resting on the Formica top. After connecting briefly to Lena, she had immediately alerted Monk and Amy. The two were up in her office, fielding calls to D.C. for the past hour, but so far there had been no news relayed to her.

Or at least nothing they're telling me.

She stared over to the large man waiting with her. Joe Kowalski had his own phone in hand, ready to answer it if his partner called with any update. He paced the room, striding back and forth like some caged beast. He seemed as anxious for any news as she. After making that brief connection to Lena, Maria had come close to collapsing, to losing it entirely, but he had held her, silently reassured her, and mumbled a promise that some colleague named Gray would find her sister.

She appreciated his attempt at reassuring her and studied him as he made another round of the room. His face was craggy, traced with the ghosts of old scars, all underpinned by a square jaw. His nose fit his features, bearing a large knot, crooked from some old break. And while he was clearly a battle-hardened man, his ears stuck out, giving him a boyish quality.

A familiar *oof-oof* drew her attention to the room's other occupant.

Baako stood before the classroom's whiteboard. He had an erasable marker clutched in his left fist. He had scrawled four large letters on the board.

LENA

Maria scooted to her feet in amazement. She and Lena had taught Baako the rudiments of spelling, a necessary part of sign language. They had used a set of plastic alphabet blocks as an educational tool, teaching him simple words, like *cat* and *dog*, along with the names of a few people who worked here: his caretaker Jack, his furry friend Tango, and of course, Maria and Lena.

Kowalski stopped next to her, looking as dumbfounded as she felt. "He can write?"

"He likes to draw, even paint, but he's never written words like this before."

Baako noted their attention, his dark eyes large, staring between them, hooting slightly, as if unsure this was okay.

It's more than okay.

"What a smart boy," Maria cooed softly.

Baako tapped a finger of his right hand to his chest, then gestured with his fingers, repeating the sign a few times. [*Love, love, love . . .*] He ended by tapping the tip of his marker under each letter on the board, then staring again at Maria.

She smiled. "I love Lena, too."

Baako must have overheard their recent conversations over the phone, recognized all the concern about the fate of Lena, and had internalized it. Perhaps sensing Maria's distress, he had reached deep inside to show how he felt, to demonstrate this latent talent, one that lay hidden until now.

She felt tears threatening, both of astonishment and love. She wiped at her eyes.

Lena should be here to see this.

Baako dropped his marker to the floor and came over to her. He hugged an arm around her waist.

"You're such a good boy," she murmured.

"Penmanship could be better," Kowalski commented.

She glanced over and saw a teasing smile on his face, belying how his eyes shone with a measure of awe as he stared at the board.

After another moment, she slipped loose of Baako's embrace. "I think we can all use some fresh air," she said, checking the time, then turning to Kowalski. "I normally take this furry fellow for a midday walk, and it looks like we're overdue."

The big man glanced to the observation window. "Where do you take him?"

"The primate center sits on over a hundred acres of woodlands. We have a regular trail we use." She patted Baako. "He loves it."

She felt a twinge of guilt, knowing in her heart how much he truly came alive when outdoors, free of this place. He belonged in the open air, not trapped down here. But she also knew that he was much more than a simple gorilla. Only here, properly taught and nurtured, could he achieve his full potential.

She sighed, not entirely convincing herself of this.

But just keep telling yourself that.

Maria cleared her throat and faced Kowalski. "You don't have to come," she offered. "If you want to join your partner up in my office . . ."

He shrugged. "I could use some fresh air."

She doubted if this was true; more likely he had been ordered to stay with her. Either way, she needed to get out of here, to escape the cloud of anxiety that had grown to fill this space over the past hour.

Better to be moving than sitting here wringing my hands.

She crossed back to the table and retrieved her cell phone, not wanting to miss any call about Lena. Baako watched her, pouncing a bit on his knuckles, plainly anticipating what was to come.

"Ready for a walk, Baako?" she asked.

He leaped high, hooting loudly, then charged alongside her as she headed toward the security cage that framed the exit door.

Kowalski trailed them. "I'd take that as a yes."

As she unlatched the cage, Baako stared back. She felt the tension vibrating through the young gorilla's body—both from excitement and from irritation that Kowalski appeared to be coming with them.

She sought to distract Baako. "How about we collect Tango from the kennels? Bet he'd like a walk, too."

At the mention of the Queensland Terrier pup's name, Baako forgot all about Kowalski. He took Maria's hand and dragged her toward the exit. She laughed and unlocked the way with her key.

Once through the door, Baako shifted closer to her. He still kept hold of her hand, something drilled into him whenever they left his domicile. He lifted his other arm and waited for the other safeguard to be implemented. She removed a pair of GPS trackers from a hook next to the door and fastened the magnetic bands around each of his wrists.

"There you go," she said. "All set."

He huffed quietly.

She led Baako and Kowalski toward the rear of the building. Baako hugged close to her, especially when they moved past the other labs that ran various research projects. Though the doors were sealed, he must have still smelled or sensed the presence of the other animals, mostly primates like him: rhesus monkeys involved in a hormone replacement study, sooty mangabeys used to evaluate the evolution of growth, squirrel and cynomolgus monkeys employed in various vaccine and neuroscience programs. The screech of a chimpanzee from behind one closed door pushed Baako tight to her side.

"It's okay," she consoled.

But was it? How disconcerting was this for him?

She finally hurried through to the kennels, where a familiar lanky form greeted them.

"Taking the big guy out?" Jack asked with a wide smile, leaning on a broom.

"Tango, too." She nodded toward a nearby room of kennels.

"I'll go fetch him," the student said. "But you should know that it's drizzling out there, and after last night's downpour, the trails are getting pretty dang muddy. Might want to pull on a set of rubber boots."

"I'll be fine." Maria turned to Kowalski, eyeing his suit and a surprisingly fashionable set of wing tips. "But maybe you'd prefer to wait here after all."

He stared down at his shoes, looking mournful. "These are hand-stitched Brunello Cucinellis."

Jack offered a suggestion. "I have an extra set of boots and coveralls. You're welcome to use them. Might be a little small, but should do."

Kowalski shrugged. "Works for me."

Maria waited as Jack led the man into the nearby locker room. She stared toward the rear loading dock that offered access to the back acres of the primate center. This delay allowed her worries to settle more heavily over her shoulders.

C'mon, Lena . . . be all right.

Warm fingers tightened on her hand.

She turned to find Baako gazing up at her. The anguished squint of those caramel eyes was easy to read.

Seems I'm not the only one worried.

11:57 A.M.

What I do for Sigma . . .

Alone in the changing room, Kowalski neatly folded his pants and draped them over the wing tips resting at the bottom of the metal locker. His shirt and suit jacket already hung from a hook inside. Standing in his boxers and socks, he lifted the set of borrowed coveralls. The kid who left them was almost as tall as Kowalski but as skinny as a beanpole. Luckily, the student preferred to wear his coveralls loose and boxy.

Sighing, Kowalski tugged into the borrowed set of work clothes. He had to inhale deeply to zip the front over his belly and chest.

That'll do, I guess.

From a bench, he lifted up the strap of his shoulder holster, weighted down by his sidearm. No way he could wear this under the coveralls, and he wasn't sure the geneticist would appreciate him carrying it openly. Monk had warned him to be discreet. So with a sorry shake of his head, he hooked the holster next to his suit jacket.

"Not like anyone's gonna let me shoot that gorilla anyway," he mumbled.

Still, his hand hovered over the butt of his weapon—a newly purchased Heckler & Koch .45. He gritted his teeth, unable to abandon it.

You belong with me, baby.

He pulled the gun from the holster and shoved it into a deep back pocket of his coveralls. The bulge was far from discreet, but what was a guy to do?

He slammed the locker closed, locked it, and pushed his feet into a cold set of rubber boots. Ready now, he headed back out to Maria. He arrived at the same time the student returned from the kennels with an exuberant gray-and-black-mottled young dog dancing at his side.

"Tango," Maria introduced the pup with a smile.

The gorilla chuffed in greeting, lifting his eyebrows high, waving his free arm.

Jack unhooked the leash and let Tango go bounding up to his friend, the pup's back end wagging as much as his tail.

"Ready?" Maria asked.

"Let's get this over with," Kowalski grumbled, following after the gorilla and dog.

Guess I'm Sigma's official pet walker now, too.

They headed to the open door of a rear loading dock. Outside, a light drizzle fell from a low gray sky. Still, the air smelled clean and inviting, free of the musky odors of animals and the ammonia scent of cleaning products.

They set off down a concrete ramp to a crushed gravel trail that led through a damp green meadow. The student, Jack, accompanied them with leash in hand. Once in the field, Maria let go of her charge's hand, and Baako went bounding across the wet grass, chased by a barking dog.

Fifty yards away rose a dark forest of pine, oaks, and white cedar.

"Is it safe to let them roam loose like that?" Kowalski asked.

She pointed to a distant fence line. "We've had this section of the field station cordoned off. While the chain link might not be an obstacle for Baako, he knows to stay within its confines. But I don't think he would ever want to escape anyway." She swept an arm wide. "Everything Baako loves is here. And despite that freewheeling carousing he's demonstrating at the moment with Tango, he's not the bravest soul. In many ways, he's a mama's boy."

Kowalski noted how her voice hiccuped over that last sentence, hearing both the affection and maybe even a little guilt. She crossed her arms as they headed through the grass, her gaze wistful upon the two animals playing together.

As they followed the pair, Kowalski asked a question that had been nagging him. "So how come you and your sister both became geneticists?"

"What? You think only men can be scientists?" She smiled softly at him, plainly teasing. "I guess it goes back to the fact that we were born twins. When you grow up with someone identical to you—while knowing you're both so different inside—such a dichotomy carries with you, makes you want to understand it better. And, in turn, understand yourself better. So over time, questions became curiosity, and curiosity drew us into our profession."

"So it's not just the sexy lab coats?" he asked, offering a small teasing grin of his own.

"Well, I didn't say there weren't perks."

By now the furry pair ahead of them approached the tree line, where a narrow trail cut into the woods. Jack trotted forward to keep the animals in sight, demonstrating the usual boundless energy of youth. Or maybe the kid just wanted to reach the shelter of the trees and get out of the rain.

Kowalski ducked his head as the light drizzle began to coalesce into heavier drops. He suddenly wished he had a thick pelt like Baako and Tango. He set a swifter pace toward the trees.

Halfway across the meadow, Jack drew to a stop ahead of them.

Kowalski's guard went up at the sudden halt; then he saw it, too. Movement in the trees, a shift of shadows. A blast of a rifle made Maria jump. He swung his arm around, scooped her around the chest, and carried her to the ground, burying her in the tall grass.

He sheltered her with his own body as another shot rang out. He saw Jack spin around, blood spraying from his shoulder. The kid went sprawling into the meadow.

"Stay down!" Kowalski hissed at Maria.

He yanked his pistol from his coverall pocket and slithered on his elbows through the wet grass toward the student. At the same time, Baako came bounding back toward them, knuckling on one arm, carrying the young dog under the other. Kowalski couldn't get out of the way in time. The panicked pair bowled over him, striking him hard enough to knock the gun from Kowalski's mud-slick fingers. The pistol went sailing into the tall grass and brush.

Goddamn it.

With no time to hunt for his weapon, Kowalski reached Jack, who lay on his back, stunned, moaning in pain. Scared eyes stared back at Kowalski. Dark shapes, all wearing knit masks, shifted out of the forest's shadows and came running low through the grass.

Kowalski glanced back to the primate center.

Too far.

Thinking fast, he wet his palm with Jack's blood and smeared it over the side of the student's face. "Hold your breath," he warned. "Play dead."

It was all he could do for the kid.

He crawled back to Maria as the dark group arrowed across the meadow, aiming for where Baako huddled with the geneticist. The gorilla's bulk was an island in this green sea.

Kowalski tugged at Maria's arm. "Leave him. If we stay in the tall grass, we might be able to—"

"Never." She yanked her arm free. "I won't abandon him."

A voice shouted. "Dr. Crandall! Come with us . . . with Baako . . . and no one else needs to get hurt!"

Kowalski bit back a curse. Apparently the bastards must've known about Maria's routine, about this daily excursion, and set up this ambush accordingly.

Maria stared toward Kowalski, looking to him for some way out.

With a groan, he demonstrated their only recourse. He lifted his arms and stood, facing an arc of assault rifles pointed at them. "Don't shoot!"

Maria hesitated only long enough to slip something from Baako's wrist and attach it to the dog's collar. "Home," she said and pointed back toward the primate center. "Go home."

The pup simply shook, too frightened to move.

As if trying to help, Baako pushed at his friend's furry rump. This seemed to work. The small dog took off, tail tucked, racing low to the ground toward the distant loading dock.

Kowalski tried to block the pup's flight with his own body and waved his arms, keeping attention fixed on himself. Maria helped by standing herself. She kept a firm grip on Baako's hand while slipping something into her back pocket. The gorilla whimpered at her side, sticking to her legs.

"I'll do what you ask!" she called out. "Just don't harm—"

Another blast rang out, cutting her off.

Kowalski turned toward one of the gunmen. He held a smoking pistol in hand, his weapon pointed down at the ground. It was the man who had called out a moment ago, the apparent leader of this group.

The bastard stood over Jack's slumped body.

Kowalski ground his teeth together as he glared at the gunman.

You fucker.

Maria moaned next to him, sagging closer to Kowalski. The leader stalked another two steps closer, his pistol lifting, the barrel steaming in the rain. The gun was pointed straight at Kowalski's chest.

Kowalski glared back, knowing what was coming.

As usual, he was wrong.

Maria stepped in front of him. "Don't! If you want my help, if you want Baako, then you want Joe, too." She elbowed him in the gut in her attempt to point at him. "He's Baako's trainer. Knows everything about him. How to keep him calm. How to get him to cooperate."

She spoke rapidly, trying everything to make him sound important. He stared down at his coveralls, at the Emory University badge on the pocket. He swallowed hard and reached toward Baako, holding out his hand, knowing this was his only hope.

Don't leave me hanging, buddy.

Baako stared back at him, his brown eyes glassy with fear, his features dripping with water. Finally a dark arm lifted, and leathery fingers wrapped around his own.

The leader stood for a long breath, studying all three of them. Then finally he lowered his pistol and turned away. "Get them to the chopper!" he ordered the others.

Kowalski blew out a breath of relief.

As the assault team closed in around their group, Baako let go of him and signed by cupping one hand under the other and lifting them both higher. But the meaning could be read as plainly in those frightened eyes.

[*Help us*]

The gorilla hugged tightly to Maria. She also looked pleadingly toward him. He knew he owed them both. They had saved his life just now.

But what the hell can I do alone?

12:23 P.M.

Monk rubbed his eyes, then returned to reading a radiologist's assessment of a CT scan of the hybrid gorilla's brain. The gross morphology was distinctly different from a regular gorilla's in many interesting ways. He perused a paragraph about the folding found in Baako's cortex. The number of surface gyri and sulci—the hills and valleys—was three times as numerous, suggesting the brain's surface area was larger, requiring it to be more tightly folded to fit inside the gorilla's skull.

It was equally fascinating and unnerving.

Behind him, Amy Wu spoke on her cell. Her phone had rung a moment ago, likely another update from her colleagues at the White House.

"Understood," she said, pacing behind him. "I'll proceed accordingly. *Zàijiàn.*"

Monk's ears pricked at her use of the formal Chinese for good-bye as she ended the call. So maybe it wasn't a call from the White House, though he couldn't rule that out. The oddity drew him to catch her reflection in a dark corner of the computer monitor. She pocketed her phone, then reached to her lower back, as if to stretch out a kink.

Her hand returned, revealing a small silver pistol in her grip.

Monk reacted instinctively to the threat. He ducked, while jerking his thighs back, sending the office chair shooting into Amy Wu. Her gun blasted explosively loud, shattering the computer monitor atop the desk as he hit the floor.

He rolled to the side as the chair struck Amy in the legs, knocking her back a step. He used the moment to yank his Glock from its shoulder holster. He pointed, half blindly, and fired, trying less to kill her as keep her off guard. Still, his round grazed her thigh. She dropped with a cry of pain to one knee, leveling her pistol at him on the floor.

By now he had enough wits to steady his Glock with both palms and point it at her. He caught her eye over his weapon, her expression cold, dropping her facade of the cooperative DARPA researcher.

They both fired at the same time.

Her round burned past his ear as he twisted to the side. She was not as quick. His shot grazed her neck, knocking her back. He lunged from the floor, his pistol raised and fixed. She glared at him and managed to swing her weapon back up. It centered on him before he could kick it away. With no other choice, he fired again, a head shot this time, taking no chances.

She collapsed to the floor, her pistol dropping from her limp fingers.

He toed it away, though he knew she was surely dead.

He reached to her body and retrieved her cell phone. She might not be able to talk, but there might be something on the phone to explain this attack.

His next thought was of more immediate concern.

Kowalski and Maria.

Someone had phoned Wu a moment ago, likely triggering this ambush.

That could only mean one thing.

I was a loose end.

Monk charged to the door, weapon in hand, and raced into the deserted hallway and down to Baako's classroom. He burst into the outer antechamber and skidded up to the observation window. The space was empty.

No bodies, no blood, no sign of a fight.

Even Baako was gone.

He searched around, momentarily confused. *Where are they?*

A shout echoed from a long hall that stretched toward the rear of the building. He ran toward it, hearing the anger, recognizing the voice of Leonard Trask, the director of this field station.

"Who let this dog loose?" the man shouted in the distance. "Get this mutt back in its kennel!"

Monk sprinted toward the ruckus. He didn't know if any of this had to do with the missing group, but Trask might know what had happened or at least offer some insight.

He passed a series of labs and ended up in a larger space bordered by rooms that held dog runs, stainless steel cages, and lockers. At the back, a loading dock's double set of tall doors stood closed. A smaller exit stood open to the rainy day.

Nearby, a dog huddled, soaking wet, trembling all over.

Trask loomed over the scared pup, pinning it against the wall with a boot. Finally a female student in an Emory University coverall came running up with a leash.

Monk joined them. "What's going on?"

Trask turned, his face red, his eyes furious. "Someone let—" His voice cut off upon seeing the pistol still in Monk's hand. "What're you doing?"

He didn't have time to explain.

The student freed the dog and hooked the leash to the pup's collar. As she did so, something fell loose and struck the concrete floor. She retrieved it and examined it curiously.

Trask held out his hand. "Let me see that."

She passed it over. "It looks like one of Baako's trackers."

Monk stepped closer. "Is she right?"

"Yes," Leonard answered with a scowl. "But what's it doing on the dog?"

The student tried to explain, looking nervous. She pointed toward the exit. "Dr. Crandall took Baako and Tango out for a walk."

"When?" Monk asked.

"I don't know. Maybe half an hour ago. I had just come on shift when Jack fetched Tango out of the kennels."

Monk stalked to the exit and stared out into the rain and across a wet meadow.

"They're probably still out in the woods," Trask said. "There's a maze of trails out there."

Monk wasn't buying it. He squinted, his gaze following a gravel path that carved through the tall grass. Something dark obscured the trail half-way across.

Damn it.

He grabbed Trask by the arm and hauled him along as he ran down the ramp and along that path. As he feared, the obstruction proved to be a body.

Trask gasped, falling back a step, refusing to draw closer. "It's Jack."

Monk searched the surrounding meadow, but there was no sign of the others. He studied the dark woods, but he knew he was too late. Whoever had called Amy Wu would have done so only after their goal was accomplished.

"They're gone," he mumbled into the rain.

Monk turned and snatched the tracker band still in Trask's fingers.

But maybe not lost.

12:48 P.M.

Baako huddles in the back of the cage, hugging his knees to his chest. The roaring noise rips into his head, yet still he hears the pounding of his heart in his ears. He wants to scream, to pound his chest, to let his terror loose. Through a nearby window, he sees the world whip past, slapped by rain. His gut churns at the reeking smell of the small space, at the bobbling of everything around him.

The only center in this storm is the familiar shape of his mother. She sits beside his cage. Her eyes are too large; her skin is too white. She breathes too hard.

He reaches a hand to her.

Mama . . .

But her arms are held behind her, tied together.

Same with the big man seated opposite her. His lips are thin and tight, his nostrils flared, his eyes poke everywhere. He looks ready to pound his chest, but his arms are also stuck behind him.

The bad shadow people, those who came with no faces, crowd the other seats. They show their faces now, peeling back the shadows. Their eyes are pinched, their skin different.

Like the woman, Mama's friend, who sometimes comes and tickles him.

But these ones are not nice like her.

Baako cowers lower, recalling how they forced him into the cage inside here, prodding him forward with a stick that burned and sparked with blue fire. Only Mama stopped them. She spoke soft words that Baako was too frightened and in pain to understand. Still, he let her guide him inside.

Then they were mean to Mama. They roughed her all over and took her phone . . . and the man's phone. Baako knows phones. He sometimes talked to his other mother, Lena, on one. He whimpers thinking of her now.

"It's okay, Baako," Mama says.

He softly hoots his disagreement.

It's not okay.

She squirms backward in her seat, reaching through the bars with her tied hands. She looks over her shoulder, her eyes on him. The fingers of one hand move, forming letters.

[Hide]

He does not understand. His mothers sometimes play hiding games with him. Like putting a banana in a box that he must turn and twist, push and prod, until he could get inside and eat it.

He draws his lips back from his teeth, showing his confusion.

She opens the fingers of her other hand. In the palm rests a circle of plastic and steel. He knows it and shows her this by cuffing his wrist with his own fingers. He remembers how she took one of the circles off and put it on Tango, then removed the second one and put it in her back pocket before the bad men came.

Her empty hand forms words again while she thrusts the circle at him.

[Take . . . Hide]

He obeys and scoops it from her fingers.

Then a voice shouts from the front. Baako is too frightened to understand, only hears the anger.

But Mama says words he knows. "Baako is scared." At the same time, she speaks to him with her fingers.

[Hide . . . Now]

Baako slinks back to the rear of the cage, unsure how to do this. He wants to be a good boy. Finally he thinks and turns from everyone. He lifts his hand to his mouth and slips the circle between his lips. He tongues it into his cheek and holds it there.

One of the bad men shoves Mama back around in her seat, but she still nods to Baako, smiling when there can be no words. He understands, knows what she means.

[Good boy]

Even the large man in the opposite seat stares at him. He does not smile, but Baako reads the approval in his face.

Baako settles back, calmer now, certain of one truth.

I am a good boy.

9

"Qǐng bú shì . . . qǐng bú shì . . ." the man pleaded, on his knees, his head bowed low. *"Shàojiàng* Lau, *qǐng bú shì."*

Major General Jiaying Lau kept her back to him, reviewing a clipboard, which held the morning reports from the installation's various lab divisions. She stood before a window that overlooked the Beijing Zoo, one of the world's largest zoos. It was also the oldest in China, dating back to 1906, when it was as an experimental farm.

How fitting a start, she thought, *considering the current project.*

Jiaying took a measure of pride, knowing all the hard work and years of painstaking detail it required to bring everything to fruition. She stared out at the park. Her view was through an upper-story window of Changguanlou, a French-inspired baroque manor in the zoo's northwest corner, built during the nineteenth century to house Empress Dowager Cixi.

She imagined the empress staring through this same window and pictured herself similarly, a queen of all she surveyed.

And in so many important ways that was true.

She might not have full control over the zoo's many exhibition halls, nor the fifteen thousand animals housed across the two hundred acres of parklands—but she had *full* authority to what lay below it, an excavation worthy of the more recent constructions built for the Beijing Summer Olympics. And her installation had a goal far more important than gaining global recognition and attention.

Jiaying closed her eyes, taking in the breadth of her project.

It had all started from a seed stolen thousands of kilometers away and planted deep underground here, where it had already taken root and promised greater glory for her country. That seed had come from a valley in southwest Tibet, not far from the borders of Nepal and India. It was a spot sacred to Buddhists and Hindus. The source of that holiness was Mount Kailash. It was the highest of the valley's snowcapped peaks, where supposedly Lord Shiva resided in eternal meditation.

She scowled at such ancient superstitions as she let out a breath, opening her eyes to the skyline of Beijing beyond the zoo's borders. She had studied at the University of Science and Technology here, where she was eventually recruited by the deputy secretary general to train at the Academy of Military Science. Her back drew straighter, remembering that honor. She had been nineteen at the time, when her future was a book of blank pages, yet to be written upon.

But that was over four decades ago.

She caught her reflection in the window, noting her gray hair, cut short and combed meticulously behind her ears. She read her past history in the lines of her face. She had no children and no husband, was married instead to her career in the military. She stood now dressed in her pine-green uniform, a single star emblazoned on her epaulets, marking her rank as *shàojiàng*, a major general in the People's Liberation Army. She polished each star every morning, but over the passing years she did so with a measure of bitterness, frustrated with the lack of additional stars to grace her uniform.

She knew her career had stagnated—both because she was a woman and because she worked within the PLA's scientific division. Still, it didn't keep her from wishing to earn additional stars, possibly even to be tapped as the PLA's military science director, a position no woman had ever attained. That was her objective, but to succeed in that next step meant first proving her worth here. She was gambling her entire career and reputation in this venture.

It must not fail.

Below her window, a blue lagoon held a plethora of long-legged cranes, their plumage glowing in shades of white and pink, all overhung by a leafy green bower dappled with flowers. She drew it all in. Beyond the lagoon rose the numerous animal halls and aviaries of the zoo, set amid faux savannahs and wound through by streams and dotted by a score of interconnected ponds. Far on the opposite side of the park stood the zoo's prized attraction and compound, drawing hundreds of thousands of visitors a year: the panda house.

Still, as magnificent as the park appeared, it was what lay tunneled and excavated *beneath* these grounds that truly housed the marvels of the natural world: over thirty thousand square meters of laboratories, pens, and climate-controlled habitats. Inspiration for this installation had come when a similar research facility was discovered hidden beneath the Baghdad Zoo, exposed during the U.S. invasion in 2003.

But her station dwarfed the feeble effort of the Iraqis, extending beneath the full breadth of the city's zoo. Initially, her facility's forays into genetic studies had been rudimentary, but as the refinements in techniques grew exponentially over the past years, so did her hopes for what she had started.

Then came a breakthrough, a discovery that changed everything, found on the sacred slopes of Mount Kailash in Tibet . . .

For more than a decade, a small anthropological research station had been established in that remote valley, studying the genomes of the local people. The site had been chosen because of the flow of pilgrims to the area, drawing people from far and wide. The anthropologists had been building a genetic database of the ancient migration patterns throughout the region. The military had funded this research to support China's claims during local border disputes, the boundaries of which were still under much disagreement, involving conflicts with India, Tibet, Nepal, and Bhutan.

Along with gathering those genetic samples, the anthropologists had also collected stories, tales of the sightings of rare animals, like the elusive snow leopard or the Tibetan blue bear. Over time, the local shepherds and herdsmen began to bring samples to the scientists: bits of fossilized bone, old ratty hides, chunks of petrified wood.

Then eight years ago, a local Tibetan herder guided one of the researchers to a cave high up the slopes of Mount Kailash, far above the snow line, grounds considered too sacred to tread. The herder claimed to have discovered the lair of a yeti, the infamous monster of the Himalayas. Such tales flourished across the centuries, rising from every country, the creature going by many different names. In Bhutan, the yeti was known as the Migo; among the Chinese mountain tribes, the Alma. But the discovery that day was not the lair of a yeti, but a cavern holding a scientific treasure far greater than any found before.

It was fortuitous that the researcher on hand was a fellow member of the Academy of Military Science. He kept his discovery secret and contacted the deputy director of the academy, who sent Jiaying Lau to investigate. Upon realizing the full implication—and the possibilities—she confiscated what was found there and brought it to Beijing, where she secretly gathered the best and brightest of the Chinese scientific community: zoologists, archaeologists, molecular biologists, genetic engineers, even experts in reproductive and developmental studies.

The zoo and her installation were the perfect place to investigate an enigma that could change mankind forever. But for this mission to succeed, especially under the timetable given her, no lapses in security could be tolerated.

"*Qǐng bú shì . . .*" the man pleaded once again.

The petitioner—a twenty-eight-year-old computer tech named Quon Zheng—had used the military's satellite communication to place an unauthorized call last night. He had been attempting to reach a girlfriend in Shanghai. While there was no nefarious intent behind the young man's action, such contact with the larger world was strictly forbidden by those employed here.

Jiaying closed her eyes, remembering that hard climb up the sacred mountain of Kailash, the supposed seat of Lord Shiva, the destroyer of illusions.

Her own family name of Lau meant to destroy.

She took strength from that.

"Take him," she ordered the two soldiers at the door. "Cast him into the Ark."

A cry rose from Quon, one of horror and fright. He did not have the clearance to fully comprehend where he was being taken, but rumors abounded in such a close-knit community, of people vanishing, never to be heard from again.

She stiffened her back as he was dragged away. She stared out at the blue lagoon at the cranes stalking slowly through the water.

A new voice rose behind her, catching her off guard. "*Chéngmahn, Shàojiàng* Lau."

The apology for the interruption was in Cantonese. Though the manner of speech was respectful, she still bristled at the veiled insult. She had been raised in an impoverished village in the Guangdong province of southern China, where Cantonese was spoken. She knew the speaker was reminding her of her humble origins, knowing Mandarin, the official dialect of China, was a second language for her.

Jiaying turned and answered crisply in Mandarin. "You are not interrupting, *Zhōngxiào* Sun." She kept her voice polite but stressed his rank—lieutenant colonel—reminding the officer of his inferior status. "What is it?"

Chang Sun gave a bow of his head before speaking. He stood as tall as she and was dressed as crisply in a khaki uniform, but he was two decades younger than her and carried all the hallmarks of youth: firm muscle, dark black hair, and an unlined face; also raw ambition shone from his eyes.

Chang was the same officer whom that Tibetan herder had guided up to the cave on the snowy slopes of Mount Kailash. His discovery there and his expanded role here earned him a promotion in rank—but like her, he wanted this venture to push him higher, even if it meant climbing over her.

"I thought you should know that my team has arrived with the package from Croatia," he said. "They are being brought over as we speak."

"Very good. And what of the other package, the one from the United States?"

"Still en route, but they should be landing within the next few hours."

She nodded her acknowledgment, giving the man grudging respect. While she commanded this installation, Chang Sun coordinated the military and intelligence facets of the operation. His role was to be her strong arm abroad—but she also recognized how much he would like to turn that upon her someday.

Knowing that, she sought to knock him down a peg. "I heard we lost our contact within the White House's scientific establishment, that she was shot during the operation in Atlanta."

Chang lowered his gaze. "A regrettable loss, but one we must now prove was worth it."

She knew this last was directed at her. As the scientific head of this project, it would be up to her and her team here to justify such a loss.

"And what of those loose ends in Croatia?" she pressed. "Have they been cleaned up?"

She kept her voice steady, but frustration still burned. Chang's intelligence sources had learned too late that the American geneticist's twin sister had been on site in those mountains. The woman had arrived a day earlier than expected. The plan had been to kidnap her from Leipzig before she left Germany. With both sisters in hand, she could have leveraged the one against the other to gain their respective cooperation. Furthermore, that lapse in intelligence required accelerating their plans to raid the U.S. primate lab. Such a rushed timetable likely contributed to the loss of their operative in the White House.

"We believe Dr. Lena Crandall is dead," Chang said, "but the search continues to corroborate this."

"And the ten men you lost out there?"

Chang sighed, showing rare irritation. "Their bodies are clean. No one will be able to trace them back to us. We've already prepared a statement of denial if any accusations are made."

"Do you have any thoughts about *who* took out your men?"

Chang shook his head, his eyes tightening with anger—not at the deaths of his comrades, but at this black mark upon his record. "Still unknown."

"Perhaps that is something you should concentrate on," she suggested, happy to direct his attentions elsewhere. She motioned to the door. "I should prepare to greet our guests."

"Yes, Major General Lau." He bowed his way out.

She returned her attention to the window, staring out at the blue lagoon as the sun rose on this new day. Still, she pictured another lake, one that lay within the shadow of Mount Kailash in Tibet: Lake Rakshastal, the Devil's Lake, named for its bitter waters and the ten-headed demon said to lurk in its depths.

She frowned at her reflection, knowing there were things worse than demons in this world.

Especially as I had a hand in creating them.

6:44 A.M.

With his wrists cuffed behind him, Quon Zheng stumbled along the hall. Two soldiers flanked him. One held his elbow; the other wielded an electric prod that encouraged him to keep moving. They moved down a long wide hall that cut through the heart of the facility, heading toward its far end, where few were allowed to trespass. Some faces stared at him as he was marched along, but those gazes quickly dropped in fear. Bodies hurriedly shuffled out of his way.

From a side hall, a cadre of four soldiers appeared, guarding a pair of older men who looked exhausted, their wrists also bound behind them. Another two soldiers carried a large coffin-like crate at the team's rear. He imagined the group had come from the military helipads that serviced this facility.

He gazed anxiously in that direction and remembered arriving here ten months ago himself, so hopeful, so proud. His eyes now clouded with tears, picturing his elderly mother, who loved to visit the tea gardens of Shanghai, and his younger sister, who doted upon her. He also remembered the glow of his girlfriend's eyes in the dark, the brush of her lips.

Voices drew his attention closer. The newly arrived captives whispered to each other in English, searching all around. The pair was rushed headlong, most likely being taken to Major General Lau's office. Quon caught the eyes of the older of the two gentlemen. The man looked equally scared, but his voice was steady, his accent British. The stranger called to Quon, perhaps sensing an ally in someone similarly under guard.

"You there! What is this place?"

Quon knew enough English to understand and forced out one word, both warning and description of this place: "*diyù* . . ." He craned back as they passed and repeated. "*Tā shì diyù!*"

The strangers were swept down the hall and away from him, but the other captive's shocked exclamation trailed back to Quon, this one's words flavored by a French accent.

"That man said . . . he said *this place is hell.*"

Quon wanted to cry out, to tell them more, but his back exploded with pain as the electric prod bit into his side. He gasped and kept his feet only because of the iron grip on his elbow.

He was half dragged, half prodded down the rest of the hall and through a warren of other passageways. In neighboring rooms, he spotted pens of sheep, even stalls holding the shaggy bulks of yaks. Finally they reached a tall archway over a large black steel door. A sign above it glowed in fiery crimson.

"No!" Quon moaned, reading the name.

The Ark.

Rumors were whispered about this vault, though few had ever seen what was hidden behind those tall steel doors.

One of the guards placed his palm on a blue-glowing reader on the neighboring wall. Moments later, the thick vault swung open with a sigh of hydraulics.

A gust of cold air reached Quon, smelling of something muskier than even the yaks he had passed. The hairs on his neck stood on end. He backed away, responding with an instinctual terror. But strong hands gripped his shoulders. His wrists were cut free, and he was shoved through the opening.

He fell to his knees just beyond the threshold, finding himself inside a cage. Beyond the thick bars, a large habitat opened, cut out of the natural bedrock. The walls rose twenty meters high, forming a steep-walled pit, the floor strewn with black boulders. To either side, the cliff faces were pitted with caves, some close to the ground, others higher up.

As he cowered, the vault sealed behind him.

His heart pounded harder in his chest.

Please, no . . .

From the caves, shadows stirred. Then closer at hand, one of the boulders shifted, unfolding to reveal an inexplicable horror.

Quon screamed, scrabbling back against the steel vault—as the door to his small cage rattled upward.

SECOND

THE RELIC OF EVE

10

Gray read the mix of hope and fear in Lena Crandall's face as he entered the small kitchen. Hand-hewn rafters supported the low ceiling, while the walls were exposed bricks dating back to the seventeenth century. The kitchen belonged to the rectory of Saint Catherine's Church in Zagreb, the capital of Croatia. The geneticist was seated at an old oak-plank table at the back. Behind her, a fire crackled and popped in a soot-blackened stone fireplace.

"Is there any news about Maria?" Lena asked.

Seichan also looked on expectantly. She pushed away from the neighboring counter and passed him a steaming mug of coffee. He accepted it, while also nabbing a cheese pastry from a platter behind her—something called *štrukli*—and crossed to the table.

"I did get an update from Washington," Gray said. "They're still monitoring the GPS tracker believed to be with your sister's party, but they're only getting an intermittent signal."

Lena lowered her eyes, her hands clasped tightly together atop the table. "Those monitoring bands were meant for short-range use. A precaution to help us keep track of Baako if he should ever lose himself in the center's woods or get beyond the fences."

Gray tried to picture that hybrid gorilla. During last night's treacherous ride over the stormy mountains from Ogulin to Zagreb, Lena had described her research study—along with its unusual subject. The raid of that primate research center had to be connected to the attack here.

But how and why?

He pictured Kowalski's face, wondering if the man was still alive.

Lena looked equally fearful for her twin sister.

He tried to reassure her. "For now the tracker is continuing to work, well enough for us to know the signal is moving west across the Pacific. We have a team already in the air, following and narrowing that gap. Once the kidnappers make landfall, we'll close a noose around them."

He avoided mentioning Painter's larger fear: that these two attacks were likely orchestrated by a faction out of China. If so, rescuing Maria's group after they reached the mainland could prove problematic at best.

Impossible at worst.

Lena raised another worry. "Those bands remain charged for only a day or so. If the batteries go out before they land, there'll be no tracking them after that."

Gray settled to a bench at the table. Painter hadn't mentioned that detail.

If he even knew about it.

Either way, there was not much more Gray could do to help. Painter had assigned him to get Lena safely back to the States. They were awaiting details and instructions concerning that itinerary.

"What about Professor Wrightson and Dr. Arnaud?" Lena asked.

He shook his head. If the British geologist and French paleontologist were still alive, they were likely long gone from the area. His priority was to maintain a low profile, to keep Lena's survival under wraps until she could be extracted. Father Novak had helped facilitate that, offering the use of his church once they had reached the city, a place to hole up for the remainder of the night. They had all gotten a few hours of sleep on some cots in a back room, but sunrise was only an hour away.

It would soon be time to get moving again.

A scuff of boots drew Gray's attention to the kitchen door. Roland Novak entered, hauling a large book—the size of an atlas—under one arm. He carried a smaller book in his other hand, along with a rectangular metallic plate. The young priest appeared haggard, with saddlebags under his bloodshot eyes. It didn't look like he had slept at all. Still, he trembled with excitement.

"You should all see this," he pronounced as he crossed to the table, drawing Seichan along with him.

He placed the larger book on the table, its giant cover bound in leather with gilt lettering spelling out its title: *Mundus Subterraneus.*

"This is a copy of a book Father Athanasius Kircher published in 1665," he stated, then placed the smaller book beside this larger volume. "And this is the tome we found in that other cave—a journal, I believe, that belonged to the reverend father."

Gray stared down at the labyrinth inscribed on its cover.

Earlier, Roland and Lena had described what they had discovered in that cavern system under the mountains: a Gothic chapel preserving the remains of a Neanderthal man, whose bones were later stolen by the attackers. The chapel also seemed to have a historical connection to this Athanasius Kircher, a seventeenth-century Jesuit priest who might have removed another set of bones, possibly those of a female Neanderthal.

Roland must have used these past hours to investigate this thread. The priest's passion—not to mention his fortitude in the face of danger— reminded Gray of a younger version of a dear friend, another Vatican priest who had died in the pursuit of ancient truths.

I could use your counsel now, Vigor.

Honoring that memory, Gray listened as Roland continued.

"Unfortunately," the man said, "whatever was written in this journal was destroyed over the centuries, leaving only a few clues."

"Like the key we found," Lena added. From a pocket, she removed a large key and placed it atop the table. Despite the aged tarnish, a cherub and an arch of skulls were clearly visible atop it.

Roland nodded. "I have no idea what lock fits that particular key, but I decided to investigate the most obvious clue first." He traced the outer edge of the labyrinth on the cover. "I thought this maze looked familiar. I believe it's a depiction of a labyrinth from ancient Crete, where according to mythology the infamous Minotaur was caged. Look at this."

The priest tugged a manila folder from the pages of the larger book and slipped free a printed page showing an old silver coin. "This was minted in Knossos, the capitol of Crete."

Gray compared the labyrinth on the coin to the maze on the book's cover. "They're almost an exact match."

"And from my research, it's not just in Crete where you'll see this labyrinth. Petroglyphs of this pattern have been carved into stones all around the globe. You can find them across Italy, Spain, Ireland, even as far north as Finland. And it's not just petroglyphs. The ancient Indian Sanskrit epic the Mahabharata describes a military formation known as Padmavyuha that is laid out in this same pattern."

"Interesting." Lena shifted the photo of the coin closer to her. "It's almost like some fundamental knowledge of this shape was shared among the ancient peoples of the world and became incorporated into their mythology. In Crete, it was the Minotaur's lair. In India, it was a battle formation."

"Possibly it represents a real place." Roland stared down at the journal's cover. "Either way, I imagine this design had to be important if Father Kircher inscribed it here. So I sought out other examples of the reverend father's interest in such labyrinths—and found many in this volume."

The priest laid his palm atop the large copy of *Mundus Subterraneus*.

Seichan settled to a seat next to Lena. "So who exactly was this priest? I never heard of him."

Roland smiled as he pulled open the cover of the large book. Gray knew Roland had been summoned to that archaeological site because of his vast knowledge concerning this Jesuit priest. If anyone knew how this all might tie together, it would be this man.

The priest stopped at a page bearing a portrait of a man in a frock and peaked hat.

P. ATHANASIVS KIRCHERVS FVLDENSIS
è Societ: Iesu Anno ætatis LIII.
Honores et observantiae ergo sculpsit et D.D.C.Bloemaert Romæ 3 May A. 1655.

Roland's words grew somber with respect. "Father Kircher was considered by many to be the Leonardo da Vinci of his time. He was a true Renaissance man, with a keen interest in many disciplines: biology, medicine, geology, cartography, optics, even engineering. But one of his greatest fascinations was languages. He was the first to realize that there was a direct correlation between ancient Egyptian and the modern Coptic languages used today. For many scholars, Athanasius Kircher was the true founder of Egyptology. In fact, he produced great volumes of work regarding Egyptian hieroglyphics. He came later in life to believe they were the lost language of Adam and Eve and even undertook to carve his own hieroglyphics into a handful of Egyptian obelisks that can be found in Rome."

Gray's interest in the man sharpened. He studied the countenance, those thoughtful eyes, flashing back for a moment to his old friend Monsignor Vigor Verona. The two men, though they lived centuries apart, could have been brothers—and perhaps in some respect they were. Both were men of the cloth who sought to understand God's creation not solely through the pages of the Bible but through exploration of the natural world.

Roland continued, "Father Kircher eventually founded a museum at the Vatican college where he taught and studied. The Museum Kircherianum contained a colossal collection of antiquities, along with a vast library and several of his own inventions. To give you some scope of that place—and of the man's significance to his time—here's an etching of that museum."

Roland returned to his manila folder and slid out another picture.

Gray examined the depiction of that cavernous domed space, all housing the life's work of one man. He had to admit it did look impressive.

Seichan appeared less stirred. "So how did this Jesuit priest end up in the remote mountains of Croatia?"

Roland gave a small shake of his head. "Actually no one knew he had been up there. From my own doctoral research into Father Kircher's history, he arrived in our city in the spring of 1669 to oversee the fortifications of Zagreb Cathedral."

Gray remembered spotting the towering Gothic steeples of that cathedral on their ride into town. They were impossible to miss, as they were the tallest structures of the city.

"Because of the ongoing Ottoman threat during that time," Roland explained, "massive walls had been built around the cathedral. Father Kircher had been personally summoned by the Holy Roman Emperor, Leopold I, to help with the engineering of a watchtower along the southern side, intended as a military observation post. But during my research, I found inconsistencies with this story, evidence that the reverend father went missing for weeks at a time while working here. Rumors were rife among the local townspeople that Kircher might have been called by the emperor for some other purpose, that his involvement with the watchtower was merely a story to cover up some ulterior motive."

"A motive that might not be secret any longer," Gray said, nodding to the journal. "But even if someone found that cavern full of bones and paintings, why would the emperor call for Father Kircher to investigate?"

"I can't say for certain, but the reverend father was known for his interest in fossils and the bones of ancient people." Roland continued to explain as he scanned through several pages of his copy of *Mundus Subterraneus*. "This work by Father Kircher covers every facet of the earth—from geology and geography to chemistry and physics. Inspiration for this undertaking came when Father Kircher visited Mount Vesuvius, just after it erupted in 1637. He even used ropes to lower himself into the smoking crater to further his understanding of volcanism."

The guy definitely put himself into his work, Gray had to admit.

"Father Kircher came to believe the earth was riddled by a vast network of underground tunnels, springs, and ocean-size reservoirs. While searching this subterranean world, he also collected thousands of fossils and documented what he found."

Roland stopped on a page showing the renderings of fossilized fish.

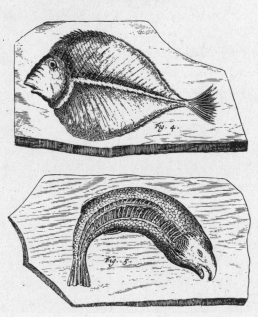

DE LAPIDIBUS.

T A B. Altera,
Piscium figuras exprimens.

"There are pages and pages of such drawings in here," Roland added. "But Father Kircher also discovered caves in northern Italy that held massive bones. They were the leg bones of mammoths, but he mistakenly attributed them to a species of giants that roamed the earth alongside early man."

Roland flipped to a page showing Kircher's attempt to capture what these mythical giants might look like and their relation in size to regular men.

Roland must have read the amused skepticism on their faces and matched it with a small smile. "Admittedly the reverend father did come to some strange conclusions, but you must understand he was a man of his time, trying to understand the world with the tools and knowledge of that era. *Mundus Subterraneus* contains many such whimsical speculations, from ancient monsters even to the location of the lost continent of Atlantis."

Gray straightened and stretched a kink from his back after leaning over the table for so long. He was losing patience. "What does any of this have to do with resolving the mystery of that cavern?"

Roland looked unfazed by his challenge. "Because I know *why* Father Kircher was summoned to these mountains."

Gray looked harder at the man, noting the return of that excited sparkle to the priest's eyes.

Roland shifted over to grasp the metal plate resting on the table and turned it over. Its silvery surface looked freshly cleaned. "This placard was bolted to the outside wall of that cavern chapel."

Gray noted the lines inscribed across the plate, all written in Latin, with a row of symbols along the bottom. "You were able to translate this?"

Roland nodded. "The message is mostly an admonishment against trespassing into those caves, a crime punishable by death."

"Why?" Seichan asked. "What did they think they were protecting?"

Roland ran a thumb under one line of Latin and translated it aloud. "'Here rest the bones of Adam, the father of mankind. May he never be disturbed from his eternal slumber . . .'" He took another breath and finished the line. "'. . . lest the world come to an end.'"

6:14 A.M.

Lena felt a prickling chill at these last words. She had also been staring at the open volume of *Mundus Subterraneus*, at the page depicting that ancient giant, while remembering the dance of shadows cast upon the cavern walls. Those dark figures had loomed large, climbing high above the herds of painted animals.

As if cast by an army of Kircher's giants.

Gray spoke, drawing her attention away from the book. "Why would Father Kircher believe those Neanderthal bones came from Adam?"

"Clearly he was mistaken, as with the mammoth bones." Roland shrugged. "Perhaps he came to that wild conclusion based on the extreme age of the bones. Or maybe it was something else he found. There were those strange petroglyphs, those star-shaped palm prints . . ."

He looked to Lena for support.

She shook her head, unable to offer any explanation, but it reminded her of another mystery. "What about the other set of remains, the ones that Father Kircher might have removed from the site? Did he think they belonged to Eve?"

"Possibly," Roland admitted. "But there's nothing written on this plate about those missing bones."

"Assuming Kircher believed they were Eve's remains, why would he take them?" she pressed. "Why not leave them to eternal rest like Adam?"

"I don't know." Roland frowned. "At least not yet."

Seichan reached and tapped the bottom of the metal sign. "What about this line of symbols?"

Lena had noted the faded row of tiny circles, too, showing a gradation of shading along their length. "They look like the phases of the moon. See how there's twenty-eight of them, the same number as a full lunar cycle."

"I think Dr. Crandall is right," Roland said. "I do know that Father Kircher became obsessed with the moon. He believed it was critical not only to the functioning of the earth—as with the ocean's tides—but also to mankind's existence. He used telescopes to create intricate maps of the moon, many of which you can find in *Mundus Subterraneus*."

As if trying to prove this, Roland thumbed through several pages until he reached a hand-drawn sketch of the lunar surface.

The level of detail for such a time—the impact craters, the mountains, the dry seas—was remarkable. Lena found herself vacillating between respect for this old priest's work and contempt for some of his more fanciful leaps.

Gray's gaze remained fixed on the other book. "Kircher clearly was trying to communicate something by leaving his journal behind in that cave full of sculptures."

Lena agreed, remembering those alcoves crusted with runnels and mounds of calcite. She pictured the broken bits found where the book was hidden. "Father Kircher didn't just take those bones," she realized aloud. "He took some object from that other cave, too, and left the book in its place. Possibly like a bread crumb for some future explorer to find."

"But what does it mean?" Gray asked.

Lena shook her head at the condition of the journal. "Whatever message he intended to leave behind was destroyed long ago." She nudged the key on the table. "But I wager it was meant to lead to whatever this key unlocks."

Gray continued to stare at the journal. Lena could almost see the gears turning behind those storm-blue eyes. He finally reached out and placed his fingertip on the date written beneath the labyrinth.

"Sixteen seventy-nine," he read aloud, then turned to Roland. "Didn't you say Father Kircher was summoned to Zagreb in *1669*?"

The priest moved closer, standing shoulder to shoulder with Gray. "That's true. I should have caught that discrepancy myself. It means Father Kircher must have returned to the cavern system a decade later—and left that book and key."

"Why?" Lena asked.

Roland eyed the group. "I don't know, but Father Kircher died the very next year. Perhaps, like you said, he wanted to leave behind some message for the future before he passed away."

Lena lifted the key, feeling its heft, the tarnished steel imbued with the weight of centuries. *What did this key unlock? What did this Leonardo da Vinci of his time hide away?*

Gray took up the journal and carefully cracked it open. He stared at the moldy wad of paper that had once held the last words of this mysterious priest. He studied the moldering imprint of the key, then examined the inside flaps of the covers. His lips suddenly drew thin. He moved closer to the fire, bringing the book near the flames—not to burn it, but for the additional light.

"There's something inscribed on the inside cover. I can barely make it out."

Roland joined him, drawing Lena, too.

She stared over Gray's shoulder. "He's right," she murmured, squinting at the faded image of a cross and what appeared to be a pair of upswept wings framing it.

Seichan came to a different conclusion. "Are those flames below the cross?"

Roland fell back a step, his eyes huge. "No, not flames. They're antlers." *Antlers?*

He gaped at them all. "I know where Father Kircher wants us to go."

6:33 A.M.

Gray watched Roland abandon the books and ancient messages and cross over to the kitchen's fridge. He retrieved a chilled bottle of liqueur, returned to the table, and placed it next to the ancient tomes, the key, and the mysterious messages written in Latin.

Seichan reached and rocked the green-tinted bottle to read the German label. "Jägermeister? If we're going to celebrate, why not break out the sacramental wine?"

"The monsignor likes a sip or two before bed," Roland explained. "The drink is very popular in Croatia. But it's not why I'm showing you this."

He turned the label toward Gray, as if the reason should be obvious.

Gray leaned down and immediately understood. "The symbol . . ."

The logo on the bottle was a stag with wide antlers embracing a glowing cross.

"The company states that the symbol represents Saint Hubertus, the patron saint of hunters," Roland explained. "Jägermeisters were German foresters and gamekeepers. Hence, the connection to the liqueur."

"But what does this have to do with Father Kircher?" Lena asked.

Roland lifted a hand, pleading for patience. "The story of Saint Hubertus pertains to a vision he had while hunting, of a magnificent stag that appeared before him with a golden crucifix standing between its antlers, but many Catholic scholars attribute the story to a saint from half a millennium earlier, Saint Eustace. According to legend, a Roman general named Placidus was hunting a stag near Rome when he had a similar vision and immediately converted to Christianity, changing his name to Eustace."

"Still," Gray pressed, "what's the connection to all of this?"

"In Father Kircher's later years, as age and decrepitude set in, he retired to the Italian countryside, where during his travels he discovered the ruins of a small church perched above Giovenzano Valley, the Sanctuary of Mentorella. It was built by Emperor Constantine to honor Saint Eustace."

Gray glanced over to the liqueur bottle and its label.

The patron saint of hunters.

Roland continued, "After discovering this forgotten church in the middle of nowhere, Kircher took it upon himself to restore it, raising funds for the task and eventually overseeing its reconstruction. It is said he was very hands-on, assisting with the engineering and managing the construction site itself, which he kept very guarded."

"You're thinking he might have hidden something there," Gray said.

"According to the historical record, he became obsessed with the place, living his final years there. He even insisted upon being buried at the sanctuary."

"Was he buried there?" Lena asked.

"Strangely enough, only his *heart*." Roland glanced around, letting the significance sink in. "Even a pope back then, Pope Innocent XIII, requested that his heart be buried there, too."

Something was clearly important about that place.

Gray picked up the old key on the table, running his thumb over the arch of skulls along its bow end, remembering the bones stolen by Father Kircher.

I'd definitely call this a skeleton key.

"It's worth looking into," Seichan admitted. He saw the glimmer of desire in her face, to be moving again rather than sitting here waiting for instructions. "We could be in Rome in less than two hours."

He was tempted—and he wasn't the only one.

"I'm willing to go," Roland said, which was no surprise. "You could use my expertise."

"And I'm going, too," Lena said, which was a surprise.

Gray was about to object, but Lena stood before the fire, looking resolute.

"Someone stole those bones from that cavern here," she said. "And we all know it wasn't because of the black market value of such relics. Especially considering the coordination of the attack here and outside of Atlanta." Her voice caught a bit as she plainly thought about her sister, but she pressed on. "There has to be some significant genetic value to those bones. I had only a brief look, but I could tell there was something *off* about the conformation of the skull. If I could get a better look—"

"She's right." Roland shifted closer to her, backing her up physically and with his words. "If we could find out where Father Kircher took the other set of bones, we might know better the reason behind the attack. I believe Father Kircher discovered something significant in those caves, and it may take someone with a greater understanding of Neanderthals and early man to discover it again."

"They're both right," Seichan conceded with a shrug. "We're missing something about all of this. And in the meantime, there's little we can do to help with Painter's operation in China."

Gray refused to relent, even outnumbered as he was now. He had his assignment to keep Lena safe.

The geneticist must have read this thought. "No one would suspect I'd be traveling to Rome," she pressed. Her eyes now held a similar glint as Seichan's, a shine of impatience and determination. "Plus I'm not about to sit idly by and do nothing while Maria's still in danger."

Before Gray could respond, his satellite phone chirped, ringing with the familiar tone for Sigma command. He answered it and heard Painter Crowe's voice.

"Commander Pierce, I've got your extraction arranged. A contact with the Croatian air force will get you all aboard a military transport headed—"

He cut the director off, eyeing the group standing before the fire. "Sir, there's been a change in plans."

7:22 A.M.

The man sat inside a small coffeehouse. He held a folded copy of a newspaper in front of him, but his eyes remained fixed through the window. Across Saint Catherine's Square stood a Baroque church of the same name, its white facade aglow in the morning sunlight. It was one of dozens of Catholic buildings across the religious city. Even from here, he could spy the twin spires of Zagreb's Gothic cathedral cutting into the bright sky.

Another two men had been posted at that larger structure, along with others at the international airport and the city's train station.

The places of Catholic worship were watched because of word that a priest had been among the party who had entered the caves yesterday. It was unknown whether the man or the American woman had ever escaped those mountains, but *Zhōngxiào* Sun had been adamant that the capital city be locked down, watched for any sign of survivors.

He did not resent the orders. A fire burned in his belly as he remembered his teammates who had died up in those mountains. Their blood called for vengeance.

Movement drew his attention away from the church to a neighboring art gallery. It was too early for the place to be opening already. From a tourist brochure he had read while waiting here, the Klovićevi Dvori Gallery was once the former monastery for Saint Catherine's. Moments earlier, a black sedan had parked near the entrance. Its engine still idled, with exhaust steaming from the tailpipe.

A clutch of four figures hurried through the gallery door to the waiting sedan. He spotted a woman among them, her blond hair a flag amid the dark clothes. When the passenger door opened, he spotted the driver inside, wearing a Croatian air force uniform.

His heart quickened at the sight, certainty settling coldly over him.

He kept his newspaper raised and picked up his cell phone from the table and tapped one button as he brought it to his ear. Once the connection was made, he spoke.

"*Zhōngxiào* Sun, I have found them."

11

The cabin steward leaned down with a tray holding a row of steaming cloths, meticulously folded into cranes. "We'll be landing in Beijing in less than an hour, if you'd like to freshen up."

Monk reached over and pinched up one of the napkins, the fingertips of his prosthetic hand registering the damp heat. "Thank you."

"And for your wife?" the steward extended the tray.

Monk turned to his traveling companion. "Dear?"

"*Búyào xièxie*," the woman politely declined, waving a palm in dismissal.

As the steward left, Monk patted his face with the steaming heat, letting it warm away some of his exhaustion.

"Is this how you usually travel?" the woman asked, smiling, lifting her dark eyes and using the back of her fingers to tuck away a fall of ebony hair from her handsome heart-shaped face. "If so, I may have to reconsider Kat's offer to join your organization."

He shrugged. "Unfortunately, our more common method of travel is usually tied up in the trunk of a car."

Kimberly Moy was the same age as Monk, but her beauty had a timelessness that made her appear much younger—which, considering their cover as husband and wife, was not exactly helping.

Still, it made the long trip all that much more tolerable.

Sorry, Kat.

His actual wife was back in D.C., coordinating efforts with Director Crowe at Sigma. Kat had recommended Kimberly Moy for this operation. They'd been friends back in their days at the U.S. Naval Academy. Kimberly eventually joined the Defense Intelligence Agency, but the two remained close allies within that clandestine world of U.S. security. Kat had vouched for her friend's skills. Beyond the woman's fluency with every dialect of mainland China, she was also a crack shot with a sniper rifle and experienced at hand-to-hand combat, besting most men in her agency.

Kimberly reclined her seat farther back. "I could get accustomed to this."

They were aboard a silver-winged Boeing 757, which had been converted by the Four Seasons resorts into a first-class accommodation of just fifty-two seats, only half of which were currently occupied. The itinerary for this semiprivate flight covered eight countries over twenty-four days. Kat had arranged for them to board the plane in Tokyo for the hop to Beijing, supporting their cover as a pair of rich Americans on a world tour.

For the moment, they had the rear of the plane to themselves.

Monk stared down at his satellite phone, which showed a map of China's coastline. Painter kept the device updated with the most current GPS feed from Baako's wrist tracker. It looked like the signal had settled at China's capital, but they were watching to see if it remained in Beijing or moved on yet again.

Monk and Kimberly's role was as a forward expeditionary force, to narrow down where the kidnappers might have taken Maria, Kowalski, and Baako. An extraction team was already en route, following on their heels via various itineraries, waiting for an order to assemble and attempt a rescue.

Monk's phone vibrated with a new incoming message. It was from Painter. He scanned through it, beginning to sense the scope of their challenge ahead. The note related all that Sigma had learned about Dr. Amy Wu, the National Science Foundation researcher who had orchestrated that ambush at the primate center. She was clearly a Chinese mole within the NSF, one who had burrowed herself as far as the White House's science council.

Her motivation for such a betrayal remained murky. Amy Wu was a fourth-generation American, an unlikely target to be co-opted by China's political ideology. Even a search of her records and correspondence showed no support for communism. Still, Sigma's financial forensics did reveal a trail of money running from Beijing through Wu's office and out to various scientific projects.

Makes no sense.

He handed the phone to Kimberly to read through the report. Once done, she gave it back. She kept her voice low, even though there was no one seated within three rows of them, and those nearby were wearing headphones and listening to in-flight entertainment.

"We've been monitoring Chinese activity on U.S. shores for decades," she said quietly. "The infiltration of their moles and spies goes well beyond the nuisance hacking that's been reported in the news. There are Chinese students in graduate and postdoctoral programs across the United States, in every technological and scientific field. They learn skills here and return to the mainland, where that knowledge is often used against us."

"Why are we allowing that?"

"Good question. The simplest answer is that we don't have enough U.S. graduates who are qualified to fill all of our PhD programs. Currently half the physics doctorates from U.S. universities are awarded to foreign nationals, most of whom take their diplomas and return home. In some regard, it could almost be considered foreign aid, as much of their education is underwritten by the American taxpayer—through grants for research, financial assistance, not to mention all the tax breaks given to colleges and universities."

"So not only are we giving them this knowledge to take abroad, we're paying for it."

"Some argue that it may be beneficial in the long run."

"How's that?"

"It can serve as a way of spreading American capitalism, business practices, even educational norms abroad. The downside risk, of course, is that we're creating our own market competitors. Scientists and engineers ultimately drive innovation—and we're shipping that intellectual capital abroad."

Monk was beginning to understand why Kat had picked Kimberly for this mission. The woman certainly knew her stuff.

"As an example," she said, "there was a Chinese student sequestered for years at Harvard, working with the best of our geneticists and bioengineers. She recently returned to Shanghai and took what she'd learned to ends considered unethical in most Western countries."

"What did she do?"

"She started a program to genetically alter human embryos." Kimberly leaned back with a sad shake of her head. "Such procedures are already banned in over forty countries—and for good reason. Such research could be construed as a first step on the road to eugenics, using science to engineer a better human. We're talking about inserting inheritable traits into the human gene pool, not only forever corrupting it, but risking a future where there will be a new class of people—those engineered to be superior."

Monk frowned. "Do you think such a goal could have motivated this current attack? Amy Wu was channeling funds into the Crandall sisters' research in the genetic origin of human intelligence."

"Hard to say. But in regards to Dr. Wu, I do suspect her loyalty was not motivated by political ideology, but by the pure pursuit of science. Research today has become more about seeing if something *can* be done versus judging if it *should*. It's knowledge for the sake of knowledge, regardless of the impact on the world."

Monk remembered Amy Wu's earlier comment regarding this subject of genetic engineering: *We certainly couldn't authorize this study using human embryos. Not without raising a firestorm of protests.* For her, steering clear of such research wasn't about the ethics of right or wrong, only about the fear of getting caught.

His phone vibrated again. A glance revealed a new text message from Painter.

SIGNAL DROPPED OFF.

TRACKER EITHER DISCOVERED OR LOST POWER.

LAST KNOWN LOCATION BEING SENT NOW.

Monk returned to the map and zoomed down upon the marked location glowing on the street grid of Beijing. Its path had stopped at a stretch of green parkland.

Leaning over, Kimberly stared down at the screen. "That's the grounds of the Beijing Zoo."

Monk nodded. Considering the enemy had a kidnapped gorilla with them, the setting made practical sense.

"What do we do next?" Kimberly asked.

He glanced up at her. "My dear wife, it looks like we'll be paying a visit to those famous Chinese pandas."

2:22 P.M.

Maria ducked under the whirling blades of the helicopter. The aircraft had ferried them from a military airfield outside of Beijing to a helipad alongside a wide river. The waterway curved past, overhung by a row of weeping willows. She had watched their approach while they descended, noting the parklands that spread to the south and recognizing cages, pens, and other large buildings. Along a maze of winding walkways, crowds of people roamed and strolled.

An animal park . . . likely the Beijing Zoo.

Once clear of the helicopter's rotors, she stretched a kink from her back. Kowalski drew alongside her, his face fixed in a perpetual scowl.

"Place stinks," he said.

She agreed. The air smelled of exhaust smoke. The city's skyscrapers across the river were sunk in a hazy yellowish fog. She had read about the air pollution problems in Beijing, but she had never imagined it was this bad. Her eyes already stung, and she had to cover her mouth to mask a deep cough.

"Keep moving," a voice commanded behind them.

She turned to face the tall, waspish form of the group's leader. While en route, she had learned his name was Gao, but she didn't know if that was his first name or last. He looked to be in his midthirties. His black hair was cut to the scalp around his ears but kept longer across the top.

Beyond his shoulders, a small forklift retreated from the rear hatch of the military transport helicopter. It carried aloft the cage holding Baako. He clutched the bars, staring toward her, his eyes scared, his lips pursed as he hooted at her for help, but she couldn't hear him over the roar of the aircraft's engines.

She took a step toward him but was blocked by Gao.

"Go," he said sternly, reinforcing his command with a pointed pistol.

The same weapon that killed Jack, she reminded herself. Fury at the cold-blooded murder of her student burned inside her chest. One fist balled up in frustration. She fixed her gaze on that bastard, letting him see her anger.

Kowalski gripped her arm and forced her to turn away and keep moving. "Another time," he grumbled under his breath. It sounded like a promise.

She let herself be led across an apron of concrete. She searched ahead, trying to get her bearings. Off in the distance rose a large arch-roofed building. A giant mural peeked above the tree line, displaying an ocean scene of cavorting seals, killer whales, and dolphins.

An aquarium . . .

But their destination was closer at hand: a nondescript concrete-block building rising two stories, its flat roof crowded with satellite dishes and antennas. A large door on the side trundled upward, revealing a freight elevator.

The forklift bearing Baako's cage whisked past them and maneuvered fully into the waiting space. Maria quickened her pace to keep up.

"Not you," Gao ordered and stepped past her. He pointed toward Kowalski. "You go with gorilla. Keep it calm."

Kowalski glanced to her. It seemed their ruse that he was Baako's caretaker continued to remain intact.

To maintain it, she gave Kowalski a small nod. "Do what you can to keep him from getting too frightened."

He lifted one eyebrow, his question plain. *Who, me?*

"Baako will need a familiar face, someone he knows," she pressed.

Even if it's someone he met only briefly.

But Baako was smart. He knew she trusted Kowalski, and the familiarity of the big man's presence should offer him a small amount of comfort, especially in such a strange environment. Hopefully Kowalski could keep Baako from panicking. She feared for his care, remembering how their captors had used an electric cattle prod on him. She didn't want Baako abused any further.

This thought raised a larger fear as she watched his cage being loaded inside the elevator. What *did* they want with him . . . or her?

Kowalski must have read the anxiety in her face. "Don't worry. I'll look after the little guy."

Without thinking, she lunged forward and hugged him. His body stiffened in surprise, but then relaxed. His arms encircled her and squeezed, showing a tenderness that belied his brutish exterior. She found the heat of his body, the muscular strength of his embrace, far more reassuring than his words.

"Go!" Gao shouted at them. He poked his pistol into Kowalski's ribs.

Kowalski let her loose and glowered at Gao, hard enough that the Chinese soldier backed up a step.

Gao shifted his gaze to her instead. "You come with me."

Another soldier bearing a rifle forced Kowalski toward the freight elevator. Maria was led toward a smaller door to the side.

"Where are you taking me?" she asked Gao.

"To see Major General Lau. To see if you will live."

2:45 P.M.

How far down are we going?

From the lurch in his stomach, Kowalski knew the elevator was descending underground, but he had no way of gauging how deep. He counted a full fifteen seconds before the car finally settled to a stop. He waited next to Baako's cage, which was still carried by the forklift. Four armed guards shared the elevator, too many for him to overpower and fight his way free.

Something tugged at his sleeve.

He glanced down to the furry fingers clutching his coveralls. A face pressed against the bars. Dark eyes looked at him.

Yeah, yeah, I know . . . you're scared, buddy.

He pulled his arm free as the elevator door rattled open. He didn't have time for distractions. He needed to concentrate, to learn the lay of the land in this subterranean complex. For any hope of escape, he had to know the way out.

A soft, frightened hoot rose from Baako as the forklift backed free of the elevator and into a cavernous warehouse. The space rose two stories, lined by row after row of shelving. Other forklifts buzzed around the room, hauling crates and boxes.

The tip of a rifle pushed Kowalski out of the elevator and set him to following after Baako's cage. He did his best to look cowed as he crossed the warehouse. He kept his shoulders slumped while he eyed the shelves for anything that might prove useful, but all of the crates and cartons were labeled in Chinese letters. No telling what each held: could be a crate full of semiautomatic rifles or a box packed with Top Ramen.

Their party exited the warehouse and continued through a maze of passageways, down ramps, and across a musky underground barnyard that held corrals of goats, sheep, and some sullen-looking sows.

What the hell is this place?

As they continued, the number of personnel—mostly wearing lab jackets, uniforms, or work coveralls—slowly waned in number until finally they reached an area bearing angry-looking red signs.

Even Kowalski could guess their meaning.

Restricted Area . . . Do Not Enter.

Their group pushed onward anyway, encountering no more people. Finally they reached a long cellblock of sorts, lined by a row of barred pens along one side, each the size of a single-car garage. The cages all appeared empty, but from the number of scratches, gouges, and stains in the concrete, they had seen some hard use.

At the far end, massive steel doors stood closed, sealed like a bank vault with a glowing crimson sign above it. One of the guards pointed toward it, but another knocked his arm down and scolded the man. Clearly even curiosity about whatever lay beyond those doors was harshly discouraged.

Kowalski squinted at it.

Interesting . . .

But it wasn't their destination. The forklift halted midway along the row of concrete cells, and the driver barked in Chinese. A guard ran forward and unlocked one of the pens, while the forklift operator lowered Baako's cage to the floor. Two other soldiers moved forward, slipping their rifles over their shoulders and pulling out electric prods. The fourth guard kept his rifle steadied on Kowalski's chest, but the man kept far enough back in case his captive should try anything.

The soldiers with the prods yelled and stabbed at Baako as he cowered at the rear of the cage. His door was yanked open, and they tried to force Baako into the neighboring pen. Kowalski could only imagine the terror in that trembling form.

"Enough!" he finally yelled. He lifted his arms, showing his empty palms in a pantomime of cooperation. "Let me get him out before you give him a goddamned heart attack."

Kowalski didn't know if any of his captors spoke English, but he made his intent clear by slowly stepping to the open door of Baako's cage and waving the furry guy toward him.

"It's okay, Baako," he said. "We'll do this together."

Whether the soldiers understood him or not, they gave him some space.

Kowalski leaned through the door. Baako panted heavily, his lips thin with terror, his gaze darting everywhere. He looked one breath away from a total meltdown.

Kowalski patted his own chest. *Look at me, buddy.*

Baako's eyes settled in his direction.

Kowalski lifted his arms and began to sign slowly, appealing to Baako's prior teaching, to use the familiar to draw him away from the edge of blind panic. He ended by crossing his fists and tapping them together at the wrist.

[*I will protect you*]

Baako continued to breathe hard, but his gaze steadied. He loosened his arms from where they were hugging his hairy knees and bumped his own fists together, grunting softly.

Kowalski nodded. "That's right."

Baako reached out a hand toward him. Kowalski momentarily flashed to his younger sister, Anne. She had often reached out to him like this, sought comfort from her older brother whenever she was scared, whether at a doctor's office or during one of his father's drunken rages.

Warm fingers wrapped around his.

That's it, buddy.

Kowalski guided Baako off the forklift, down to the floor, and over to the concrete pen. From one cage to another.

One of the guards barked at them. Fingers tightened to a crushing level on Kowalski's hand. He gritted through the pain and waved his free hand at the group of soldiers.

"Just get the hell back!" he scolded as he walked Baako into the pen.

It was a pitiful confinement. The concrete floor was covered by a skim of scattered straw. A bucket in the corner was half full of greenish water. There were no toys to play with, no ropes to swing from, nothing to distract from the grim surroundings. Worst of all, a set of steel manacles hung ominously from the rear wall.

A guard called to him, softer at least this time. The man waved, ordering him out.

Kowalski stared down at the fingers still holding tight to him.

Fuck it.

He sank to his rear end on the cold concrete and patted the straw next to him, urging Baako to join him, then called to the soldier, "I'm staying."

Better here than anywhere else.

The soldier huddled with his comrades; then they seemed to reach some consensus. One of them picked up a woven bushel that held bundles of bruised bananas, carrots, and branches of leaves. He dropped it across the threshold, then kicked it closer to them. Another soldier clanged the door closed and locked it with a large key.

"Guess they got the message," Kowalski mumbled to himself.

The forklift reversed away, drawing the soldiers along with it. A set of double doors was slammed closed behind them as they retreated out of the cellblock, but not before Kowalski spotted one of the soldiers taking up a post outside.

So they're not taking any chances with their new prisoners.

Kowalski freed his hand from Baako's fingers and stood back up. He glanced to the other end of the hall, toward that sealed steel vault. He noted a palm reader glowing beside it, and a row of cameras hanging along the roof outside the cages, their lenses pointed toward the pens.

Baako also used the opportunity to take in his surroundings, sniffing at the air. Then he lowered his nose closer to a dark stain beneath the straw. Whatever he smelled caused him to retreat away.

Kowalski didn't blame him. It looked like dried blood.

To distract Baako, Kowalski hauled up the bushel of food and joined the ape. "Not exactly pizza and beer, but it'll have to do."

He lowered the container, pulled out a banana, and offered it. Baako sank to his haunches, turning a shoulder, refusing. The ape hadn't eaten since he was captured. Maria had gotten him to drink a little, but that was about it.

"You gotta eat," Kowalski said.

Baako turned back and touched his lips, his eyes still scared.

Crap, forgot about that tracker band . . .

Kowalski shifted to put himself between the cameras and Baako. He held out his hand. "It's okay. Spit it out."

Baako understood enough to obey. The saliva-soaked band dropped into his palm. Keeping his back to the cameras, Kowalski examined it. The green light that normally glowed from the GPS unit was barely lit. It was running out of juice.

Not that it's doing any good buried under all of this concrete anyway.

Kowalski swore under his breath.

Baako chuffed worriedly, ducking his head lower, perhaps believing Kowalski was mad at him.

"It's not you, buddy." He pocketed the tracker away, forgetting about it for now. At this moment, he had a more immediate concern. "Let's get you something to eat."

He held out the banana again but only got a forlorn look from his cellmate. His sister, Anne, had often made a similar face when he tried to get her to eat. Sometimes her anorexia was secondary to pain, but more often than not it was a reflection of her brother's pitiful attempt at cooking.

Kowalski dropped down next to Baako. He put the banana on his lap, then lifted his arms to the side, balling his fists and flexing his biceps.

[*You must be strong*]

He repeated the sign, altering it slightly, by forming claws of his hands, then clenching them into fists.

[*And brave*]

He finally pinched his fingers and brought them to his closed lips.

[*So you must eat*]

Baako looked at the banana. Kowalski picked it up, peeled it, and offered it again.

Baako finally reached over and took it. He put the peeled end between his lips, then mimicked Kowalski's first sign, raising his fists and flexing his arms. He finished by pointing at Kowalski.

[*You be strong, too*]

Baako bit through the banana and held out the other half.

Grimacing, Kowalski stared down at what was offered, then simply shrugged.

What the hell . . .

He took the banana, peeled it the rest of the way, and popped it in his mouth.

A guy's gotta eat.

3:13 P.M.

Where are they taking me?

Fearing what lay ahead, Maria moved through an opulent hallway. The walls were covered in a crimson silk print, the lintels of the windows gilded in gold. Underfoot was a handwoven rug that looked like a tapestry.

Where am I?

After being separated from Kowalski and Baako, she had been taken down an elevator by Gao to a subterranean complex beneath the park, where another soldier met them with an electric vehicle and drove them through the underground facility. As they were swept along, she had caught glimpses through windows into large laboratories. She recognized equipment used in genetic research: thermocyclers for amplifying DNA, hybridization ovens for incubating nucleotide probes, centrifuges for the fractionation of macromolecules. One room even had a SequiGene Vertical Gel Apparatus, identical to her own at her lab, used for sequencing DNA.

Finally they reached another elevator, and Gao forced her at gunpoint into the cage, which rose up into this older building. From the scrolled woodwork and antique furnishings of this structure, it felt as if she had been transported from the modern age to the seventeenth century. Along the length of the hallway, small windows offered views down to a lagoon holding flocks of wading birds, and beyond the trees, the rest of the animal park.

So I'm still on the zoo property.

Ahead, a man stood post before a closed door, dressed in a khaki uniform and tall black boots. Though several years older than her, he was handsome in a roguish way, a feature magnified by his warm smile as he greeted them—or rather, greeted her companion.

"Gao, *huānyíng huí jiā, dìdi*."

Gao holstered his pistol and hugged the other. "*Xiè xie,* Chang."

From the informal and affectionate embrace, she guessed they were brothers, recognizing now the family resemblance. As they continued speaking in hushed tones, she noted the subtle deference of Gao to his older brother—not just because of the age difference, but likely also because his brother had a higher rank.

Finally the senior brother—Chang—knocked on the door, got a muffled response, and opened it. Chang entered first, then Gao pushed her forward to follow.

She remembered Gao's earlier warning about where she was being taken.

To see Major General Lau. To see if you will live.

Maria had been expecting to be interrogated by some stoic-faced older member of the Chinese Army. Instead, as she stepped in the room, she found a thin woman in a starched green uniform standing behind a broad desk. She had a chestful of colorful ribbons and the epaulets of her jacket carried two stars. From her gray hair and the lines on her face, Maria guessed her to be in her midfifties.

And the woman was not alone.

Two older men—neither of them Chinese—also shared the space, seated on a neighboring sofa. In addition, two armed guards flanked the broad window behind the general's desk.

The older of the two men rose to his feet. Confusion and shock registered in his eyes as he fixed his glasses more firmly to his face and studied her up and down.

"Lena?"

Maria had grown accustomed to this confusion and corrected the man. "Lena is my twin sister . . . I'm Maria."

"Of course, of course," the man said, sinking back down, looking abashed at his mistake.

She didn't need to hear his British accent to know this must be Professor Alex Wrightson, the geologist who had discovered the cavern system in Croatia. Monk had shown her pictures of the two kidnapped researchers back at the primate center. The other was plainly the French paleontologist, Dr. Dayne Arnaud. Though he was a couple of decades younger than the geologist, at the moment he looked as haggard and aged.

The woman stepped around her desk. "Dr. Crandall, I'm a great admirer of your work. I am Jiaying Lau, major general of the People's Liberation Army."

The general held out her hand. Maria took it, not wanting to be rude to the woman who would decide her fate.

Jiaying's gaze shifted next to Gao and his older brother. She said something swiftly in Mandarin and pointed back toward the door. Chang voiced some objection, looking perturbed, but he was overruled by his superior. He left stiffly with Gao in tow.

Witnessing their irritation, Maria felt incrementally warmer toward her host.

Still, Maria cleared her throat and took the offensive. She kept her back straight and her voice firm. "How do you know about my work?"

Jiaying waved her to a chair opposite the sofa. "Who do you think financed your research?"

The shock more than the invitation dropped Maria heavily into the seat. "What . . . what do you mean?"

"Your advocate with the National Science Foundation, the woman who sat on the White House's science council and helped you and your sister with your research grants—"

"Amy . . ."

Jiaying bowed her head in acknowledgment. "Dr. Wu was well paid to facilitate the flow of money from the Academy of Military Science here in Beijing to your primate center in the United States. It was a shame to lose her."

Lose her?

Maria tried to keep her face dispassionate while her mind did cartwheels trying to absorb all she was being told. If this story was true, it meant she and Lena had been working for the Chinese all along. They were puppets whose strings were being pulled by Amy Wu.

How could that be?

Maria had considered Amy a friend. But instead, the woman was some sort of mole. As her breathing grew more labored, Maria wanted to lower her head between her knees. She remembered how hard Amy had pushed her and Lena, driving them to work faster, to set aside their initial misgivings about producing a gorilla hybrid model to test their theories.

Maria had always harbored a distaste at the idea of using great apes in research. She'd had heated debates with Amy on this very subject. Apes were intelligent animals with a rich emotional and cognitive life. They showed self-consciousness, with an ability to understand their individual role in the past and future. What right did humans have to imprison them and torture them in the name of science?

Still, in the end, Amy had found ways to persuade her, to allay her concerns, to wheedle her into pushing past the boundaries of her own comfort.

Yet look what I did.

Deep down, Maria knew Amy was not fully to blame. She had let herself be won over because she had *wanted* to know the truth herself, to prove her hypothesis concerning the Great Leap Forward. But most of all, she had wanted to see if she could succeed where so many others had failed.

Including the Chinese.

She and Lena had developed innovative hybridization and germ-line engineering techniques that were still unpublished and proprietary. Not even Amy had been fully informed.

Thank God.

Maria began to understand why she had been kidnapped, but such techniques were more Lena's specialty than hers. Her sister was the technical expert, dealing with this project at the molecular level. Maria's role was more about tackling the bigger picture: the raising, educating, and testing of Baako.

"We hope you'll be willing to continue your research here," Jiaying said, confirming Maria's fears. "I understand your distaste for our methods in bringing you and your test subject to our shores. But we're both scientists, searching for the truth. Ultimately, what does it matter if your research is conducted here or in the States? If you cooperate, you could have a wonderful life, with the full resources of the Chinese government at your disposal, with none of the red tape or ethical limitations that bound your hands in the United States."

Maria tried to look interested instead of horrified.

"Of course," Jiaying added, "this applies to your sister, too."

"Lena?"

Before Maria had been kidnapped, she had been awaiting word from Croatia about a search-and-rescue effort to extract her sister from some flooded caves. She had heard nothing after that.

"Is . . . is she still alive?" Maria gasped out.

"She has been spotted in Zagreb," Jiaying confirmed. "We hope to facilitate a reunion of you and your sister soon."

Maria clutched her hands in her lap to keep them from shaking. She glanced to the two men.

Professor Wrightson offered her a wan smile. "As long as she's still alive, there's always hope."

Dr. Arnaud would not meet her gaze, clearly not as optimistic.

Maria sought to change the subject. "Why did you raid those caves to begin with? Was it just to grab my sister?"

"Actually we had intended to extract her in Germany, at the Max Planck Institute. But due to foul weather, she ended up leaving a day earlier than expected. Such are the whims of fate, spoiling the best-laid strategies."

"Then what did you want out of those caves?"

"Let me show you."

Jiaying encouraged her to cross over to a long plastic transport case resting beside the sofa. The latches were already undone, so the general merely flipped open the lid. Maria stared inside. She immediately recognized the fossilized remains of a skeleton nestled inside. Despite her heart thudding in her throat, she could not discount a spark of professional interest.

She dropped to a knee to better examine the skull, amazed at the preservation. "These bones, they're not human . . . or rather not *Homo sapiens.*"

"Neanderthal," Wrightson corrected her.

Frowning, she reached a finger toward the brow ridge. "No, I don't think so. At least not completely. The facial bones are too flat. And what I can make of the molars, they appear too small."

She glanced up to find Jiaying smiling at her.

But it was Dayne Arnaud who spoke, the paleontologist's tone mournful. "I noted the same. And after taking meticulous measurements, I believe we're dealing with the remains of a hybrid, some offspring very close to the original mating of an anatomically modern human and a Neanderthal."

Maria sat back on her heels. "If you're right—"

"It would be the first ever discovered," Arnaud finished. "A specimen of astounding rarity, found in *immaculée* condition. Professor Wrightson radiocarbon-dated the remains to the last glacial period, around forty thousand years ago."

The geologist nodded. "But what's most intriguing are the contradictions regarding—"

"Enough, Alex," Arnaud cut him off sharply. "No one cares about such anomalous details."

Wrightson looked ready to object, but instead settled back and crossed his arms. Clearly the two researchers were accustomed to bumping heads.

Arnaud closed his eyes, then opened them, plainly trying to regain his composure. "It was because of this miraculous find that I reached out to the Max Planck Institute. And why I specifically requested your sister come to Croatia."

"Because of our research on Neanderthal hybridization," Maria said.

The paleontologist nodded. "I believed at the right facility there would be a great chance of extracting substantial DNA and wanted her expertise."

Maria understood. Such a discovery could unlock everything, offering a road map to what humans were as a species, to where we came from.

If Lena and I had such a sample . . .

Jiaying drew her attention away from the scientific potential and back to the immediate threat. "We learned of Dr. Arnaud's discovery through one of our operatives already studying at Max Planck and acted quickly. Perhaps too hastily."

Maria gave a small shake of her head at the efficiency of the Chinese system of moles and spies. She knew Chinese students were enrolled at technical universities across the United States and abroad, but apparently many of them also had their ears to the ground, ready to alert the powers that be of any significant discovery.

Jiaying continued, "Such a boon as this could shorten our own research by a full decade, if not more. Especially with the right team in place."

She bowed her head toward Maria and the others.

Maria stood. "What exactly are you trying to accomplish here?"

"Better I show you."

Jiaying waved her toward the door. The two men also stood to follow.

Wrightson rose with a groan, palming his lower back. "No rest for the wicked."

Arnaud pushed past him gruffly.

"I hope to enlist your cooperation," Jiaying told Maria. "And Dr. Arnaud, your expertise as a paleontologist could also prove beneficial. But Professor Wrightson, we have little need for a geologist, even one of your esteem. But maybe you can serve in another capacity."

The old man looked baffled.

Jiaying removed her sidearm, pointed it at Wrightson, and fired.

The puzzlement never left the geologist's face as he collapsed back onto the sofa, a small hole smoking in his forehead.

The sudden blast in the small space deafened Maria. She stumbled backward, close to falling, but Jiaying kept her upright by gripping her arm. Maria looked aghast at the Chinese general, immediately realizing the intent behind Jiaying's brutal action.

It was a lesson.

Maria understood.

Be useful . . . or be dead.

12

Gray drove their Mercedes SUV up another switchback into the Prenes-
tini Mountains. Though it had taken them only an hour to travel from
Rome's airport to these highlands, it was like entering another era. The
bustle of Rome had fallen behind them as they climbed into the farmlands
and vineyards of rural Italy.

Seated behind him, Lena Crandall had her window rolled down,
taking in the fresh warm air of this spring day, but her eyes remained
haunted, concerned for her sister. Upon arriving in Italy, they had received
word that the GPS tracker being monitored by Sigma had finally died,
placing the last known location of Lena's sister somewhere in Beijing.
Monk had just landed to continue the search for the kidnapped group.

In the meantime, Gray's party had their own quest.

Father Roland sat in the backseat next to Lena. He had his nose buried
in a small tourist guide, while balancing an iPad on his knee—where he
had stored all of his information concerning Father Athanasius Kircher.
The priest had purchased the booklet when they made a short stop at the
village of Guadagnolo for lunch, dining at Ristorante da Peppe, a quaint
family-run establishment with a roaring fireplace that was overhung with
strings of handmade sausages. Roland had also used the time to make inquiries with the local diners concerning their destination: Santuario della
Mentorella.

The Catholic sanctuary—the ruins of which had been discovered and restored by Father Kircher—lay at the neighboring summit of Mount Guadagnolo. It was perched like an eagle's nest a few kilometers higher up the peak, clinging to a spur of rock overlooking the surrounding Giovenzano Valley. Legend stated that it was upon that spur that Saint Eustace had his vision of a stag bearing aloft a glowing cross between his antlers.

Gray pictured the faded drawing in Father Kircher's journal.

Let's hope this isn't all a wild-goose chase.

As he finished the final switchback, a cluster of stone buildings with clay tile roofs appeared ahead, crowning the top of the peak. He passed a traffic sign written in Polish, Italian, and English.

Seichan, who was seated in the passenger seat with an elbow out the window, frowned at the sign. "Why is so much around here written in Polish?"

She was right. Even in that small village where they'd stopped for lunch, there had been a bookstore with a prominent display of Polish books.

Roland explained, "Back in 1857, Pope Pius XI granted this church to the Congregation of the Resurrection—a Polish order. But what's interesting is that Pope John Paul II often visited this shrine, even coming here immediately after his election to the papacy. As did his successor, Pope Benedict."

"So Father Kircher left his heart here," Gray commented. "As did a pope from back then. And now the popes of our time make this place their first pilgrimage. Definitely sounds like there's something important about this place."

Roland raised his tourist guide. "It also says here that the holy relics of over two hundred saints are interred at this sanctuary."

Lena turned from the window, clearly drawn by this strange fact. "Why so many?"

"Probably because most people believe this church to be the oldest Marian sanctuary in the world."

Lena scrunched her brow. "Marian sanctuary?"

"It's a site dedicated to the Madonna, to the Virgin Mary," Roland explained. "The shrine dates back to when Emperor Constantine first founded it, some time in the fourth century. The Benedictine order oversaw this place for almost a thousand years before it finally fell into disrepair. In fact, it's believed Saint Benedict spent time here in seclusion and prayer, living inside a cave just steps from the sanctuary's church. You can still visit that grotto."

"I think I've had enough with caves for a while," Lena said, which earned a rare snort of amusement from Seichan.

Gray drove the last length of the winding road, passing a small cemetery, to park in a nearly empty lot next to a convent. The sanctuary's church sat nearby. Its nondescript Romanesque facade hinted little at the significance of the site. Above the simple wooden doors, a rosette-shaped window reflected the sunlight, while below stood a bronze statue of a pope, with an upraised arm in blessing.

"This is the place?" Lena asked, sounding disappointed.

Gray climbed out and surveyed their surroundings. Whatever this church lacked in grandeur, the view from the rocky spur made up for it. The sweep of mountains faded into the distance to the north and south, while to the east, a wide valley opened, dropping far below in cliffs and forests to distant tilled fields.

The others joined him.

"We should check out the church first," Roland said. "The nuns here are likely to know more about the mysteries of this place than we'll find in any tourist guide."

The priest marched toward the door, adjusting his white Roman collar. Gray followed with the two women, letting Roland take the lead. If anyone could pry secrets out of a local nun, it would be a priest of the same faith.

With the sun directly overhead, the day proved to be warm and bright, fading the cold and stormy mountains of Croatia into a distant memory. Still, Seichan kept a wary watch on their surroundings, glancing frequently toward the lone road that led up here. When they reached the church door, she hung back.

"Something wrong?" he asked.

"The approach here . . ." She narrowed her eyes. "There's only one way up or down."

That was true. They were isolated up on this peak. It would be easy to get pinned down here. After Croatia, he didn't blame her suspicions. He shifted his light jacket, feeling the weight of his SIG Sauer holstered at his shoulder.

She noted the small movement, meeting his eyes. "I'll stay out here. Let you all poke around on your own."

He appreciated her caution. While there was no evidence they had been followed, why take any chances? He touched her hand, thanking her. His fingers brushed along the inside of her wrist, remembering kissing that tender flesh—but now he felt the steel hilt of a sheathed dagger hidden under her cuff. It reminded him of the true nature of the woman he loved, that mix of tenderness and steel.

That was Seichan.

Roland tugged open the door to the church.

"Get to work," Seichan whispered throatily to Gray. The smoldering emerald of her eyes held both a challenge and a threat: *Don't leave me waiting for too long. Who knows what mischief I'll get into?*

11:21 A.M.

As Roland entered the church, he dipped his fingers into the font just inside the door and whispered a small prayer. He dabbed himself with holy water in the sign of the cross. As usual, he felt reverence and awe upon stepping into a house of God. Even the soft fragrance of old incense greeted him like a dear friend, blended with the vanilla-scented smoke from votive candles.

While the sanctuary appeared drab on the outside, inside, the white plaster walls seemed awash with sacredness, arcing high into Gothic buttresses. Wooden pews led toward the altar, while on a landing overhead rose a magnificent eighteenth-century pipe organ. To the side, a few windows shone with stained glass, illuminating centuries-old frescoes and paintings. But it was the main altar that held the true treasure of the Sanctuary of Mentorella.

In an alcove behind the altar rested a large wooden statue of the Madonna. It dated back to the twelfth century, a carving of Mary seated on a throne, cradling the infant Jesus. Both she and the child wore crowns embedded with gems and pearls. Tall bronze lamps flanked the figure, illuminating it, making the sculpture appear to glow from within, as if the wood itself was suffused with holiness.

He headed toward it, drawn by its beauty.

Lena broke the spell as she spoke behind him. "Where do we even begin this search?"

His feet slowed, reminded of the task at hand: to hunt for what Father Kircher had removed from those caves. He allowed Lena and Gray to draw abreast of him in the center of the nave. He searched around, noting how few people were here. A pair of tourists—a husband and wife—made a slow ambulation along the perimeter of the pews, where a lone elderly woman, her hair tied in a scarf, knelt with her head bowed in prayer.

The only other person present was a woman in a black nun's habit. She stood to the side of the altar with her arms crossed, her hands hidden inside her sleeves. Considering the age of this convent, he would have expected to find an old nun in attendance, but instead the woman appeared no older than her twenties. Her hair was tucked and hidden under her wimple, but her bright blue eyes sparked with youth. Her gaze flicked to his Roman collar and gave a demure bow of her head, acknowledging his station.

"Let's see if she can help us," Roland said and continued between the pews toward the altar.

"*Dzie dobry,*" she greeted them in Polish, then repeated in Italian. "*Buongiorno.*"

He smiled at her attempt to accommodate all visitors—or at least those that must drop in here the most often. "*Lei parla inglese?*" he asked in Italian.

"Of course, Father, most certainly," she said, her Polish accent still present. "In fact, I spent two years in Atlantic City. As a blackjack dealer."

Roland laughed. "Not exactly the usual path to serving our Lord."

She offered a shy grin, her gaze dropping in embarrassment. "It was a good job, paid well, and it let me see more of the world."

"I understand," he said, encouraging her with a warm smile as he made their introductions. "And may I ask your name?"

"Sister Clara."

"Excellent. Sister Clara, we were hoping you might help us."

"In any way I can, Father."

"We've traveled all the way from Croatia to study more about this sanctuary. We're specifically interested in information about the priest who oversaw its reconstruction in the seventeenth century."

"You mean Father Kircher."

Roland felt a measure of shock, but then realized any nun here would certainly know this place's history in detail.

"Yes, precisely," he answered. "I teach at a Catholic university in Zagreb and did my doctoral thesis on the reverend father. I came here to learn more about his later years, to discover why he became so focused on rebuilding this sanctuary, specifically why he took such a personal involvement. I had hoped that perhaps you and your sisters might know more than could be found in any textbook."

"Even if it's just legend or rumor," Gray added. "Anything that might direct us to discovering more about his work here."

Sister Clara pointed to the marble floor in front of the altar. "We can perhaps start right here. Father Kircher's heart is buried at the foot of this altar, per his request to the pope. He wanted the grace of the Madonna to always be shining upon him."

Lena spoke up. "So Father Kircher was obsessed with the Virgin Mary."

"*Revered*, I believe is more accurate. It was why he petitioned to rebuild this sanctuary. Because it was the oldest site of worship for the Holy Mother."

Roland glanced quizzically at Lena, seeing some glimmer of realization shining in her eyes. He pulled her and Gray aside and asked softly, "Lena, what are you thinking?"

"Eve was a woman, the *mother* of us all," she whispered. "If Father Kircher was seeking a place to venerate her, too . . ."

This would be the perfect place to inter her bones.

"But if you're right, how might he have hidden such a grave? How would he have marked it?"

Gray offered a solution. "Didn't you mention that Father Kircher had a great fascination with hieroglyphics, that he even carved some of his own symbols into ancient Egyptian obelisks?"

"That's correct, but what does that have to do—"

Gray pressed on. "And didn't he come to believe that hieroglyphics might be the lost language of Adam and Eve?"

Shock and possibility widened in Roland's eyes. He looked upon the American with more respect.

"Let's find out," he said and crossed back to Clara. "Sister, when the reverend father oversaw the reconstruction here, I understand that he laid some of the bricks himself and also had a hand in restoring the artwork and ornamentation."

"That's true."

"Fascinating. And I know this may sound odd. But is there anywhere on these grounds where he might have had hieroglyphics inscribed as decoration?"

Clara's brows rose in surprise. "As a matter of fact, yes, Father." She turned to a side door to the church. "Up in the Chapel of Saint Eustace. I can direct you there if you'd like."

Roland inclined his head, trying to keep calm. "We'd be most grateful."

She led them past the altar to a small wooden door and held it ajar for them. Sunlight streamed inside from a small courtyard behind the church. A crushed gravel path led through a wild garden of olive trees and rose-bushes, set among a scatter of marble statuary.

"If you follow this path," she instructed, "it will take you to a fork. To the left, steps lead down to Saint Benedict's cave, but to the right, you'll find the Scala Santa, the Holy Ladder. Those set of marble steps climb up to the Chapel of Saint Eustace."

Gray headed out first, nodding to Clara. "Thank you, Sister."

Clara stopped Roland with a touch on his arm before he left. "You asked about *legends* concerning Father Kircher." She nodded in the direction of the solitary chapel sitting at the highest point of the summit. "It is said that Father Kircher worked on that building with a single mason. The only other person he ever allowed up there during its construction was a friend, a bishop named Nicolas Steno. According to our records, Bishop Steno and Father Kircher spent much time together here, and in fact it was the bishop who carried Kircher's heart to the Sanctuary of Mentorella upon the reverend father's death."

"That's indeed most interesting," Roland said. "Thank you, Sister."

With a small smile, she bowed her head, retreated back inside, and shut the door.

As he headed after Gray, Lena kept alongside him. "What was that about?"

"Maybe nothing, but I came across the name Nicolas Steno during my studies of Father Kircher. He was a Danish scientist, several decades younger than Father Kircher. They worked in the same circles and became close friends. But what's most interesting is that Steno's field of study was what would be called paleontology today. The study of fossils, old bones, et cetera."

"You're thinking if Father Kircher took possession of what he considered Eve's remains that he might have involved his friend."

They reached the fork in the path and met up with Gray. Roland pointed to the steep stone staircase winding up to the right. "From Sister Clara's account, it sounded like those two men were up to something secret involving that chapel."

Gray had stopped to study the other path, the one that led down to a cliff face with a dark vertical cut in it. "That must be the famous grotto." He pointed to a glass-enclosed shrine at its entrance, full of a jumble of skulls and bones. "But what's that?"

"An ossuary," he explained. "According to the guidebook, it holds the relics of monks and friars who once served here. The inscription on its marble pedestal reads: *Remember: what you are, we were. What we are, you will become.*"

"True, I guess, but definitely morbid." Gray turned toward the flight of marble steps and headed up.

Lena followed but glanced back at the ossuary. "Let's just hope we don't *become* that anytime soon."

Roland smiled. *That was also true.*

Gray led them up the precariously steep ascent of the Scala Santa. Underfoot, the steps were made of white marble, worn smooth by the passage of many sandals, boots, and shoes over the ages. A low wall on the left was all that kept climbers from a fall down the cliff on that side.

"I can see why they call this a Holy *Ladder*," Lena commented, huffing from the effort.

Roland wheezed, "It's meant both as a challenge and to humble those pilgrims seeking to reach the chapel."

"Certainly does its job."

Roland stared up as he climbed, shading his eyes with a palm. The small tile-roofed chapel looked austere and simple silhouetted against the blue sky, clinging to the spur overlooking the next valley. Four arched windows faced each of the cardinal directions.

Roland found himself winded by the time he reached its door. He stopped to catch his breath, taking in the panorama of white rocky cliffs and fir-covered slopes. A slight breeze carried the fresh scent of pine. He finally faced the door of the chapel, feeling a flicker of unease.

What had Father Kircher hidden here . . . and why?

11:48 A.M.

Lena followed Roland across the threshold into the shadows of the small chapel. After such a difficult climb, she had expected to discover something grand and stately, but the interior was spartan. The only adornment was a small marble altar on the far side, holding a scatter of guttered candles below a simple stone crucifix. The room was little larger than a two-car garage, with arched windows open to views in all directions.

Roland stared up at the roof, at the crisscrossing of stone arches above. "This is the same pattern of brickwork we saw in that chapel in the caverns."

He was right, which made her wonder. If that cavern chapel had been built to inter the bones of a Neanderthal male, was this same construction some clue about what had been done with the female's remains?

Roland searched around. "Sister Clara said there were hieroglyphics to be found up here."

Gray stalked along the perimeter of the room, running his fingers along the walls below the windows, peering closely. "All of these bricks are faintly inscribed with writing. They circle the room, row by row. The topmost appears to be Latin. Below that is Greek."

Lena joined him as he dropped to a knee.

"This next level is carved with Chinese characters." Gray glanced back at them. "And at the very bottom are strips of Egyptian hieroglyphics."

Roland crouched down. "It's almost like he layered them by age. Going back in time."

Lena ran her fingertips along that bottommost level, examining the carving, impressed by Father Kircher's ability to mimic this writing. She worked around the walls, studying the triple lines of hieroglyphics that ran along the walls near the floor.

Roland crawled beside her. "One of Father Kircher's greatest published works was a three-volume epic titled *Oedipus Aegyptiacus*. It was his major treatise on Egypt, hieroglyphics, and ancient knowledge. He merged Greek myths, Pythagorean mathematics, Arab astrology, biblical accounts, and even alchemy, all in an attempt to comprehend the universal source of all knowledge."

"Like some grand unifying theory of intelligence," Lena said.

Roland nodded.

Lena felt a sudden kinship with this historical figure. *Maria and I were researching the same, to discover the true source of human intelligence.*

Gray scanned the ribbons of hieroglyphics. "Can you translate any of this?"

Roland frowned. "It's likely all meaningless. Father Kircher believed he had a discovered a way to decipher hieroglyphics, but in the end, he was deceiving himself."

"Then what do we hope to gain from all of this?" Lena asked.

With no answer apparent, silence settled over them.

After a few minutes, she was about to admit defeat when Gray stirred. He shifted closer to one section of the wall. "Look over here. In the middle row, at this pair of antelopes. Notice the one on the right with the raised horns."

He rubbed his thumb there to better reveal a pinkie-sized divot centered between the horns. He glanced back at them. "It's almost like a hieroglyphic representation of Saint Eustace's symbol. The stag's antlers and the cross."

"Like what we found drawn in the back of Kircher's old journal," Lena said, leaning closer. "But what does it mean?"

Gray pivoted to face her and held out his hand. "Can I see that key you found?"

Lena understood and fished it out of her pocket, then handed it to him.

Gray positioned the tip of the key near the indented mark between the horns. It appeared to be the same diameter. "Notice how there's a half inch of clean rod at the end of the key, almost like a steel punch."

Roland looked doubtful. "You're thinking of using it to unplug this hole."

Gray took out a pen and dug at the divot. "There's definitely looser material packed in here." He rubbed at some of the debris generated between his fingers. "Fine sand and maybe wax."

Roland swallowed and rubbed his chin. "Try it."

Gray shifted around, positioned the key's tip into place, then used the heel of his hand to strike a hard blow. With a grating of stone, the key sank to the level of its first toothed bit. He pulled it back out, then blew at the newly created hole.

"I think that did it," he said. "The impact even broke away part of a vertical slot along the bottom. Looks like it would accommodate the protruding teeth of the key."

To make sure, Gray slipped a dagger from a boot sheath and used its sharp point to clean out the slot. Once satisfied, he tested it with the key. He had to push and prod—then finally it sank fully away, teeth and all, coming to a stop at the skull-adorned crown of the key.

Gray gave them both a questioning look.

Surely this lock won't work after so many centuries, Lena thought.

"Do it," Roland instructed, his eyes shining with hope. "Beyond studying lost languages, Father Kircher was a master engineer, concocting all sorts of mechanical devices from magnetic clocks to windup automatons. He even had statues at his museum in Rome that would talk, amplifying the voices of someone in another room."

Given the okay by the priest, Gray tightened his grip on the head of the key and gave it a firm twist.

Lena held her breath, not sure what to expect.

A jarring clank echoed from the wall. Then a large marble slab at the foot of the chapel's altar dropped away, swinging on hidden hinges to form a ramp leading down. A waft of rock dust blew up from below.

Lena stood but kept warily back from the hole. Roland stepped to her side as Gray removed the key and joined them.

The ramp led to a shadowy set of stairs hidden under the altar. They looked hewn out of the mountain bedrock, descending steeply away.

"It's almost like a dark mirror of the Holy Ladder outside," Roland whispered.

Lena had a larger concern.

But where does it lead?

12:18 P.M.

Seichan kept in the shadows of the convent walls. The midday sun hung in an achingly blue sky. She watched a hawk slowly circle on the thermals rising from the warming mountains. The air smelled of fresh pine, along with a hint of rosemary from the convent's nearby gardens. She could faintly hear voices of the nuns inside the building, their words rising and falling in a prayerful cadence.

She tried to imagine what it would be like to live a life of such seclusion and isolation, to be at peace with oneself and one's god. Her upbringing had been full of terror and desperation as she scrabbled for life in the slums of Southeast Asia. From there, she had been recruited, trained in a brutal manner to grind away the little humanity that was left in her. Only lately had she come to reconcile her past, to set herself on a path to right the wrongs she had committed and to find a semblance of peace.

A peace she still mistrusted.

She knew how easily it could all be taken away.

She glanced toward the church, to the chapel higher up the hill. She had watched Gray climb up there with the others a few minutes ago. She did not doubt his love for her, nor could she deny how she felt about him. But as much as she tried to hide it—and she was good at putting on other faces—she could not discount her wariness when around him. It was some combination of fear at losing him coupled with the guilt that she did not deserve him.

Or any of this new life.

The bang of a door drew her attention back to the church. A middle-aged couple headed toward the small parking lot. The woman slipped her hand in her husband's, as naturally and easily as a bird landing on a limb. The wife said something that made the man smile. As they walked, they drew imperceptibly closer. It was a dance older than time, driven by their paired hearts beating together, synchronized by the passing years into a perfect rhythm.

She shifted, stiffening her back. The sight irritated her—not because she envied them, but because she didn't. She found them naïve, blissfully ignorant of the harsher realities of life. For her, such peace was an illusion, a purposeful blindness, like blinkering a horse's eyes to keep it from spooking at the dangers around it.

In the end, the only true and lasting peace was found in death.

And I don't intend to go without a fight.

An echoing rumble drew her attention away from the couple and toward the lower road. A tourist bus slowly trundled a switchback, heading up. It was painted a bright crimson, with a stylized dragon emblazoned on its side. She had seen similar buses across Europe, full of camera-toting Asian tourists who flocked together as a group, clinging to their own culture as a wall against foreign influence. She knew some of the tour companies even discouraged their clients from sampling local cuisine, preferring instead to stop at noodle shops or Asian restaurants.

Though the sight of such a bus was common throughout Europe, Seichan still slunk deeper into the shadows of the convent. She knew a Chinese faction had kidnapped Kowalski and Lena's sister and likely orchestrated the ambush in Ogulin.

As a precaution, Seichan maneuvered over to a narrow window, open to the soft breezes across the mountaintop. The voices of the nuns in midday prayers grew louder, rising from deeper within the centuries-old structure. Earlier, she had canvassed the area, making a full circuit of the grounds, surveying various vantages of approach and escape.

Crouched now, she listened for the crunch of gravel under the bus's tires as it pulled into the parking lot. She took that moment to leap up and drop cleanly through the convent window into the empty room beyond. Safely ensconced out of sight, she spied as the bus heaved to a stop amid a cloud of dust and exhaust.

After a moment, the doors sighed open, and people began piling out, stretching, yawning, and checking cameras. The tour guide—a hummingbird of a woman in a bright crimson jacket that matched the bus's exterior—opened an umbrella of the same color. She used it both to shade herself and as a focus of attention as she chattered loudly in Mandarin, trying to herd her charges together. After a bit of wrangling, she began to march her clients toward the wooden doors of the church.

Seichan studied the tourists. They were all Chinese, ranging in age from young children to bent-backed elders. Clearly this was no assault team. Still, such a crowd offered the perfect cover for anyone who wanted to get closer to Seichan's group. She observed each member closely, paying attention to how they moved, who they talked with, how they interacted.

Six men—all in their late twenties or early thirties—made her uneasy. They did not walk together, nor did they converse with anyone else. Instead, their eyes swept the mountaintop a little too purposefully, and one gaze settled for several seconds too long on their parked Mercedes SUV. As that figure turned back around, she noted a telltale bulge under his light jacket.

It could be a camera—but she wasn't buying that.

She ducked away, struggling for a plan, yet knowing one certainty.

The time for peace was over.

12:32 P.M.

Gray led the others down the dark staircase. The way was narrow and treacherously steep, requiring them to proceed single file. He lit their path with a penlight while Lena trailed behind, using her cell phone to help illuminate her steps. The air was several degrees cooler than the sunlit chapel above and also drier than he had expected.

Like entering a dusty Egyptian tomb.

Roland ran his fingers along the wall. "If I had to guess, I'd say this must lead to some cavern within the mountain, similar to Saint Benedict's grotto."

In another handful of steps, the priest's estimation proved to be true as Gray's light vanished into a cave. It was small, no more than five yards across. As he stepped off the last stair, his bootheel sank into what appeared to be a layer of crushed gravel over the floor. He moved aside to let the others join him. The crunch of their steps was loud in such a confined space, but not enough to cover the others' gasps of shock.

Lena lifted her cell phone higher.

Roland wavered where he stood, looking close to falling to his knees.

Across the cavern, seated on a throne carved from the bedrock, was a bronze figure of the Virgin Mary. It was a perfect replica of the wooden Madonna in the sanctuary's church—from the bejeweled crown atop her head to the infant Christ cradled on her lap.

"She's beautiful," Roland murmured.

Lena spoke, tempering his enthusiasm. "But it's not what we came to find." She searched around at the rock walls of the cave. "It's just another chapel. Maybe a private place for Father Kircher to pray to the Virgin Mary."

"Still, to discover such a holy place, one hidden for centuries . . ." Roland's voice was full of passion, sounding close to tears. "It's miraculous."

Gray stepped closer, washing the beam of his penlight over the figure. "For now I'm less concerned about miracles than I am about answers. Like, why did Father Kircher hide this statue down here?"

He stared up into those serene eyes of the Madonna, remembering how Sister Clara had said Kircher wanted his heart to be buried in the church beneath that holy gaze.

There must be more here.

He looked down at his toes, sweeping at the gravel. The granular material did not look like debris from the construction, but more like kitty litter. The motion drew Roland's attention from the statue.

Gray leaned down and pinched up some of the grains, rolling them between his fingers. "It's like what I felt plugging the keyhole above. Some sort of sand."

Roland bent down and examined it himself. "Not sand," he concluded, a soft smile on his face as he looked back up. "Silica."

"Silica?" Lena asked.

"A form of silicon dioxide," Roland explained. "Like you find in those desiccant packets inside pill bottles, used to keep things dry."

No wonder the air down here felt so arid.

"The material was a scientific curiosity during Father Kircher's time," Roland continued. "He wrote chapters on its synthesis and drying properties. He even used it to help preserve some of the inner workings of his mechanical devices."

Lena glanced back to the stairs. "Like the locking mechanism above."

Roland nodded.

"Maybe not just that," Gray added. "Father Novak, didn't you tell us that Kircher built moving statues, some of which were featured in his museum?"

Roland's eyes widened. "You don't think . . ." He turned toward the bronze sculpture of the Madonna. "It couldn't be."

Only one way to find out.

Gray crossed to the statue and searched with his penlight, suspecting what he would find. He discovered it in the crown atop Mary's head: a cross-shaped hole framed by a crescent of jewels below it.

Like a rack of antlers.

Roland made the sign of the cross, whispering a prayer.

Lena looked no less stunned.

Gray handed his penlight to Roland and retrieved Kircher's old skeleton key. He had to lean on the statue's lap to reach up to the crown.

"Careful," Roland warned.

He slipped the key into the cross and seated it fully in place. He turned it a full revolution—but nothing happened. He tried it again to no better effect.

"Maybe it's broken," Lena said, crossing her arms nervously.

Gray repeated his effort, noting a slowly growing tension with each turn. "It feels like something's tightening inside."

"Keep it up," Roland encouraged, his eyes shining with hope.

Gray obeyed, continuing to turn the key, feeling that tautness increase with every revolution. He understood what Roland was hoping for.

I'm winding something up.

Soon he had to fight the key to turn it, the tiny steel skulls biting into his fingertips. Then finally something popped inside the statue, ringing the bronze like a bell.

Startled, Gray stumbled back a step, yanking out the key.

Roland grabbed his elbow—not to keep him on his feet, but in shock. "Look!"

A ticking whir sounded from the statue, and a dark line split the Madonna from crown to foot. The statue opened on its own, unfolding into two halves, like some bronze sarcophagus.

This time even Gray gasped along with the others.

Nestled within the hollow sculpture were the remains of an ancient skeleton. But this was no pile of limbs and skulls. The bones here had been carefully rearticulated and wired together in bronze, positioned exactly like the Madonna. The figure was seated serenely, with those bony sockets staring down at them, overhung by thicker brows, marking her as uniquely different from modern man.

"We found her," Lena whispered. "We found Eve."

"That's not all," Roland said, shuffling forward. "Look at what she's holding."

In one arm, she cradled a yardstick-long staff of bone across her lap, mimicking how the Madonna had held the infant Jesus, but this wasn't what drew the most attention. Balanced on the figure's knee was a ball of rock about the size of a grapefruit.

Gray shone his light upon it, revealing details carved over half its surface, showing star-shaped craters and smooth planes of lakes.

"It's a sculpture of the moon," Roland said. "Mapping its near side perfectly."

Lena drew even closer. "Impossible."

Gray didn't understand the severity of their reactions. Roland had shown them Father Kircher's drawings of the lunar surface earlier. Such knowledge shouldn't have warranted the shared looks of disbelief on their face.

"What's wrong?" he asked.

Lena glanced back at him. She had to swallow before she could speak. "There are darker pieces of calcite still stuck on the back side of the sphere."

Gray frowned, not understanding.

"This *isn't* from Father Kircher's time," Roland explained. "This must've been taken from that niche in the prehistoric sculpture gallery we told you about. It was clearly broken free from the millennia of calcite dripping and frozen over it."

Lena pointed. "Which means this model of the moon must be tens of thousands of years old."

Gray stared harder at that mystery.

That *was* impossible.

Roland fell back a step, lifting a hand to his brow. "No wonder Kircher became so obsessed with the moon, with searching for the source of ancient knowledge. Like us, he had to recognize the impossibility of this discovery."

"Maybe that's why he sealed up that cavern system," Lena said. "And stamped it with that stern warning against any trespass."

"And why he hid everything down here in the end," Roland added.

Lena touched the priest's arm. "In doing so, Kircher proved himself to be a *true* scientist. He protected and preserved what he found for posterity."

Roland sighed. "He must have spent the latter years of his life investigating all of this in secret. Revealing what he knew to only a handful of his closest colleagues. And while he likely never fully understood his discovery, he clearly came to revere it."

Gray studied the beautiful craftsmanship of the mechanical Madonna and couldn't disagree.

Lena lifted a hand toward the long staff resting in the Neanderthal woman's skeletal fingers. "I think this is carved out of ivory, maybe from a mammoth tusk."

"What is it supposed to be?" Gray asked.

"I don't know. Maybe a crutch. From the arthritic changes in some of the bones, she was very old when she died."

Gray stared at that staff, sensing there was more here than just a prehistoric cane, especially as prominently as it was displayed here. He could even see faint notches along its length, like some prehistoric yard-stick.

Lena leaned closer. "Look. The pinkie on this hand is callused from an old break."

"A broken finger." Roland peered over her shoulder. "Same as those palm prints we saw above her gravesite."

"And in that cavern of niches and statues. Which means it's all the *same* woman. She must have made that wall painting and likely sculpted that representation of the moon."

Gray hung back as they focused fully on the skeleton. From his van-tage, he noted something the other two had missed. The inner surfaces of the two halves of the hollow bronze Madonna offered more mysteries. On one side, a map had been inscribed into the metal. Gray could make out a large island, but any further details were too faint to discern from this distance.

On the other half of the shell, a leather-bound book rested in a bronze sleeve. The top half was visible, showing a familiar labyrinth gilded on the cover.

As he shifted his penlight to better illuminate the book, the motion drew Roland's eye. The priest exhaled sharply, recognizing what Gray al-ready understood.

Roland's hands reached for it, but then fell back away in caution. "It's a copy of Kircher's journal."

Before they could decide what to do next, Gray's phone buzzed in his pocket. He answered it, only to be immediately cut off by Seichan.

"I've been trying to reach you," she said in a rush. "We've got company."

13

April 30, 5:04 P.M. CST
Beijing, China

"According to the zoo map," Monk said, "the gorilla habitat should be around the next bend."

He and Kimberly continued along a tree-lined path, winding past Plexiglas-enclosed monkey cages. With the collar of his jacket pulled high, he kept a grip on Kimberly's hand as they strolled through the Beijing Zoo, continuing their charade of husband and wife.

He glanced at his watch.

They had entered the park fifteen minutes ago, passing through a tall set of arched gates, magnificently carved with a riotous display of dragons. That majestic introduction had not prepared Monk for the shabby conditions of the park inside.

A majority of visitors aimed for the zoo's greatest attraction, the Panda House, which was conveniently positioned near the main gate. That exhibit looked modern and inviting, housing China's national treasure: the giant pandas. Resisting the tidal pull in that direction, he and Kimberly had continued deeper into the park.

What they found beyond the Panda House was not only disheartening but heartbreaking.

Monk skirted past an exhibit holding a troop of golden-haired monkeys. The glass was filthy, the pen inside just as dirty. Worst of all, several visitors had ducked under the rail barrier and were rapping at the glass, yelling and taunting—which only seemed to terrorize the animals inside.

From the little he had seen of the rest of the park, such behavior seemed perfectly acceptable. Certainly no attendants came forth to scold anyone. Back at an open-air pit that held a Mongolian she-bear, the floor of her featureless concrete pen was littered with refuse tossed down at the poor creature: candy wrappers, cups, napkins. Monk had watched a laughing teenager pour a bottle of Coke over the despondent bear's head. He had to restrain himself from bumping the kid over the rail into that pit.

Kimberly must have sensed his growing aggravation. "I know it's disillusioning," she whispered. "The lack of upkeep, the shameful behavior of the visitors, the sorry state of the habitats—"

"*Sorry* is hardly the word I'd use." Monk waved back. "This place is a hellhole."

"It's just a reflection of the times in this country," she said, trying to calm him down. "Yes, this is backward for a zoological park in the modern age, but from what I read before landing here, there's already talk of moving the park out to the suburbs, where land is cheaper and where the animals will have larger habitats."

"Why wait so long?" he asked. "After all the money the Chinese government poured into their Olympic village, they should have done something about this place. If nothing else, police it better. The government certainly has no problem with pushing the populace around. So why tolerate that?"

He pointed to a tourist who was kicking at the grate to the habitat of a red fox, which quivered and cowered on the far side.

"What's wrong with these people?" he muttered.

"You must remember, to the Chinese, animals are still considered food, medicine, or entertainment. The signs on the cages once listed which parts of the animals were the tastiest and which made the best medicines." She cocked her head toward Monk. "So you see, things are getting better already."

Disgusted, he increased his pace toward the great ape section of the park. The zoo was due to close in an hour, and he wanted to canvass as much of the grounds as possible before they were forced to leave. But with the zoo encompassing over two hundred acres, they had to use their time judiciously. The plan was to concentrate their search on the great ape exhibit. If Baako had been taken to the zoo, it was the most logical place to look first.

After the park closed, he and Kimberly would make a circuit of the zoo grounds from the outside to search for any sign of Kowalski and Maria Crandall. Back at Sigma, Painter was continuing to monitor for any further blips from the GPS tracker while Kat prepared a detailed map of the immediate area, both above- and belowground.

Monk stared at his toes. From a preliminary briefing by Painter, the park had many subterranean facilities, but the extent of them was not fully known.

Kimberly noted his attention and guessed his thoughts. "Anything could be down there," she said.

"What do you mean?"

"Another popular tourist destination in Beijing is the Dìxià Chéng, the Underground City. Built as a bomb shelter for the populace back in the seventies, it covers eighty square miles and is said to have over a hundred entrances, most of which are hidden in shops or along streets. Though a small area is open to the public, the rest remains secret."

Monk tried to picture such a massive infrastructure buried under his feet. "Do you think it could extend this far?"

"Possibly. It does link most of the major city sites: the railway station, Tiananmen Square, even the Forbidden City."

Monk rubbed his chin in thought. It could definitely be worth investigating.

"Look," Kimberly said, drawing his attention back up. "There are the chimpanzees."

Monk searched around. It seemed they had finally reached the region of the park that housed the zoo's great apes.

The chimp enclosure looked little better than the others he'd seen. The glass was smudged. The cages had exposed piles of dung dotting the floor, along with standing pools of urine. The animals inside looked despondent, slumped on the concrete, picking at themselves. Patrons pounded on the glass and hollered for attention.

A lone gorilla sat in a neighboring pen. His cage was little more than a concrete cell. The large beast squatted in a corner, his back turned from the assault on his cage. Monk could not imagine such a life, one of isolation, lacking proper mental stimulation, all compounded by the nonstop taunting. If this was happening in China's capital city, he feared what he would find at the smaller zoos of this country.

Kimberly kept her voice to a whisper as she searched the neighboring cages. "I see no sign of Baako."

As much as Monk wanted to find the kidnapped research animal here, a part of him was glad. No living creature deserved to be treated like this.

Perhaps sensing his sympathy, the gorilla turned toward Monk, those large dark eyes looking lost and forlorn. Large nostrils flared, sniffing the air. Then, with a heavy huff, he turned back to the wall.

Sorry, big guy, if I could rescue you I would.

"This is a dead end," Kimberly said.

He agreed. "Let's get out of here."

Before I shoot someone.

He continued with Kimberly, winding their way back toward the main gates. Beyond the exhibits, the parklands themselves were quite handsome, with creeks lined by willows, large blue ponds holding wading birds, and a generous number of wooden pavilions and painted colonnades.

Still, such beauty was not enough to mask the torment found here.

Monk grew ever grimmer, weighed down by their failure to discover any sign of the kidnapped group. Still, he clung to a bit of faith.

Maria and Baako were not alone.

C'mon, Kowalski, give us some sign.

5:18 P.M.

"Do it," Kowalski growled.

He signed the same to his cellmate, keeping his back to the overhead camera outside the concrete pen. He wasn't sure if anyone was watching them, but he couldn't take that chance.

Baako stared over at him, looking reluctant.

Kowalski made the okay signal with his fingers, encouraging the gorilla's cooperation. This had to look good. He had spent the past hour, slowly gesturing as furtively as he could, trying to get Baako to understand.

He signed again.

[*You must, buddy . . . if you want to see Maria again*]

Kowalski wasn't sure how much his hairy companion understood, but this plan was their only hope.

Baako hesitated, hooting in worry and fear. Then the gorilla's hand rose and tapped a thumb against his chin, his fingers splayed stiffly. He grunted questioningly at Kowalski.

[*For Mama?*]

"That's right," Kowalski said, realizing he must be talking about Maria.

The kid's actually pretty damned smart. Maybe this will work.

Kowalski stepped closer, tilting his chin slightly. Baako met his gaze. Kowalski nodded.

Now or never, little guy.

Baako swung his arm high, then whipped it back around, striking Kowalski across the face. Nails gouged his cheek. The blow was harder than Kowalski had expected. He went toppling backward, wondering if his head was still on his neck.

Baako cringed, cowering down slightly.

Kowalski rolled to a seat and scooted on his butt away from Baako while gesturing low. [*I'm all right*] He then curled his fingers at Baako, motioning for him to come again.

Baako charged. Kowalski didn't have to fake looking scared as he hastily retreated. The gorilla was a lot stronger than he looked. Baako barreled into him, striking a shoulder into Kowalski's chest and slamming him against the bars.

Kowalski gasped to loosen his lungs from the impact, then hollered as loudly as he could. "Hey! Someone help! Get me out of here!"

A moment later, the door at the end of the block of pens crashed open. A glance over his shoulder revealed two uniformed men rushing toward him. One carried an electric prod, the other a rifle.

He bit back a groan. He had hoped only *one* guard would come, someone he could overpower, allowing them both to escape.

So that meant going to plan B.

Before the guards reached him, Kowalski lifted both arms to his chest and jiggled his arms. While the motion might look like he was guarding himself in fear, it was actually a simple sign.

[*Be aggressive*]

Baako needed no coaxing to appear angry. His eyes flashed with fury at the sight of the soldiers, at the crackle of the electric prod. He took a firm stand two yards away. Leaning on the knuckles of one arm, he pounded his chest with the other fist. He also bared his teeth in a fearsome display.

"Let me out of here!" Kowalski yelled.

The guard with the cattle prod fumbled a set of keys into the lock and yanked the door open. In his other hand, he brandished the sparking end of his electric weapon at Baako. It allowed Kowalski a chance to roll out of the cage. He grappled with the man in his haste to escape until he was shoved away.

The other soldier stood well back, his assault rifle held at his shoulder, swinging his aim from Baako to Kowalski and back again.

Kowalski gestured surreptitiously to Baako, lowering a palm.

[*Back down*]

Baako huffed loudly, looking irritated, but he swung away and retreated on all fours to the back of the pen.

The guard shut the door with a loud clang and relocked it.

Kowalski fingered the deep scratches on his face, rubbing the blood around to make it look even worse. "Thought he was going to kill me."

The two soldiers spoke rapidly to each other in Mandarin. Only now did Kowalski recognize the guard with the cattle prod. It was that jackass, Gao, the head of the group who had kidnapped them all. The bastard must have returned from wherever he had taken Maria and come to check up on his other prisoners.

Gao spat through the bars at Baako, then waved Kowalski forward, threatening him with the prod. The guard with the rifle flanked his other side.

Kowalski kept his arms half raised, doing his best to look sheepish. "Take me to Dr. Crandall. She should know about all of this."

He got no acknowledgment, so he simply let himself be marched out of the cellblock. Before the door closed, he glanced back at Baako, feeling guilty about abandoning the little guy. He clenched both of his raised fists and clutched them to his chest.

[*Be brave*]

5:22 P.M.

Baako watches the big man leave, sees the door close. He remembers the man's last words, but he finds nothing but fear inside him. It does not help that his sharp nose catches the scent of blood under his fingernails. His breathing comes harder, forcing him to drop to the ground.

He hugs his knees, wishing it was Mama he hugged.

He looks slowly around the room. There are no toys, no drawing board, no ropes. He stares toward the food in the bucket, but he has no hunger.

Only fear.

He keeps his back to the far corner, turned away from the stinking pile, where the man made him go. There is no toilet here like back home. He feels shame—not only because he was taught not to go on the floor, but because he knows what is hidden in there, put there by the man.

He huffs his confusion, his frustration.

He thumbs his chin, rocking in place.

[Mama, Mama, Mama…]

Then a loud noise erupts—a roaring, a fierce bellowing. It comes from the big shiny door at the other end of the room. Red letters shine on a sign above it, angry like a warning. Something bangs heavily against that door.

Baako goes still, afraid to move, fearful of attracting whatever screamed like that. His tiny hairs quiver with warning. He hears blood in that roaring, as surely as he smells it from his fingertips. His two mothers told him stories at night, often with pictures. Some had monsters in them: shadows lurking under a bed or trolls hiding under bridges.

Trolls eat goats, *he remembers Mama telling him.*

He does not know what made that bellow. It goes silent again, but Baako fears he might be a goat in this story.

He turns from that shiny door and toward the double doors at the other end of the room, where the big man vanished, but he thinks of another.

Mama, where are you?

5:42 P.M.

Maria paced the length of the octagon-shaped room. The floors were polished concrete, the walls a featureless white plaster. All around, glass-enclosed alcoves held ancient artifacts and tools, their antiquity in direct contrast to the modern sterility of the place.

Dr. Dayne Arnaud stood before one of the cases, slightly bent at the waist, his hands clasped behind him. The paleontologist studied a fist-size stone, chipped into a prehistoric hand ax. But from the haunted expression on his face, he likely had little interest in what he was looking at and sought only to distract himself from the situation at hand.

She understood. The brutal and sudden execution of Professor Wrightson weighed upon them both.

She glanced to a pair of armed guards flanking the exit. Jiaying Lau had escorted her and Dr. Arnaud down into the subterranean complex beneath the zoo and abandoned them in this museum room, promising to return shortly.

That was over an hour ago. By now Maria's nerves were stretched as tautly as piano wire. She finally stopped next to the French paleontologist.

Maybe if we compared notes . . .

"Dr. Arnaud," she said, drawing his attention. "Do you have any thoughts or theories about what might be going on here?"

He glanced to the exit and gave a small shake of his head.

She sighed, trying to sort things out. "Clearly this must be some sort of covert genomics project, one tied to ancient DNA, but there's something else going on here, something the Chinese are still keeping under wraps. After they kidnapped you and Professor Wrightson, were you able to overhear anything?"

"*Hélas, Docteur Crandall,*" Arnaud started, then firmed his lips and switched to English. "I'm sorry. But unfortunately I know no Mandarin, so the little that I overheard was meaningless to me."

She was in the same boat.

"But," he said, sweeping an arm, "from the collection gathered here, I can make some suppositions."

"What do you mean?"

"Let me show you."

He marched her over to one of the larger alcoves. On a shelf, illuminated from panels at the back, rested a massive skull, far larger than any human's, but with similar conformations.

Something in the ape family, she guessed.

When Arnaud spoke, she heard the envy in his voice. "Nothing like this skull has ever been found. At least not this intact."

"What is it?"

"An extinct species of gorilla. *Gigantopithecus blacki.* Such beasts roamed the highlands of southern China and Vietnam until they died off a hundred thousand years ago."

She eyed the size of the skull. "It must've been massive."

"*En effet,*" he agreed. "It stood three meters tall and weighed as much as five hundred kilograms."

She tried to imagine such a half-ton beast.

"All we know about the species," Arnaud continued, "comes from a handful of molars and a few fragments of jaw. The first teeth were found back in 1935 at an apothecary shop in Hong Kong."

"As in a drugstore? What were the teeth doing there?"

"In Chinese medicine, fossilized bones were often pulverized into a powder to formulate elixirs."

"But what's all of this have to do with what's going on here?"

He stared around at the collection. "From this specimen and several others, I would wager someone has made a discovery of astounding importance, a cache of fossils and relics that could potentially rewrite what we understand about our early history."

She frowned at the gorilla skull. "What do you mean, *our* history?"

"Like I said, *Gigantopithecus* went extinct only a hundred thousand years ago, making it a contemporary of early man in this region." He moved to another alcove. "And look at all of the bone, antler, and stone tools on display here. From my estimate, they all date to the Upper Paleolithic."

She slowly nodded. She knew that period well from her own research. It was when Neanderthals coexisted with humans, along with a handful of other hominin tribes still in existence: the Denisovans, the hobbit-like *Homo floresiensis*, even a few surviving *Homo erectus* relatives.

It was a pivotal moment in human history.

Arnaud directed her next to a stone figure. It was a crude depiction of a gravid woman squatted around her large belly. "Such Venus figures began appearing in the Upper Paleolithic. The Venus of Willendorf, the Venus of Laussel, et cetera. If you look closely, you can see traces of red ocher painted on this figurine, a clear sign of ritualistic behavior."

"So you believe this entire collection all came from a relatively narrow sliver of history?"

"Not only that, but also the same *place*. From the presence of that intact *Gigantopithecus* skull, I'd say these artifacts all came from southern China, maybe up in the Himalayas. Which brings us to this unusual item." He shifted her over to another case, to another skull, this one much smaller. "Notice the blend of archaic features and modern anatomy found in this specimen. The flat face, the thick skull bones, the broad nose."

"It looks human."

"But not quite." He glanced over to her. "This skull belongs to a cave-dwelling people, a tribe who were only recently discovered in the southern provinces of China. They're called the Red Deer Cave people, and their existence still baffles paleontologists and archaeologists."

"Why?"

"Because they shouldn't exist. For the longest time, it was accepted that Neanderthals were the last of our closest relatives to survive, dying off some thirty to forty thousand years ago. But the bones of the Red Deer Cave people date back only eleven thousand years."

Her eyes widened. That was a mere blip in geological time.

"Most paleontologists believe they're a subspecies of human, a cross-breed of *Homo sapiens* and a more ancient hominin tribe, the Denisovans, further proving our ancestry is much more blended than previously suspected."

She already knew this to be true. It was well documented that humans carried the genes from both Neanderthals and Denisovans, the percentages of which varied by regions. But much still remained a mystery, like the fact that a recent comprehensive study suggested our genetic ancestry owed a debt to a *third* archaic group, one as yet unknown.

The possibilities intrigued her.

If that puzzle could be solved, what might be learned about our true past?

"Do you think that's what the Chinese are exploring here?" she asked. "Trying to piece together the genetic root of what makes us human?"

"I don't know." He swept his gaze across the room. "But from the pristine condition of these fossils and relics—all marking such a significant moment in time—the Chinese discovered something important, something they judged valuable enough to keep hidden from the rest of the scientific world."

She considered the cost involved in the construction of this buried laboratory complex. It must have been substantial, on a par with the Manhattan Project. But even more disconcerting was *who* was running it all.

She glanced to the uniformed guards. "If you're right about this discovery, why is it being run by a division of the Chinese military?"

Arnaud furrowed his brow. "Perhaps they are seeking a way to weaponize what they found."

Maria took in a deep breath, horrified at what that might mean.

"Then again, Dr. Crandall, was not your own research funded by DARPA, the U.S.'s military science division?"

That was certainly true.

Are my hands any cleaner?

Her funding came from a division of DARPA called the Biological Technologies Office, whose mission statement was to explore the boundary between the biological and the physical sciences. Before accepting DARPA's grant money, she had read up on other BTO projects, many of which involved enhancing soldiers in various ways: from advanced prosthetics to cortical implants. But one of the projects also sought ways to increase human intelligence through genetic manipulation. She suspected her and Lena's research with Baako was linked to that long-term goal.

She closed her eyes, unable to deny the truth any longer. Like it or not, the world was in the midst of an escalating *biotechnological* arms race. And she and Lena were a part of it.

But who were we truly working for? She pictured Amy Wu's smiling face. *Was it China or the United States?*

She breathed harder, realizing now she would have no choice in the matter going forward, not if she wanted to live. She remembered the lesson in the brutal execution of Professor Wrightson.

Be useful . . . or be dead.

She stared toward the exit, knowing the one person who would decide her fate.

As if responding to her summons, the door opened and a figure entered, followed by an armed Chinese soldier. But the newcomer wasn't the one whom Maria had been expecting.

Kowalski lumbered into the room. He cast a scowl back at the man with the pistol—it was that bastard Gao—then turned to Maria. His left cheek looked freshly bandaged, and he was wearing a new set of gray coveralls.

"There you are," he grumbled.

"What happened?" She studied his face. "Is Baako—"

Kowalski fingered his bandage. "He freaked out. Attacked me."

Maria felt her heart skip a beat, but then Kowalski flattened his fingers and scooped them under his chin, signing to her.

[*I'm lying*]

He stared pointedly at her. "We should both go down there and try to calm him."

Before she could respond, Gao prodded Kowalski deeper into the room. "The major general says for you all to wait here."

Kowalski's jaw tightened with frustration.

Seems we're not going anywhere yet.

With no more explanation, Gao swung away and stormed out of the room. Clearly something had the Chinese soldier agitated.

"What was that all about?" Maria asked Kowalski.

Kowalski looked grim and kept his voice to a whisper. "I think they may be onto us."

6:05 P.M.

"I'm certain my brother left no trail for the Americans to follow," Chang Sun insisted. The lieutenant colonel stood at stiff attention, but his eyes blazed with anger. "I would stake my life on it."

And I will hold you to that, Jiaying thought.

She stood inside the complex's security office. Earlier she had received a warning from the Ministry of State Security, which oversaw intelligence operations for the People's Republic of China. From rumblings within the U.S. intelligence services, it seemed the Americans suspected who was behind the attack on the primate center. And if so, she had to assume the Americans might be sending assets to investigate.

If they aren't already here . . .

To ramp up the facility's security, she had personally come down to this office, into the heart of the section run by Chang. It was a purposeful trespass to demonstrate her fury, a sign that she lacked confidence in the lieutenant colonel's ability.

She swept her gaze across the bank of monitors covering the three walls. Technicians were normally seated at the U-shaped desk below those monitors, observing the feed from the various cameras positioned throughout the underground complex and the zoo above. She had ordered everyone out to have this private conversation with Chang.

She let the man stew upon her rebuke, staring instead at the monitor that showed Dr. Crandall's gorilla seated sullenly in his pen. "And you had that beast's body and cage thoroughly scanned for any hidden electronics."

"Gao saw to it personally just now. After he strip-searched and did the same to the zookeeper. There's nothing. Like I said, there was no failure on my brother's part that could have led the Americans to look toward our shores."

"But according to the Ministry of State Security, they are doing exactly that."

"Then it must have been something the Americans learned from that mole in the White House's science division. Who knows what Dr. Wu told them before she died or what the Americans learned afterward?"

Jiaying recognized this was a likely scenario. Thankfully, Dr. Wu knew no details about these labs. Still, Jiaying refused to loosen the noose from around Chang's neck or his younger brother's. Not until she was fully satisfied that the Americans knew nothing about this facility.

"What about Dr. Crandall?" Chang asked.

Jiaying shifted her attention to another monitor, one showing an overhead view of the room holding the American geneticist and the French paleontologist. They had just been joined by the tall zookeeper, led there by Gao.

"I will bring a technician with me when I rejoin her and scan her there," she said. "I still have much to discuss with her."

"Do you believe she'll cooperate?"

"That will depend to a large extent on whether you are able to secure her sister. How are matters proceeding in Italy?"

Jiaying took pleasure in pointing out another of Chang's failures. Apparently Lena Crandall had survived the caves of Croatia and was on the run with a small group whose identities and loyalties remained obscure. Jiaying was still mystified by the strange path that Lena and these others had taken in Italy.

It made no sense.

Why had they gone to that remote Catholic sanctuary?

Chang spoke stiffly, "All should be resolved within the hour."

"Let's hope in a satisfactory manner. I suggest you concentrate on that and leave the matter of Maria Crandall's cooperation to me."

Jiaying glanced over to another screen. The monitor was dark. It required a special key to access that feed, a key only she and Chang possessed. When activated, it offered a view down into the Ark. With the two sisters in hand, the problems facing the facility could be resolved more quickly.

Then again, if need be, Jiaying could manage with only *one* of the sisters.

She turned to Chang and fixed him with a cold stare. "See that our perimeters are continually monitored, especially for any foreigners."

"And my brother?"

She turned and headed toward the door. "An agent from the ministry will be here shortly to interrogate Gao. Once finished, have your brother dismissed from the premises until we fully grasp the breadth of his failure."

"But—"

"Are you questioning my orders, *Zhōngxiào* Sun?"

She felt the other's gaze burning a hole into her back. She preferred to keep those two brothers apart, to keep Chang isolated from any support. The lieutenant colonel would tread more carefully and respectfully, knowing his brother's career could be in jeopardy.

"*Bù, Shàojiàng* Lau," he said.

She smiled, hearing the obeisance in Chang's voice.

That's more like it.

She headed out, determined to bend another just as firmly to her will.

6:18 P.M.

Maria stood with her arms outstretched to her sides as an electronic wand was passed over her body by a technician in a white lab jacket. Major General Jiaying Lau stood to one side with her arms crossed. The woman had asked her to submit to this search but had never explained why.

Not that I can't guess.

The Chinese must have caught wind of the possible presence of the GPS tracker, but the haphazard search suggested they were unsure. It felt more like they were covering their bases. She glanced over the top of the technician's head toward Kowalski. He looked unperturbed. Surely the guards had already searched him and likely used the wand on Baako, too.

The technician said something in Mandarin to Jiaying, bowing his head slightly and stepping away. She could guess what he was telling his superior: *All clear.* So what had happened to the tracker? Had Kowalski found a way to hide it in Baako's cell? Or had Baako swallowed it?

She had so many questions, but Jiaying had returned before she could get anything further from Kowalski.

The major general stepped forward. "With that matter settled, Dr. Crandall, let us continue our earlier conversation regarding the research being conducted here. I believe that once you fully appreciate what we're trying to accomplish, you'll want to be part of it."

Like hell I will, she thought, but she turned and looked about the octagon-shaped room full of fossils, specimens, and relics.

"If I had to hazard a guess," Maria said, "your project must involve building a stronger soldier through genetics."

Jiaying showed no reaction, beyond the slightest bow of her head. "Perhaps on the surface that is our goal. But the biggest advances in science have always been driven by the baser needs of the world."

"In other words, necessity is the mother of invention," Maria quoted.

"Such has been true since the beginning of time. But all too often what the military funds in secret eventually reaches the larger world. Look at the global Internet. It started as a small U.S. military information web, but soon expanded to change the world. Similarly, the hurdles we leap here today will alter the path of humankind tomorrow."

"But you're talking about seeking ways to permanently alter the human genome. Who knows what detrimental effects that could have in the long run?"

Jiaying sighed. "You're not thinking rationally. Human activity has *already* been altering our genome. Smoking tobacco causes mutations in human sperm. Older men who father children have a higher likelihood of passing on similar mutations. The only difference is that those mutations are *random*. Why not take control of such damaging consequences to our genome?"

"That's the key word. *Control*. What you're talking about is a slippery road toward eugenics, where human life will be engineered, where babies will be designed, and where the weak will be weeded out or reduced to a second-class level of humanity. No good can come from it."

"No good? We could erase inheritable diseases, cure cancers, prolong life, and yes, we could even improve on nature. Since when is nature infallible? Why is it so horrible to imagine humanity taking the reins of its own evolutionary future? Even your own country has not officially banned the investigation of such pursuits."

Maria knew that all too well. Her own research could be construed as a step in that direction. What was the ethical difference between creating Baako in a lab and doing the same with a human life?

Into the silence that followed, Dayne Arnaud spoke up. "But, Major General Lau, you discovered something that set you on this path. Something significant enough to risk building this complex in secret. May I ask what it was?"

"Thank you, Dr. Arnaud, for reminding me. That was why I brought you both down here." She walked toward the wall opposite the exit. "Are you familiar with Mount Kailash in southern Tibet?"

"Non," he said. "I am not."

"It's a holy mountain in the Himalayas, a site of worship for both the Hindu and Buddhist faiths. It is upon that peak that the god, Lord Shiva, is said to reside in perpetual meditation. Pilgrims have been venturing there for centuries. Then eight years ago, a Tibetan herdsman who was looking for a lost sheep discovered a group of caves upon its slopes and brought a local anthropologist to examine what he found."

Maria searched around the room. "And that is where you collected all of this?"

"Those caves and some others found in neighboring peaks." Jiaying reached the wall and placed her hand on a nondescript patch. A square glowed to life, revealing a hidden electronic palm reader. "But it was in that first cave, the one discovered by the herdsman, that we found this."

From the wall, a secret drawer slowly slid open. It was wide and deep, like a large coffin. Its interior flickered to life, steadying into a soft illumination.

"The herdsman believed he was taking the anthropologist to the cave of a yeti," Jiaying explained. "And maybe he was not entirely wrong. Perhaps the bones we found have some bearing on the myths of such a creature roaming the snowy highlands. Or maybe even such caves gave birth to the legends of a slumbering god residing within that mountain. But in the end, the truth was far more exciting and illuminating."

Jiaying stepped aside so Maria and Arnaud could examine what was found. Kowalski even shouldered forward to take a look. A gasp immediately rose from the French paleontologist. Maria lifted a hand to her throat, strangling back her own surprise.

Within the drawer rested the complete skeleton of an anthropoid figure. The conformations of the skull were remarkably similar to modern humans, only with larger brows and a double sagittal crest crowning its cranium. But what truly garnered such shock was the skeleton's sheer *size*. The frame stretched over eight feet long, topped by a skull twice as large as a typical human's.

It was the bones of a veritable giant.

Kowalski scoffed, "That can't be real."

"It is," Arnaud said in a hushed, awed voice. "I've seen cranial fragments of this hominin before, but nothing this complete. The older nomenclature classified such remains as *Meganthropus,* or Large Man."

"Well, that pretty much fits this guy," Kowalski muttered.

Arnaud continued, "Most paleoanthropologists have now settled on the name *Homo erectus palaeojavanicus*, believing the hominin to be an offshoot of our older relative. Remains of these particularly large descendants of *Homo erectus* have been found throughout Southeast Asia."

"How much did this specimen weigh when he was alive?" Maria asked.

Jiaying answered, "From the density of the long bones and the size of the skull, we estimate he weighed somewhere between three hundred and three hundred fifty kilos."

Kowalski looked questioningly at her.

"That's six to eight hundred pounds," Maria explained.

Twice that of a typical gorilla.

"But from what I can tell," Arnaud interrupted, glancing toward Jiaying, "there are several *uncharacteristic* features in this specimen, conformations different from the typical *Meganthropus*."

Jiaying bowed her head in acknowledgment. "You are correct. From our comparative study, we believe this specimen is the result of interbreeding between *Meganthropus* and early humans. Hence, we've given it the name *Homo meganthropus*. This assessment is further supported by its genome, which we've fully mapped."

Maria could not hide her shock. "You mean you were able to recover salvageable DNA?"

"Indeed."

Maria looked closer and spotted several small drill holes in the pelvis and tibia. She straightened as a sudden realization dawned on her. She could barely get out any words. Geneticists and anthropologists had already hypothesized that an unknown *third* hominin contributed DNA to the modern human genome and that it was most likely some unclassified offshoot of *Homo erectus*, like these remains. Even more significantly, from studies of genetic drift, those same researchers estimated that this unknown tribe lived somewhere in central Eurasia.

She stared down into the drawer.

Am I looking at that specimen now? Is this our long-lost relative?

Arnaud followed that same thread, but from a different angle. "If you're right about this species interbreeding with early man, what time frame are we talking about? Surely you've dated these bones?"

"We have. They're approximately thirty thousand years old."

Even Kowalski understood the implication. "So you're saying these giants definitely roamed the world with us."

"For a period of time," Jiaying agreed. "And considering all the yeti sightings throughout the Himalayas, maybe they're still around. Stories persist in remote villages of yetis stealing women, mating with them, and having offspring. So who knows?"

The general smiled softly, her eyes twinkling with amusement at such superstitions. But Maria wondered if there couldn't be a kernel of truth in such stories, some race memory or legends going back to that time period. Even in the Old Testament, giants of two to three meters were stated to be living alongside early man.

"Did these big guys only live out this way?" Kowalski asked. "In China?"

"We have no way of knowing for sure," Jiaying answered.

"Or maybe we do," Arnaud said. "A countryman of mine back in 1890, an anthropologist named Georges Vacher de Lapouge, discovered a grouping of Neolithic bones at Castelnau-le-Lez in France. They became known as the Castelnau Giant, because the figure stood three meters tall. The bones were studied at the University of Montpellier by zoologists, paleontologists, and anatomists—all confirming Vacher de Lapouge's discovery. Similar bones were later discovered in France while workers were excavating a reservoir, with skulls twice the average for a typical man. All of those discoveries dated back to the last glaciations of Europe, around the same age as the bones in this drawer."

"So what became of these giants?" Kowalski waved an arm over the sheer length of the skeleton. "Something tells me our puny ancestors didn't wipe these guys out . . . at least not without help."

"We may have simply outsmarted them." Arnaud leaned over the case, studying the skull more closely. "From the cranial capacity of this specimen, this creature wasn't likely all that intelligent. Probably smart enough to be a tool user, to employ fire, similar to *Homo erectus*. But not much beyond that."

Maria frowned, glancing back at the rest of the room. "Then where did all of these other artifacts come from? The bone and antler tools, not to mention that Venus figurine. Are you saying they're not the handiwork of this hybrid?"

"I can't imagine they are," Arnaud said, straightening back up.

"And you would be right," Jiaying confirmed. "We've had half a decade to piece together much about this tribe's behavior, studying its caves, investigating nearby clans of other people."

"Like the Red Deer Cave people," Arnaud said, looking over at the smaller skull.

Jiaying nodded. "The advanced tools you find here were produced by that tribe, but we discovered several caches of the same weapons and artifacts in the caves of Mount Kailash. Along with these . . ."

She touched another panel and a piece of the wall slid up to reveal a shelved alcove behind glass. Halogen lights illuminated a collection of charred and broken pieces of skulls, along with fragments of pelvises and femurs. It was like a peek into a charnel house.

"Deep within the *Meganthropus* home caves, we found a crude crematorium. From the ashes, we pulled out these burnt bones of Red Deer Cave people."

Maria could not hold back the disgust. "Are you saying these *Meganthropus* hominins were cannibals?"

Jiaying faced them. "From our archaeological research, the tribe definitely appeared to be warlike savages. They were certainly preying upon their neighbors, a behavior likely born of an ingrained xenophobia. And while *Meganthropus* didn't have the innate ingenuity to manufacture their own tools and weapons, they were not above stealing such items, assimilating them."

"But what became of them?" Maria asked.

"We believe their warring eventually turned inward, leading them to consume themselves. In that same crematorium, we found the burnt skull fragments of other *Meganthropus*."

Maria let out a long breath.

So they were eating their own.

Arnaud offered one last insight. "Perhaps such behavior is why we've discovered so little evidence of this tribe's existence. If they cannibalized and burned their dead, it would be harder to leave a lasting mark in the fossil record."

"Which is why this rare find is so important," Jiaying said. "It offers us the chance to reach deep into our common genetic heritage, to extract genes that have been proven to be compatible to modern man, lost sequences of DNA that could benefit humankind."

"Benefit?" Maria asked. "How?"

"From the very existence of *Homo meganthropus*, we know we could be stronger, larger. It's only a matter of recovering that ancient potential."

"In order to engineer a better soldier," Maria realized aloud.

"You are thinking too small. At your own Harvard University, geneticists have isolated *ten* naturally occurring gene variants that hold the potential to benefit all of mankind. For example, one of them confers greater bone density, making limbs harder and tougher to break. Another variant protects against Alzheimer's. A third reduces the risk of heart disease." She pointed to the open drawer. "So why not take full advantage of *this* genetic resource? Why not tap into that ancient potential for the betterment of all?"

"Because of that." Maria nodded to the case of burnt bones. "Raw power—without the intelligence to wield it—is a recipe for disaster."

Rather than challenging Jiaying, her comment drew a smile from the woman. "Precisely, Dr. Crandall."

Maria blinked a few times, suddenly knowing why she had been brought to this lab, why the bones of that Neanderthal hybrid discovered in Croatia were so important. Her own research dealt with the evolutionary root of intelligence, that unique sequence of genes that uplifted early man from his hominin ancestors.

She gaped down at that open drawer. Apparently the Chinese had discovered the *brawn*; now they wanted the *brains* to go along with it.

Before she could protest, the door opened behind them. Chang stalked into the room. He ignored everyone else and fixed his gaze upon the major general. He spoke rapidly in Mandarin, plainly excited.

Whatever he said widened Jiaying's smile.

Maria's heart raced faster.

Anything that made that cold woman happier could not be good for us.

After the brief exchange, Jiaying turned to Maria.

"Dr. Crandall, I have wonderful news. It appears your sister will soon be joining us."

14

"What do we do next?" Lena asked.

A few minutes ago, in the silence of the small cave, she had overheard Seichan's warning over Gray's phone: *We've got company.* Gray now stood at the base of the steps that led up to Saint Eustace's chapel. He clutched a black pistol in one hand, guarding the only way out of here. She eyed that dark climb. Even if they reached the chapel above, what could they do? They'd be trapped atop the summit with the enemy waiting below.

"Did you finish your photos?" Gray asked.

She lifted her cell phone. "Yes."

After Seichan's call, Lena had taken a flurry of snapshots, capturing Father Kircher's Eve from as many angles as she could manage in the short time. She tried to record every detail of the skeleton, along with the relics clutched in those bony hands: the moon sculpture and that strange staff. She also took photos of the hollow bronze statue that had hidden those remains for centuries.

Roland spoke as he retreated from the figure of the Madonna. "I'm done here, too."

He held up the leather-bound journal of Athanasius Kircher, showing the gilded labyrinth on the cover. He had slipped it free from the metal sleeve on the inner surface of the hollow statue.

Roland pointed to the other half. "Lena, were you able to get a good shot of this map?"

"I did my best, but it's inscribed rather faintly."

"No matter," he said, herding her away. "I've seen something like this before. Let's go."

She sensed that something deeply disturbed the priest, but she had no time to question him. They quickly joined Gray by the stairs.

"All set," Roland said, though he stared longingly toward the bronze Madonna. He had taken several measurements. He had also slipped free that stone sculpture of the moon and stored it in a satchel over his shoulder. Still, he looked reluctant to abandon Kircher's Eve.

Even with her heart pounding in her throat, Lena appreciated his hesitation. She wished she could have collected those bones, to preserve them for a future genetic assay, but the skeleton had been rearticulated with thick bronze wire—not only bone to bone, but also secured to the framework of the mechanical sculpture. Without wire cutters and time, she had to be satisfied with what she had archived on her phone and with what Roland had gathered. If they survived this, she could always return later.

"Follow me," Gray said as he mounted the steps and began to climb. "But keep some distance. Let me check out the situation topside first. Wait for my signal before showing yourselves."

They continued single file. Lena breathed heavily, with Roland rasping behind her. Gray ascended more swiftly, not making a sound. He had clicked off his penlight, so the only illumination came from the square of light marking the trapdoor in the floor of the chapel.

Gray reached the exit well before them. He stopped to inspect the thick marble tile that formed the ramp up to the chapel. Lena huffed to within four steps of his position.

Gray glanced down to them and pointed to the wall. "I found a lever over here. I think it can be used to manually raise and lower the ramp."

"What do you want us to do?" Roland asked.

Lena could guess, which Gray confirmed with his next words.

"One of you keep a hand on it. If there's trouble I can't deal with, you pull the lever and stay hidden below."

"What about you?" Lena asked.

"I'll do my best to lead the enemy away. If I can't make it back, you all wait until after nightfall and sneak out."

Limned against the light above, Gray's face was all shadows. It was impossible to tell how confident the man was about this plan.

"Roland," Gray continued, "do you still have that secure telephone number to D.C.?"

"I do."

"If we get separated, use it. Director Crowe will help you both get somewhere safe."

Rather than reassuring her, these backup plans only made Lena more anxious.

Roland's voice cracked with the same heightened tension. "O-okay."

Gray nodded, then twisted around and dashed low up the ramp.

Lena climbed the last steps and took a position beside the bronze lever sticking out of the wall. She gripped it with both hands, finding a bit of confidence in its solidness. She stared down at Roland, his face awash in the light from above. His eyes shone with fear. Beyond his shoulders was only darkness.

Her fingers tightened on the lever.

Please, God, don't let me have to pull this.

1:02 P.M.

Gray slid next to the door of the chapel. He kept out of sight of the steep set of stairs—the Holy Ladder—that led up here from the main church. He touched the throat mike he had taped over his larynx.

"Seichan?" he whispered. He used a finger to seat the radio earpiece more firmly in place, listening for any response.

There was none.

Where are you?

While waiting for Roland and Lena to finish their work below, he had tried to contact Seichan several times—both on the radio and over the satellite phone. After her initial message, she had gone silent.

Something's wrong.

He shifted over to a neighboring window and rose high enough to peek past a corner. The vantage was less exposed than the doorway. Below his position, the white marble steps of the Holy Ladder blazed under the midday sun. The stairs were empty for the moment, but from his lofty position, he had a clear view down into the garden courtyard behind the church. A clutch of people gathered there around the red umbrella of a tour guide.

Before going silent, Seichan had reported on the arrival of a busload of Chinese tourists—who came with a suspicious group of at least six men.

Down below, the tour guide lowered her umbrella and pointed toward the chapel.

Gray tightened his jaw.

Are the tourists heading up here?

He willed them to remain in the courtyard. He didn't want to put any civilians at needless risk, especially if he had to shoot his way off this rocky spur of the mountain.

Then movement drew his attention. From the rear door of the church, the familiar figure of Sister Clara stepped into the sunlight. A pair of Chinese men accompanied the nun. She shaded her eyes and lifted an arm toward the chapel. The men looked in his direction.

Gray slunk farther back, cursing the nun's goodwill. Had the men inquired about their group or was Sister Clara merely telling the story of the chapel, the legend of Saint Eustace? One of them finally bowed his head in thanks to Sister Clara. The other headed off and confronted a pair of dark figures waiting at the fork in the path. Words were exchanged; then the same pair headed down the path toward Saint Benedict's grotto, clearly ordered to search the hermit's old cave.

The man who gave the order was rejoined by his partner, who lifted his gaze toward the chapel.

Gray ducked completely out of sight.

So that accounts for four of the assault team.

He guessed the other two were still in the church or out front, covering the escape routes off the mountain. The enemy intended to lock the summit up tight. The only other way down from here was straight over the cliff.

And here I am without a parachute.

A muffled whisper rose from the hole in the floor behind him. He caught only a few words, but the note of inquiry was easy to recognize. Roland and Lena wanted to know what was going on.

"Stay below," he warned as he dropped flat to his belly next to the door.

He kept his SIG Sauer extended ahead of him, aiming toward the two men as they began the hard climb toward the chapel. He weighed the option of simply rolling over to the trapdoor and hiding below with Roland and Lena, but clearly the enemy knew their targets were on the mountaintop. He feared what would happen if the assailants failed to find them, what they might do to the civilians or the group of nuns at the convent.

Plus Seichan was still down there somewhere.

Knowing that, Gray needed to stay in place, to back her up.

Halfway up the stairs, the man in the lead unzipped his thigh-length jacket, revealing Kevlar beneath and a compact assault rifle slung across his belly. He raised the gun, keeping it hidden from below with his body. Gray recognized a ZH-05 rifle, the latest hardware of China's special forces. The weapon came equipped with a laser-guided grenade launcher.

Then if that wasn't bad enough . . .

In the courtyard below, the tourist group drifted away from their guide and began to separate: some heading upward, others moving down toward the grotto. If Gray opened fire on the stairs, he risked a stray round cutting into those civilians.

He needed a new plan.

Gray glanced over his shoulder. The chapel had four windows, each open and facing a different cardinal direction. He had to get those two men in here, away from the civilians. He belly-crawled away from the door and aimed for the altar directly behind him. Above it, a window opened onto the mountain spur on that side. If he hid outside and waited for the men to enter, he could hopefully ambush the pair.

But first he had to make sure Roland and Lena remained safe.

As he reached the trapdoor in front of the altar, two pale faces stared back up at him. "Close it up," he ordered. "We've got company coming."

Though plainly frightened, Lena nodded and hauled hard on the bronze lever. It refused to budge. Lines of strain creased her forehead as she struggled with the centuries-old mechanism.

Roland squeezed next to her, adding his strength—then something finally gave way. The floor jolted and the ramp began to rise with a rhythmic ticking of gears.

Satisfied, Gray ran toward the window above the altar.

At least they would be safe.

Now to find Seichan.

He vaulted onto the altar and leaped for the sill of the open window. As he flew, a gun blast sounded behind him, coming from outside. Landing in the open window, he twisted around.

A dark object came whistling inside.

Grenade.

He barely registered it, already moving. The small 20mm grenade struck the roof and ricocheted off. It hit the top of the altar, then bounced and rattled over its edge.

With no other choice, Gray flung himself out the window—but not before he caught a glimpse of the grenade dropping through the trapdoor before it closed.

Cursing, Gray hit the ground outside and flattened to the granite mountaintop. He covered his head as the detonation shook the ground under him. Tiles broke off the chapel roof and shattered all around.

He pictured Roland's and Lena's scared faces.

What have I done?

1:08 P.M.

What did you do, Gray?

Seichan crouched in a small cave as the explosion subsided. The flames from a dozen small candles and votives continued to shiver from the quake, dancing her shadows across the stony walls of Saint Benedict's grotto. She kept her legs braced for another breath, her muscles bunched to make a leap for the sunlit exit.

Outside the cave, screams rose as the tourists reacted to the explosion, likely fleeing from the vicinity. *Good*, she thought grimly. With the crowd gone, there'd be less risk of collateral damage from the firefight to come—and it would come.

Once she was satisfied that the cave roof was not about to come crashing down, her concern returned to Gray. He must have been the target of that explosion, but she had no way of making radio contact with him inside this cave.

So first things first.

She dropped to one knee and yanked her steel dagger from the neck of her dead assailant. His cohort lay sprawled a yard away, his neck slashed from ear to ear. Earlier, she had guessed the enemy would search this dark grotto and so had set up her ambush. She had hoped to take out at least *one* of the enemy.

Two was even better.

She had already dispatched a *third*, a guard left near the parking lot. She had no trouble getting close to him, approaching him from his blind side, from the convent where she had been hiding earlier. Caught by surprise, he had reacted too slowly. Afterward, she had hid his body under the tourist bus and had circled the church to set up the trap in the grotto.

Preparing to continue her assault, she wiped the bloody dagger clean on the victim's chest and slipped it into her wrist sheath. She tugged a sleeve over the weapon to hide it. As an extra precaution, she reached under the dead man's jacket and removed the pistol hidden in a shoulder holster. She shoved the weapon into her belt at the base of her back. Once ready, she smoothed her disheveled clothes, checking how she looked.

At least *black* hid the few drops of blood splatter.

Seichan adjusted the wimple of her nun's habit. Earlier, while hiding in the convent when the bus of Chinese tourists arrived, she had searched the rooms until she found the garment in a closet and had quickly donned the disguise. What better way to get a drop on the enemy than to play a simple nun, especially here on church grounds?

Satisfied with her look, she headed toward the exit. As she stepped out of the cave and back onto the sunny path, she came upon a young Chinese mother and her four-year-old daughter. The pair sheltered behind the grotto's glass ossuary, as if the bones of the dead friars would protect them. The woman's eyes met hers, her expression frightened, her arms clutching tightly around her child.

"*Xiūn?, jiu ming!*" the woman pleaded in Mandarin.

Sister, help me!

Maintaining her guise, Seichan pointed toward a gate in the church fence that led out to the parking lot. She kept her voice soft, consoling her in Mandarin. "Get to the front, my child. Don't stop. Keep heading down the road."

The woman only clutched her daughter more tightly, clearly too scared to move.

Seichan rolled her eyes and took a more direct approach. Through a slit in the habit, she removed her stolen pistol and waved the barrel at the gate.

"Move! Now!"

That worked better.

Like a spooked jackrabbit, the woman bolted with her child.

With the way finally clear, Seichan stalked to the fork in the path. She now had a clear view to the chapel above. She spotted a pair of men running up the steep steps. One carried a pistol; the other hauled a smoking assault rifle. The two reached the chapel and dropped to either side of the door, their backs to the walls.

Her heart quickened, anxious for Gray.

She raised her pistol, but the men were too far away for any chance of a decent shot. So she touched her throat mike.

"Gray, are you okay?"

His voice came back immediately, whispering in her ear as he subvocalized into his mike. "Still alive, if that's what you mean."

Relief flooded through her, but she spoke tersely. "You've got two men about to knock on your front door."

"Got that. Can you handle any others? We need a way off this rock."

She glanced toward the church. "Working on it."

The last assailant must still be holed up in the sanctuary, which was a problem with the tourists hiding inside. A glance to the church's rear courtyard revealed the gardens had mostly emptied out. The tour guide remained in the open, looking anxiously up toward the chapel. The tiny woman clearly recognized the threat, yet bravely tried to get the last of her clients into the church.

Through the open door, Seichan spotted a crowd milling inside.

This is not going to end well.

She tucked her hands—including her stolen pistol—into the wide cuffs of her habit's sleeves. She bowed her head and hurried toward that rear door, hoping her disguise held out long enough for her to surprise the remaining assailant. She did not want a firefight to break out inside that packed sanctuary.

The tour guide spotted her and motioned for Seichan to hurry. The woman still held her umbrella aloft, hiding less from the sun than from the gunmen above.

Seichan increased her pace.

As she neared the door, rifle blasts drew her attention back to the mountaintop chapel. One of the men strafed his automatic weapon through the open doorway, while the other ducked low and rolled into the chapel.

She fought against a desire to sprint up there to help Gray, but she had her own assignment. As she neared the sanctuary door, a dark figure burst out into the courtyard from the nave of the church. Seichan immediately recognized the man. The spatter of fresh gunfire must have drawn her target out. He came barreling toward her, oblivious to the threat in front of him.

She smiled, pulled out her stolen pistol, and emptied most of the clip into his chest. The impact of the barrage stopped his charge. She placed the last round through the center of his forehead. He teetered in midstep, his expression shocked—then toppled backward to the gravel path.

She tossed the spent weapon and reached through a slit in her habit. She tugged free her SIG Sauer from a hip holster—a precaution in case there were any other men. Earlier she had identified at least six, but there could be more.

In the end, she was correct about the number of *men*.

The tour guide lowered her umbrella between them, as if sheltering behind it. Seichan met the woman's eyes over the top edge—and saw no fear there.

Not good.

Seichan immediately recognized her mistake.

Apparently I'm not the only one in disguise.

Seichan leaped to the side as bullets ripped through the umbrella fabric, chasing her to the ground. A round struck her SIG Sauer, knocking the weapon out of her grip.

The woman twirled the umbrella and closed in on her.

1:12 P.M.

As gunshots echoed up from below, Gray skirted low around the outside of the chapel. A man called from inside, likely telling his partner that the place was empty. Gray heard the confusion in their voices. The pair must be equally mystified at the lack of damage inside the chapel from the grenade.

Gray had his own worries about that blast, about the fate of Roland and Lena.

Reaching the window on the south side, he popped up with his SIG Sauer and fired at the man inside the chapel. He squeezed his trigger twice, aiming both times for a head shot, knowing the enemy had body armor under their civilian clothes. Both rounds struck true and dropped his target to the ground. He ducked away as a spray of automatic fire ripped through the window, coming from the doorway.

Gray retreated back the way he had come, putting the chapel between him and the shooter. The window above him faced the front door. He pictured the gunman sheltered there, watching all three windows for any movement.

Gray propped his back against the wall. He held his pistol in both hands, clutching it to his chest, readying himself for the challenge, to see who was the quicker draw in this standoff.

Then a series of loud blasts rang out—three of them.

A small grenade came sailing through the window over his head. It struck a boulder ten yards away and came bouncing back toward him. He imagined similar missiles flying out the other two windows. Apparently his adversary was trying to blow him out of hiding.

It certainly worked.

With the first grenade rattling back toward him, Gray had no other option but to twist around and dive for the window above. He leaped headlong over the sill as the grenades exploded in a series of chest-thumping booms outside. As he flew through the air, he kept his arms ahead of him, cradling his pistol between his hands and firing toward the doorway.

His opponent never flinched from the barrage. The gunman lay on his belly, hiding behind the doorframe, his assault rifle chugging rounds into the chapel. Gray felt something burn across his bicep as he hit the marble floor and slid sideways into the body of the first assailant he had shot.

Gray lay on his back, using the dead man's mass as a shield, and fired over the form.

The situation was plainly untenable—which proved true with his next breath.

A familiar sharp retort echoed from the doorway. A grenade shot past his nose, hit the altar, and ricocheted straight toward him. Anticipating such an assault this time, Gray flung the dead body over him, caught the skittering grenade with the dead man's chest, and smothered it with the body.

Gray huddled on top, curling his limbs in tight to keep the dead man's body armor between him and the grenade. From a corner of an eye, he saw his assailant fling himself away from the doorway, hiding from the blast to come.

The explosion tossed Gray high. He flew upward amid a cloud of blood and smoke. Then he crashed back down. But rather than hitting the floor, he fell through it as the concussive force of the grenade had shattered the thick marble slab that covered the hidden stairs.

He struck those dark steps hard.

Deaf and dazed, his ears aching, Gray clawed back to his knees, then his feet. He teetered atop the debris and lifted his head through the hole. Smoke obscured the shadowy interior of the chapel. A rectangle of sunlight glowed through the pall, marking the doorway. A shadow rose into view there.

His opponent.

Safely hidden in the smoke, Gray took his time and lifted his SIG Sauer. He had managed to keep the pistol still clutched in his right hand. He did his best to steady his aim and emptied the last of his rounds at that shadow.

With grim satisfaction, he watched the dark form slump to the ground.

Good enough.

Gray's legs gave out and he fell sideways, sprawling across the top of the dark stairs. His vision blurred, but then a bright light grew from below, revealing two watery shapes.

Hands clutched his shoulders.

"Gray?"

It was Lena.

He forced his breath out, his lips forming a name.

"Sei . . . chan . . ."

1:15 P.M.

The next round clipped the wing off an angel statue in the garden.

Nine . . .

As Seichan hid behind the statue, she kept count of the number of shots fired by the Asian assassin with the umbrella. If the weapon was the same design as the one Seichan had stolen from the dead man in the grotto—a Chinese QSZ-92—the dual-stack magazine held fifteen rounds, which meant her opponent still had plenty of ammunition left.

Seichan had spent the past two minutes in a fierce game of cat and mouse with the deadly woman across the church's gardens. Loud explosions interrupted their battle, echoing down from the chapel above. Seichan took advantage of those blasts to dive from cover to cover, to draw her opponent to waste more shots.

All the while, she did her best to quell her fears for Gray, to ignore the chatter of automatic fire from up there. She needed her full attention at hand. This assassin was disciplined and well trained, with a heart as cold as her own.

Seichan caught glimpses of the woman as she danced through the gardens and shielded her form with an expert twirl of that infernal umbrella. Her adversary appeared to be no older than twenty, maybe even younger. Her straight black hair was cut in a severe line across her forehead and along the bottom of her ears. Seichan estimated her height was at best five feet, all of it lithe muscle, a frame built for speed, which the woman used to her advantage.

Seichan had tried repeatedly to reach the SIG Sauer that had been knocked out of her grip, but her opponent kept her away from the pistol. Left with only her throwing knives, Seichan had already flung *two* at the woman—the first sliced through the umbrella's fabric but failed to find a target behind that shield; the second was blocked by an expert twirl of the umbrella's steel ribs.

Crouching behind the angelic statue, Seichan reached under the torn edge of the nun's habit and slipped her last blade from an ankle sheath.

Got to make this count.

She used the blade's polished steel surface to spy upon her opponent without exposing herself. In the mirrored reflection, she watched the woman drift closer, angling wider for a better shot. Her body was entirely hidden behind the umbrella, her dark eyes occasionally flashing from around its edges, never at the same place twice.

Beyond that threat, Seichan had a clear view to the rear door of the church. It was still partly ajar. Shadows milled inside. People were clearly too frightened to flee out into the open with all the gunfire and explosions. She heard children crying, parents trying to hush them. She imagined calls were already being placed to local law enforcement.

But help would not arrive in time.

Knowing that, Seichan waited until the woman stepped back onto the gravel path, then made her final move. She feinted to the left side of the statue, as if trying again to go for her abandoned pistol, drawing her opponent that way. Then she rebounded back in the opposite direction, spinning under the left wing of the angel.

As she dove out of hiding, she whipped her dagger low. It flew from her fingertips, sailed under the umbrella, and caught the momentarily duped woman in the calf.

Seichan hit the ground, rolled on a shoulder, and slid behind a cement planter. She peeked through the thorns of a rosebush to see her adversary stumble several steps back along the gravel path. Still the woman made no sound, no complaint, and kept her body fully shielded behind the umbrella. Even as she retreated, she fired through her umbrella at Seichan. Though she was shooting blind, two rounds still successfully pelted into the planter.

The woman was damn good.

But I'm better.

As her opponent finally halted and gathered herself to resume her assault, she had come too close to the open door to the church—where Seichan had wanted her to be after spotting an ally inside. With the assassin's focus fixed on Seichan, the woman had failed to note a dark shadow slip from the doorway behind her.

Seichan smiled with satisfaction.

I'm not the only nun you should've been worried about.

Sister Clara descended upon the woman. She swung a heavy brass crucifix in one hand and coldcocked the woman from behind.

The assassin dropped her umbrella. A gust buffeted it and rolled it across the gardens. The woman crashed to her knees, then to her side.

Seichan dashed forward, snatching up her pistol from the ground with one hand. As she reached the assassin's side, she noted those dark eyes had rolled white. Blood seeped thickly into the gravel. Still, the woman's chest heaved up and down.

Alive.

But not for long.

Seichan aimed her pistol toward that pale forehead, but Sister Clara stepped between her and her target.

"No," Clara said.

Seichan stared daggers at the nun, but Clara refused to back down. Seichan read both the resolution and the compassion in the young woman's face. The nun might be incited to violence to protect the innocents inside, but she plainly drew the line at cold-blooded murder.

Seichan growled her frustration, but she also owed the nun for her help. Plus she recognized that they could possibly get information out of this assassin when she woke up. Given the opportunity, Gray would want to interrogate her.

Seichan glanced up toward the chapel. It was still shrouded in smoke. The gunfire had ceased a minute ago. But what did that mean?

Impatient and worried, Seichan picked up the assassin's weapon, still hot from the gunplay, and shoved it toward the nun. "Do you know how to use this?"

Clara backed a step. "Yes, but—"

"Either guard her or I shoot her."

Clara swallowed and took the weapon. Seichan waited until the nun had the pistol pointed at the limp figure of the assassin. Only then did she twist away and sprint up the steep stairs. With every step, the fears she had held in check burned brighter in her chest.

You better be okay, Gray.

1:18 P.M.

Roland climbed out of the secret tunnel and back into the chapel. He reached an arm down and helped Gray out, half pulling his dazed form free of the dark well. The man's clothes were shredded, his skin bled from a hundred cuts. A scalp wound ran with a heavy flow of crimson down one side of his face.

But you saved our lives.

Gray crawled to the altar and settled on his backside. He sucked on the water bottle Lena had handed him below. She stood guard by the door now.

"There's a nun coming," she said, sounding worried. "With a gun."

Roland felt his heart quicken.

Gray rolled to his knees and yanked out his pistol.

Lena turned to them, her voice brighter now with relief. "It's Seichan."

Gray fell back to his rear and mumbled, "Thank God."

A moment later, the woman's shadowy form wafted through the smoke and fell into the chapel like a dark falcon. She seemed to take everything in with a glance, her gaze settling on the blasted hole in the floor.

"Looks like you've been busy," she said.

"And apparently you have a new vocation," Gray rasped out, eyeing the shreds of a nun's habit. "Gotta say, the outfit sort of works for me."

Roland frowned at the improper exchange, but he also recognized it as a coping mechanism. He read the concern between them, the shine of love that ran deeper than mere professional partners.

"Enough sitting around," Seichan said. She crossed to Gray and brusquely offered a hand to help him up. "Time to get off this mountaintop before anyone else shows up."

He smiled through the blood and let her haul him to his feet. "Thanks, dear."

"Someone's got to keep pulling your ass out of the fire."

"You're a little late for that." Gray hobbled toward the door but glanced back to the secret stairs. His expression looked confused. "That first grenade, the one that fell through the trapdoor before it closed—what happened?"

Lena answered. "It dropped straight past us and rolled down those steep stairs."

"It exploded in the cavern below," Roland said. "My head's still ringing from that blast."

"But at least we still have our heads," Lena added.

"What about Kircher's Madonna and the skeleton?"

"We checked . . . before you came crashing back down to us." Roland shook his head. "The grenade must have exploded at the feet of the Madonna. We found the bronze statue toppled on its side, crushed and charred."

Lena sighed heavily. "The bones fared worse. Blasted to dust and burnt slivers. Still, we have what we collected earlier. Hopefully we can—"

A single gunshot cut her off, cracking loudly across the summit.

Roland swung toward the door, but Seichan burst past him, shoving Lena deeper inside the chapel.

Seichan pointed her pistol toward the stairs—then cursed brightly.

Roland shifted to a window, which offered a view down to the church courtyard. The dark form of a nun lay sprawled on the garden path. He caught a glimpse of a smaller shape vaulting over the fence and vanishing away.

"What's wrong?" Lena asked.

Without any explanation, Seichan simply lunged out of the chapel and fled down the Holy Ladder toward the church.

Gray limped forward and headed after her. "Stay here," he ordered them.

Left alone, Roland eyed Lena.

She bit her lip, then shook her head. "Screw that."

While those might not be the words he would've chosen, he agreed with her sentiment. He had his fill with hiding in the shadows, waiting helplessly. Resolved, he and Lena headed out of the smoky chapel and into the sunlight. They ran together down the stairs.

Still, Seichan reached the courtyard well ahead of any of them. She dropped to a knee beside the sprawled body. It was Sister Clara. Seichan kept her weapon raised in one hand while checking the nun with her other hand.

Roland and Lena reached the courtyard only steps behind Gray, who wobbled on his feet from the exertion.

"What happened?" Gray asked, hurrying forward.

Seichan turned to them. Her face was a storm of emotions, most of them dark and angry. "That bitch used my own dagger," she explained, clearly distraught. "Must've pulled it out of her leg and stabbed Sister Clara. I didn't think to take it before going to check on you."

Roland imagined Seichan's concern for her partner had contributed to that lapse. He kneeled next to Sister Clara. He was relieved to see the young nun was still alive, but she was gravely wounded, her face a mask of pain. Blood soaked through her habit, rising around the steel hilt of a blade sticking out of her stomach.

"Tried to shoot her . . ." Clara wheezed, clutching Roland's sleeve. "Too fast."

"It's okay," he consoled her.

Clara's eyes implored him. "Forgive me, Father."

"There is nothing to forgive, my child." Roland looked up at the others, unsure what to do.

Sirens sounded in the distance, rising up from the valley below. A pair of nuns pushed out of the rear door of the church. One carried a red plastic first-aid kit.

"We have to clear out of here," Seichan warned, standing up.

Lena looked reluctant. "But Sister Clara . . ."

Roland gripped the nun's fingers, also refusing to leave her side.

"I don't think anything vital was hit," Seichan said. "She should live until help arrives."

Her words were callous, but Roland also heard the pain and guilt in her voice.

Fingers tightened on his hand. Sister Clara stared up at him, then to the others.

"Go," she whispered weakly but with clear resolve. "Whatever those *potwory* were after, stop them."

"I promise," Roland said.

Lena also nodded.

With Clara's permission granted, Roland stood and stepped aside, leaving the young nun to the care of her fellow sisters. He faced Gray and Seichan. He was uncertain where all of this would lead, but he held firm to one clear conviction.

I will not break that promise.

15

"Now where are they taking us?" Kowalski grumbled under his breath.

Maria shook her head, as much in the dark as he was. She sat next to the big man in the back of an electric cart that whisked through the depths of the subterranean complex. She noted Kowalski picking at the bandage on his face, remembering his story of Baako attacking him. She also remembered his furtive signal that undercut this story.

[*I'm lying*]

Worry for Baako burned in her gut, along with guilt. She pictured her little boy alone in this strange foreign place. He must be terrified. She wished she could go to him, console him, but that was not where they were headed at the moment.

After revealing the fossilized bones of the newly discovered hominin species—*Homo meganthropus*—Major General Jiaying Lau had ordered them to be transported to a new destination. The general sat in front beside the driver, talking on her cell phone. From her clipped and angry tones, it sounded like she was browbeating the caller.

Finally the electric cart slowed before a tall set of double doors. A familiar figure in camouflage-colored fatigues waited for them, standing stiffly, his expression stoic. It was Gao's brother, Chang Sun.

Jiaying twisted in her seat to face them. "Remain here."

The general climbed out of the cart and drew Chang several steps away.

"Where does she think we can go?" Kowalski said, slumping deeper in his seat.

A second cart pulled up behind them, carrying Dr. Dayne Arnaud and a pair of armed soldiers. Arnaud was prodded out of his cart and marched over to them. The paleontologist eyed the tall set of double doors. A steel track system ran along the ceiling and passed through the top of those doors.

Arnaud sighed. "It appears we are getting closer to the reason you were brought here, Dr. Crandall."

Maria sensed the same. After seeing those remains, she knew the Chinese must be pursuing ways to harvest specific sequences of DNA from the giant's bones, all in order to engineer a stronger soldier.

But how far along had they gotten?

Arnaud crossed his arms, likely worried about the same. "As I understand it, your research—and your sister's—was all about proving that the Great Leap Forward in human intelligence was due to the introduction of new genes gained from the interbreeding of early man with Neanderthals."

"That's basically our hypothesis. That this hybridization produced a small tribe of individuals who were capable of greater intuitive leaps, who looked at the world differently than either of their parents."

"And it was from these few unique souls that the Great Leap Forward was driven."

She heard the incredulous tone in his voice and pushed back against it. "Multiple statistical models support such a theory. Knowledge is like a virus, capable of growing exponentially under the right circumstances. It would take the creativity and innovation of only a small population of super-enhanced individuals to alter the world: to spread new insights, to share new tools, to teach new methods of art and ritual. In fact, it's one of the dangers of exploring this path. If such super-enhanced individuals could be engineered today, the result would be world-altering."

"Or *-ending*," Arnaud added, staring toward Jiaying. "Especially in the wrong hands?"

Maria understood.

"How close were you and your sister to achieving this goal?" he asked.

She pictured Baako, a model of that same Neanderthal hybridization, and the astounding learning curve he had already demonstrated. While she and Lena had made significant steps in that direction, much still remained unknown.

She admitted that aloud. "Genes that affect intelligence are still poorly understood and likely involve a complicated interaction of multiple sequences. What we are exploring is a new frontier."

"But you and your sister are pioneers who have begun to blaze a trail into that territory." His gaze remained on the pair of Chinese officers. "Now you must be wary of who follows."

As Maria watched, the exchange between Jiaying and Chang grew more heated. She heard Lena's name several times amid the flurry of Mandarin. Clearly something had gone wrong. But what did this mean for the fate of her sister?

Kowalski mumbled under his breath, "Sounds like the shit hit the fan out in Italy." He crossed his arms with a slight satisfied sneer to his lips. "And I can guess who was throwing that shit around."

7:29 P.M.

"And you have no idea where they've gone?" Jiaying asked. She kept her arms crossed, waiting for Lieutenant Colonel Chang to explain his latest failure.

He kept his head bowed, his silence answering her question.

The recent intelligence out of Italy was bleak. Not only had Lena Crandall slipped through the snare set up by Chang's handpicked team, but SISMI—the Italian Intelligence and Military Security Service—had recovered the team's bodies.

"The Italians may have their suspicions of who sent those men," Chang said, "but we still have full deniability. The men I commissioned were ghosts, shadows with no official record with the People's Liberation Army. And no locals were killed, so the matter can easily be spun as a terrorist attack against a Christian target."

Though Chang's assessment would likely prove correct in the long run, it still did not diminish his larger failure. Maria's sister had once again escaped.

Knowing this, Chang attempted to dilute his culpability by spreading the blame wider. "If you had told me that you had an asset on site, perhaps the operation would've had a more positive outcome."

Jiaying set her lips into a hard smile. "*Duì,*" she agreed. "But at least First Lieutenant Wei *survived* that assault, and she is in active pursuit of the targets as we speak."

First Lieutenant Shu Wei was one of the youngest members of the Chengdu Military Region Special Forces, a unit code-named Falcon, which specialized in target acquisition, along with sabotage operations and offensive strikes. Shu Wei was also Jiaying's niece, daughter to her sister. Jiaying had used her contacts in military intelligence to covertly enlist Shu Wei for this mission, to infiltrate and intervene as necessary.

Jiaying continued, "First Lieutenant Wei has also learned *who* is accompanying Lena Crandall and that Croatian priest. They're Americans, likely a covert group tied to their military. From talking to a nun prior to your assault, Wei also learned what Lena's group was searching for."

"What was that?" Chang asked, his tone more subdued now.

"Information regarding a seventeenth-century priest named Athanasius Kircher."

Chang frowned, plainly confused—as was Jiaying, but she maintained a passive expression as she continued.

"Wei will be pursuing this course. To determine how this unusual angle of investigation might threaten our goals . . . and to eliminate Lena Crandall."

"But I thought we wanted to capture the geneticist alive."

"After so many failures on your part, I've come to the conclusion that such a plan is too risky. To safely acquire her requires a delicacy that we can no longer afford. So Shu Wei is gathering a strike team from her own unit to hunt down and eliminate this threat once and for all."

Chang straightened his back. "Then with my support, I'm sure—"

She turned on a heel, dismissing him. "That won't be necessary. Clearly you have more than enough to handle on site here."

She walked away, imagining his face going dark. She took a final moment to goad him further.

"With your attention fully focused here, I have confidence that you can at least keep our facility secure." She glanced back to him. "Of course, any further failure will require a harsher reprimand."

She nodded toward the double doors.

Though Chang's face remained angry, his eyes shone with a measure of fear as his gaze flicked in that direction.

Good.

She turned to Maria and the others.

Now to teach these newcomers the consequences of failure.

7:27 P.M.

Here comes trouble.

Kowalski watched the Chinese general stalk back over to their group. The woman looked much too pleased with herself for his liking.

"Come," she said as she rejoined them. "Let me show you what we've accomplished—and how you might help."

She waved for them to follow her while brusquely ordering their two armed escorts to fall in behind them.

"Guess this isn't an optional tour," Kowalski said to Maria as they set off after the general.

She didn't respond, but he read the nervousness in her pale face. She fingered the tattoo of the double helix under her ear, marking her profession and likely the source of her worry. The Chinese wanted her genetic expertise for something—but what?

Jiaying crossed to the tall set of steel doors, which glided open before her. A puff of air washed out, bringing with it the musk of animals, along with the scent of antiseptic and bleach.

Beyond the threshold, a white room full of stainless steel equipment stretched half the length of a football field. One side held a towering wall of cages; along the other wall stretched a row of ten steel tables. The place reminded him of an oversize morgue. Except the closest pair of tables had been equipped with elevated stirrups, like something one might see in a gynecology office.

One of these tables appeared to have been recently used. A white-smocked worker was using a small hose to wash blood and tissue down the inclined table, jetting the gore into a stainless steel bucket at one end. Even more disturbing, stacks of glass jars were lined on a counter behind the table. Organs floated inside, including what appeared to be an oversize heart.

Kowalski swallowed back his disgust and looked away.

As they entered, technicians scurried about performing other chores, most of which seemed to involve getting clear of Major General Lau's way.

Maria studied the stainless steel cages to the other side. Several held what Kowalski would expect to see in such a research lab: white rats twitching pink noses at them; a pen of rabbits; and a lone chimpanzee who huddled near the back of a larger cage. The latter's arms had been shaved to his pits, along with the crown of his head.

Before Kowalski could even wonder about the reason for such a hair-cut, the answer appeared in the next cage. A young chimp stared at them, its large brown eyes tracking them as they passed. Eyes were all the poor creature could move. A perforated steel shelf had been clamped around its neck, clearly meant to immobilize it and to keep it from reaching higher than its shoulders. The need for such a restraint was obvious. The top of the chimp's skull was missing, exposing the surface of its brain. A pincushion of colored electrodes protruded from that moist pink surface, wired to equipment hanging outside the cage. A small whimper continually flowed from its lips, which were stretched tautly over its teeth.

"Motherfu—" he started, then clamped his mouth shut as General Lau glanced back to them. Now was not the time to offend their host—at least not yet.

"It's a vivisection lab," Maria whispered, her eyes glassy with shock and maybe a few tears.

In the next cage, a small ape—maybe an infant gorilla—clung to a wooden pillar with a ratty rug tacked to it, as if the object were its mother.

The Frenchman slowed enough to look closer at the tiny figure, its frightened face tucked hard to its only solace in this place of horrors. Arnaud's brow furrowed as he cast Maria a worried look, but before he could speak General Lau hurried them deeper into the lab.

"This way," she insisted.

Her goal appeared to be a large window at the far end of the lab. It encompassed the entire back wall. A larger chamber, lit from above, opened beyond the thick glass.

They were marched forward.

"Thanks to the techniques you and your sister perfected, Dr. Crandall," General Lau said, "see what we've been able to accomplish already."

As they reached the window, Kowalski stepped closer, flanked by Maria and Dr. Arnaud. He stared down into the cavernous space and couldn't hold back an outburst this time.

"You motherfuckers . . ."

7:48 P.M.

Monk sat with Kimberly Moy on a bench in the parklands that bordered the Nanchang River. The dark waterway, lit by occasional streetlamps, cut directly through the center of the Beijing Zoo. Nearby, a ferry stop, closed at this hour, offered tours through the park and out to the Summer Palace. Monk had a nice view along the river's course, which was periodically forded by arched stone bridges.

"What do you think?" Monk asked softly.

Kimberly rubbed her calf. It had been a hard three hours of walking: first through the park, then afterward on a slow circuit around the outside. They had finally reached the northernmost edge of the park, having made almost a complete circle around the zoo grounds.

Without looking up, she said, "Definitely one of the Chinese army's newer helicopters. A Z-18A utility chopper, if I'm not mistaken, for transporting troops and cargo."

Definitely large enough to haul a crated gorilla.

Monk had noted the helicopter parked on a pad in this nondescript corner of the park, not far from the zoo's large aquarium building. From outside the fence, he had only caught glimpses of the aircraft's bulk. Trying not to arouse suspicion, they had continued to this riverside park and settled on the bench, where they still had a patchy view of the military chopper.

"Lots of activity going on over there," Monk commented.

Over the past ten minutes, they had watched uniformed men come and go, mostly loading crates into the back of the helicopter. They seemed to be readying to take off. Fearing the Chinese might be moving the kidnapped party again, Monk kept close watch for any sign of an armed escort leading a group toward the aircraft.

"Wish I could get closer," Monk mumbled. "To make sure they're not already aboard."

"And do what?" Kimberly asked. "That area is crawling with personnel. Until we get verification that the kidnapped party is still here, you'd only risk exposing yourself for no good reason."

She was right, but he hated sitting idly, waiting for some sign.

A loud trundling sound drew his attention to the neighboring road. A large armored personnel carrier, emblazoned with a prominent red star, sped past them and skidded to a stop before the northern gate into the park. Soldiers offloaded out the back, while another popped up through a roof hatch to man a heavy artillery gun. The troops spread out before the gate. Shortly thereafter, two pairs of soldiers began to march off in either direction, clearly beginning to canvass the zoo's perimeters.

Monk imagined the other gates of the park were being similarly bolstered and guarded.

He nudged Kimberly. "How's that for a sign that our friends are still holed up somewhere on those grounds?"

She nodded. "But it may also be a sign that Chinese intelligence knows that we're here. Or at least suspects something."

She took his hand. He knew what she was silently telling him.

Time to go.

Monk stood up with her and began retreating through the riverside parkway as a pair of the soldiers strode toward their position. He kept close to Kimberly, playing the casual tourist. Hand in hand, they ambled along the river, heading away from the zoo grounds. Monk kept the collar of his jacket up and his face turned away from the soldiers. At any moment, he expected to hear a shout, an order to stop, but instead a roaring grew behind him, accompanied by the familiar bell-beat of heavy rotors.

"Don't look," Kimberly said, squeezing his hand.

Monk felt no need to glance over his shoulder. He could readily picture the helicopter rising from its concrete pad and climbing into the night sky. He didn't know if Kowalski and Maria were aboard that aircraft, but he still felt a sinking sense of defeat in his gut.

With no other path open to them, Monk and Kimberly continued away from the zoo, driven off by the soldiers. Even if Kowalski and Maria were still on the premises, with the park being locked down now by the full force of the Chinese military, the prospect of rescuing them grew slimmer.

"What now?" Kimberly asked.

"We wait," he said, not liking his answer. "We have to hope Kat and Director Crowe can get some new blip from that GPS tracker. Otherwise, we're screwed."

Earlier, he had fielded a call from Painter, who had informed him that the extraction team for this operation had landed in Beijing, arriving on different flights from various routes. The five commandos were slowly gathering at a rendezvous point, in anticipation of the go-ahead from Monk about a rescue mission.

He scowled.

Looks like we'll all be waiting a bit longer.

Once far enough away, Monk looked back toward the zoo.

What the hell is going on over there?

7:50 P.M.

Maria struggled to understand what she was seeing.

It can't be . . .

She stood with Kowalski and Arnaud before a curved set of windows that overlooked a habitat the size of a basketball arena. The space appeared to be dug out of the native rock, with the walls pocked by dark caves. But her focus remained fixed to the bottom of the pit.

Three stories below her, massive hairy beasts shambled or squatted amid faux leafless trees made of concrete, several of which looked to have been broken into pieces by the habitat's occupants. Each figure appeared to tower eight to nine feet in height, likely massing out at half a ton each, easily twice the size of the typical mountain gorilla. Their legs looked as thick around as tree trunks, their arms only a little thinner. A few lumbered about by leaning on their knuckles, but the largest stood upright, exposing its full height and the silver hue to its coat. It stared up at them and bared its teeth in a silent roar, exposing yellowed fangs as long as an outstretched hand.

The silverback stood guard over a recent kill, clearly feeling threatened by the onlookers. The torn body at its feet still had bits of a shredded uniform, not unlike the coveralls of the workers she'd seen here.

Before she could look away, the upraised beast reached back, grabbed something, and flung it toward them. She fell back a step as it struck the window, both astounded at the display of strength and horrified at the sight of the severed arm slapping against the window and sliding down in a bloody smear across the glass.

The violent act broke through her shock.

"What . . . what is this?" she asked.

Major General Lau answered, "We call it the Ark, a crucible to observe our creations. It's not unlike your classroom back at the primate center."

Maria refused to accept such a comparison. She gave a small shake of her head, trying to clear her dismay. "They're gorillas . . ."

"Hybrids," Jiaying corrected needlessly.

Maria had already recognized that these were not ordinary apes. She remembered studying that massive skull of the prehistoric gorilla, *Gigantopithecus blacki*. These creatures were comparable in size and shape, but she knew what lurked below was not that monstrous species brought back to life.

Arnaud spoke up, allowing Maria a moment to get her bearings. "I can only imagine that to create these specimens, you must have spliced in DNA from that *Meganthropus* specimen you showed us earlier."

Jiaying bowed her head in agreement. "To accomplish that, we used various techniques, refining them over the years through trial and error. We eventually employed protocols developed by the Crandalls, which accelerated our program. But whereas Maria and her sister extracted Neanderthal DNA to create their hybrid, we sequenced the genes from the bones of *Meganthropus*." She waved to the window. "Still, like the Crandalls, we chose to use gorillas for our initial model. The results are as remarkable as we had hoped. Even the musculature of these specimens has proven to be extraordinarily powerful: easily *twice* that of a typical gorilla, and *ten* times that of an ordinary man."

Maria's breathing grew heavier with dismay and horror. The general's cold words echoed in her head: *We even employed protocols developed by the Crandalls.*

She stared down as the massive silverback bent over its kill and lifted what appeared to be a chunk of liver to its muzzle, gnashing into it.

What have Lena and I done?

"Of course before we move into human studies," Jiaying continued, "we must iron out several key issues."

Maria glanced to her. "What issues?"

"The beasts here have proven to be more savage than a typical gorilla, often killing each other unless we provide them with an ample food supply."

Maria recalled the story of the *Meganthropus* tribes, how they had preyed upon neighboring clans, along with their own people. It seemed the geneticists here hadn't just passed on that tribe's genetic brawn to these hybrids, but also its cannibalistic ferocity.

Maybe the two even run hand in hand.

Jiaying fixed those cold eyes upon Maria. "That is why we need your help. To find a way to balance what we've accomplished here with the heightened intelligence you've instilled into your research subject."

Maria pictured the gentle soul of Baako. She could not ever imagine finding a way to *balance* his sweetness with what crouched inside this bloody Ark.

She said as much aloud. "To accomplish what you're asking, it would take filtering through hundreds of different variables, not to mention an untold number of epigenetic factors that could further complicate matters. It could take decades of trial and error to achieve such a goal, if it could even be done at all."

"So we believed, too," Jiaying admitted. "It was why we continued to fund you and your sister's research through back channels."

Facilitated by Amy Wu, Maria thought bitterly.

Jiaying straightened her back. "Then we got word of Dr. Arnaud's discovery in the mountains of Croatia."

Arnaud looked equally offended that his research could be connected in any way to the horror show here. "What does my discovery have to do with all of this?"

"Because of the genetic possibility locked in those bones, the bones of a first-generation hybrid between early man and Neanderthals. If we could successfully harvest DNA from those remains, we would have a chance to search and isolate the specific genetic factors that heightened such a hybrid's intelligence."

Maria crossed her arms, realizing the woman was likely right. With access to such unique DNA, defining and extracting the specific code that lay at the core of mankind's evolutionary Great Leap Forward could be possible.

Or at least vastly accelerated.

Maria began to understand the scope of all of this. Whoever controlled this rare genetic repository would have a great advantage in the bioengineering arms race that was sweeping the globe. Those bones could prove to be the Holy Grail of the next stage of human evolution. And it wasn't just the Chinese. Even DARPA's Biological Technologies Office had set a goal to unlock the genetic code of human intelligence.

No wonder the Chinese had acted so quickly and so harshly. The endgame here was not about a single country's dominance; it was about controlling the very reins of mankind's future.

"And then there's Baako," Jiaying added, drawing back Maria's full attention.

Kowalski also reacted, his face hardening. "What about him?"

Jiaying returned her attention to the window. "Besides the aggression issue, we ran into another difficulty, a reproductive problem. While the female hybrids are fertile, all the males are sterile."

Maria knew this was not unusual. Hybrids between closely related species were often infertile, like the mating of a donkey and a horse, which produces a mule. Male mules are uniformly sterile, while the females are sometimes still fertile.

Arnaud brought up a detail even more relevant to the situation. "Most paleontologists believe the same might be true for Neanderthal hybrids. The males were probably sterile, whereas the females could still perhaps produce viable offspring."

"If this is correct," Maria added, "it would mean the Neanderthal genes we humans carry today had to come from those hybrid *females*, not the males."

"And that's why Baako is so important," Jiaying said. "I understand that your research subject has been tested and found to be capable of reproducing."

Maria held up her hand. "Not necessarily. So far, *genetically* it appears that is the case, but we can't know with absolute certainty, since Baako is only three years old. He's still sexually immature. It will take another three or four years before we can definitively judge his fertility."

"Perhaps," Jiaying countered, "but we're not looking for Baako to mate physically. We only need to sequence that reproductive viability locked in his Y chromosome. Of course, even more important are those unique Neanderthal genes that have been shown to enhance his intelligence."

Maria felt a sinking feeling in her gut.

Poor Baako . . .

"Then again," Jiaying continued, "we could have gained all of that from a few cheek swabs and blood samples. And that's exactly what we'll do, along with bone marrow biopsies. But his true value lies in our being able to access the unique architecture of his brain. It could prove invaluable to have a living subject to study and analyze in regard to the expression of those unique genes."

"You intend to study his brain?" She pictured the series of MRIs that had been performed on Baako since he was an infant. "To see how it develops further?"

"Correct. But you and your sister have been too conservative in your approach. We believe a more invasive study will bring us more comprehensive results." Jiaying glanced back to the chimpanzee whose exposed brain was wired with electrodes. "We've found we can keep such specimens alive for up to two years. And in a larger subject, we believe we can extend that time frame by at least twofold."

Maria realized they intended to perform the same surgery on Baako. "No," she blurted out. "I won't allow it."

"It will happen whether you *allow* it or not. The veterinary surgeons are preparing everything as we speak."

"When?" she asked weakly.

"He'll be taken to surgery in the morning, after he's had the night to rest from his travels."

Desperate, Maria sought any way to stop this from happening. "If . . . if you do that, I won't cooperate with any further work. You'll have to shoot me."

Jiaying flicked her gaze to Kowalski. "If it comes to that, you won't be the first I shoot. And I'll not be as merciful as I was with Professor Wrightson."

Maria glanced to Kowalski.

He shrugged. "Let them do their worst."

Despite his bravado, she saw the tip of his tongue lick his bottom lip, a nervous tic.

But Jiaying was not finished. She nodded to their armed escort and force-marched them back to the wall of cages. They stopped before the chimpanzee, which mewled in fear and distress. Jiaying reached to a piece of equipment hanging outside the cage and twisted a dial.

The chimpanzee jerked in its restraints, an ear-splitting screech bursting from its small chest. Its eyes were wide, protruding from its skull, likely blinded by pain.

"Stop it!" Maria yelled.

Jiaying simply stood there, oblivious to the suffering.

Another was not.

Kowalski suddenly lunged backward, faster than she could have imagined. He barreled into one of the guards and hooked an arm over the rifle barrel. Though the weapon still remained strapped to the guard's shoulder, Kowalski reached back enough to pull the trigger.

The rifle blasted loudly.

The round shot between the cage bars and exploded half of the chimp's skull. The screaming cut off and the body slumped, hanging limply by its neck.

Kowalski immediately lifted his arms high and stepped to the side. Both rifles pointed at him. Even Jiaying had her own pistol in hand. Maria waited for the man to be executed.

Instead, Jiaying holstered her weapon. "I see your zookeeper has as tender a heart as you." The general faced Maria. "But he will not be able to help you with Baako. If you wish the animal to be kept as comfortable as possible throughout all of this, I will expect not only cooperation from you—but also *results*."

She waved for the guards to escort the group from the lab.

"It's been a long night," Jiaying said. "You'll be taken to your room."

Maria resisted. "Wait! I want to see Baako. To spend this last night with him."

Jiaying stared hard at her.

"Please," she begged.

"If you do any harm to him," she warned, glancing back to the dead chimpanzee, "even an inappropriate act of mercy, another will take his place."

Jiaying turned her gaze upon Kowalski.

Maria hadn't even considered committing such an act, so she simply nodded.

"I want to go, too," Kowalski said, touching his bandaged face. "To help keep Baako calm, to protect Dr. Crandall if necessary."

Jiaying sighed, plainly done with arguing. "So be it. I'll have bedding brought to you. But know that you will be watched throughout the night."

Maria reached and touched her fingertips to Kowalski's hand, silently thanking him. As soon as they passed through the gliding doors of the vivisection lab, everything suddenly struck her at once, overwhelming her.

What are we going to do? How can I face Baako, knowing what is going to happen to him in the morning?

Her legs weakened; her knees began to shake.

Then a strong arm slid around her waist, keeping her upright.

"We'll get through this," Kowalski whispered.

"How?" She looked up at him.

He shrugged. "No idea."

"Then what—"

"Just thought that's what you needed to hear."

Oddly, she was strangely comforted by his honesty.

He half lifted her into the waiting electric cart. "Let's go check on that big kid."

8:44 P.M.

Baako spots his mother as soon as the double doors open. Joy bursts in his heart at the sight of her. He bounds to the bars and clings to them, hooting at her, letting her know how happy he is.

As she draws closer, she hugs her fists to her body in a sign he knows well.

[I love you]

He drops from the bars, bouncing on his back legs, and repeats her sign.

[Baako loves Mama]

She smiles but not as big as usual. He sees sadness in the corners of her eyes. He sniffs and catches a whiff of her fear. It makes him slap his upper arm with his other hand. He does this only when scared.

She sees this and taps her wrists together.

[You're safe]

She waits for one of the bad men to open the door. He hates the smell of these others. A long black stick pokes between the bars and spits fire at Baako. He fears it and drops back, but he growls deep in his chest and shows his teeth.

Finally the door swings wide and Mama enters. She comes with another, the big man who can talk with his hands. Yesterday Mama signed his name in letters [J-O-E]. *It was back at home, where Baako had his television, his bed, his toys, and his best friend, Tango.*

Baako is glad Tango is not in this bad place.

Mama comes and puts her arm around him. She squeezes and makes sounds that are warm and full of love. He hoots softly back to her. She leans back. He sees tears on her face. She wipes them with one hand, but more come. She turns away. He chuffs at her, reaching to her cheek with the back of his hand.

Mama likes when he does this.

But she does not smile now and does not kiss him on the nose. Instead, more tears roll from her eyes.

He lowers his arm, then the big man—Joe—squats before him, leaning on the knuckles of a hand like Baako. With his other hand, he signs and speaks the same.

[Are you okay?]

Baako shakes his head. He turns so Mama can't see and waves his fingers in front of his chest. [Scared]

Joe moves closer. His big hands shape words.

[We'll be brave together . . . you and me]

Joe points to Mama.

[For her . . . okay]

Baako nods and repeats the last gesture. [For Mama]

A large hand reaches to Baako's shoulders. Strong fingers squeeze hard—but Baako knows it is not meant to hurt him. Baako stares into the man's eyes, then presses his two fists together, stirring them between them.

[Together]

Joe grins and speaks words that Baako knows. "That's right."

By now, the bad men have left, but they had tossed in two curled-up rolls. They are red and smell like feathers. It reminds Baako of his pillows back home. Mama once scolded him for using his teeth to rip the pillows open to get at those feathers.

Mama and Joe untie the rolls, shaking them so they spread long.

Curious, Baako nudges between the two.

Mama signs to him, leaning her head on an open palm.

[They are beds]

Baako coughs, disbelieving her. Sometimes Mama teases him. Still, she shows him a zipper. He tries it himself, pulling it back and forth.

Joe says something that makes Mama laugh. It is good to hear. Joe then shows Baako how to unzip one of the beds. Once it's open, the man slides his body inside, limbs and all, and pretends to sleep.

Baako sniffs at the edges, while Joe and Mama talk too fast for him to understand, but he perks up whenever he hears his name. Mama eventually gets him to eat some more bananas; then she wiggles into her own bed.

Baako stares at the two of them, picking at a zipper.

Joe pulls a hand from under his bed and pats the space between him and Mama.

Baako understands and carefully steps there. He circles a few times, making Joe grunt when he accidentally steps on him. Then Baako settles down, curling between them.

Mama kisses him on the forehead like she always does at night. He wiggles closer to her, and she puts her arm around him. He sighs in contentment.

For the first time here, he feels safe.

Still, he snakes a hand toward Joe.

The man's eyes shine in the dark back at him. Then with a low grumble, a big hand slips out between the zippers and finds Baako's hand. Fingers wrap around his fingers. They squeeze once, then relax—but don't let go.

Joe shakes his head, burrowing deeper. Muffled words flow out. "Happy now?"

Baako stares at their joined fingers, reading the silent message there, as clear as any moving arms and hands. It is one word and a promise.

[Together]

He closes his eyes and answers Joe with his heart.

Yes.

16

"We believe the Chinese still have Kowalski and Maria Crandall stashed somewhere on the zoo property," Painter said over the secure line.

With the phone by his ear, Gray stood at a third-story window of the Pontifical Gregorian University. The vacant office belonged to one of Roland's old colleagues, another medieval historian who was on sabbatical at the moment. After escaping the mountains, Roland had suggested holing up here to regroup for the afternoon and assess what to do next. The priest also wanted to use the university's vast library to research something that he believed could be important to all of this.

Gray had used the time to report to Sigma headquarters. "What about that GPS tracker?" he asked. "Have you been able to pick up any more pings off of it?"

"No, but considering the heightened military presence around the zoo, the Chinese are likely aware that we know of their involvement. At least, that's Kat's assessment after hearing from Monk."

Gray was sure Kat was worried about her husband—and with good reason. Monk's face was not one that would exactly blend in with the populace of Beijing.

Concerned, Gray asked, "So what's Monk's next move?"

"I've ordered him and his partner to hang back, to avoid arousing further suspicion. Kat is doing what she can through back channels to learn more. But at the moment, we're in the dark about the particulars behind their attack on U.S. soil."

Not to mention the assaults out here.

Gray's face and limbs were covered with a patchwork of small bandages, and what wasn't covered felt bruised and battered. He tried to make sense of it all.

"The Chinese clearly wanted those bones discovered in the Croatian cavern," he said. "And somehow it's connected to the Crandalls' research into the genetic source of human intelligence."

"That's likely true. We know the Chinese were secretly funding the Crandalls' research, bankrolling it through an operative in the National Science Foundation, Dr. Amy Wu. But beyond that, we're operating in the dark. We need to know what was so important about those bones. It seems that discovery set all of this in motion."

"We're working on some leads out here," Gray said. He had already informed Painter about what they had found at the Sanctuary of Mentorella and its connection to Father Athanasius Kircher. "At the moment, the Chinese are pursuing this matter purely from a *scientific* perspective, but we may be able to learn more by following the *historical* bread crumbs left behind by Kircher."

"Why do you believe that?"

"Because Kircher was clearly onto something, something he deemed important enough to preserve, yet alarming enough to make sure it was kept well hidden. If we could learn what that was, we might get a jump on the Chinese—or if nothing else, we could gain a better understanding of their interest in those bones and the Crandalls' research."

"You might as well do what you can," Painter said, though his voice sounded doubtful. "Right now we're in a standoff, so I suppose any new intelligence could prove useful."

"I'll keep you updated."

Gray signed off, but he remained at the window, studying the streets below. It didn't appear they had been followed out of the mountains, but he knew one of the Chinese team—a woman—had survived, fleeing on foot. Kat had been monitoring local law enforcement chatter coming from the area. It seemed a farmer outside the village of Guadagnolo had reported the theft of a motorbike from his barn.

It couldn't be a coincidence.

He searched the roads below the window for that stolen motorbike, but every other vehicle was either a Vespa or some other cycle. As he stood at his post, he noted an upper-story window to his right. The facade of bricks around its frame were slightly blackened, and the panes of glass had been recently replaced. He could almost hear that old explosion from months ago. The window marked the former offices of Monsignor Vigor Verona, an archivist for the Vatican and a professor at this university.

A sense of foreboding settled over Gray's shoulders, remembering the loss of his dear friend—and, of course, Vigor's niece. A pang of guilt lanced through him.

Rachel . . .

A hand touched his shoulder, making him flinch. He had not even heard Seichan approach. He had thought she was in the next room, keeping watch on Lena as the woman napped on a couch.

Seichan wrapped an arm around his waist and turned him from the window. She stared deep into his eyes, easily reading him, knowing his regrets.

"My mother once told me the world is full of ghosts," she whispered. "And the longer you live, the more haunted you become."

"Mine just told me to sit up straight and keep my elbows off the table."

Seichan only sighed at his attempt to defuse the moment. She leaned up and pressed her lips to his mouth, silencing him. He felt the warmth of her, tasted her, inhaling the slight hint of jasmine off her skin. She withdrew enough to speak, her breathy words rising between them.

"The ghosts are there to remind us that we still live, that we still have hearts that beat, flesh that burns, lungs that gasp for air." She let her lips brush his again. "Never forget that . . . or those deaths have no meaning."

Gray pulled her closer, held her tighter, felt her heartbeat against his ribs as he kissed her deeply.

I won't forget.

A key rattled in the door lock behind them. Gray broke free of their embrace, his hand settling to his holstered pistol. Seichan took a step away, a steel dagger already glinting in her fingertips. The door swung open, revealing the disheveled form of Father Novak.

Struggling with an armload of books, Roland failed to note their wary stances. "I think I found something that might be important."

5:52 P.M.

The commotion woke Lena, startling her into an immediate panic. With her heart pounding, she shifted up on an elbow on the sofa. She recognized Roland's excited voice rising from the next room.

He must have learned something.

Earlier, she had wanted to go with him when he left—if nothing else, to see the famous Gregorian library for herself—but the stacks of rare books that he had intended to search were off-limits to the public.

She rubbed her eyes, surprised that she had actually fallen asleep, if only for a brief and fitful time. When she had first tried closing her eyes, she was certain her fear for her sister would keep her awake.

Must be more exhausted than I thought.

She glanced at the slit-like window of this small private space of Roland's colleague. It was little bigger than a closet, with a sofa and a small prayer bench under a cross. It felt less like an office space than a monastic space for contemplation.

Drawn by the excitement she heard in Roland's voice, she stood and crossed to the door. In the next room, a small desk stood under a larger window, which was flanked by tall bookcases full of dusty volumes. In the center of the room rested a wide library table, with a cluster of mismatched chairs around it. The lingering odor of old pipe smoke and tobacco was stronger in here, as if Roland's colleague had just stepped out.

"Come see this," Roland called to her, stacking books on the library table. "If I'm right, it's simply amazing."

Stoked by the fervor in his voice and manner, Lena's interest quickened.

Roland reached into his jacket and carefully removed the old journal of Father Kircher, the one found inside the bronze Madonna at the chapel. He reverently placed it on the table next to the other books. The gilt labyrinth shone in the sunlight streaming through the window.

Gray joined them at the table while Seichan remained near the window, her eyes on the streets below. The woman's guarded manner was a reminder of the threat that still hung over their heads. It dampened Lena's curiosity, but only slightly. She knew the best way she could help Maria was to piece together the mystery behind all of this.

She stared at Kircher's journal, suspecting the answers might be found within those old pages. While driving to Rome, she had managed to get a brief look inside. The pages were scrawled with a meticulous script, all in Latin, set amid pictures, maps, and pages full of numbers.

"So were you able to learn anything from Kircher's journal?" she asked.

Roland frowned. "Actually I've barely had a chance to give it more than a cursory review. It will take many hours, if not weeks, to fully understand the message locked within these pages. But I have made some headway."

"Then what were you looking for in the library?" Gray asked. "You never made that clear."

"I wanted to research that map inscribed on the inside shell of the bronze Madonna." Roland pulled out his iPad from his satchel and placed it on the table. "It looked familiar. I recognized it from an earlier work by Father Kircher."

Roland woke up the device and pulled up the photo that Lena had taken of the map.

It showed what appeared to be an island, with crudely delineated rivers and a couple of mountains.

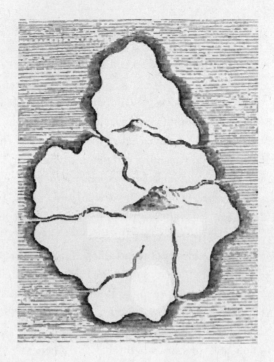

"What's that supposed to represent?" Gray asked.

Roland looked up, his face brimming with amazement. "You won't believe unless I take you through it. I hardly believe it myself."

Lena shifted closer. "Tell us."

Roland tapped the iPad screen. "I recognized this map as soon as I saw it. A fuller version can be found in Kircher's volume, *Mundus Subterraneus*."

Lena remembered Roland showing them pictures from the Jesuit priest's book, a volume full of illustrations both practical and fantastic.

"Let me find it." Roland sifted through the records he had stored on the device concerning Father Kircher, including a full collection of his books. "Here it is."

They all stared down at a map copied from one of the pages of *Mundus Subterraneus*.

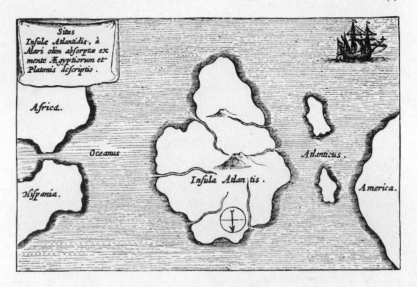

The island featured in the center was definitely the same one carved into the bronze shell. Only here there were more details, including names and a legend at the top, written in Latin.

Lena couldn't decipher much, except for the name written on the island in the center. "Is that what I think it is?"

Roland grinned and read the legend at the top. "*Situs Insulae Atlantidis, a Mari olim absorpte ex mente Egyptiorum et Platonis descriptio.* Or translated, 'Site of the island of Atlantis, in the sea, from Egyptian sources and Plato's description.'"

"This is meant to be Atlantis?" The incredulity in Gray's voice was easy to hear.

"That's right. According to what Kircher wrote in *Mundus Subterraneus*, this map was compiled from charts found on ancient papyruses he had discovered during his research concerning Egypt and from information gleaned from Plato's writings. By Plato's account, this island was home to a technologically superior race, a people who were also great teachers. Similarly, the Egyptian papyruses also spoke of the godlike residents of this island, who came bearing gifts of knowledge and wisdom, teaching the most ancient pharaohs."

Lena recognized how much this sounded like her and her sister's theory: that mankind's Great Leap Forward was propelled by a small group of unique individuals.

"You must understand," Roland continued, "the legend of these great and mysterious teachers is not limited to the Greeks and Egyptians. Ancient Sumerian texts also make mention of the existence of a race of tall beings whom they called Watchers. You'll find these same Watchers mentioned in Jewish texts, even the Bible. But the most pertinent account comes from the Book of Enoch. According to that ancient text, it was a Watcher named Uriel who taught Enoch about the movement of the stars. The same text names other Watchers, along with the sciences they taught."

He pulled one of the books from the pile, opened to a tagged page, and read aloud from it. "'Semjaza taught enchantments and the cutting of roots . . . Baraqijal astrology . . . Kokabel the constellations . . . Araqiel the signs of the earth . . . and Sariel the course of the moon.'"

Roland lowered the book. "So you see this same mythology persists throughout ancient cultures." He turned to Lena. "And in regards to your research into hybrid species of early man, the Dead Sea Scrolls references the interbreeding of these Watchers with other humans, mentioning children born of those unions."

Lena swallowed, taking it all in. In her mind's eye, she put flesh on the bones of Kircher's Eve, wondering if these ancient hybrids between Neanderthal and early man might be the source of such legends.

Intrigued, she asked, "So did Father Kircher come to believe Eve was one of these Atlanteans, these ancient Watchers? Is that why he inscribed that map inside the bronze shell that housed her bones?"

"Possibly. Think about it. After the Madonna was sealed closed, Eve's empty eye sockets would have forever looked upon that island, a place Kircher might have believed was Eve's former homeland."

"But that's a pretty large leap for Kircher to make," Gray commented. "To tie these bones to the mythology of Atlantis."

Lena disagreed and pointed to the sculpture of the moon resting on the library table next to Roland's satchel. "Kircher stole that from the prehistoric sculpture garden we found in those caves. Like us, he surely recognized that whatever people lived in those caves were much further advanced than anyone could expect or imagine. Remember how Kircher mistook the bones of a mammoth to be the remains of some extinct species of giant? It would not be hard for him to make a similar fantastical conclusion in regards to these bones."

"Only in this case," Roland said, his eyes gleaming, "the reverend father may have been correct."

Lena turned to him, unable to hold back her own disbelief this time. "What are you talking about? How can that be?"

Roland looked down at the map glowing on the screen, then back at all of them. "Because I know the location of Atlantis."

6:07 P.M.

Roland took a small amount of guilty pleasure at their shocked expressions. "Like I said, let me walk you through it all. Then you'll better understand the message left by Father Kircher."

He tapped and zoomed in on the island of Atlantis found in *Mundus Subterraneus.*

"If you look at the compass rose on the reverend father's map, you'll see the arrow is pointing *downward*, indicating this chart was drawn with north pointing *down* and south *up*."

"The reverse of most maps," Lena commented.

"That's right, and it wasn't unusual for that time period to have maps occasionally drawn in this manner." He danced his fingertips across the screen of his iPad and brought up a picture he had rendered while down in the university library. "I took the liberty of flipping the map around and labeling the surrounding continents in English."

He showed the others the result.

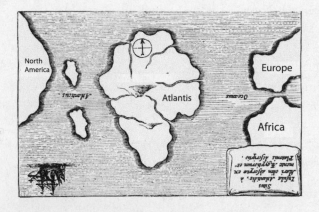

Gray studied it for a breath. "If I'm looking at this right, it appears the island of Atlantis is drawn somewhere in the middle of the Atlantic . . . or at least somewhere between North America and Europe."

"Which supports what Plato wrote in his dialogue *Timaeus*." Roland grabbed a copy of the Greek book from his pile and read from a marked passage. "As Plato describes it, Atlantis lies beyond 'the straits which are by you called the Pillars of Hercules' . . . which in modern times are the Straits of Gibraltar."

"Placing Atlantis outside the Mediterranean," Gray commented.

"Correct." He pointed down at the book in his hand. "But Plato also states here that this island is 'larger than Libya and Asia put together.'"

Gray frowned. "That would make Atlantis less of an island and more like a continent."

"And what *continent* lies outside the Straits of Gibraltar and close to North America?"

Gray rubbed his chin. "The only other continent out there is South America."

"Exactly."

Gray lifted his brows skeptically. "So you're claiming the *island* of Atlantis is actually the *continent* of South America?" He pointed to Kircher's map on the screen. "While I can appreciate that the coastline of this island does resemble South America, it's drawn in the middle of the Atlantic."

Roland understood his hesitation, having gone through the same intellectual cartwheels himself. "You have to keep in mind," he warned, "that what's illustrated here was derived from older maps. So perhaps those ancient cartographers got the continent aligned wrong, or maybe they put it there as a place of prominence, to better highlight the features of that landmass."

Roland reached to his iPad and brought up another pair of images he had created. "If you look at these side-by-side silhouettes that I compiled, you can see the resemblance is more than just the coastlines. Even the river deltas and mountains seem to match up between the two."

"He's right," Lena said, leaning closer, comparing the two maps. "The Amazon . . . the Orinoco . . . and the other major rivers. They do line up."

Gray waved dismissively. "Still, it makes no sense. If South America was once Atlantis—home to some great empire of godlike teachers—how come there's no evidence of their prior existence?"

"Who says there's not?" Roland pulled a recent archaeology magazine from his stack of books and slapped it on the table. "In early 2015, a team of Honduran archaeologists, aided by British SAS soldiers, discovered the ruins of a lost city buried in the rain forest. They believe they had found Ciudad Blanca, the legendary White City of Gold, a complex built by a mysterious pre-Columbian civilization that vanished long ago. The only firsthand account of this city came from a conquistador, Hernán Cortés, in letters to the Spanish king back in 1526. He told the story of a miraculous place whose inhabitants were said to be descended from a Monkey God, and whose children still bore monkey-like features."

"Monkey-like features." Lena straightened, a thoughtful expression fixed on her face. "If some conquistadors did encounter an existing tribe of hominins—or even hybrids like Eve—I could see them mistaking them for some relation to primitive primates."

"And that's only one story," Roland said. "Satellite mapping and ground-penetrating radar is slowly stripping away what's hidden under the jungles of that continent, revealing layer upon layer of ancient civilizations, some ruins predating the Aztecs, Incas, and Mayas by millennia."

Gray continued to look unconvinced. "You actually believe one of these lost civilizations was the home of the Watchers?"

"Possibly. If this civilization was advanced enough in navigation and sailing, they could've periodically sent out emissaries, offering new tools, teaching new techniques. Maybe some settled in foreign lands, had children, and became assimilated into the many ancient cultures." Roland tapped the map on the screen. "Or maybe here was where they eventually retreated and hid."

Lena slowly nodded her head. Still, she had one more concern. "But didn't Plato describe Atlantis being destroyed, sunk under the sea? As far as I can tell, South America is still there."

Roland waved a hand across the books before him. "You must take into account that these Greek and Egyptian stories were written by people who could not truly fathom something as large as a continent in the oceans beyond the straits of Gibraltar. Also, upon closer reading, the cataclysm described by Plato actually sounds more like the sinking of an island *city*, or possibly an isolated piece of a larger landmass that was destroyed by earthquakes and flooding."

"Still," Gray pressed, "even if Father Kircher believed those bones he interred under that chapel belonged to Eve and had a connection to these ancient Watchers, where do all these conjectures about South America get us?"

Roland smiled. "They get us to that city, to that lost home of the Watchers, to the very heart of the mystery that Kircher spent the last eleven years of his life investigating—all of which may help explain *why* the Chinese stole those bones and kidnapped Lena's sister."

6:12 P.M.

Gray sighed, hearing in Roland's last words an echo of his earlier conversation with Painter Crowe: how following the *historical* path left by Athanasius Kircher might lead to the very answers they needed to get an upper hand on the Chinese.

With a measure of impatience, he motioned for Roland to continue, sensing the priest had more to reveal. "Go on," he ordered. "If Kircher spent the last eleven years of his life secretly studying this mystery, what else did he discover?"

"It wasn't so much what *he* discovered as what his dear friend Bishop Nicolas Steno discovered."

Gray remembered that name from Sister Clara's account of the building of the Sanctuary of Mentorella—how Bishop Steno was the only colleague whom Kircher would allow to visit the construction of the chapel that hid Eve's bones. The younger man was also a budding paleontologist, with an avid interest in fossils and old bones.

Roland picked up Kircher's book from the table. "According to this journal, Kircher sent the young Nicolas out into the world to follow up on leads. The reverend father needed a younger man's eyes and strength to extend the investigation abroad. To Crete, to Egypt, to Africa, and eventually as far as the New World."

"What was he sent to look for?" Lena asked.

"For the truth behind those bones." Roland lifted the journal higher. "Though I've not had a chance to fully review everything packed in here, I did read through correspondence, copied by Kircher into these pages, all written by Nicolas Steno, including several maps of his travels. One of those maps caught my eye, one that may tell us where to go from here."

Gray stepped closer. "What did you find?"

"To understand that, you have to see this first." Roland used his iPad to pull up a new image. "Here is another map, one that Father Kircher drew in *Mundus Subterraneus*. This one clearly depicts the continent of South America in more detail."

Gray studied it, confused. "Didn't Kircher publish this book well before he ever found Eve's bones?"

"He did," Roland admitted. "He actually constructed this map in attempt to describe the unique hydrology of that continent, to show how the rivers flowed out of the Andes and down to the sea. But note the large crater-like feature drawn in the center of the Andes."

"What about it?" Gray asked.

"Father Kircher hypothesized that the Andes hid a great reservoir, a massive underground sea that supplied this continent with its water."

"Okay," Lena said tentatively. "But what does that have to—"

"Then look at this." Roland cut her off and opened Kircher's journal. "I found this illustration among the correspondence from Nicolas. It's a copy of a section of the same map, but overdrawn with something that I think bears on all of this."

Roland placed the journal on the table so all could see.

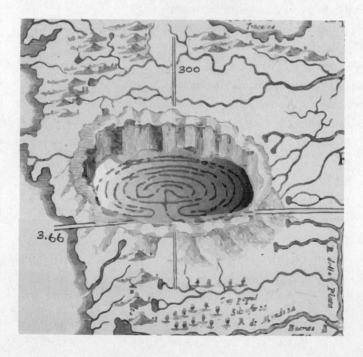

It did indeed appear to be a closer view of that same subterranean lake; only this time a new illustration lay atop the water, almost shimmering there.

Lena gasped softly. "That overlaid image—it's the same one from the journal's cover."

Roland nodded. "The famous Minotaur's labyrinth from Crete."

Gray recalled Roland's history of this maze, how that same pattern had been found carved into rocks discovered not only in Crete, but also in Italy, Spain, Ireland, and as far north as Finland. The pattern was even described in an Indian Sanskrit epic.

Roland faced them all. "I believe Nicolas Steno—following the clues found in Croatia and driven by the insights of Father Kircher—discovered the ancient home of these lost Watchers, marking it here with this labyrinth."

Gray stared at the vast lake depicted on the drawing. "You mentioned before that the sinking of Atlantis might actually be the story of a drowned *city*." He pointed to the open journal. "Are you saying that might be the place?"

"Possibly. At least Kircher believed so, but of course he might have conflated the reports from Nicolas Steno with Plato's ancient tale. But either way, Nicolas discovered something in those South American mountains, something that ties all of this together."

"If only we knew where that place was," Lena said, her voice tinged with awe. "Can you imagine if we could go there?"

Roland glanced to her. "We can."

"How?" Gray asked.

He tapped the illustration of the crater with a fingertip. "Because I know exactly where that is."

Gray studied the map and understood. "The lines that crisscross over that site. They're numbered."

"Marking longitude and latitude. During Father Kircher's time, latitude lines were calculated similarly to how we do today, but longitude used the Ferro Meridian instead of the Prime Meridian."

"And you were able to convert them?" Gray asked, noting the twinkle of excitement shining brighter in the priest's eyes.

"Not only that, I plotted the location." Roland returned to his iPad and pulled up a map with an arrow pointing to the coordinates.

"It's in Ecuador," Gray said.

Roland nodded. "Deep in the Andes Mountains. About fifty miles due south of Cuenca."

Lena shared Gray's skepticism. "But how can we really know if any of this is significant? I mean, that looks like it's in the middle of nowhere."

Roland's eyes shone brightly. "Because we're not the first ones to follow Kircher's bread crumbs to that area of the country."

"What do you mean?" Gray asked, unable to hide his surprise.

"From my own doctoral work, I know that there was another Catholic cleric—a monk named Father Carlos Crespi—who became enamored with Athanasius Kircher back in the early 1900s. The man even *emulated* the reverend father by pursuing the sciences as devotedly as he did his religion. Father Crespi was an avid botanist, anthropologist, historian, and musician. He eventually started a mission in Cuenca, where he served for fifty years until his death."

"Cuenca?" Lena said, staring down at the map of Ecuador. "It's right near that spot."

"Exactly. It always struck me as strange that such an accomplished and knowledgeable man as Father Crespi should choose such a remote village in the Andes to spend the rest of his life. That is, until now."

"You think he went out there because of Kircher?"

"In the rare stacks of this library, there are still scores of the reverend father's collected works, most dating back to when the Museum Kircherianum closed its doors here at the university. It included a vast collection of his correspondence: notes, letters, replies, even early drafts of his work, some of which were never published. Most of it was forgotten for centuries and never cataloged. Until the project was undertaken by one man."

"Let me guess," Gray said. "Father Carlos Crespi."

"He helped organize a majority of it, along with restoring and preserving most of those old letters. Including many from Nicolas Steno."

"So you're thinking that Crespi gleaned something from those letters that led him to Ecuador."

"I can't imagine he grasped the true breadth of all of this. But he must have believed there was something important worth investigating."

"So he set up that mission in Cuenca?" Lena asked. "As a cover?"

Roland winced slightly. "No. I believe he saw an opportunity to pursue this line of interest while also following a true calling to help the natives of that region. In the end, he was deeply loved by those he served."

"And what of his quest concerning Kircher?" Gray asked. "Did it ever lead anywhere?"

Roland smiled enigmatically. "It led to a mystery that has baffled archaeologists for decades, one that would eventually end with a British expedition into the Ecuadorian Andes, involving over a hundred soldiers and scientists, all led by a famous American hero."

An American hero?

"Who *are* you talking about?" Gray asked.

Roland hefted the sphere of rock from the tabletop, balancing the sculpture in his palm, showing its perfect rendering of the lunar landscape across half its surface.

"The expedition was led by Neil Armstrong," he answered with a broad smile. "The first man to walk on the moon."

Before Gray could respond to this news, a sharp, angry shout rose behind him.

"That bitch!"

Gray turned to see Seichan spinning from the window and waving them all away.

"Run!" she shouted, her eyes panicked.

6:22 P.M.

Seichan vaulted over the corner of the desk.

A breath ago, she had spotted a clutch of nuns in dark habits exiting through the main entrance of the Vatican's university building. She had barely given them a second glance until one broke away, stepping with a slight limp toward a parked motorcycle. The oddity was enough to draw her attention. At the curb, the nun suddenly turned, parted her robe, and pulled free a compact assault rifle.

As the woman spun and pointed the barrel toward the window, Seichan caught a glimpse of the face hidden under the habit's wimple. It was the Chinese assassin. Apparently the woman had shed her disguise as a tour guide and had assumed the role of a nun, stealing a page out of Seichan's earlier playbook.

As Seichan skidded over the desktop, the windowpane shattered behind her. A dark object shot high overhead and ricocheted off a rafter.

Grenade.

Ahead of her, Gray was already in motion. He grabbed Lena around the waist with one arm and snatched Kircher's book from the table. He barreled into Roland and drove the priest toward the office door.

Seichan would not make it.

Once past the desk, she hit the floor, skidded low on her back, and slid under the library table. She spun and kicked the table's edge, sending it toppling over on its side, a shield between her and the grenade as it struck the floor to the far side of the desk.

The explosion rocked the room, the concussion pounding her head and popping her ears. The force of the blast shoved her and the table toward the door, amid a rain of wooden splinters and a cloud of choking smoke.

Gray had made it out to the hall, sheltering beyond the threshold. He grabbed her ankle and dragged her free of the office.

She rolled into a low crouch, scanning both directions for any other threat. She spotted no one. This section of the university building was secured with a passcode-locked system—but after such a commotion, Seichan knew any safeguards could be easily circumvented during the chaos to come.

Which was likely the intent.

Someone wanted them smoked out into the open.

Gray came to the same conclusion. "We need a way out of here!" he shouted above the ringing in her ears. "But not any of the usual exits."

"The basement!" Roland pointed down the hall. "There's a service tunnel, part of an old Roman aqueduct. It leads to an exit several streets over."

"Show us," Gray said, setting them in motion.

Seichan followed, but something nagged at her. She glanced back at the dark cloud rolling out the office door. She remembered the flying debris of the blasted desk, but the explosion had been mostly smoke and noise.

No shrapnel.

Gray noted her starting to lag. "What's wrong?"

She turned back around, unsure, and waved him forward, certain of only one thing. "Let's get the hell out of here."

7:31 P.M.

First Lieutenant Shu Wei sat on the idling motorcycle at the rendezvous point near Piazza Navona. With the sun sitting low on the horizon, shadows filled the square ahead. Tourists and locals idled and chattered, drifting toward open-air restaurants for dinner.

No one paid her any attention.

Over the past hour, she had shed her disguise and disposed of her rifle, all the while maintaining contact with the three men assigned to her in Rome. She now listened to the phone at her ear as a secure connection was made to Beijing.

A stern voice answered. "Report."

She recognized the brusque tone of Major General Lau and stiffened her back as if her aunt stood before her. "The targets are on the run. Unfortunately the men posted at the exits report no sign of them leaving the building."

"That is indeed unfortunate."

Shu bristled at the anger she heard in the other's voice. After events up in the mountains, she had barely had any time to set up a proper ambush. Still, it was only through her resourcefulness and quick thinking that they had gained even this advantage.

Before escaping the mountain and stealing the motorbike, she had planted a tracker in the wheel well of the lone car still in the lot. It had allowed her to shadow her targets and close in on them once they reached the congestion of Rome. She had caught up in time to see the foursome entering the university building.

Afterward, it had been easy to incapacitate a nun in an empty hall, hide her body in a closet, and don the stolen habit. It took little effort from there to inquire about the arrival of such a battered and unusual group, to discern where they had gone. Then she had caught sight of the Croatian

priest heading down to the library. Taking advantage of the opportunity
to eliminate one target immediately, she had followed him, but before she
could slip a dagger between his ribs, the priest had entered a section of the
library where she couldn't follow.

Still, she had gleaned enough from his inquiries at the front desk
to tell he was investigating something quite diligently. She remembered
that the nun who had attacked her back in the courtyard of the Sanctuary of Mentorella had told her this group had been inquiring about
a seventeenth-century priest.

Apparently that investigation was ongoing.

While Shu had waited for the priest to return from the stacks, she had
called Major General Lau and reported on what was happening. As ever,
her aunt was not one to dismiss the variables in any equation. Lau had
ordered her to discover what the others were searching for here, clearly
fearful of being blindsided by whatever information this group sought to
uncover.

So Shu bided her time in the main library. After nearly an hour, the
Croatian priest finally reappeared and headed up to the secure section of
the university that housed the professors' private offices. Shu had wanted
to eavesdrop on the group, but entry to that area required an access code.
And without a laser microphone, she had no way of listening at the window from the streets below.

Major General Lau had suggested Shu flush the targets out into the
open, to set them running, to follow them wherever that path might lead.
The smoke grenade had accomplished the first half, but her targets proved
to be resourceful, vanishing unseen into the shadows before she could
reach the office.

"If you've lost them," Lau warned over the phone now, "there will be
repercussions, even for a niece I hold so dear."

"It is no matter," Shu said.

"Why is that?"

Shu looked down at her other hand, at the object she had recovered
from the office during the bedlam that followed the explosion of her

smoke bomb. She flicked the switch, and the iPad glowed to life. The device belonged to the priest, left behind in the group's haste to escape.

Shu stared down at the last image viewed by the others, still frozen on the screen, and smiled as she answered her aunt.

"Because I know where they're headed."

THIRD

THE LOST CITY

17

Whatever you do, don't move.

Kowalski lay perfectly still in his bedroll. He had awakened a few moments ago to find his arm pinned under the bulk of the gorilla. Baako snored gently, curled into a ball with his head nestled in the crook of Kowalski's arm. Maria slept on Baako's other side, spooning the little guy from within her sleeping bag. One of her arms was draped over the gorilla's shoulders with her fingertips resting on Kowalski's cheek.

He feared waking them, knowing the horrible day that awaited them both. Though he didn't know the time, he suspected it was early morning. According to Major General Lau's timetable, someone would soon be collecting Baako for his operation. Kowalski pictured the tortured chimpanzee, trussed up with its brain exposed and wired to monitoring devices.

Fuckin' bastards . . .

He stared at the small face on his arm, noting the tiny twitches of Baako's eyes as he dreamed. Past the gorilla's shoulders, Maria breathed evenly and deeply, her lips slightly parted. Slumber relaxed her features, making her appear even younger. He found himself fixated on the length of her eyelashes.

His heart ached to keep them safe, but all he could do for now was let them sleep, to have this final moment of peace together . . . if only for a little longer.

He extended his gaze beyond the cage to the row of cameras posi-

tioned along the ceiling. He followed them back to the large steel doors at
the other end of the cellblock. A crimson sign glowed from the shadows
back there. He squinted at those letters.

方舟

Though he didn't read Chinese, he was certain they were the same
characters he'd seen back at the vivisection lab, hanging above the curve of
windows that overlooked the habitat of the gorilla hybrids. Yesterday, as he
had eyed those lumbering beasts, he had spotted a steel door at the ground
level of their pen, sealed off by a cage of thick bars.

That's gotta be the same door.

He studied the pens that made up this cellblock. He now understood
the heavy gouges in the concrete, the thick manacles hanging from the
walls.

They must do tests on those creatures here.

He remembered the tallest of the bunch, the gorilla with a broad back
of silver fur, how easily it had tossed that bloody arm up at them, fury
glowing in those eyes and reverberating from its howl. The beasts might
be naturally savage, genetically prone to hostility and aggression, but
Kowalski was certain of one other detail about them.

They're damned pissed at their makers.

And probably for a good reason.

As if sensing his thoughts, an exceptionally loud roar burst from back
there, ululating up into a piercing scream.

Maria's body jerked at the noise, her eyelids popping open, her face
wrenching with fear as her brain fought to catch up. Baako responded in
kind, balling tighter for a clenched moment, then exploding to his feet in
a low, wary crouch. He chuffed his anxiety, his gaze sweeping everywhere
at once.

"It's all right," Kowalski told them both.

Yeah, it was a lie, but what the hell else was he going to say?

Maria took several shaky breaths, then sat up and placed a hand on Baako's hip. "Calm down," she cooed to him. "I'm here."

Baako hooted once, then lowered to his haunches. With his large brown eyes fixed on the steel door, he hugged one arm nervously around his hairy knees and reached back for Maria.

She took his hand and pulled him closer.

Kowalski used this moment to wiggle out of his bedroll and slowly climbed to his feet, stretching kinks out of every muscle in his body.

"What time is it?" Maria asked.

He shrugged. "Morning, that's all I know."

She licked her lips and looked to the other side of the cellblock, to the double set of doors that opened out into the rest of the subterranean facility. Though she didn't say a word, he read the worry shining from her face. She pulled Baako more firmly to her side, as if by sheer will alone she could keep him from harm.

Baako shivered under her arm, clearly sensing her tension and fear.

She turned to Kowalski. "What are we going to do?"

"You're going to cooperate," Kowalski answered her bluntly, seeing no reason to sugarcoat the situation. "Any other course will only get you killed, and Baako will still end up under the knife. At least with you alive, you can be there for him—even if worse comes to worst."

His words did nothing to dim that shine of dismay in her eyes. And he didn't expect they would. He spoke more for the benefit of those who might be watching and eavesdropping on their cell.

Let them think we're going to play ball.

He shifted his back to the cameras and lifted one hand. He wanted to offer Maria a measure of hope, though it was admittedly a thin one. He formed three letters with his fingers.

[GPS]

A deep crinkle formed between her brows as she tried to understand. He knew she must have wondered what had happened to Baako's wristband with the GPS unit embedded in it. He had kept quiet about its fate until now, fearing any hint might expose his actions yesterday.

He glanced over to the cold pile of dung in the corner of the cell. He was glad the maid service in this place was so lax, not that the Chinese would have discovered anything in that pile except for some ground-up bits of rubber.

Yesterday, while he and Baako had eaten—or mostly pretended to—Kowalski had had the gorilla bite apart the band, enough so that Kowalski could peel out the GPS unit. The electronic device was barely the size of penny. Once it was removed, Kowalski had Baako hide the excess bits of chewed-up rubber in his dung. Afterward, Kowalski had secretly planted the device in a place where it had the best chance of being ferried up to the surface, where hopefully the unit's signal would be detected again.

He touched the bandage still taped to his face. He pictured Baako's faux attack, remembering his own fumbling flight from the cage, how he had bobbled into the guard who had opened the door to let him out. With the guard focused on the angry gorilla, it had been easy to slip the GPS unit into the pocket of the man's uniform. With luck, the guard would exit this place when he got off duty, returning aboveground. If anyone was still monitoring that tracker, it would lead them to that man—and hopefully to this place.

Kowalski kept his hand shielded by his body and formed three more letters with his fingers, naming that guard.

[*GAO*]

8:23 A.M.

Kat spoke rapidly, her voice rushed with excitement and urgency. "We just picked up a ping off the tracking band."

"Where?" Monk asked.

"I'm sending you the location and real-time plotting of its path right now."

As Monk waited, he looked out the window of the hotel, which was located less than half a mile east of the Beijing Zoo. He had requested a room on the highest floor, which afforded him a view all the way to the spire of the aquarium and the zoo's northern gate. Over the past night, he and Kimberly had taken shifts to monitor the military presence over there, watching with binoculars for any significant change in troop movements.

Overhearing the phone conversation now, Kimberly pulled on her jacket. A moment ago, she had been speaking to her husband back in Virginia, her voice turning warmer, a soft smile playing about her lips. Monk could tell when the woman's three-year-old daughter was put on the phone. Kimberly's words became even sweeter, higher-pitched. Monk had two daughters of his own and easily recognized that mix of worry and love.

"You should have the information now," Kat said.

Kimberly joined him, looking over his shoulder at the phone's screen. A small glowing blue dot marked the first reappearance of the tracker's signal, and a dotted line continued in a path across a map of Beijing.

"That's odd," Kimberly murmured.

Monk glanced to her.

"That first ping is about a mile southeast of the zoo." She swung around and opened her laptop. Her fingers danced across the keypad, bringing up satellite maps and various data windows. Finally she made a small, disgruntled sound.

"What is it?" Monk asked.

"That location is a former restaurant. It was shuttered back in 2012 and never reopened." She closed her laptop and pointed to the door. "Let's grab our gear and go."

He understood her haste as another blue dash slowly extended the trail across the city map. They had to reach that path before the signal vanished again.

Monk grabbed his pack and joined Kimberly at the door. They hurried to the elevator and dropped down to the lobby. Once in a taxi, Kimberly offered her assessment.

"For the signal to have reappeared so far away from the zoo, I wager that restaurant must be the site of one of the entrances that leads down to the Dìxià Chéng, the Underground City."

Monk remembered her telling him about the old warren of cold-war-era bomb shelters that extended for almost a hundred square miles beneath Beijing, connecting most of the major city sites.

"So you're thinking they've moved Kowalski and Maria through those tunnels?"

"It only makes sense. In the past, the Chinese army often used those tunnels to hide their troop movements. Back in 1989, the army transferred soldiers through those same passageways during the Tiananmen Square crackdown, to hide their maneuvers from the rest of the world."

"And I imagine those same passageways could be used to transport construction equipment just as readily, allowing the Chinese to construct new underground facilities without the world growing any wiser."

"It wouldn't be hard to pull off. Some of those tunnels are said to be as wide as four-lane highways, large enough to accommodate tank battalions."

As the taxi turned a corner, Monk monitored their progress. "We're just a quarter mile away."

Kimberly leaned forward and spoke rapidly to the taxi driver in Mandarin, pointing where they wanted to go. She then settled back to her seat.

"Looks like we're headed toward a residential district," she said. "One of the old *hutong* neighborhoods."

"*Hutong?*"

"They're neighborhoods made up of narrow streets and alleys, formed by a maze of interconnecting *siheyuan*, the traditional Chinese courtyard homes. I've ordered our driver to get us as close as possible. Then we'll have to continue on foot."

Monk frowned. "Why would they be moving Kowalski and Maria through such a residential area, especially if Baako was still with them?"

"I don't know. But it's a concern." She turned and eyed Monk up and down. "As is your appearance in such a neighborhood."

He nodded. *I won't exactly blend in there.*

"Hang on." Kimberly shifted around and began pulling items from her backpack. She passed him a ball cap with Chinese characters embroidered on it, a pair of dark sunglasses, and a blue paper surgical mask. "Put these on."

Monk fingered the mask. He had seen many locals wearing them as protection against the ubiquitous air pollution in Beijing. The cap, sunglasses, and mask would do a fair job of hiding his features, especially if he kept his head down.

As he tugged the ball cap over his bald scalp, Kimberly barked again to the driver and pointed to the next intersection.

Looks like this is where we get off.

Kimberly offered Monk one last bit of advice. "Let me do all the talking from here. These neighborhoods are notoriously insular and wary of strangers, especially foreigners."

The taxi stopped at the curb. Kimberly paid the driver in cash, and they both climbed out. Monk took in his surroundings. Across the street spread a typical commercial area of Beijing, with tall hotels surrounding a large pedestrian shopping center.

Kimberly led Monk in the opposite direction, into an alley lined by brick walls. It was so narrow the two of them could barely walk shoulder to shoulder. Within steps, it felt like he had left the modern world behind and entered a sliver of Beijing's past. The outermost layer seemed to be made up of tiny shops, selling tobacco goods, antiques, or brightly colored candy. The next layer felt more personal, as communal teahouses took over the storefronts and the scent of burning incense rose from a small neighborhood temple.

"A little farther," Kimberly whispered under her breath after glancing surreptitiously at his phone's map.

As they moved into the heart of the *hutong*, Monk caught occasional glimpses into the residences' courtyards, spotting small gardens, overloaded clotheslines, and a number of pigeon coops.

Shadowing his phone with a palm, Monk noted that the signal had rounded a corner ahead and was now coming *toward* their position. He showed the screen to Kimberly.

She searched around and tugged him into a small art shop. It was barely large enough for the two of them. They had to squeeze between racks of calligraphy brushes, stacks of paper, inkwells, and stamping stones. The proprietor—a small wizened woman who could be anywhere from sixty to a hundred years old—smiled, showing only gums.

Kimberly spoke softly to the old woman, her tone deeply respectful. With his back slightly turned from them, Monk concentrated on his phone, watching both the screen and the open doorway.

Finally, the moving blue dot reached their position—and passed. At the same time, a tall figure wearing a PLA uniform strode across the storefront and continued down the alleyway.

Monk waited several breaths, watching for any other soldiers or some sign of an armed escort covertly leading Kowalski and Maria through this neighborhood. The only others who appeared were a chattering line of small kindergarten-aged children, likely heading to school.

Monk glanced back to Kimberly and motioned for her to follow him. He exited the shop, hearing Kimberly offer parting words to the proprietor in apologetic tones. Back in the narrow street, Monk nodded toward the soldier as the man turned the next corner.

"Signal's coming from that guy," Monk whispered as they trailed behind the children.

Kimberly searched behind her, then back to the next corner. "What do you think?"

He knew her concern.

This could be a trap.

Someone could have found that tracking device and was using the soldier as a decoy to lure anyone who might be monitoring its signal.

Like us.

Monk weighed the risks as he followed their target. The smart move would be to pull back and reassess the situation, but after nearly a day of wringing his hands and waiting, impatience trumped caution. He knew that the best chance of rescuing the others was during the first twenty-four hours. The dead student found in the meadow of the Yerkes Primate Center was testament to the ruthlessness of those running this operation.

For all I know, that soldier could be the one who shot the young man.

"Well?" Kimberly asked.

Monk increased his pace, knowing there was only one way of truly getting any answers.

"Let's take him down."

9:02 A.M.

Maria tensed as the double doors at the end of the hall banged open. She gained her feet, stepping between Baako and the cage door. A forklift appeared, carrying the same crate used to transport Baako yesterday.

"Looks like our time's run out," Kowalski mumbled, his face dark with anger.

A four-man team of soldiers accompanied the forklift. They all carried rifles, but one held an electric cattle prod.

Baako pushed against Maria's side, cowering at her thigh, clearly remembering that crate and the pain of those fiery shocks. He reached an arm to Kowalski, silently asking for protection.

Kowalski took Baako's hand and faced the group that came forward.

As the forklift drew abreast of their pen, another soldier hopped out of the cab. He called an order to the driver, who lowered the crate toward the ground. Maria recognized Chang Sun, dressed in a crisp uniform, his black hair slick and wet as if freshly showered. She was surprised to see the man instead of his younger brother, Gao. From the man's scowl and stiff back, he was clearly irritated at being assigned the menial task of fetching Baako.

He waved a guard to unlock the cage and barked to the one holding the cattle prod. Both soldiers snapped to obey. The cage door was quickly opened, while rifles bristled toward them and sparks spat from the end of the electric prod.

By now Baako was quaking all over. Kowalski winced, glancing down to his hand, which was being crushed within Baako's frightened grip. Still, the man didn't let go. Instead, he stepped forward and confronted Chang.

"You're not putting him in that crate again," Kowalski said. "He stays with us."

Chang's scowl deepened.

Maria stepped forward and supported Kowalski's position. "If Baako's undergoing surgery this morning, getting him too stressed could have adverse consequences. I'm sure Major General Lau wouldn't—"

Chang cut her off, yanking out a large pistol holstered at his waist. Maria immediately realized her mistake. She shouldn't have mentioned Lau, remembering the friction she'd witnessed between the two officers. She also recognized the weapon in Chang's grip. It was a tranquilizer gun.

Kowalski lifted his free hand, ready to press their case. But before he could speak, Chang aimed his pistol—and fired.

The feathered dart shot between her and Kowalski and struck Baako in the shoulder. He yelped and swatted at it, knocking the needle free. But it had already delivered its dose. Hooting in fear, Baako let go of Kowalski's hand and retreated toward the back of the pen.

Maria went after him.

Kowalski followed at her heels, swearing sharply.

She dropped to her knees as Baako huddled in the corner. He balled up tightly, his dark eyes wide and shiny with panic. She scooped him to her chest, cradling him.

Kowalski joined her. "It's okay, little guy."

Baako turned to the man. With shaking limbs, Baako lifted his fists, tapping the knuckles and swirling them slightly.

[*Together*]

"I'm not leaving you," Kowalski promised. "We're a team."

"That's right," Maria said, not sure how much Baako understood, but infusing as much reassurance into her voice as possible.

Baako's gaze swung between the two of them, his eyes already glazing over as the sedative began to take effect. From the rapid response, she imagined the dart had contained M99, a potent tranquilizer commonly used on zoo animals.

As Baako began to slump, he unfolded his fists and formed an OK sign with his fingers before he then swept his hands out into a new sign. His gaze wavered between her and Kowalski. Even weakly delivered, she recognized that faltering sign.

She caught Kowalski's eye, seeing that he also understood.

Baako was correcting the man's earlier words. Instead of *We're a team,* Baako signed *We're a family.*

"You got that right, little guy," Kowalski said firmly.

As if knowing his message was understood, Baako's head fell back, and his limbs dropped heavily to the cold concrete.

Footsteps approached behind them.

Maria glanced over her shoulder to find Chang standing there.

"He's calm now," he said with a slight sneer of disdain. "No stress."

Kowalski lunged to his feet, about to tackle the officer. But Chang held his ground and swung the dart gun toward the big man's chest. Maria grabbed Kowalski's forearm, urging him to restrain himself. M99 was highly lethal to humans; even a couple drops could kill almost instantly.

Kowalski continued to glare, but he settled more heavily to his heels.

Chang's gaze turned to Maria. "You will come with us." The dart gun poked toward Kowalski. "He will stay here."

"No way," Kowalski warned darkly.

Maria took his wrist, knowing this was not a battle they could win. "It's okay. I can look after Baako."

Kowalski breathed hard through his nose, looking ready to argue, but even he must have realized the futility of it. With a huff, he mumbled, "Fine."

With the matter settled, three of the soldiers pushed into the pen and manhandled Baako's bulk over to the forklift. Maria followed, cradling Baako's head, making sure he wasn't banged up by the rough treatment. Though she knew he was in store for much worse this morning.

She pictured the brutalized chimp from yesterday. As much as that treatment had horrified her, she could not escape her own shame. Was her treatment of Baako any kinder? She had kept him caged, letting him out for the occasional romp in the woods and testing him at every turn.

She remembered his last sign.

[*We are family*]

Tears rose as guilt squeezed her heart. As he was rolled limply into the crate, Maria rested a palm atop his head, knowing how special he was.

You should be free.

A soldier forced her away from the crate, and the barred door was slammed shut with a rattle of steel. Chang marched her toward the exit as the forklift followed them.

She glanced back to Kowalski, who stood alone in the pen. His gaze was hard upon her, silently urging her to stay calm. As added measure, he lifted his hands and repeated Baako's sign.

[*Family*]

She nodded to him, taking his message to heart. They were all in this together. Still, a fear followed her through those double doors, a premonition of doom. The feeling persisted as they headed toward the vivisection lab.

How can any of us survive this?

9:07 A.M.

From a block away, Monk watched their target cross the street. It looked like he was headed toward a five-story apartment complex on the edge of the *hutong* neighborhood.

Home sweet home.

Kimberly realized this, too, and they both increased their pace to close the distance. They didn't want to lose the man within that sprawling complex. The signal of the GPS unit was only so precise. If they lost sight of their target, it could be difficult to discern his exact apartment.

They followed the soldier across the street, dodging the bustling flow of morning traffic. Ahead, the man stopped at the small courtyard entrance to the complex.

Monk hadn't anticipated that. With no other choice, they continued on their path toward him. They couldn't risk raising suspicions by suddenly stopping or turning around.

Kimberly pointed toward a bus stop bench in front of the complex.

Monk kept his head lowered and adjusted the surgical mask higher up his nose. They crossed within steps of their target and settled to the bench. Kimberly kept at Monk's shoulder, taking his hand as if they were a couple heading to work.

In the reflection off a window of a parked car, Monk watched the man strike a match and light a cigarette. The soldier had purchased the fresh pack from one of the *hutong* shops. His attitude to the proprietor had been brusque, bordering on rude. The soldier was clearly agitated. He took several long drags on the cigarette, then pulled out a cell phone.

Kimberly's fingers squeezed tighter on Monk's hand. The soldier spoke loud enough to be easily overheard, his tone full of anger and frustration. Clearly something or someone had royally pissed the man off.

Monk pictured Kowalski. He knew from experience how exasperating the big guy could be at times—but also surprisingly clever, too. It must have been Kowalski who had planted that tracker on the soldier, using the man as a courier for the GPS unit to bring it aboveground.

Now to turn that to our advantage.

Kimberly leaned closer, resting her cheek on Monk's shoulder as if she was exhausted. She whispered in his ear. "He's talking to his brother. From the sounds of it, the guy here must've been kicked out of his workplace pending a military review. Said he was interrogated for hours by someone from the Ministry of State Security."

She paused, listening further. In the reflection, Monk saw the man drop his cigarette and grind it under his heel. With a final angry burst, the man cut off the call and headed into the complex.

Monk waited until the soldier was out of direct sight before rising with Kimberly.

She kept close to his side. "Sounds like someone has it in for this guy. Maybe his brother, too. Someone named Lau. A woman who outranks them both."

Monk took in this information, wondering if that friction could be used to their benefit.

"If I had time to check my intelligence sources," Kimberly continued,

"I could probably figure out who that woman was. Might give us a clue as to what's going on here."

"First things first," Monk whispered.

They rounded the corner into the central courtyard. It was open to the sky above, with tiers of railed walkways lining the inside of the space.

Their target crossed to a set of stairs and headed up.

Monk kept to the corner. He dropped to a knee to retie a shoelace while watching the soldier. The man reached the second floor gallery and set off down the row of apartments, finally stopping at the seventh door. Standing there, he reached into a pocket and pulled out a set of keys. As he did so, something silvery flew out, glinting brightly in morning sunlight. It dropped to the man's feet, drawing his eyes and raising a deep frown on his face.

Monk pulled back out of sight. He stared up at Kimberly, reading the same realization in her face.

It had to be the GPS unit.

We've been made.

9:10 A.M.

Maria watched helplessly as soldiers hauled Baako out of the crate and dropped him onto a wheeled gurney. They then rolled his limp form toward the towering doors of the vivisection lab. She kept alongside him, making sure he was still breathing. Fear drove her heart into her throat, along with a grim realization.

Maybe it would be better if he died on the operating table.

Such an end would be far kinder than the miserable existence that awaited him after the surgery. Tears again threatened, but she fought them back, refusing to give in to defeat.

Past the doors, the vivisection lab was far busier than before. Most of the activity surrounded one of the stainless steel tables. A team in blue scrubs prepped a pile of surgical packs. One tool, sterilized and sealed inside a crinkled plastic bag, caught her eye.

A battery-powered bone saw.

Her knees weakened at the sight.

Two of the operating team came forward to relieve the soldiers of their burden. They rolled Baako to the station and slid the gurney next to the operating table.

Maria hurried to stay with him, fearing that they would drive her off. Instead, one of the nurses came forward and handed her a cap and surgical mask. The offer indicated she would be permitted to observe Baako's procedure—his *mutilation*, she reminded herself. The nurse must have recognized her distress and gently touched her elbow in sympathy before returning to her duties.

Maria stood there with cap and mask in hand, suddenly wanting to flee, to turn her back on what was about to happen. But instead she lifted the elastic blue cap and snugged it over her head, tucking in loose strands of hair.

I won't abandon you, Baako.

She stepped forward as he was dragged from the gurney to the table. His wrists and ankles were secured in padded restraints, an act that she found odd. She shifted forward until she could grip his hand. She felt the thick leather pads of his fingers, ran her thumb over the line of fur at the edge of his palm. It was baby soft, a reminder that he was really just a child. She remembered holding this hand in the past, gently bending those fingers, teaching Baako his first words.

One of those was *Mama.*

Tears rolled down her cheek now. She couldn't stop them. She couldn't even wipe them away, refusing to let go of Baako's hand with both of her own.

Oh, my sweet boy, what have I done?

A commotion drew her attention back to the tall doors of the lab. The familiar figure of Jiaying Lau appeared. Dayne Arnaud accompanied her. The French paleontologist looked haggard with bags under his eyes. He nodded his head at something Jiaying was saying.

Maria kept hold of Baako as she faced Jiaying.

The major general looked well rested, a small smile of satisfaction fixed on her face. As she arrived, she spoke to a tall man in surgical scrubs, likely the head surgeon. They exchanged a few words, then Jiaying nodded and dismissed the man back to his preparations.

She continued over to Maria. "It appears we're right on schedule this morning. I appreciate your cooperation."

Cooperation?

Maria wanted to tackle the woman, gouge her eyes out. Instead, she glanced over to Arnaud, whose face mirrored her own dread.

Jiaying surely sensed her mood, but chose to ignore it. "At the moment, it's your *further* cooperation that I'd like to discuss."

"I'm not leaving Baako," she said firmly.

"And I wouldn't expect otherwise, Dr. Crandall. In fact, the surgical team believes you can be of great help this morning."

She frowned. "Help? How?"

"They'll be performing a modified version of the Montreal procedure, where the craniotomy and electrode placement will be done with the patient awake."

"Awake?" She could not keep the horror from her voice.

Jiaying lifted a palm, trying to reassure her. "It is safe and relatively painless." She pointed to the lead surgeon. "Dr. Han will use a drug to reverse the tranquilizer, then switch over to a propofol intravenous drip. After applying a local anesthetic scalp block, they'll be able to perform the craniotomy under a light sedation. Once the brain is exposed, they'll fully wake the patient. And that's when your expertise will be needed."

"For what?"

"To talk to your research subject."

Despite the brutality of it all, Maria understood what was being asked of her. "You want me to challenge Baako with questions as you stimulate various parts of his brain with electricity."

She nodded. "From those responses, the research team will build a highly accurate map of the brain's architecture. It will help them plant those electrode needles in the most critical sections for future neurological testing."

Maria swallowed. As appalling at it sounded, it made cold clinical sense. She tried to imagine Baako awake, with his head clamped to this table, his skull cut open. No wonder they had put him in ankle and wrist restraints. He would be terrified, looking to her for solace and comfort.

How can I face those eyes, so full of trust and love?

She wanted to refuse, but she also knew she had to be here for Baako. Still, a moan escaped her. "Please, don't do this."

"I do not discount your concern, Dr. Crandall, but science must be dispassionate. We each have a role to play here." Jiaying motioned to the French paleontologist. "This morning, Dr. Arnaud will be doing a thorough analysis of those hybrid Neanderthal remains found in Croatia. Once we're finished here, I'll need you to join him, to help harvest as much viable DNA from those bones as possible."

By now Maria had begun to tune Jiaying out. She couldn't think beyond what was about to happen to Baako. Nothing else mattered.

Fingers suddenly gripped her arm, snapping her attention back to Jiaying, who continued speaking. "—to ensure your cooperation."

"What?" she asked with a confused shake of her head.

Jiaying drew her by the arm toward the back of the vivisection lab. "I was explaining that there would be a price to be paid for failure. But perhaps *showing* you will have more of an impact."

Maria was taken to the windows that overlooked the grim habitat known as the Ark. Once again, she found herself staring into the boulder-strewn pit. She searched below but failed to spot any of the hybrid creatures. Likely they were slumbering in those dark caves that lined the walls. Still, she noted the pile of broken bones on the floor, all gnawed clean. She remembered the severed arm being flung against the window. A smear of dry blood still stained the glass.

Then movement drew her attention to the side, toward a cage in front of the massive steel door below. That vault eased open, and a tall figure was shoved into the waiting cage. He fell to his knees as the door resealed behind him. His face turned up toward the windows.

Kowalski . . .

"We'll have little need for your gorilla's caretaker after this morning's

operation," Jiaying explained. "Except as an incentive to your cooperation."

Maria understood, her gaze returning to the pile of bones.

I help them . . . or Kowalski dies.

A small sound drew her attention back to the lab. She turned to find
Baako stirring on the table. A bleary, frightened hoot escaped his throat as
he tugged at one of his wrist restraints. They must have already given him
the reversal drug to the tranquilizer, partially waking him.

Jiaying looked in the same direction. "Time to get to work, Dr. Crandall."

9:19 A.M.

Now or never . . .

From the apartment courtyard below, Monk watched the soldier bend
down and reach for the GPS unit. They were running out of time to act.
Monk knew they only had a narrow window before their target figured
out what had been planted in his pocket.

Monk started to lunge toward the stairs, but Kimberly grabbed him
by the arm.

"Let me," she whispered. She drew him back and stepped forward.
"Follow my lead."

As Monk trailed her, she set off at a brisk but unhurried pace toward
the staircase. Once there, she climbed the stairs, all while chattering angrily back at him in Mandarin, plainly chastising him. While this was
clearly an act—playing the angry wife to a recalcitrant husband—her eyes
cast daggers at him, urging him to keep his head down, his manner calm
and subdued.

Monk tipped the brim of his cap lower. Over the years, he had learned
a life lesson from Kat. *A wife is always right.* And in this case, even an *in-
vented* one.

They reached the gallery that ran along this level of the complex.
Apartment doors stretched ahead. Still scolding Monk, Kimberly contin-

ued toward the soldier, who was on one knee, examining the GPS unit in his fingers.

With his head down, Monk glanced around, noting several other residents leaning on railings or smoking and gabbing with neighbors. In the courtyard below, a handful of children laughed and played at a small swing set.

Monk recognized how foolhardy his first impulse had been. If he had charged headlong toward his target, all hell might have broken loose. Or at the very least, their cover would have been completely blown.

Though at the moment, *both* outcomes were still a distinct possibility.

Ahead, the soldier took out his cell phone, preparing to report on his discovery.

Not good.

Kimberly reached his side first, barking at him to get out of her way. Apparently she was as skilled at delivering a tongue-lashing as she was with her espionage talents.

The soldier rose quickly and mumbled apologetically. He turned to his apartment door and jangled his keys into the lock. As he pushed the door open, Kimberly shouldered into him from behind and knocked him sprawling across the threshold. She followed him inside.

Monk dashed to keep at her heels.

"Close the door," she ordered as she stepped forward and kicked the steel-shod toe of her boot into the soldier's forehead. His head snapped back, and he went limp—out cold for the moment. "Get his weapon. Haul him inside."

Kimberly stepped past his prostrate form and withdrew a Glock from a holster under her jacket. She quickly swept the one-bedroom apartment, while Monk stripped the soldier of his sidearm. He then grabbed the man by his shoulders and dragged him into the living room. The motion drew a moan from their captive.

"Patient's waking up," Monk whispered.

Kimberly tossed him a roll of duct tape. Monk wasn't sure if she had found it or if she simply had it on her. The woman was spookily prepared.

Monk taped the man's mouth, then wound several loops around his wrists and ankles. As Monk trussed up their captive, Kimberly searched the soldier's body, removing items from various pockets of his uniform: a folded map, a chain of electronic keycards, a wallet.

She checked the latter. "Say hello to Gao Sun. From his papers and rank insignia, he's a first lieutenant in the Chinese army."

By now, the man had grown clearheaded enough to glower at them. Monk kept a knee on his throat, putting firm pressure there.

"What now?" he asked. "While this isn't my first rodeo, you obviously know this country far better than I do."

She studied their prisoner. "He's not likely to give up anything vital. From what I read about the events in Croatia, the Chinese assault team members committed suicide before allowing themselves to be captured or interrogated."

"So what do we do with him?"

She lifted her Glock while taking a pillow off the sofa. "We can't risk him getting free or someone finding him."

Monk wondered if she was truly hard-hearted enough to kill the man in cold blood. "Wait," he warned.

He stood and crossed back toward the door. He retrieved the cell phone the man had dropped. He tried to access it but found it locked.

Kimberly noted his frustration and held out her hand. "Let me see it." He passed her the phone.

She examined it. "It's fingerprint protected." She turned to their captive, and with Monk's help, got his thumb on the sensor. The screen bloomed to life. She swept through a few screens, then nodded. "I can change the password manually from here, so we can access it whenever we want without needing his fingerprint."

"Perfect."

She passed him back the phone. "What do you want to do with it?"

"To buy a bit of insurance." Monk stepped back, accessed the phone's camera feature, and snapped a shot of the duct-taped form of Gao Sun.

"What are you doing?"

"You mentioned this guy's last call had been to his brother. From the content of that conversation, I wager his brother must also work at that place under the zoo. Having possession of Gao might come in handy."

"You may be right." She crossed to a table holding a set of framed photos and picked one up. "I saw this earlier."

Monk stared at the photograph of two men, arms around each other's shoulders, smiling broadly, both in uniforms. One was Gao. "That other must be his brother," he said.

With a nod, she pulled free the photo, folded it into a pocket, and tossed the empty frame on the sofa. "How do we proceed from here?"

Monk pulled out his satellite phone. "Time to rally the troops that Painter sent. I'll assign someone to babysit our friend here while we go check out that entrance into the Underground City."

"It's sure to be a maze down there."

"But we know where to head—*toward* the zoo."

"Let's hope that's enough."

Monk agreed, appreciating the enormity of the search ahead of them. As he dialed the phone, he hoped they weren't too late already.

Hang in there, Kowalski . . .

9:28 A.M.

With his back to the steel door, Kowalski tried to ignore the stench of the habitat around him. It smelled of meat gone bad, mixed with an unwashed muskiness. The cloying reek was reminiscent of his days mucking barns at the Riverdale Stables in the Bronx for extra cash, specifically when an old mare had died in her stall during a summer heat wave.

Still, it's not the stink that'll kill me.

He placed a hand on the archway of rock that separated the steel door behind him from the wall of bars in front. Heavy tracks outlined a door of his cage. He pictured that tracked section trundling upward, exposing him to what lurked inside the Ark.

Earlier, he had spotted Maria at the curve of windows high above, standing alongside the uniformed figure of Major General Lau. He was certain the Chinese were using him as leverage against Maria.

He stepped to the bars—each as thick around as his wrist—knowing his fate if Maria didn't cooperate.

This assessment was reinforced as shadows stirred from a cave ten yards away. A large shape shambled into view, knuckling on both arms. The gorilla's fur was as black as soot, thick and heavy over its shoulders, sleeker over its hindquarters. The beast had to weigh over seven hundred pounds, most of it muscle. Its forehead came to a peaked top above prominent brows. It sniffed a couple of times at the air, then lowered that dark gaze toward him.

Kowalski noted a shiny metal band around its neck, weighted down by a steel box at the hollow of its throat. He guessed it was a shock collar for controlling these beasts.

He retreated a step, keeping away from the bars.

The small movement produced a dramatic reaction. The gorilla charged toward him. Kowalski cringed, fearing that massive creature could barrel straight through the bars. But at the last moment, the beast skidded on its hind legs, turning slightly to come to a rest on its rear.

It leaned that flat face against the bars, huffing strongly enough for Kowalski to feel the draft on his cheeks. It then howled, its maw stretching wide enough to bite a basketball in half, baring foot-long yellow fangs. The bellow shook his rib cage, pounded his skull.

Kowalski clamped his hands over his ears.

And here I was starting to like apes.

Then suddenly that massive shape fell away from the cage—or rather, it was *knocked* away. Another took its place.

Kowalski recognized the silvery sheen to the fur of this newcomer's back. It was the beast he had noted yesterday, the one ripping into the remains of some lab worker. This fellow was easily half again as big as the other, weighing over a thousand pounds. The first gorilla rose from where he had been bowled aside and reared up on its hind legs, thumping its chest with the palm of one hand.

The older silverback grunted once in that one's direction. The result was immediate. The black-furred gorilla dropped to all fours, twisted around, and retreated.

Apparently the boss of this joint had made his point.

The silverback turned back to Kowalski and settled to its haunches, staring straight at him. There was no outburst, no howl, no threat—just that steady unblinking gaze. It was far more unnerving, especially with the glint of malicious cunning in those eyes.

Kowalski kept his back against the steel door, taking the measure of the other. The silverback sat there, nearly unmoving. Only its thick chest rose and fell in an easy rhythm, the very picture of patience. He couldn't imagine the Chinese wanting to engineer smarter versions of these half-ton monsters. Especially as this beast's plan was easy enough to read and practically flawless.

It needed only to wait for the dinner bell to ring.

18

The pilot of the Gulfstream G650 radioed back to the cabin. "Folks, just a heads-up. We'll be landing in Cuenca in thirty minutes."

Gray glanced out the window to the low-hanging moon in the night sky. He checked his watch. Though the flight time had been nine hours, with the time change, they would be landing only an hour later from when they had left Rome.

He glanced back to the spacious cabin appointed in leathers and exotic woods. The cabin could accommodate a dozen people, but at the moment, it was only the four of them. At the back, Roland was once again buried in a pile of books, though most of his time was spent with his nose stuck in Kircher's journal. Lena assisted him with his research, the two often murmuring with their heads bent together. Seichan had spent most of the flight dozing on a reclined seat across the aisle from him. She rolled to her side with a grumble of irritation at the pilot's interruption.

Gray appreciated her exhaustion. He had also taken a four-hour nap, knowing they would have to hit the ground running once they reached the remote town of Cuenca, located high up in the Andes. He had been in contact with Painter a few minutes ago, learning that the fate of Kowalski and Lena's sister remained unknown, but Monk was following up on a possible lead. That left Gray to pursue the historical trail left behind by Father Kircher, to search for a lost city in the jungle.

From Kircher's journal and annotations on his map, his colleague Nicolas Steno had ventured out to South America and returned with the rough coordinates of the city's possible location. Despite Kircher's belief, Gray still doubted that this city of ancient teachers—those *Watchers* mentioned in ancient texts—was truly the mythic site of Atlantis. So he had used the remainder of the flight to pursue his own research into the history of this region.

Motion drew his attention to the back of the cabin. Lena came forward with a book in hand. "Roland wanted me to show you this before we landed," she said as she joined him.

She settled into the seat opposite him and placed the book on a small table bolted between them. She opened to a page displaying a rock with a labyrinth carved into it. It was the same maze gilded on the cover of Kircher's journal, a pattern found throughout the world at various ancient sites.

"This is a piece of polished diorite," Lena said, "discovered in the jungles near Cuenca where we're headed."

Gray leaned closer. *So the labyrinth was found even here.*

"A native tribesman gave this carved stone as a gift to Father Crespi."

He looked up. "The missionary? The one who came out here because of his own interest in Athanasius Kircher?"

She nodded. "His mission was located at the Church of María Auxiliadora, or Mary Our Helper. Another church dedicated to the Virgin Mary, like the Marian sanctuary where Kircher hid Eve's bones." She let that sink in before continuing. "Over the course of his fifty years here, until his death at the age of almost ninety, he accumulated a vast collection, artifacts given to him by the Shuar natives of the region. He stored the collection at the church, some seventy thousand items in all."

"Where did such a haul come from?"

"According to the tribesmen, they were taken from an extensive cavern system buried under the jungle. Roland believes these artifacts came to Father Crespi's doorstep not by mere chance, but because the priest had made inquiries of the natives about such a place in the jungle."

"But he didn't have the coordinates we have now."

"He didn't. Likely Father Crespi had gleaned enough from his research about Kircher to bring him to this general region."

"But not to the doorstep of this lost city." Gray nodded to the book. "What else was given to him?"

Lena flipped through the book, showing him other artifacts: seven-foot-tall mummy cases that looked vaguely Egyptian, full suits of Incan parade armor, shelves of Ecuadorian pottery, rolls of silver and gold sheets adorned with images that seemed incongruous for the area.

Lena pointed out those anomalies. "According to archaeologists who examined the collection, the motifs and representations of many of the artifacts seemed to better fit other cultures—Assyrian, Babylonian, Egyptian."

She opened to a picture of a copper sculpture of a winged man with a lizard's head. "For example, this is clearly the figure of Nisroch, a god of ancient Assyria, a Mesopotamian civilization dating back four thousand years ago." She turned next to a set of golden plaques covered in a linear script. "And here are samples of proto-Phoenician writing. Experts have identified other pieces of the collection bearing Egyptian hieroglyphics, Libyan and Punic writing, even Celtic symbols. Father Crespi became convinced that these objects were proof of a *connection* between a lost civilization hidden in these jungles and the rest of the ancient world, a connection that predated recorded history."

She fanned through the book, stopping at another set of photos. "Even stranger, the natives also brought him steel-hard copper gears, along with strange brass tubes that showed no rifling. All examples of a metallurgy beyond the local tribes' technical abilities to produce."

Gray took the book and looked through more photos of Father Crespi's collection. Much of it was gold tablets and scrolls, depicting a kaleidoscope of astrological figures, pyramids, and gods. One gold plate even showed a bent-backed figure writing with a quill pen.

He shook his head. "Surely some of this must be fake."

Lena shrugged. "Father Crespi admitted as much, believing that over time the natives might have crafted some of these gifts to please him. But even he could tell the forgeries from authentic items. I mean, who would freely give up so much gold just to fool an old priest?"

As proof, she flipped to a page that showed a yard-long golden crocodile with large rubies for eyes. It had to be worth a small fortune, certainly not something a native would craft as a simple forgery.

"Whatever happened to Father Crespi's collection?" he asked.

"That's a mystery all its own. After he died in 1982, his collection was quickly dispersed. Most of it ended up locked away in museum vaults on order of the Ecuadorian government. You can only view them with special permission. Other pieces ended up at an Ecuadorian military base of Cayambe, deep in the jungle."

A military base?

Lena glanced to the rear of the jet's cabin. "And according to Roland, rumors persist that some key pieces were taken and shipped off to the Vatican."

Gray leaned back in his seat. "If that's true, it sounds like Father Kircher wasn't the only Catholic priest who was trying to keep something secret."

But what were they trying to hide?

"For any more answers," Lena said, "we'll have to find that cavern system noted on Kircher's map, the one marked with a labyrinth."

From across the aisle, Seichan spoke with an arm over her eyes. She must have been feigning sleep while he and Lena had talked, eavesdropping on their conversation. "All of this sounds like nothing more than folktales, rumors, or treasure-filled dreams."

"Maybe not," Gray said.

Seichan lowered her arm and turned toward him, arching an eyebrow doubtfully.

While the others had studied various pieces of the puzzle, he had spent the past few hours researching the possibility of the existence of a lost city buried in the jungles of these mountains.

"It's been well documented," he said, "that a vast cavern system *does* tunnel through the Andes in this area, stretching an immeasurable distance. Large sections of it were photographed and mapped by the British-Ecuadorian research team back in 1976."

"The one headed by Neil Armstrong," Lena said.

"He was the honorary president of that expedition. While they found no lost city, the group did discover the remains of an old tomb in those caverns, along with identifying hundreds of new species of plants, bats, and butterflies."

Seichan rolled her eyes. "Still, like you said, they found no lost city. And like I said, it's folktales."

"I'm not so sure. There's a persistent legend about this region, of secret caverns that hold a vast library of metal books and crystal tablets. According to accounts of a man named Petronio Jaramillo, a Shuar tribesman took him to those caverns when he was a teenager. This was back in 1946. Afterward, fearful that it might be looted, he kept its location secret for decades. He finally agreed to guide a handful of people to its location, but only with the assurance that Neil Armstrong would participate in this latest venture, too. Then in 1998, within weeks of this scheduled trip, he was assassinated outside his home."

Lena cringed. "Assassinated?"

"Some believe it was done to silence him. Others that he was murdered while someone tried to extract his secrets. Either way, the location died with him."

Lena took the book from the table. "Do you think Father Crespi's collection could have come from that same place?"

"Possibly. From there or maybe from tunnels that connect to that lost library."

Seichan stretched in her reclined seat. "So why did that assassinated guy insist that Neil Armstrong be part of this new expedition?"

Gray shrugged. "It could be the man wanted someone whose status and name were beyond repute. Or maybe there was another reason. I still find it odd that Armstrong would've agreed to be a part of *either* expedition. He wasn't an archaeologist. And after the Apollo 11 mission, he became somewhat of a recluse, doing only a handful of interviews. So why become involved in any of this?"

"I think I may know," a voice said behind him.

Roland had quietly joined them, his eyes glassy with exhaustion and amazement. He clutched Kircher's journal to his chest while gazing toward a window, where a full moon was perfectly framed.

"Why?" Lena asked him.

"Because of the moon . . . it's not what we think it is."

9:02 P.M.

Roland ignored their incredulous reactions. He struggled to find the words to explain what he had found buried within Father Kircher's journal.

No wonder the reverend father had kept all of this secret.

Just forty years prior to the reverend father's discovery of Eve's bones, the Inquisition had sentenced Galileo to death for daring to suggest that the earth was not the center of the universe. The revelations written within Kircher's journal would have equally doomed the man and anyone associated with his discovery.

"If the moon isn't what we think it is," Gray asked, "what is it?"

Roland lifted Kircher's book. "The reverend father came to the conclusion that the moon is *not* a natural object." Before anyone could object, Roland stood straighter. "And I agree with him."

Seichan pulled her seat upright and swung around to face them all. She pointed toward the window, toward the full moon. "You're saying that's not real."

Roland sank into a seat amidst the group. "I spent all night researching details I found in Kircher's book. Seeking ways to disprove his conclusions. But instead, I only found more corroboration."

"Maybe you'd better take us through this," Gray said, nodding to the book. "What did you learn?"

"It's not just what I found in the reverend father's journal." He looked to the shining face of the moon. "Have you never wondered why during a total solar eclipse the face of the moon fits *exactly* over the surface of the sun? Doesn't that perfect visual alignment seem like an odd astronomical coincidence?"

From the others' expressions, he saw that this odd fact had escaped them.

Like it does most people.

"That phenomenon happens because the moon is 400 times smaller than the sun, while sitting 1/400th of the distance between the earth and the sun." He shook his head at the amazing relationship. "And that's not all. The moon precisely mirrors the annual movement of the sun. A *midsummer* full moon will set at the same angle and place on the horizon as a *midwinter* sunset. Again, doesn't that symmetry seem to defy coincidental chance?"

"But that doesn't make it fake," Lena said softly, as if talking to a madman.

And maybe I am . . . maybe I've fallen too far down the rabbit hole.

Still, he refused to relent. "Researchers aren't even sure how the moon formed. The current hypothesis is called the Big Whack theory, that some object the size of Mars impacted with the earth early in its formation and knocked enough material into orbit that it formed the moon."

"What's wrong with that theory?" Gray asked.

"Two things. *One*: astronomers all agree that such a planet-sized impact would have set the earth spinning faster than it does today. To compensate for that and to make their theory work, they hypothesized a *second* impact to our planet, this one striking from the opposite direction with the same force."

"To brake the faster spinning of the earth." Gray's brow furrowed at the improbability of such an event.

"Even astronomers admit there is *no* actual evidence of such an impact having occurred. Which brings us to the second problem of the Big Whack theory. It concerns the strange *amount* of material ejected from the earth that coalesced into our moon."

"How is it strange?" Gray asked.

"Because once the dust settled, the earth ended up with a circumference precisely *366 percent* larger than the moon's. Doesn't that percentage seem odd to anyone?"

"The number 366." Lena frowned. "That's almost the same as the days in a year."

"In fact, the earth rotates 366 times during one trip around the sun." Roland looked down at the journal in his lap and traced a finger along the labyrinth of ancient Crete gilded on the cover. "It's why the Minoan astronomer-priests of Crete divided a circle into 366 degrees. The Sumerians did the same, further dividing the degrees into 60 minutes and subdividing those minutes into 60 seconds."

"Like we do today," Lena said.

"Except we rounded this to an even *360* degrees," Roland corrected. "But back to the moon. There are other oddities concerning our sister satellite: how it's lighter in mass than expected; how its gravitational field has stronger and weaker patches; how its core is abnormally small. Yet without this strange moon, there would be no life on this planet."

Lena frowned. "Why's that?"

"Biologists believe that the gravitational pull of the moon—which produces tidal changes and tidal pools—is probably what helped early aquatic life transition onto land. But more important, astrophysicists know that the mass of the moon orbiting our planet helps to stabilize the earth's axis, to keep it at a slightly tilted angle toward the sun. Without the moon's presence, the earth would wobble more, leading to extreme fluxes in temperature and weather, making it almost impossible for complex life to form."

"So without the moon, we wouldn't be here," Seichan said. "But at the same time, its perfect symmetry and existence defies rationality. Is that what you're saying?"

Roland shrugged, letting them reach their own conclusions. "Maybe that's why Neil Armstrong became involved in all of this. Maybe he experienced something during his time on the lunar surface that compelled him to pursue this line of investigation."

Gray frowned, glancing toward the full moon framed in the jet's window. "NASA's missing two minutes," he mumbled.

Everyone stared at him.

"What missing two minutes?" Seichan asked.

9:07 P.M.

Gray wasn't sure how much weight to give to Roland's revelations. Still, Neil Armstrong's puzzling participation in this archaeological expedition reminded him of another mystery concerning the Apollo 11 mission.

"I heard a story from a colleague, an astrophysicist who worked at NASA," Gray explained. "During the televised moon landing, a pair of cameras supposedly overheated, resulting in two minutes of radio silence. Afterward, sources claimed that NASA was covering something up, something Armstrong and his fellow astronauts witnessed upon landing. This was substantiated later by a retired NASA communications engineer, who admitted that the event was deliberately staged to hide something found on the lunar surface."

"What?" Lena asked. "Like extraterrestrials?"

"That's one of the theories floated." Gray turned to Roland. "But others believe they were covering up some mystery tied to the moon itself."

"Maybe they were right." Roland admitted. "Father Kircher certainly became convinced there was something miraculous about the moon. He spent pages and pages exploring this possibility in his journal."

"What else did he learn?" Gray asked.

Roland gripped the old book with both hands. "Most of it centers on the strange symmetries between the earth and the moon. For example, can you guess how many times the moon orbits the earth over the course of 10,000 days?"

No one bothered to answer.

"It's 366 times," he said. "And that number is important in so many other ways. You could almost consider it the fundamental code for our planet. And that's been known for far longer than you could imagine."

"How long?" Gray asked.

"Do you remember that staff we saw with Eve's bones?" He pulled out his phone and brought up the photograph that Lena had taken of the remains, showing those bony hands clutching a length of carved mammoth tusk. "The reverend father named this *de Costa Eve*, or the Rib of Eve. And if you look closely, you can almost make out small gradations inscribed along its length."

He zoomed in and passed the image around.

"What about it?" Gray asked.

"It's marked that way because it's an ancient measuring tool."

"To measure what?" Seichan asked.

"Everything. It may be the key to our very world."

Gray gave him an exasperated look, but Roland forged onward.

"Back at the chapel in Italy, I measured the staff's length," he said. "It's 83 centimeters long."

Gray shrugged. "So just shy of a meter or yardstick."

"That's right, but—"

"Oh, my God!" Lena suddenly blurted out, cutting him off and drawing their attention. "That length! I know what you're getting at. It's not a regular yard like we use today. It's a *megalithic* yard."

Roland nodded at Lena. "Precisely. I came across that same term while cross-referencing some of Kircher's claims."

"What's a megalithic yard?" Gray asked, searching between Roland and Lena.

Lena spoke excitedly. "There was a Scottish engineer back in the thirties. I can't remember his name . . ."

"Alexander Thom," Roland filled in.

She nodded and rushed on. "He was surveying megalithic ruins throughout Scotland and England and noted how those prehistoric builders had laid out their giant stones along lunar or solar lines. Curious, he did a statistical analysis of ancient Neolithic sites across both the UK and France and noted a strange anomaly. Basically they all seemed to have been constructed using a standard unit of measurement."

"The megalithic yard," Roland explained. "It's the same length as the staff held by Eve. That length appears again and again throughout history and cultures. The old Spanish vara, the Japanese shaku, the gaz of the Harappan civilization of ancient India . . . they're all very close in length to this megalithic yard. Even going back to the ancient Minoans of Crete. A thousand Minoan feet is equal to 366 megalithic yards."

"That number again," Gray mumbled.

"And if I remember right," Lena added, "the area found within the sarsen ring of Stonehenge is exactly a thousand square megalithic yards."

Seichan turned to Lena. "How come you know so much about all of this?" she asked, plainly wondering how a geneticist had come upon such knowledge.

"Maria and I had studied markers such as this, indications of knowledge spreading globally during Paleolithic times. All of this ties to our hypothesis that there was a small band of people who helped with mankind's Great Leap Forward, guiding the path to modern civilization."

"Like the Watchers that Roland mentioned before," Gray said. "Those otherworldly teachers from ancient scripture."

Seichan scowled. "So what you're saying is that some universal unit of measure was shared between societies, spread by these Watchers."

Gray stared down at the phone's screen, at the bones of Eve. He studied the unique features that marked her as a hybrid between early man and Neanderthals.

Am I looking at the face of one of those Watchers?

He finally returned his attention to the others. "But what's so important about this length? Why is it the *key* to the world, like you said before?"

Lena stepped up and tried to explain. "Because the megalithic yard was calculated from the dimensions of the planet . . . specifically on the *circumference* of the earth."

"Even Father Kircher came to realize this." Roland opened the journal to a page of calculations surrounding an illustration of the sphere of the earth. "You can see here how the reverend father divided the circumference of the earth into 366 degrees, then sliced those degrees into 60 minutes, then again into 60 seconds. Here at the bottom you can see his final calculation, where he determined the length of *1 second* of the earth's circumference."

He tapped that final number.

36.6 Costa Eve

"It's that same sequence again—*366*," Gray noted.

Seichan stared down at the page, too. "But how could these prehistoric people have come to know the circumference of the Earth and calculate something like this?"

"Most likely by indirect means. All of this could have been derived by simply using a string, a pebble, and a pole." Roland turned to another page in the journal showing a crude pendulum. "Father Kircher diagrammed it out here, using the planet Venus as a positioning point."

"Roland may be right," Lena added. "We already know ancient builders were wise to the movement of the stars, and many early cultures revered the planet Venus. Take, for example, the Neolithic ruins of Newgrange found in Ireland. Its builders positioned its doorway to allow Venus to shine its light inside their structure on the winter solstice."

Gray sat back. "So you believe that somebody calculated this megalithic length based on the circumference of the earth and eventually shared it as a universal unit of measurement."

"That's what Father Kircher believed," Roland said. "He recognized these bones were ancient, that there was something not quite human in their conformation, and that the artifacts found with the remains—the length of ivory, the perfectly sculpted sphere of the moon—showed advanced knowledge of astronomy."

Gray sat back. "And after coming to this realization, he secretly sought to learn more about these people."

Roland nodded. "But being a pious man, he also sought support from religious texts. He came to believe that the Bible also hid clues about those special numbers we were talking about."

"How do you mean?" Gray pressed.

9:09 P.M.

Roland swallowed, almost fearful of revealing the ultimate truth he had discovered in Kircher's journal. He imagined the reverend father must have struggled even more.

"Are you familiar with the term *gematria*?" he finally asked. After getting shakes of heads all around, he explained. "It's a Babylonian system of numerology that was adopted by the Hebrews, where each letter is assigned a number, giving words extra meaning based on those numbers. It became the root of a medieval cabalistic system of interpreting scripture. Later, Christians also embraced this mystical way of looking at the Bible. And as Father Kircher was a mathematician, such numerology would have interested him. From the ramblings in his journal, he became fixated on one specific number and its connection to the Bible."

"What number?"

"A prime number. 37." He returned again to the page showing the length of Eve's Rib tied to circumference of the planet. "At first I thought Father Kircher was merely rounding this number—36.6—to an even 37, but he also references what Lena and I saw above the grave of Adam back in Croatia."

He flipped through the images on his phone until he came across the splay of palm prints above the Neanderthal male's grave.

"If you count the number of prints, you'll find 37 of them." Roland turned to Lena. "You also took a picture of a similar star-shaped petroglyph above Eve's grave, but those palms were more numerous. I don't have that photo, but could you count the number of prints that make up Eve's star?"

Scrunching her brow, Lena pulled out her own cell and searched until she found the proper image.

She tallied the number of prints and lifted her face when done. "There's *73*."

Roland nodded. "Father Kircher noted the same in his journal."

"The numbers 37 and 73," Gray said. "They're mirrored prime numbers."

"What Father Kircher called *stella numeros* . . . or star numbers, because of the patterns they formed." Roland fanned through a section of the journal. "He also used gematria to tease out hidden messages from the Bible, coming to conclude that the number 37 was fundamental to understanding the Holy Scriptures."

"How so?" Gray asked.

"A few examples. The word *faith* is used 37 times in the Gospels. Also if you convert the Hebrew word for wisdom—or *chokmah*—into its cabalistic equivalent, you get the numerical value of 37." He glanced to Lena.

"You've been searching for the roots of human intelligence. And the only word found in the Bible that equals 37 is *chokmah*."

Her face grew thoughtful. "Wisdom."

He turned to the others. "Father Kircher lists many other such biblical ties to the number 37, but his most compelling comes from the very first line of the Bible, from Genesis. *In the beginning, God created the heaven and the earth.*"

Roland revealed a journal page with the same verse written in Hebrew, under which the reverend father had inscribed the numerological equivalent for each Hebrew word.

בראשית ברא אלהים את השמים ואת הארץ
296   407   395   401   86   203   913

"If you total up this line of cabalistic numbers," he said, "you get 2,701."

Gray frowned. "How's that significant?"

Roland turned to the next page and revealed what Father Kircher had calculated.

$$2701 = 37 \times 73$$

Gray shifted closer. "It's those same mirrored primes multiplied together."

"The reverend father's star numbers." Roland nodded. "Such a discovery seems beyond pure statistical chance, especially given that Father Kircher pursued this a step further. He found out that if you took this same verse, multiplied each *letter's* value by the number of letters, then divided that figure by the same with the *words'* values, he came up with another number that defies rational explanation."

Roland handed the journal to Gray so he could double-check the reverend father's mathematical calculations and the final number circled at the bottom.

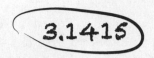

Gray's voice rang with a note of astonishment. "That's pi."

"A number that was well known during Father Kircher's time."

Lena sat back, speaking softly, almost distracted. "Maria and I studied the history of pi for our dissertation about the roots of intelligence . . . using it as a marker for the evolution of knowledge. The earliest approximations of pi actually go back to the Babylonians."

Roland took back the journal. "So it appears that not only are those star numbers buried within the first verse of Genesis, so is the numerically significant value of pi."

Gray reached forward and took the book. He flipped back to the page to the earth's illustration. He tapped the final calculation written on the bottom: *36.6 Costa Eve.* "As you mentioned, this also rounds up to 37. A number that—if you're right—seems to connect the sun, moon, and earth together with the precision of a Swiss clockmaker."

Lena's face had gone noticeably paler. "It might not just be the *stars.*"

They all turned to her.

"That same number is also buried in our *genetic code.*"

9:12 P.M.

Lena had been fearful of broaching this matter. As soon as she had heard about the significance of the number 37, she had recalled something she had read in an academic journal back in 2014. While she had wanted to dismiss the article as a statistical anomaly, she now began to wonder.

Roland stared at her. "What are you talking about?"

She looked down at her hands. "Nearly all life on the planet uses DNA as its coding material, but there's a code within that code, one that is beyond mutation and change. It's the complex set of rules that govern how DNA produces proteins. Recently a biologist and mathematician, working together, discovered a series of perfect symmetries buried in that code. A pattern all based on the multiples of a single prime number."

"Let me guess," Gray said. "37?"

She nodded. "I remember one example from the article: how the atomic mass of every amino acid that makes up our bodies—all twenty of them—is a multiple of 37." Lena gave a small shake of her head. "The odds of this pattern emerging by random chance were calculated to be one out of a decillion, which is 1 followed by 33 zeros."

"So in other words, *slim*," Seichan added.

Roland frowned. "You don't even have to look so *microscopically* to see that connection to our biology. All you have to do is consider the normal temperature of the human body." He stared across the group. "It's *37* degrees Celsius."

Silence settled across the cabin.

Gray finally spoke, his voice hushed. "If all of this is true, we're talking about a single number that defines everything. Connecting our DNA and our bodies to the very movement of the sun, moon, and earth."

"But what does it all mean?" Seichan asked.

He shook his head, as much in the dark as everyone else.

"If there are any answers," Roland said, "they'll be found here."

The priest had shifted again to Kircher's journal, returning to an image he had shown them earlier. It was the section of South America with a labyrinth drawn atop a subterranean lake. It was where Kircher believed Atlantis was hidden. Lena recalled the history of this region, hinting at a lost city buried under the mountains, a place of inexplicable treasures, where ancient libraries stored books of metal and crystal.

Could there truly be such a place?

Seichan echoed this question. "How can you be so certain about all of this?"

Roland pointed to the journal. "Look where we're headed, at the *latitude* marked on the map."

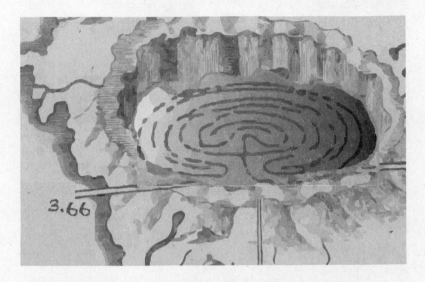

Gray leaned closer and read those coordinates aloud. "3.66."

Roland smiled. "Anyone want to claim that's random chance?"

The pilot radioed back. "Buckle up, folks. We're beginning the final approach into Cuenca."

Lena twisted around and peered out the window. Ahead, the dark forest vanished into a patch of brightly lit homes. She returned her focus to the spread of jungle and the sharp-edged peaks in the distance. Somewhere out there could be hidden the greatest discovery in mankind's history.

Still, a part of her wished the plane would tip on a wing and head away, knowing all the bloodshed that had led them here, reminding herself that Maria was still in danger.

Lena drew her gaze up to the moon, at the mystery hanging in the night sky. Beyond all the talk of calculations, she remembered Roland's first comment about how the face of the moon perfectly covered the sun during a total eclipse. It was a symmetry of orbital movements and celestial sizes that defied common sense. Yet it had hung there for millennia, offering up this miracle to whomever dared to look and wonder.

She also recalled Gray's comment earlier, about how all of this—the sun, the moon, and the earth—seemed designed by a Swiss clockmaker.

A chilling question rose to her mind.

If true, who was that clockmaker?

The jet shook as the landing gear was engaged.

Maybe we're about to find out.

10:03 P.M.

Inside the shadowy hangar that neighbored the main airport of Cuenca, Shu Wei stabbed her dagger under the cowering man's ear, angling the blade up. His mouth opened to scream, but death claimed him before any sound could escape. His body toppled backward, sliding off her knife and collapsing to the concrete floor.

She turned away, wiping the blood from the blade with a rag. She had gained the information she needed from the man. Her targets had flown off in a rented helicopter forty-five minutes ago, heading out into the jungle. The group had left with only a hired pilot, destined for a site deep in the mountains, where they were scheduled to meet with a pair of local guides of the Shuar tribe.

She tugged free an iPad from a pocket inside her jacket. It was the device she had discovered in the smoky university office back in Rome. It belonged to Father Roland Novak. During the flight here, a digital forensics expert had reviewed everything on the unit's drive. Most of the information pertained to a medieval priest, Athanasius Kircher, including vast volumes of the man's work. Little of it seemed pertinent to this hunt, except for the image she had viewed from the start. She brought up the screen again.

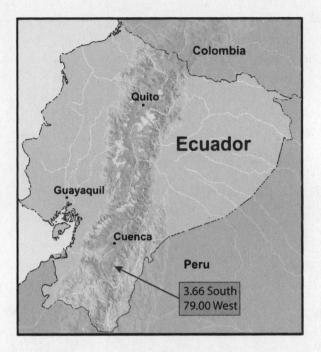

It was a map of Ecuador, with a specific spot pinpointed on it.

Her target's rented helicopter was flying to a site near that same location.

She frowned, wishing the group had waited until morning before beginning their jungle search. She had hoped to narrow the gap with them
here in Cuenca, to ambush them while they slept.

Still, she had prepared for this eventuality.

She crossed to the ten men assembled near the hangar door. She had
handpicked each member of the strike team. They all belonged to the
Chengdu Military Region Special Forces, all part of her current unit,
code-named *Gǔ*. They had earned that title, *Falcon*, due to the unit's notorious ability to hunt down and eliminate their targets with the ruthlessness
of a true bird of prey.

I will not dishonor that name this night.

Her second-in-command joined her. Sergeant Major Kwan stood a head taller than her, his limbs thick with muscle, his face crisscrossed with old scars, his dark hair tied in a short tail. Many called him the Black Crow, due to his penchant for taking trophies from those he killed: rings, wedding bands, snips of hair, even a pair of slippers. She had once asked him about this quirk. It wasn't to glorify the kills, he had told her, but as a measure of honor, respecting the lives of those he took.

Over time, she had grown to trust the man, more than any other. He in turn never showed any resentment of her position, age, or gender, a rare and welcome sentiment.

"The helicopter is fueled," he said, his voice deceptively soft and quiet for such a rocky countenance. "Engines are being warmed."

She nodded her approval, staring past the tarmac to the dark mountains.

Then let the hunt begin.

19

It's okay, baby. It's okay.

Maria clasped tightly to Baako's hand. Because his wrist was bound in restraints, all she could do was squeeze his fingers. The heat of his skin was feverish. Though his eyes were glazed under a light sedative, he still silently pleaded with her, trying to understand what was happening to him, wondering why she was allowing this to be done to him. Tears rolled down from the corner of his lids. He could move little else with his skull clamped to the operating table by a ring of stainless steel.

An electric shaver glided across his scalp, wielded by one of the nurses.

It had been almost ninety minutes since she and Baako had been delivered to the vivisection lab. The preoperative preparations were interminable, involving a comprehensive physical, multiple blood tests, even an MRI. As the procedures ran on, Major General Lau had finally left with Arnaud, escorting the French paleontologist away to begin his study of the Neanderthal bones stolen from Croatia.

Then moments ago, a lab tech had returned with the results of a spinal tap. The lead surgeon—Dr. Han—had reviewed them. With everything seemingly in order, he had given the go-ahead to proceed with the surgery.

As the nurses continued their preparation of Baako, Dr. Han waited with a syringe of lidocaine, ready to perform a local anesthetic scalp block once they were finished. Other members of the team began to open surgical packs.

Baako hooted hoarsely at her.

"I know you're scared," she whispered to him. She bent down and kissed his fingertips. She let go of his hand long enough to cross her fists and press them to her chest.

[*I love you*]

She took his hand again—just as one of the nurses tested a piece of equipment. The ripping buzz of the surgical bone saw made her flinch. Baako reacted more severely. He bucked in his restraints, both straining to see what was making that noise and to escape it. His frightened grip came close to breaking her fingers.

Still, she held firmly to him. "Baako, I'm here. Look at me."

His panicked eyes swiveled wildly but finally settled on her.

"That's right. I'm not leaving you."

More tears wet his cheeks. He mewled softly, the sound shredding her heart.

She struggled for any way to offer him solace, her mind whirling with thoughts of breaking him free. But she knew the futility of such hopes. There were guards posted outside the lab. Also, during Baako's MRI, Maria had returned briefly to check on Kowalski, whose life balanced on her cooperation. He was still trapped in that cage on the ground level of the habitat. Except he was no longer alone. A large male silverback squatted before the door to his confinement. Other hybrid beasts stalked behind the leader of the pack.

Knowing the fate that awaited Kowalski if she did not cooperate, Maria had no choice but to be compliant, to do what was expected of her.

What else can I do?

She stared into Baako's eyes, willing him all her love, trying to maintain a brave face for him. But she knew his senses were far more acute, his well of empathy as deep as any human's. In his pained gaze, she could see his effort to communicate with her. But with his arms locked down, he was all but mute. While he could spell a few words with his fingers, he could not express the true depth of his fear and confusion, which only seemed to heighten his distress.

Baako's fingers squeezed incrementally tighter on hers. He pressed his lips together and halted his soft mewling for a single breath, then continued again—only this time the sound coalesced into two repeated syllables.

"Ma . . . ma . . ."

Maria swallowed, feeling her legs give way. Even the surgical staff heard this utterance. Faces turned to the patient on the table. Murmurs of amazement spread among them. While gorillas did not have the vocal apparatus for true speech, Baako clearly had the ability to mimic a sound he knew well, one imprinted on his heart.

"Mama," he repeated, his gaze fixed to her.

Maria could restrain herself no longer. She collapsed to her knees, her cheek pressed against Baako's fingers. Sobs racked through her, rising out of the depths of her soul.

Somebody help us.

11:08 A.M.

"This search could take all day, if not all week," Monk said.

He stood at the threshold of Dìxià Chéng—Beijing's Underground City—and studied the arched passageway that headed off from the bottom of the stairs. The tunnel was painted hospital white, stained with streaks of green mold. The floor was swamped in ankle-deep black water. He was happy to be wearing the paper mask over his nose and mouth, imagining what pathogens must be wafting about this claustrophobic place. Even through his mask's filter, the air reeked of algae, fungus, and rot.

Kimberly handed back his phone. "I doubt this will help us find our way through here."

The phone's screen glowed with a spotty diagram of this subterranean warren, a map supplied to them by Kat. His wife had compiled a rough composite of the eighty square miles that made up the Underground City, leaning on her sources in the intelligence community. But Dìxià Chéng had been dug out a half century ago, and over time it been sliced and diced apart by the ongoing extension of Beijing's subway system.

In the end, Kat admitted, *the map's only our best guess.*

To make matters worse, her sources had found no evidence that the Underground City actually reached the Beijing Zoo, which lay a mile or so off from the shuttered noodle shop overhead.

After ambushing Gao Sun, Monk had gathered Painter's extraction team to this shop. It was the first location where the GPS signal had reappeared. They had broken into the abandoned restaurant through a rear window, and after a quick search, they discovered a set of stairs in the basement leading down to the Underground City. According to Kimberly, this access point was one of a hundred entrances into the sprawling maze.

But the steel door found at the bottom of the steps looked new, clearly a recent addition. It was electronically locked, but a swipe of the magnetic keycard taken from Gao Sun had successfully opened it.

The capture of Gao Sun also proved to be a source of additional information. Through her contacts, Kat was able to discover his brother's name: Chang Sun. The man was a lieutenant colonel with the PLA, trained at the Academy of Military Science. His immediate superior, Major General Jiaying Lau, also came out of that same academy. Kat had forwarded a photo of the woman, standing stiffly in a starched pine-green uniform. The major general was likely the source of the griping and anger displayed by Gao during his earlier phone conversation with his brother, Chang.

So it seems we now know the major players, but how do we find the bastards?

A splashing drew Monk's attention forward. One of the extraction team returned out of the darkness. Monk had sent four commandos forward to canvass the immediate area. The fifth was back at Gao's apartment, babysitting and safeguarding that extra bit of insurance.

"All clear," the man reported. "But you should see what we found."

The five men handpicked for this mission by Painter were all Chinese American Army Rangers chosen for their ability to blend as seamlessly as possible into the populace. To further disguise their presence on foreign soil, they were all outfitted with PLA uniforms, including Monk and Kimberly.

When in Rome . . .

"Show me," Monk said.

The ranger—a stocky sergeant named John Chin—led the way down the flooded tunnel, passing by cramped rooms full of rusted skeletons of bicycles and mold-encrusted pieces of furniture. The narrow tunnel slowly sloped upward, taking them out of the water and onto drier ground. The perpetual gloom dissipated as a glow grew brighter ahead.

Monk soon found himself standing with the other rangers: two steely-eyed brothers named Henry and Michael Shaw—and a smaller commando who went simply by Kong. Monk wasn't sure if the latter was his actual surname or a nickname based on the man's size.

Kimberly gasped slightly, surprised by what lay at the end of the narrow passageway. It had emptied into an enormous tunnel, large enough to allow a tank to roll down the center of it. The walls and arched roof were painted a spotless gray, lit by a rail of sodium lights overhead. The tunnel stretched in both directions, burrowing north and south, fading around curves in the distance.

"I'm guessing this is the right road," Monk commented. "And lucky for us, Gao left us transportation."

A Chinese army jeep—a BJ2022 half-ton off-roader—sat parked next to the smaller tunnel. It was painted green with a crimson PLA star emblazoned on the front doors. Gao Sun must have parked the vehicle here before heading up top and walking the rest of the way to his apartment.

Kimberly reached into a pocket and pulled out the set of keys taken from their captive. "So who's up for a road trip?" she asked with a small smile, which spread across the assembled group.

They quickly loaded inside. Kimberly took the wheel. If they ran into trouble, her pretty face and quick tongue were their best assets to get through any checkpoints.

Monk climbed in the back, squeezing between the Shaw brothers in order to better hide his presence. As extra insurance, he tugged his cap lower and his mask higher. Still, he knew such efforts would survive only the most casual inspection.

So be it.

He leaned forward and pointed to the north, in the general direction of the zoo. "Head out. Let's see where this road takes us."

The engine roared to throaty life, trebling off the concrete walls.

He sank back into his seat.

And let's hope we're not too late.

11:14 A.M.

Baako feels the fire burst atop his head.

He thrashes in panic and pain, but his arms and legs are stuck. He can't move his head. All he can do is roll his eyes, trying to see. He had watched the tall man lean over him with a needle in his fingers.

Baako knows needles. Mama sometimes poked him, giving him treats afterward: bananas covered in honey.

But this hurts more . . . so much more.

He looks to Mama now. She holds Baako's hand. She says soft words, but her cheeks are wet. He smells her fear. The scent cuts through the sharper smells and finds him, pushing his own terror higher.

Mama, make it stop. I'll be a good boy.

But it doesn't stop. The needle sticks him again and again around his head, leaving behind a pool of fire each time.

Finally the man goes away.

Mama pushes closer. "You're okay," she tells him.

He must believe her, but he swallows and swallows and can't make the pounding in his ears stop. Then slowly the fire fades across the top of his head, leaving a coldness that makes his skin feel dead and thick.

He doesn't like this any better.

"You're my boy," Mama says. "You're my brave boy."

She says these good words, but her eyes weep. She brushes his brow, but by now that coldness has seeped even there. He can barely feel her fingertips.

"Sleep now, my little boy," she whispers to him, like she did so many nights back home. "I'll be here when you wake up."

She looks at the tall man who plays with a milky bag that connects to Baako's arm by a plastic rope. Baako feels everything grow lighter, like he's floating. He remembers a blue balloon that Mama let him play with. Outside, the string had slipped from his fingers, and the balloon went up and up into the sky.

He is that balloon now.

Mama's face blurs and fades away.

He hoots, trying to tell her to stay.

Mama, don't go.

Then blackness.

11:28 A.M.

As Baako's body slumped to the tabletop, Maria finally let go of his hand. She stepped from the table and hugged her arms around her chest, shivering with cold certainty. She had watched the terror and agony as Baako endured the anesthetic scalp block. But at least he was now asleep, sedated under the short-acting effect of the propofol drip. His chest rose and fell evenly, looking peaceful for the moment.

But such rest would not last.

The operating team—which consisted of two surgeons and three nurses—was already draping his form. They would keep Baako sedated only long enough to slice a flap of his skin off his scalp and perform the craniotomy. Once his skull was cracked open and the brain exposed, the drip would be turned off, and Baako would waken in a matter of minutes.

Then his true nightmare would begin.

Unable to watch these final preparations, she strode back to the curve of windows overlooking the hybrid habitat. She placed her forehead against the glass, staring below. Kowalski remained trapped in the cage by the habitat's exit, while the hulking occupants of the pit waited at the threshold, led by the massive silverback. Behind the bars, the big man looked like a rag doll compared to the half-ton beast.

Maria wondered how the researchers controlled such aggressive specimens. She placed her palms against the glass. Was this barrier even thick enough to prevent them from battering out of there? Surely they could climb the rocky walls to reach the height of these windows.

A scuff of shoes drew her attention around. One of the nurses—a young woman with bright eyes—joined her, sipping from a glass of ice water, taking a break before the final stage of the operation. It was the same nurse who had showed a bit of sympathy when Maria had first arrived. The woman nodded to the window, perhaps noting her attention.

"They cannot reach here," she said. Her words were whispered, but not as if she were afraid of sharing secrets. She seemed naturally soft-spoken. She pointed to a row of large boxes positioned below the level of the windows. "They broadcast on a frequency coded to the animals' collars."

Maria had noted the steel bands around the hybrids' necks. "They're shock collars?"

"That is correct. The signal generates a shield over the habitat, just under the level of the windows."

Maria nodded her understanding. If the beasts climbed too high and reached that invisible barrier, they would be jolted with electricity and driven back to the floor.

"And for emergency . . ." The nurse pointed to the left, to a locked cabinet holding a tranquilizer rifle. There was a latched gate in the neighboring pane of the observation window. "But do not fear. The guns have never been used. You are very safe."

Maria did not bother to point out the irony of this last statement. She stared down at Kowalski. He spotted her and lifted an arm. She placed her hand on the glass again, trying to reassure him that she was doing her best to keep him safe, too.

Behind her, Dr. Han barked out an order, making the nurse jump. The woman gave a hurried bow toward Maria—then dashed to obey her superior. Maria turned and saw that Baako was now fully draped. The surgical team stood off to the side, scrubbing up for the procedure.

A cold dread settled over her.

So it begins.

11:35 A.M.

"Well, that doesn't look good," Monk said from the backseat.

As Kimberly rounded the jeep past a long curve, a wooden barricade cut across the wide tunnel ahead. It was topped by rolls of razor wire and had a sentry shack guarding the gateway through it. Beyond the barrier, a small parking lot held a handful of jeeps and motorcycles.

"What do you think?" Kimberly asked as she slowed their approach.

"That barricade pretty much matches the southern border of the zoo overhead," he said. "So I'm guessing that's where we need to go."

During the drive here, Monk had been monitoring their progress via an accelerometer built into his satellite phone, but after the first quarter mile, their path had shot beyond the boundaries of Kat's map, passing into no-man's-land. Along the way, countless smaller passageways branched off, including a tunnel or two even larger than this one. It was a veritable maze. With no road signs to guide them, they had simply continued along a path that best aimed for the park.

At least it seemed to have worked.

But now a new challenge presented itself.

Up ahead, the road through the barrier was blocked by a row of waist-high steel pylons. A sentry stepped out of the guard shack to meet them.

Showing no hesitation, Kimberly glided their vehicle toward the gateway. As she braked to stop before the line of pylons, the sentry came forward to meet her, looking bored and unconcerned. He likely recognized the vehicle, so didn't bother to unhook the assault rifle from his shoulder.

Clearly this buried station did not get much action.

The sentry reached the vehicle and leaned over to the driver-side window.

Monk kept his head low, pretending to be half asleep, just another soldier reporting for duty. Kimberly spoke firmly to the sentry, twisting away from him as she reached for her knapsack, feigning an attempt to find papers or orders.

While she did so, the man poked his head through the window and took stock of the others in the jeep. Monk felt one of the Shaw brothers shift a hand to his sidearm.

Hold steady, he silently urged the ranger.

Before anyone else could make a move, Kimberly lashed out and hooked her arm around the sentry's neck. Catching him off guard, she easily jabbed his throat with a syringe, and an explosive puff of CO_2 pneumatically injected a powerful sedative into his bloodstream. She held him for the several breaths it took to knock him out.

Sergeant Chin used that time to hop out of the front passenger seat and rush to the guard shack. He searched the panel inside, then hit a button with his fist. The pylons blocking the way lowered into the road. He hurried back, then took the limp form of the sentry and hid it inside the shack.

"He'll be out for at least an hour," Kimberly said as she eased the jeep through the barrier. "But we'll need to move fast. It won't be long before someone finds this gate unguarded."

Outside their vehicle, Chin continued on foot, flanking their route toward the parking lot, watching for any other soldiers. Beyond the parking lot, the tunnel ended at a towering set of roll-up doors, tall enough to accommodate a double-decker bus. A dump truck stood backed up to that door, suggesting it was a loading dock for this facility. Chin popped up to check the truck's cab, then dropped and signaled the all clear.

Kimberly parked their jeep, and they all off-loaded. She pointed to a smaller door to the left of the larger one. A blue key reader glowed next to the knob.

She pulled out Gao's keycard again. "Let's hope this works here, too."

"And pray there's no additional biometric sensors," Monk whispered. "Palm readers, retinal scans."

Kimberly shrugged. "If necessary, we can always drag that sentry over here. Use his hand or eye."

True . . .

Monk appreciated the woman's ability to think on the fly. Kat chose well in picking her. Kimberly crossed to the key reader and waved Gao Sun's stolen card over the glowing surface.

The lock disengaged with a sharp click.

"Simple enough," he muttered.

She tugged the door open—only to find herself facing a startled man in a blue workman's uniform. His cap bore the same insignia as on the dump truck's door. The worker fell back in surprise, mumbling apologetically. His gaze swept across the assembled group of uniformed figures and moved out of their way.

Kimberly gave a small bow of her head in thanks and stepped through. Monk hung back, adjusting his sunglasses higher on his nose, praying his use of shades in this underground world didn't set off any alarm bells in the man—but it wasn't *that* man Monk should have worried about.

Chin followed Kimberly. As the sergeant crossed the threshold, Monk noted the change in the key reader next to the door. Its glow flared from blue to an angry crimson.

His heart sunk.

Oh, crap.

A loud klaxon erupted from sirens above the doorway and spread off into the distance.

Kimberly swung around, her face registering shock, but also understanding. The doorway must have sensors built into it, requiring anyone passing through to have a keycard on their person.

The truck driver tried to flee, but Chin pistol-whipped the man from behind, dropping him with a single blow.

Kimberly waved to Monk, staring upward. "Get inside! Now!"

A heavy security gate had begun dropping across the doorway. The Shaw brothers dashed across the threshold. Monk followed, rolling on a shoulder to get under the lowering barrier. The last of them, Kong, lunged with surprising speed, diving on his belly and sliding under the edge. Then his belt snagged on the door's metal sill, stopping him midway.

Panic etched the man's face.

No, you don't.

Monk snatched the gate's bottom edge with his prosthetic hand and braced himself against the grind of gears, knowing he could hold out for no more than a breath. Chin grabbed Kong's arms and yanked the man through the narrowing gap, falling backward and using his body weight to haul his smaller teammate to safety. The metal barrier dropped with a resounding clang at Kong's heels, sealing them in.

As the alarm bells continued to ring, Monk tossed aside his sunglasses and faced Kimberly with a heavy sigh.

So much for simple.

11:42 A.M.

Maria stared at the tableau before her.

With the first wail of the sirens, the surgical team had frozen in place around the operating table. Dr. Han stood poised with a blade in hand. He had just made his first incision across Baako's shaved scalp.

Maria could not take her eyes off the trickle of blood that trailed from the three-inch-long cut. She felt numb all over, barely registering the alarm. Still, her mind whirled, wondering what had happened.

Faces turned to the tall doors at the other end of the vivisection lab. Concerned murmurs rose from among the team, plainly unsure if they should proceed with the surgery or not.

Before anything could be settled, Maria made the decision for them. Reacting more than thinking, she rushed the table, determined to protect Baako, even if it only meant delaying the inevitable. She kneed Dr. Han behind the legs, dropping him to the floor, while snatching the scalpel from his fingers. She grabbed the back collar of his scrubs and pulled him close.

She poised the tip of the blade at his carotid.

"Wake Baako up!" she yelled at the remaining staff.

Dr. Han struggled as his initial stun wore off. She stabbed the point of the blade through his skin, drawing blood. He stiffened again.

"Now!" she hollered.

Finally one of the team moved. It was the nurse who had shown her kindness earlier. The young woman shifted around and clamped shut the sedative drip.

"Pull his catheter, too," she directed the nurse. She then glared at the others. "Free him!"

No one moved, so she twisted her fist in Dr. Han's scrubs and pushed the blade tip deeper. He gasped in pain, then shouted at his staff, clearly ordering them to obey. Like Maria, he probably realized there was nowhere she could go with the patient. So why not cooperate?

As she continued to threaten with the blade, the surgical drapes were yanked off Baako's form, and the leather straps unbuckled from his limbs.

"Bandage up his incision," she ordered the assistant surgeon, her voice growing meeker, more uncertain as her initial adrenaline surge began to wane.

Still, the doctor obeyed and closed the wound with butterfly bandages, then taped gauze sponges over the site. By the time he was finished, the sirens had gone silent.

In the quiet, the others looked at her, waiting for her next instruction.

Maria faced them, overwhelmed by one question.

What do I do from here?

11:44 A.M.

Major General Lau stood in the eye of the storm.

Upon first hearing the alarms, she had followed protocol in the event of a security breach and proceeded directly to the communication room of the complex. Six men manned the curve of tables under a wall of video monitors. The largest screen glowed with a three-dimensional map of the facility's four levels, encompassing miles of tunnels and hundreds of acres of research labs, office and storage spaces, living quarters, and countless other rooms and miscellaneous halls.

The site of the breach was at the complex's southern gate, where the facility merged with the old warren of bomb shelters and tunnels of the Underground City.

"How many intruders are there?" Jiaying demanded of Chang Sun.

"Unknown for the moment." The lieutenant colonel cupped an earpiece as he monitored reports from the security teams closing in on that location. With his other hand, he pointed to a grid of monitors. "We're pulling feed from the nearby cameras now."

On the indicated screens, images rolled in reverse. Finally, one of the technicians raised a hand.

"Over here," Chang said.

She joined the lieutenant colonel at that station. The technician ran the footage from the moment of the breach. The feed came from a camera facing the loading dock. She watched a group barge inside and assault a worker at the threshold.

Chang reached past the tech's shoulder, froze the image, then tapped each of the faces on the screen. Blue boxes outlined them and zoomed into fuzzy close-ups.

"Six of them," he said, finally answering her earlier question. "One woman, five men. All wearing army uniforms."

Jiaying leaned closer. "Are they our people?"

She did not dismiss the possibility that the Ministry of State Security had ordered a covert challenge to the base's security. Still, she sensed this was no drill.

Chang offered corroboration by pointing to one of the outlined faces. The man had removed a pair of sunglasses, revealing his foreign features. "They're Americans," he said, glancing over to her. "I'm sure of it."

Anger burned through her at such a trespass. "Where are they?"

He sighed in exasperation. "After the breach, they moved beyond the surveillance net around the loading bay door. But they can't stay out of sight for long. If another camera fails to pick them up, one of my teams will flush them out."

"How many security personnel do you have on the premises?"

"Over a hundred." Chang straightened. "And with all gates locked down and extra guards posted, they're trapped inside. It's only a matter of time before we find them."

She nodded, forcing her breath to slow. While she was perturbed at this assault, a part of her was relieved. She had suspected the Americans had sent operatives here, but until this moment that threat had been hypothetical, an unknown variable beyond her control. Now it had become quantifiable, a hazard she could eliminate, possibly even turn to her advantage.

"*Zhōngxiào* Sun!" a technician called out sharply to Chang.

Jiaying crossed with the lieutenant colonel to the new station, hoping the intruders had been spotted. But the screen revealed a view into the vivisection lab. She frowned at the sight of Maria Crandall holding a hostage at knifepoint, clearly interrupting the surgery.

Jiaying shook her head sadly at the woman's misguided efforts, clearly ignited by her compassion for her test subject.

I expected better from a fellow scientist.

Then again, too often Americans had proven themselves to be soft when they should be hard. They were too coddled, too certain of their superiority, too blind to the new millennium's shift of global powers.

Unlike in China, where hard lessons were taught at a young age.

It seems your education is sorely lacking, Dr. Crandall.

"Connect me to that lab," she ordered.

Chang instructed the tech, who tapped a few keys, then handed back a wireless microphone. "You'll be able to hear any responses over the monitor's speakers."

"Very good." She lifted the microphone to her lips. "Dr. Crandall, if I could have your attention."

On the screen, Maria backed a step, dragging the surgeon with her. She glanced toward the ceiling speakers.

"I see you appear panicked, but let me assure you that the sirens are merely a drill," she said, using the lie to smother any hope of rescue. "Still, I should inform you, as a matter of protocol, all rooms are locked down."

This last was *not* a lie.

There was nowhere Maria could go.

"You and your test subject will be fine, Dr. Crandall. Unfortunately the same cannot be said for your companion."

Maria glanced back toward the wall of windows behind her.

"You were given ample warning," Jiaying said.

Now it's time to learn your lesson.

11:55 A.M.

Kowalski kept to his feet inside the small cage, unnerved by the sudden silence after the blaring sirens. He had been penned in here for nearly three hours, coming to view his prison as nothing more than a vending machine for the beasts outside. When the sirens first erupted, he had been certain it was the dinner bell being rung, marking his end.

And he wasn't the only one bothered by the noise.

The klaxon—echoing loudly across the cavernous habitat—had roiled up the massive gorilla hybrids. Some retreated for the shelter of the caves, their heads bowed away from the noise. Others shifted closer, tightening around their leader. The half-ton silverback continued to squat outside the cage door, clearly unperturbed by the ruckus. The only sign that the beast had heard anything was when it had glanced over a shoulder and glared toward the windows.

Even Kowalski had stared up toward the curve of glass, hoping to catch sight of Maria, wondering the same thing over and over again.

What's going on up there?

By now he feared the surgeons had finished with Baako's operation. He wished he could console Maria, to offer her his support, as meager as it might be. He also tried not to think about Baako's fate, which only served to tighten the knot of anger in his gut.

Motion drew his attention back to the furry mountain at the door. The silverback had begun to rock slowly on its haunches. Kowalski met its dark gaze, which never left his face.

It's like the bugger knows something.

Kowalski pressed his back more firmly against the solid steel behind him, wishing he could melt through it. Then a loud grind of gears erupted above him—and the cage door began to trundle slowly upward along its tracks.

Oh, shit . . .

20

In the copilot's seat, Gray searched the jungle below their rental helicopter as it swept higher into the mountains. Though it was an hour shy of midnight, the brilliance of the full moon glistened off the dark green canopy, which was woven through by swaths of silvery mists. The terrain below looked untouched by man, broken into deep crevices and pierced by jagged outcroppings of granite.

He glanced at the aircraft's altimeter. The small town of Cuenca, from which they'd departed, lay at the eight-thousand-foot level. Where they were headed now—some forty miles due south of the town—was even higher in the Ecuadorian Andes.

Lena's voice reached him through the radio built into his headphones. "It's hard to believe anyone would build a city way out here."

"It's not that implausible," Roland argued. "During my research, I discovered Ecuador has many attractive qualities. First, its soil is exceptionally fertile due to the amount of volcanic activity, which makes it perfect for farming. The region's also the site of *four* ancient migration routes through the Andes, connecting the Amazon rain forest to the Pacific Ocean. It's the literal crossroads of this continent. Even the Inca empire settled on Cuenca as their northern capital."

"Sounds like a popular place," Seichan mumbled with thick sarcasm.

Roland ignored her and continued, "More significant, Ecuador is the *only* source of balsa wood in the world."

"Balsa?" Lena asked.

"The lightweight material was used to construct the old seafaring boats of this region, going back millennia. So if someone was looking for a temperate place to make their home and possibly serve as the launching pad for a migratory culture, Ecuador would suit them perfectly."

Gray took this all in, picturing such a lost civilization, remembering the book Lena had shown him, full of photos of Father Crespi's collection, antiquities that seemed to have come from all corners of the world.

"And last of all," Roland said, "in the ancient Amerindian tongue, the phrase *Old Andes* translates as *Atl Antis.*"

"Atlantis?" Lena said, her voice a mix of shock and doubt.

Even Gray looked over his shoulder to search Roland's face for any sign that he was joking.

Roland merely shrugged. "That's what I read."

The pilot cut in, his English thickly accented by Spanish. "That clearing up ahead, señor, is as close as I can get to the coordinates you gave me."

Gray returned his attention to the mist-shrouded forest. He spotted no break in the canopy ahead. The terrain looked as inhospitable as ever. Then he made out a tiny pit within that tumultuous dark green sea.

He couldn't possibly mean—

"You can land this bird there?" Seichan asked, clearly incredulous.

"*Sí*, no problem."

The pilot dove the small aircraft toward the small glade. It was open to the sky, but surrounded by towering trees. Mists filled the clearing, erasing any sign of the ground.

Gray clutched a handgrip as the pilot swung the helicopter around, bringing it to hover above the opening. He then swiftly descended. The rotor wash whipped the surrounding branches, which appeared to be only inches from the whirling blades. The pilot looked unperturbed as he continued down, sinking the aircraft into the mists.

Blind now, Gray held his breath, waiting for the rotors to dice into the trees and send them plunging to a fiery crash. Instead, after a stomach-sinking drop, the skids safely kissed the ground.

The pilot looked toward him and repeated. "No problem."

Easy for you to say . . .

Relieved, he clapped the pilot on the shoulder, silently thanking him, then turned to the others. "Everybody out." He checked his watch. "Our guides should be here soon."

I hope.

While en route, Roland had made contact with Father Pelham, the priest at the Church of María Auxiliadora in Cuenca, the man who took Father Crespi's place at the mission. Like Crespi, the current father was well regarded and loved by the local Shuar tribes. With the support of the Vatican behind him, Roland was able to get Father Pelham to contact a nearby Shuar *centro*, a village of some twenty families not far from where they wanted to go.

If anyone knew this terrain and its secrets, it would be the local Shuar.

But gaining their cooperation from here might prove to be a challenge. The tribes were notoriously suspicious of foreigners. People still vanished within these forests, succumbing to predators, poisonous snakes, or disease. But no one denied that a few of those travelers likely met their ends at the hands of the tribesmen in the darkest corners of the jungles, where headhunting and cannibalism continued. Even the occasional *tsantsa*, or shrunken head, made its way to the black market from these shadowy forests.

As they all unloaded, Lena pulled deeper into her jacket. "It's so cold."

Roland agreed with her. "Certainly not the steamy jungle I expected."

"It's the elevation," Gray explained, waving an arm toward the towering canopy shrouded in mists. "At this height in the mountains, the jungle turns into a cloud forest."

The air was also incredibly thin, forcing him to breathe harder.

Stepping away, Seichan stared off into the darkness beyond the reach of the helicopter's lights. "It's like another world."

Gray unsnapped a flashlight from his belt and shone the beam into the forest. It illuminated the heart of a lush green landscape. Cloud forests were notorious for their damp abundance, and this was no exception. The trunks, branches, and vines were covered in feathery crusts of mosses. Orchids grew on every surface in myriad shades and subtle curves of petals. Ferns sprouted not only from the ground but also from branches overhead. Even the leaves dripped with algae.

And throughout it all, wisps of mist and shreds of heavier fog hung in the air or gently snaked through the branches and canopy. The air here was exceptionally thin, making his lungs strain and his heart beat faster. Still, the soft breezes easily carried forth the rich scent of loam underfoot, interlaced with the flowery perfume of night-blooming flowers.

It *was* another world.

To enter here felt like trespassing.

As the helicopter's engines quieted down to cooling ticks, the forest came alive with the burring buzz of insects, the brittle knock of branches in the canopy as something fled their arrival, and the occasional spirited call of a bird. It was a reminder that it was not only *green* life that thrived here. These forests were home to large predators, like jaguars and anacondas, but also tapirs, sloths, peccaries, and all manner of monkeys.

A flock of parrots took wing from the forest edge and spiraled across the glade, calling down their complaints before vanishing again.

Lena tracked them, then stared over to Gray. "It's beautiful."

"And dangerous," Seichan warned her, clearly trying to dampen the geneticist's enthusiasm, to keep her focused. "Such beauty is nature's way of luring you into a trap."

Lena looked aghast.

Gray hid a smile as he sidled next to Seichan. "Maybe ease up a bit. Remember we need the others' help."

She slipped her hand into his, leaning closer. "We also need them *alive*." She raised her lips to his ear, her breath warm on his neck. "Besides, I *was* being easy. I didn't even mention the snake tangled in the branch above her head."

Gray looked up and searched until he spotted an emerald length spiraled along a limb. "Poisonous?" he asked.

"From its triangular head, some sort of pit viper." She nestled closer as he tried to pull away and warn Lena. "Don't worry. It's too cold at the moment to be a threat."

Gray was not entirely convinced. Doubts weighed on him. "Maybe it would be better to wait until morning before traipsing into the jungle with some headhunters."

Seichan pulled back and stared at him. "No, you were right before. We've spent ten hours getting here and shouldn't waste any more time. Besides, if we discover this lost cavern system, it won't matter if it's day or night once we're underground."

True, but first we have to find that place.

"We've got company," Roland said, moving closer to the two of them, drawing Lena with him.

To their right, two figures stood quietly at the forest's edge. Gray could not say how long they had been there. It was as if they had suddenly materialized out of the shadows.

Wary, he signaled the others to stay put and advanced toward the pair.

The taller appeared to be a Shuar elder. His face was pocked with tribal scars and traced with geometric tattoos across his cheeks, chin, and forehead. His gray hair was braided behind his gaunt shoulders. He stood bare-chested, except for an elaborate neckpiece of feathers, seedpods, and what appeared to be bones.

Next to him was a smaller figure, a boy of twelve or thirteen. His dark hair was shaggy and unkempt. Though barefoot like the older man, he wore baggy shorts and a green T-shirt with a Notre Dame leprechaun on it. He offered Gray a wide, enthusiastic smile, a counterpoint to the grave countenance of the elder.

"Hello," Gray said and introduced himself. "Do you speak English?"

The boy nodded. "I am Jembe." He waved to the older man. "This is Chakikui. I will speak for him, tell him what you say."

"Thank you," Gray said, glad to have a translator. "Do you know Father Pelham at the Church of María Auxiliadora?"

The boy's grin grew even larger. "I like him very much. He taught me English and Spanish at the mission school."

Good. A personal connection might help.

"Father Pelham told us that you might be able to guide us to some caves in this area."

Jembe nodded his head vigorously. "Caves, yes. Many caves under the mountains."

The elder interrupted, speaking dourly, never taking his eyes off Gray.

Jembe listened, then translated. "Uncle Chakikui says he knows the caves you seek."

Gray let out a breath, reassured.

"But he will not take you," the boy added, looking stricken. "If you try to go there, our tribe will kill you."

With his message given, Chakikui turned and headed back into the forest, drawing Jembe with him, who cast an apologetic look back toward Gray.

He watched the pair vanish into the darkness.

So much for that personal connection.

11:22 P.M.

"Wait!" Roland yelled. He rushed forward upon hearing the elder's declaration and warning. "Please!"

He joined Gray, who stopped him from plunging into the forest after the pair.

"Careful," Gray warned. "Those two may not have come alone. If you spook them, you could get an arrow in the chest."

Roland refused to relent, stepping in front of Gray. "I am Father Novak," he called out into the darkness. "I've come a long way. Please!"

Not knowing what else to do, Roland opened his jacket and exposed the white Roman collar of his station. If Father Pelham was well regarded, perhaps that respect might extend to another who wore that collar.

He waited, standing there with his chest exposed, all too cognizant of Gray's earlier warning.

Finally, without even a rustle of leaves underfoot, the shadows co-alesced into the returning figures of the elder and the boy.

The older tribesman stepped forward, his gaze fixed to Roland's collar. He spoke sternly, but with a measure of forbearance.

Jembe translated. "Chakikui says he will listen. Because priests have shown kindness to our tribe."

Roland recognized the boy's use of the word *priests* . . . as in plural. The elder was certainly old enough to have been alive during the time when Father Pelham's predecessor ran the mission in Cuenca. He decided to play that card now.

"You knew Father Carlos Crespi," he said. He noted the elder's eyes narrow at the mention of the missionary's name and pressed his case. "We come this night to honor the good father's memory, to hopefully carry on his duty in these forests."

Jembe relayed Chakikui's skeptical response. "Many come after the gold."

"Not us," Roland insisted. "We come for knowledge. To find a city of ancient teachers, a place of learning."

He pulled out Father Kircher's old journal from the inside of his jacket and showed the gilded cover to Chakikui and the boy. The elder's attention focused on the labyrinth, his eyes narrowing again, as if in rec-ognition.

Interesting . . .

"We have heard stories of caverns that hold many books like this," Roland said, remembering Petronio Jaramillo's tale of a lost library buried underground. "Can you take us there?"

The elder spoke, giving a disconcerting shake of his head. Jembe looked equally grim as he translated. "Chakikui says he took another to those caves. Long ago. He says it was a mistake."

Roland glanced at Gray. *Could this be the same tribesman who took Jaramillo to those caves back in the forties?*

"It is forbidden to go there," Jembe said, continuing to share the elder's words. "Even to honor Father Crespi." The boy made the sign of the cross at the mention of the father's name. "May he rest in peace."

Roland sighed and wiped his brow, struggling to find a way to convince the elder to cooperate. He had noticed during this entire exchange that Chakikui's eyes kept returning again and again to the book in his hand.

Hoping it might be the key to gaining the elder's support, he held forth the journal. "Another reverend father wrote *this* book. Hundreds of years ago. Like Father Crespi, he sought out this lost city of ancient teachers." Roland flipped through the pages until he came to the map of South America with a labyrinth marked on it. "He said for us to seek out this place."

Chakikui stepped closer, holding out his hand. Roland let him have the journal. The elder searched through other pages. He paused at a page where Father Kircher had copied down the star petroglyphs found above the graves of Adam and Eve.

Chakikui whispered to Jembe.

The boy turned hopefully toward Roland. "Chakikui asks who is this other father? He says there is *one* name—another father from long ago—that will open the path to those caves."

Roland felt a surge of relief and certainty. "His name is Father Athanasius Kircher." He pointed to the journal. "Those are his words, his writings."

Chakikui closed the journal and handed it back to Roland. He turned away, casting back a final verdict, which the boy shared.

"That is not the one."

The pair began to head into the forest again.

At a loss for words, Roland did not know what else to do to convince the man.

Gray pushed past Roland. He reached for the elder's shoulder, but then retracted his hand before making contact, fearing such physicality might be mistaken as a threat.

"Wait," Gray blurted out. "This other father . . . Was his name Nicolas Steno?"

Roland stiffened, realizing his mistake.

Of course.

Father Kircher had never set foot on this continent. He had been too infirm in his later years, so he had sent an emissary, a younger man capable of such a hard journey, his dear friend Nicolas Steno. But could it be possible for the oral history of the local Shuar tribe to still remember such a man, to still revere his name?

The answer came as Chakikui faced them again, his eyes glinting brightly. "Nikloss . . . Steno?" he said, searching their faces.

Roland nodded.

Chakikui let out a long breath, as if he had been holding it for decades. He then whispered to the boy.

Jembe nodded as the elder turned away. "He will take you to the home of the ancient ones, to the city of the Old Andes."

Roland barely heard the boy's translation. Instead, the last words of the elder rang in his head. He had recognized Chakikui's use of the Amerindian translation of Old Andes.

Atl Antis.

He turned to the others, who all wore varying looks of shock, having heard it, too.

Could it be true?

11:58 P.M.

Lena followed behind Gray and Roland, with Seichan trailing them all.

After they had trekked through the rain forest for forty minutes, all of her clothes clung to the crevices of her body—not from sweat, but from the perpetual cold dampness trapped under the high canopy. The moisture dripped from branches, pooled under mats of decaying leaves, and hung in the air. With every breath, she drew in that clamminess. Even her lungs had begun to ache, as each inhalation grew more ragged in the thin air.

She strained to keep close to Gray, who carried a flashlight. It cast enough light to illuminate their way through this green tunnel under the canopy. Still, her eyes often drifted to the darkness to either side. The forest rustled, creaked, and buzzed, breaking out occasionally with the sharper hoot of a monkey or a whistling cry of a bird. Her thoughts ran with other imagined threats hidden behind that cloak of darkness, mostly dwelling on snakes.

The shifting tendrils of mist only added to her unease.

Makes the whole forest feel like it's moving.

A sudden cry pierced the night, full of leonine rage, sounding both distant and close at the same time. She stumbled forward to get closer to the others.

Jembe drifted back to her, leaving the older tribesman to continue leading them through this trackless forest. "Jaguar," he informed her. "Lots of them around here. But they won't come closer. We are many and making lots of noise."

Lots of noise?

Barely anyone said a word for the past fifteen minutes. All she heard was the sound of breathing and the soft squelch of their boots in the damp loam.

Jembe patted her arm, his eyes shining on her, plainly infatuated. "I protect you," he offered. "I'm fast. Like my name. It means humbird."

"Hummingbird?" she asked with a smile.

He bobbed his head proudly, imitating the flit of a bird with one hand. "Very fast."

"I'm sure you are."

They continued on for what seemed like miles, traipsing up steep paths and winding down switchbacks. Twice they had to ford fast-flowing streams over moss-slick rocks. The last time the water had been thigh-deep.

Then slowly a louder roaring grew ahead of them.

What now?

Before they could reach the source of that thunderous rumbling, Chakikui drew them to a stop at the crest of a ridge. Jembe translated his warning.

"Past here, the land is forbidden. Guarded by . . ." Jembe struggled for the word. "By devils."

As proof, Chakikui stepped to a tall standing stone at the ridgeline. Its surface was encrusted with lichen, but the side facing them was clear enough that they could recognize a crude figure engraved into the rock. The petroglyph had been drawn by scraping through the dark outer varnish of the boulder to reveal the white stone beneath, casting a ghostly quality to the image.

"A devil," Jembe said, scowling at the depicted beast.

The figure stood upright on its hind legs, with claws raised high, growling menacingly at them.

Lena pushed forward. "It's not a devil," she said with awe. A fingertip traced the muzzle and the rounded ears; then she glanced to the others. "It's a cave bear. Similar to what we saw painted underground in Croatia."

Roland nodded. "She's right."

She shook her head. "But the Paleolithic territory of *Ursus spelaeus* did not extend to South America," she whispered. "This image shouldn't be here."

"Unless someone drew it from memory," Roland offered.

She stood up and stared past the crest. Beyond the totem marker, more boulders were strewn down the steep slope ahead. Even from her perch, she spotted other petroglyphs scratched into those rock faces. Most of the designs were abstract: geometric shapes, fanciful whirls, even what appeared to be sticklike writing. But there were also many more animals: snakes, birds, jaguars, monkeys, and a giant horned and hoofed beast that could be a bison.

No wonder such a place spooked the local tribes.

Chakikui blocked them with an arm, relating another reason for the forbidden nature of this area. Jembe explained, "Father Nikloss Steno. Long ago, he say to let no one come here. Not unless they know his name."

"Why?" Gray asked.

Chakikui frowned and answered with the boy's help. "Dangerous." The elder patted his bare chest. "To body and to spirit." He waved to encompass more than the forest. "And to world."

The elder stared at Gray, clearly seeing if he still wanted to continue.

"I understand." Gray waved onward. "Show us."

Before obeying, Chakikui raised his hands to his mouth and let out a sharp whistle, not unlike a birdcall.

Jembe explained, "He sends the others away. Back to our village. They cannot come with us."

Lena peered into the dark forest.

Seichan looked unsurprised. "We've been followed since we left the helicopter. I figure at least a dozen."

Shocked, Lena continued to stare over her shoulder as they all headed down the slope, following Chakikui.

Roland hiked beside her. He swept an arm to either side of their path. "According to Jaramillo's account of his journey to the lost library, the trail to its entrance led through a maze of carved boulders." He pointed toward the distant roaring of water. "A path that ended at a storm-swollen river."

As Chakikui continued down, the canopy began to thin overhead, shredding apart to allow the bright face of the moon to show in glimpses and pieces.

Lena craned up at the brilliance, happy for the extra light, but also weighed down by Roland's earlier assessment of that satellite. She remembered the strange synergy of alignments and proportions that defined the relationships of the earth, moon, and sun.

Roland noted her attention skyward. "Makes me wonder again about Neil Armstrong's involvement in all of this."

"How so?" she asked.

"Maybe he truly did experience something strange up there." He gazed in wonder at the moon. "Maybe that was what drew him to join that British expedition? A desire for the truth. We know he had been in touch with the first expedition's organizer, a Scottish engineer named Stan Hall—a man who had also been in contact with Petronio Jaramillo. Hall was also the one organizing the second expedition with Armstrong before Jaramillo was assassinated."

By now any further discussion became more difficult as the roar of water grew deafening. Ahead, the river came into view, shining silver in the moonlight. It cascaded along a series of cataracts down a rocky cliff and pooled into a crystal-clear basin. From there, its course continued over another sheer drop, becoming a thunderous waterfall that disappeared into the forest far below.

Gray checked his satellite phone as they neared the riverbank.

"Strange," he muttered.

Lena moved closer. "What?"

"The GPS shows we're generally right on the mark. At the same longitude and latitude noted on the map in Kircher's journal. Except look at this." He tapped a compass in the lower right corner of the screen. "This is a magnetic reading, not the result of any satellite feed."

Lena saw that the needle jiggered clockwise and counterclockwise, spinning erratically.

Before anyone could comment, Jembe called to them. He stood with Chakikui beside the wide pool. Misty droplets from the cataracts sparkled over their figures.

As she and the others joined the pair, Chakikui pointed to the other side of the river, to a cliff face that rose on the far side.

"The entrance is through there," Jembe explained.

Lena squinted but failed to see anything but sheer rock.

Roland let out a small groan. They all turned to him. "Look near the waterline. I can make out a shadow of a tunnel entrance. Only the top foot of it is showing. I think that's what they're talking about."

"So the entrance is flooded," Gray said.

"What else did you expect?" Seichan said with a sigh. "If this is Atlantis, wasn't it supposed to have been sunk under the water?"

Gray gave a sorrowful shake of his head. "Looks like we're going to have to swim."

Lena's reaction was stronger. Her breath quickened and her heart began to pound with trepidation. She remembered another set of flooded tunnels, a place she had barely escaped from the first time.

Roland must have sensed her fear and offered his support. "At least this time we're not being shot at."

12:04 A.M.

The wind whipped and snapped at Shu Wei's clothing as she fell through the well of mists. She studied her landing zone, searching through goggles fixed with night-vision equipment. The gear was toggled and attuned to pick out heat signatures.

Below her, the largest object glowed a fiery crimson, marking the location of her target's helicopter, its engines still warm, casting off a discrete signature against the cool background of the cloud forest.

Smaller pools of fire marked the other members of her strike team as they spiraled down, parachuting into the forest clearing.

Finally, a brighter spark bloomed at ground level. It marked a flare ignited by her second-in-command, Major Sergeant Kwan. He had landed and was signaling the all clear.

She pulled her chute's cord and heard the satisfying flutter of fabric unfurling above her head. Then her body yanked hard into her rig's straps as the canopy snapped open. Her plummet from the single-engine jump plane far overhead braked swiftly. She expertly manipulated her lines to follow the others in a tight spiral into the small clearing.

Moments later, she skirted past the glowing bulk of the helicopter and landed with a soft bump to the forest floor. Cutting loose her canopy, she shed her rig, removed her goggles, and took in the scene that presented itself.

Major Sergeant Kwan knelt over a body sprawled facedown beside the aircraft. A shotgun rested a meter from the figure's outstretched arm.

Kwan straightened. "I had no choice but to take out the pilot."

She frowned. It was disappointing. She had hoped to interrogate the man before dispatching him. But ultimately it wouldn't matter.

"The targets are already gone?" she asked.

He nodded and stood, but not before she noted him pocketing a locket of hair, a trophy he must have cut from the pilot's head. With each death, the Black Crow always demanded his toll.

She didn't scold him for it and stayed focused on the task at hand. "How far ahead are they?"

"Best estimate. No more than forty minutes."

So, closer . . . but not close enough.

Still, she was content with their progress. The team could have come by helicopter and made better time, but the noise would have carried far, alerted their quarry. It was worth the sacrifice of minutes to maintain their cover.

"We've already disabled the aircraft," Kwan said. "The enemy won't be leaving the way they arrived."

They won't be leaving at all.

She stared off into the shadowy forest. Her team would go dark from here, moving forward with night-vision gear.

"Have Zhu and Feng head out," she ordered.

The two were her team's best trackers.

Kwan gave a bow of his head and headed off to get everyone ready.

Shu Wei stood quietly, listening to the whisper of wind, the whirring of gnats, and the twitter of distant birdsong. She imagined the number of predators hidden in the dark forest, while certain of one detail . . .

The true threat to her targets had just arrived.

With everyone ready, Kwan eyed her, awaiting her signal.

Very good.

She stepped into that shroud of darkness.

Now to end this.

21

I have to do something . . .

Maria stood with her back to the arch of windows that overlooked the hybrid habitat. She kept her fist snarled in the collar of Dr. Han's scrubs and a scalpel held at his neck. From the corner of her eye, she had watched the grate to Kowalski's small cage begin to rise, exposing him to the beasts below.

The giant silverback still remained squatted on his haunches a yard away, patiently waiting for its meal to be let loose.

Maria searched for a way to help Kowalski. Her gaze settled on the locked cabinet that held a double-barreled tranquilizer rifle. She called over to the surgical team, pressing the scalpel more firmly to Dr. Han's throat.

"Someone unlock that case!" she ordered.

A figure rushed forward. It was the young nurse who had shown herself to be the most cooperative of the group. She reached the case, tapped a code into its electronic lock, and opened the door.

Maria shoved Dr. Han away. As the surgeon stumbled and fell to his knees, she tossed the scalpel aside and snatched the double-barreled rifle from its rack. She had been trained with such weapons as part of her orientation at the primate center. She quickly checked to see if the rifle was preloaded. She was relieved to find a pair of feathered darts resting in the chambers of the two barrels.

Still, she grabbed and pocketed another pair of capped darts from a tray on the cabinet's bottom shelf, then secured the rifle and pointed it at the surgical staff. "Stay back," she warned.

A small groan drew her attention to the operating table. Baako stirred and lifted his bandaged head from the crown of stainless steel that had once trapped his skull. His eyes fluttered as the short-acting sedative cleared his system. Dazed, he rolled and fell off the table, but he had enough wits to catch himself. He landed on all fours and twisted in her direction.

The nurses and surgeons cleared out of his way.

"Baako," she called to him. "Come to Mama."

He hooted and scrambled toward her, staying low, still woozy.

Not daring to wait any longer, she swung to the gated casement built into one section of the observation windows. She struggled with the latch, trying to free it while staring below.

By now the door to Kowalski's cage stood fully open. The big man remained within the shelter, his back to the steel door. The silverback had also stayed put. It still squatted at the threshold, like a cat crouched at a mouse hole, waiting for its prey to run out.

But Maria knew this standoff could not last.

As she continued to fight the latch, Baako reached her side and leaned hard against her hip. Perhaps noting her attention, he lifted his face enough to peer below, too.

"C'mon," she said, swearing at the damned latch.

The young nurse joined her. She shifted Maria's panicked hands aside and freed the casement with an experienced series of turns and tugs on the latch. The two-foot-wide window slid open.

"Thank you," Maria mumbled.

She lifted the rifle through the opening, but she had taken too long.

Down below, Kowalski burst out of his cage.

12:07 P.M.

Bring it, you fucking monkeys . . .

Kowalski dove low through the open door. He had waited as long as possible, knowing the patience of the beast outside would not last forever. When a low rumble of irritation had flowed out of that massive chest, Kowalski took this as a signal. As the silverback lifted an arm and reached toward the cage, Kowalski was already in motion.

He ducked that meaty paw and rolled under the raised arm. Once past the mountainous bulk, he shoved to his feet and leaped away.

Other beasts crowded their leader, but Kowalski's sudden flight had them momentarily confounded. *Momentarily* being the operative word. Still, some were startled enough—likely still on edge from the blaring sirens—to stumble out of his way. Or maybe they feared the silverback enough not to claim the prize that the massive beast had set his sights upon for these past three hours.

No matter the reason, Kowalski took full advantage of it to break through the cordon of muscle, bone, and teeth and get into the clear.

Behind him, an ear-shattering bellow erupted.

He didn't have to glance back to know its source. Instead, he sprinted for the section of the habitat that offered the best refuge, where boulders littered the floor amid concrete trees.

A new noise rose in counterpoint to the roar: a heavy thumping.

Kowalski reached the rock-strewn section of the habitat and skidded around, coming to a stop. The silverback stood before the open cage. Thwarted, it had reared up on its hind legs, pounding its wide, leathery chest with both fists in a dramatic display of gorilla rage. Ropes of spittle flew from its lips as it bared razor-sharp teeth evolved to rip flesh from bone.

Panting, Kowalski crouched. He struggled for his next move, expecting that half-ton bulk to come charging in his direction, as unstoppable as a freight train under a full head of steam. He searched for any place to hide, even for a breath or two.

I have to keep clear of that—

Then something barreled into him from behind, shattering his ribs with a cracking flare of agony. The impact tossed him headlong across the floor. He twisted in midair and crashed down onto his uninjured side. Beyond his toes, he spotted a familiar black-furred gorilla, the same one who had confronted Kowalski at the cage door earlier, before being shoved aside by the silverback.

Apparently the bastard still held a grudge.

12:08 P.M.

The howl of fury echoed up to Maria's perch at the open casement window. It rose from the dark-furred gorilla hybrid who had bowled into Kowalski, knocking him out of his hiding spot. The beast vaulted over a boulder and dove at Kowalski, going for the kill.

Maria jerked her rifle's aim from the silverback to the more immediate threat. She fired at the younger male gorilla, but feared she was already too late.

Kowalski rolled to the side at the last moment, just missing getting smashed under the plummeting bulk of the gorilla. Still, as the beast landed, it lashed out with a hand and grabbed Kowalski's thigh. His body was whipped forward like a rag doll.

Maria centered her rifle and peered through the telescopic sight, unsure if the first dart had struck the beast. She squeezed the trigger again. The rifle blast stung her ears, but she resisted blinking, concentrating. This time she spotted red feathers sticking out of the neck of the gorilla.

The male let go of Kowalski and pawed at its throat, knocking the barb away.

Its face swung up toward her, guessing the source of the assault. It rose to its feet and roared at her—then stumbled back. Tripping a step, it dropped heavily on its haunches.

For the tranquilizing effect to be that fast, her first shot must have also hit it. She hurriedly cracked the rifle open and reached inside her pocket for another load of darts. In her fumbling haste, one of them slipped between her fingers and dropped to her toes. Swearing, she slapped the other one into the weapon's chamber.

On the floor of the habitat, the young male collapsed to its side, its huge limbs going slack. But that beast wasn't the only threat.

Before she could finish fully reloading, the silverback bellowed its rage, rising to its full height. Even now Maria balked at its sheer size. While she understood the genetics that had birthed such a monster, her mind still struggled to accept it. She pictured the giant bones she had been shown yesterday, of *Meganthropus*, one of man's earliest ancestors, and recognized it wasn't only that hominin's massive *size* that had been engineered into these hybrids—but also its savage and xenophobic nature.

The silverback lowered to a fist and charged toward Kowalski. The man was still down on all fours, rattled and bruised. There was no way for him to get out of the way in time.

She fought her rifle through the window and fired the one loaded dart at the thundering beast, but the gorilla was moving too fast. She caught sight of a red bolt of feathers ricocheting off the limb of one of those faux trees.

Damn it . . .

She lunged for the other dart abandoned on the floor, but she knew she could never reload in time.

Someone else realized the same.

Before she could stop him, Baako leaped from her side and flung himself headfirst through the window. At the last moment, he hooked a hand on the sill, swung around, then dropped in a series of halting falls toward the floor, catching brief fingerholds on the coarse-hewn rock wall.

Maria called down to him. "Baako! Come back!"

For the first time in his young life, Baako ignored her.

12:09 P.M.

Monk huddled with Kimberly in the empty office. Sergeant Chin guarded the door while the Shaw brothers and Kong kept watch out in the halls.

"How much longer?" Monk asked.

Kimberly tapped furiously at a keyboard. She had already wired and plugged her satellite phone into the computer terminal via a side port. "Okay, I've accessed the security cameras. While I can't shut them down, I can *add* to their feed."

"Do it."

She brought up her phone's video folder and broadcast a stored file into the security camera's feed. "This should do it."

Monk nodded, clutching the radio in his hand. He had secured it from a guard whom they had ambushed shortly after entering the facility.

"I'm also going to scroll information at the bottom of the image I'm sending out," Kimberly said. "It'll list your radio's secure channel."

"You can do that?"

As answer, she simply frowned back at him.

Monk held up his other palm. By now he should've known better than to question his partner's abilities. "Okay, then let's hope this broadcast reaches the right audience."

12:10 P.M.

It appears I must do everything myself.

Jiaying Lau leaned on a table, her nose not far from the monitor's screen. She did her best to ignore the chaos inside the facility's security hub. She had already fielded calls from the Ministry of State Security and the deputy director of the Academy of Military Science. Word of the security breach had plainly extended beyond the borders of the facility.

She could guess the source of that leak.

Behind her, Chang Sun shouted orders into a radio, lighting a fire under the teams who were searching for the intruders. When he found them—which he would with time—he would certainly use their capture to make himself look good, while undermining her role. She could all but smell the ambition wafting from the sweat on his brow.

Still, she kept her focus on another potential embarrassment, another black mark threatening her record. On the monitor, she had watched everything tipping toward ruin within the vivisection lab. Dr. Crandall had secured a tranquilizer rifle and was attempting to aid her companion in the Ark. The matter should have already played out to its bloody end, a necessary lesson for Maria.

Then, even worse, Baako had leaped through the window and dropped into the heart of the Ark. Jiaying had spent considerable resources to obtain that unique specimen, including losing a valuable covert asset in the process. To end up with her prize torn to pieces by her own hybrids could prove more than disastrous to her career—she could end up with a bullet through her skull for this failure.

She pounded a fist on the table, intending to deal with this situation personally. But before she could turn away, a smaller window popped up in the corner of the monitor. She leaned closer. The new grainy video showed a soldier strapped to a chair. A pistol was pressed to his temple by a captor who stood out of view.

"Enlarge that image," she ordered the tech.

Murmurs rose behind her, coming from the other stations. A glance around revealed the same video playing in the corner of *all* of the camera monitors. Chang joined her, his eyes pinched with confusion.

"What is this?" he asked.

"You tell me." She pointed to the screen. "This is your system."

"Someone must have hacked into it."

He shifted closer as the technician zoomed into the new feed. The image grew enough to reveal the face of the threatened soldier. Jiaying recognized the familiar features, even with a mouth gag in place.

"Is that your brother?"

Chang balled a fist at his side. "Gao . . ."

Jiaying pointed to the scrolling number at the bottom of the screen. It was a demand to call a secure radio channel. She could guess who would answer that call.

"Can you trace where this is coming from?" Jiaying asked.

Chang exhaled sharply. "Yes. It will take a minute or so."

But would the Americans still be there by then?

Chang gripped the technician's shoulder, both urging him and threatening him to obtain that information swiftly. The man typed vigorously, chasing through screens.

Jiaying glared at the monitor. "As I suspected all along, it appears your brother *was* the source of the leak. Whether inadvertently or not, he must have led the enemy to our doorstep."

Chang seethed, clearly recognizing the same.

She turned and jabbed a finger into the lieutenant colonel's chest. "So clean up your brother's mistake. Lure those intruders out into the open by any means necessary and eliminate them." She glanced toward the feed from the Ark. "I'm heading off to protect our assets before all of this comes to ruin."

She stormed out of the security hub, intending to regain control, but her mind already ran through various contingencies if matters grew out of hand.

During the construction of this facility she'd had countermeasures covertly built into the infrastructure. She would not be brought down. She would not suffer the dishonor of this facility being wrested from her hands.

If I fall, we all do.

12:12 P.M.

The radio buzzed in Monk's hand.

Looks like it's showtime.

He climbed into the electric vehicle they had commandeered: a military green truck with an open bed in the back. Sergeant Chin took the wheel, while Kong and the Shaw brothers hauled the unconscious Chinese driver into a neighboring lab.

Monk lifted the buzzing radio as he joined Kimberly in the front seat. "Call's coming on the secure channel. Seems your message was received."

He leaned closer to her as he pressed a speaker button so his partner could listen in and translate if necessary.

A voice answered sharply in Mandarin.

Kimberly whispered. "He's demanding to know who we are."

Monk lifted the radio, trusting the caller spoke English. "You know who we are. And I'm guessing this is *Zhōngxiào* Sun." He hoped he had pronounced the rank of lieutenant colonel correctly. "Brother to Gao Sun."

There was no response. As radio silence stretched, Monk tapped Chin's shoulder, setting the truck in motion once the Shaws and Kong were aboard, jumping into the back bed.

Monk cast a worried glance toward Kimberly.

If this didn't work—

Then an answer came, the speaker's words stiff with fury. "This is Lieutenant Colonel Sun. If you wish to live, you will turn yourselves in immediately . . . and free my brother."

Monk heard the catch in the other's voice at the end.

Good.

Kimberly had obtained additional information about the two brothers from her intelligence sources. Chang was the older of the two, married, with a young daughter. Gao was single. The pair had lost both their parents when they were teenagers and joined the army shortly thereafter, rising within the same unit. Kimberly estimated that such a tragedy and circumstance likely bonded the two very closely.

Now to turn that to our advantage.

Monk raised the radio. "If you ever want to see your brother alive again, you'll listen to what I have to say."

As he waited for a response, the truck swept down a long hallway, passing a series of sophisticated labs, chock-full of stainless steel equipment and cages. So far they had encountered only a handful of personnel. It seemed the alarms had triggered some sort of facility lockdown.

"What are your demands?" Chang asked tersely.

"Simple. You help us. We help you."

Another long pause, then Chang's voice returned, softer now. "How?"

"If you assist us, we will leave your brother safe, and with ironclad intelligence that will implicate Major General Lau as a co-conspirator in all of this. She will be the scapegoat. For every *win* you help us achieve over the next hour, she *loses*."

Monk held his breath. The success of this plan hinged on the animosity between Chang and his superior, but would professional ambition outweigh loyalty in this regard?

"How do I know you can do what you claim?" Chang asked.

"Have we not penetrated your facility?" Monk asked. "That should be proof enough of our skill and expertise."

"But why should I trust you?"

"You don't have much choice. If we fail to give an all clear to our operatives in Beijing, your brother's body will be discovered near the U.S. embassy, with clear evidence that he was trying to escape to that safe zone." Monk ratcheted up the threat. "And on his remains will be found evidence implicating you and your wife as American spies."

Monk let that sink in for several breaths, then finished. "Listen. If we get what we want, you turn out to be a hero, while Major General Lau is taken down. We fail, and you suffer along with your family, while Lau basks in the glory of stopping us. The choice is yours, *Zhōngxiào* Sun."

This time, there was not even a pause. "What do you want me to do?"

Monk grinned at Kimberly, then spoke. "Tell us where the others are and clear a path for us to them."

Kimberly had her satellite phone out. She pulled up a schematic of the facility that she had hacked from a computer terminal earlier.

As Chang passed on the necessary information, she nodded. "Got it," she whispered. "I know where they are."

"What else?" Chang asked bitterly.

"Just one more thing."

"What?"

Monk told him, then signed off.

Kimberly faced Monk, letting out a long sigh. "Can we trust him?"

He pointed ahead. "We're about to find out."

As they set off on the path given them, another worry set in.

What if we're already too late?

12:13 P.M.

The ground trembled as the massive silverback pounded toward Kowalski. Still, on his hands and his knees, he couldn't do much more than brace himself against what was to come. Still, he rolled toward the snoring bulk of the younger black-furred hybrid sprawled to his left, doing his best to seek any shelter.

Fat lot of good it'll do me.

Then a screeching howl echoed throughout the habitat, seeming to come from every direction at once as it reverberated off the rock walls. The cry was full of anger and threat.

Now what?

He lifted his head to see the silverback skidding to a stop a yard away. It leaned on one arm while craning around for the source of the sound.

Kowalski did the same while taking the chance to retreat farther back, crawling toward the boulder pile in the center of the habitat.

Then he spotted a dark shadow bound away from the wall below the observation windows. The shape moved swiftly, leaping and racing toward Kowalski. It took him half a breath to recognize Baako.

No . . .

What was he doing down here?

With a final hurdle, Baako landed in a crouch next to Kowalski. Panting, the little guy faced the mountain of muscle only yards away. He lifted to his feet and thumped his chest with both fists, challenging the alpha beast of this habitat.

Not smart, kid.

"Baako, go!" Kowalski yelled, waving an arm, which triggered a fresh flare of agony from his broken ribs. "Get outta here!"

Baako held his ground.

The silverback remained rooted in place, clearly trying to comprehend this intrusion into its domain, not to mention the defiant posturing of such a small creature. But the confusion quickly wore off, replaced with irritation and anger.

A bellow burst from its wide chest. The half-ton beast lunged forward and lashed out with a thick arm—but Baako was no longer there.

The young gorilla leaped high, springing and somersaulting over the silverback's shoulder to land on the monster's rump.

The silverback reared up, flinging around.

Baako jumped away as another arm came swinging at him. This time he failed to get completely out of the way in time. An elbow clipped his hip and sent him flying. Still, he managed to twist before landing and rolled on a shoulder, tumbling across the floor.

The silverback thundered after him, pounding its fists into the rock.

The other denizens of the habitat—initially stunned by the strangeness—slowly reacted. With the silverback's attention diverted elsewhere, they closed toward Kowalski.

Not good.

He continued his retreat toward the boulder field while watching Baako flee from that avalanche of muscle and claw behind him. Kowalski reached the rock pile and ducked behind a boulder. In one hand he grabbed a chunk of stone and in the other a concrete limb that had broken off one of the fake trees. He intended to go caveman on these monsters if necessary.

He flattened his back against the rock, noting Baako had begun to slow, clearly tiring out. The silverback now huffed at his heels.

Kowalski cringed, afraid to watch; then Baako juked to the left, ducking clear of the other's path. The silverback could not turn so swiftly. The momentum of all that mass could not match Baako's lithe agility. Still, the silverback heaved around and skidded through loose shale, bunching its tree-trunk-sized legs under its bulk. Before even coming to a stop, it bounded after Baako, who was unfortunately aiming straight for Kowalski's hiding spot.

Kowalski rose into view, waving Baako off, pointing to the open window.

"Get your ass up there!"

Like everyone else in his life, Baako ignored him.

The little guy made a final leap in his direction, his arms straining for Kowalski, but luck and speed could last only so long. The silverback caught Baako by the ankle and swung his small body to the side, ripping Baako away from Kowalski's reach.

No!

12:14 P.M.

Pain rips through Baako's leg as his body is wrenched around. The rock walls blur. Still, he knows he must keep struggling. Deep in his chest, he knows anything else is death.

Still caught, his body is flung high above the monster. The beast is a horror out of one of Mama's bedtime stories. It intends to swing him down and smash him to the floor. Knowing this, Baako wriggles around and bites the hand clamped to his ankle.

A roar rises; the grip loosens.

Baako yanks free and tumbles toward the ground. His arms and legs flail, seeking some way to catch himself. Then monstrously powerful fingers snatch him around the waist, grabbing him out of the air, squeezing so hard that he cannot breathe.

The monster has him again, bellowing with rage and blood. Jaws open wide. Fangs dive for Baako's throat. His eyes roll in terror, finding a face far above, so scared like him.

He gets enough breath to hoot to her.

Bye, Mama . . .

Baako's final feeble bleat reached Maria, shattering her heart.

She squeezed her rifle's trigger in a maternal need to protect, but the pin struck an empty chamber. She had already used the last of the tranquilizer darts, reloading three times during the brief battle below. She had concentrated her fire upon the silverback, but the beast had moved too fast, escaping the darts. The only shot that had struck home was one that hit a lumbering female that had gotten too close to Kowalski's hiding spot.

The sting of that impact had been enough to frighten the creature away, but it would take another minute or so for the sedative to knock it out.

That's if one dart was even enough for such massive beasts.

With an empty rifle and no more ammunition, she could do nothing but watch the silverback prepare to rip out Baako's throat.

Suddenly a large rock flew through the air and struck the silverback between the eyes. The beast paused long enough to look up, more surprised than hurt by the assault.

Kowalski mounted one of the boulders, bearing aloft a club of concrete.

"Pick on someone your own size, you furry bastard!"

12:15 P.M.

Not that I'm your size . . .

Even standing on the boulder, Kowalski was dwarfed by the towering silverback. It still clutched Baako, the little guy forgotten for the moment.

"C'mon!" Kowalski challenged the beast, beckoning with his weapon, hoping it would let Baako go.

The silverback stepped toward him, then stumbled slightly to the side. It caught itself by grabbing at one of the concrete trees. Branches snapped under its teetering weight. The beast fell to a knee.

What the hell . . .

The rock he'd pitched couldn't have done *that* much damage. It was like wafting a pea at a bull.

Still, the silverback let go of Baako and planted a fist on the ground to keep itself upright. Free now, Baako scampered over to the boulders.

Kowalski glanced around. The other beasts had frozen in place, apparently intimidated by their alpha being so stunned. The silverback dropped to a hip, weaving in a struggle to stay up. Only then did Kowalski note the bloom of red feathers sticking out of the silverback's rump.

He glanced to Maria. Had she managed to nail the bastard after all? But she looked equally shocked.

She shouted down to him and pointed toward the steel door. "Run! One dart's not enough to knock it out!"

12:16 p.m.

Maria realized what must have happened. Earlier, she had never found the tranquilizer dart she had dropped on the floor. She now understood what had become of it.

Before Baako had leapt into the Ark, he must have snatched the abandoned needle. Back in Lawrenceville, she had taught him about tranquilizer guns, as they were used as a common means of restraint at the primate center. She had wanted him to understand that the animals incapacitated in such a manner were not dead, but only sleeping.

Still, she was never sure how much he had understood.

Apparently it was enough.

Below, the silverback continued to totter, struggling to shake off the sedative's effect.

Taking advantage of the situation, Kowalski and Baako took off toward the steel door that led out of the Ark. As they ran, the other gorillas began to stir, drawn by the motion, likely growing more confident with the silverback incapacitated.

She swung to the young nurse who had helped her before. "You have to get that door open for them."

The nurse looked forlorn. "I cannot. Not from up here. Someone has to be down there and place their palm on the reader outside."

And we're all locked in here.

With a sinking heart, she turned back to the window. Kowalski

and Baako continued their flight for the door, drawing the hybrids after
them.

But they're going the wrong way.

12:17 P.M.

As Kowalski dove into the cage that enclosed the exit door, he heard his
name shouted, in a voice full of urgency and fear. He glanced over his
shoulder.

Maria called to him. "I can't open the door from up here! You have to
get back to me."

Something tumbled out the window and unfurled along the rock wall.
A fire hose.

She clearly wanted them to climb out of here.

Easier said than done.

Kowalski lowered his gaze to the growing wall of fur and muscle gathering outside the cage. There was no getting through that crowd. While he
might be able to create enough of a distraction to allow Baako to make a
break for it, he doubted the young gorilla would leave his side.

Baako tugged on Kowalski's arm, drawing his attention. The gorilla
splayed out his thumb and pinkie and thrust his hand down in a clear sign.

[*Stay*]

Before Kowalski could react, Baako bounded out of the cage and
loped straight toward the herd. He favored one leg, but he still managed
to leapfrog through the group at the last moment, agilely avoiding a few
surprised attempts to grab him.

So much for not abandoning me.

As the hybrids closed toward him, he tried tugging at the cage door,
but it was locked in its tracks.

Then a fearsome bellow shook through the cavernous habitat, rising
from that monstrous silverback.

Kowalski retreated to the steel door, consoled by one thought.

At least Baako got away.

12:18 p.m.

Baako drops the broken stone club and flees.

A breath ago, he had snatched the tool from the floor and crossed to the monster. He found its eyelids hanging low, its breathing deep. Without slowing, Baako had leaped and swung the length of rock with all the strength in his arms. The club had shattered across the ridge above those dull eyes, snapping them fully open again.

Earlier, he had wanted it to go to sleep; now he needs it awake.

A roar chases Baako across the floor again. Pain shoots up his right leg, so he runs on all fours, needing to go fast. The monster rages after him.

He flees not toward Mama . . . because Mama is safe from the monsters.

Instead, he heads toward another member of his family.

Kowalski gritted his teeth, expecting the worst as he heard the silverback thundering again in his direction. He did not expect to see Baako suddenly vault over the wall of hybrids that held him trapped. The young gorilla hurtled past that group, struck the floor, and shot headlong into the cage.

Kowalski caught Baako in his arms, but the impact slammed him against the steel door, knocking the air from his lungs. Still, he hugged tightly to Baako.

Past the kid's shoulder, the mass of gorilla hybrids shattered apart as the silverback burst through them like a freight train. Still dazed, the beast could not stop fast enough and crashed sidelong against the opening of the cave door.

Kowalski cringed from the impact of that mountain of flesh, fearing it might still crush them. Instead, the silverback's bulk rebounded off the wall, bowling more of the hybrids out the way.

Baako grabbed Kowalski's hand and tugged him toward the open doorway.

He understood.

Let's get out of here while the getting is good.

They fled past the stunned bulk of the silverback and through the chaotic confusion of the others. But he knew such turmoil wouldn't last forever.

He raced across the floor, ignoring the agony lancing from his left side.

When they reached the wall under the windows, Kowalski scooped Baako by the waist and tossed him onto the fire hose. Furry hands caught hold, but Baako glanced back, hooting his worry.

"Go! I'm right behind you!"

As proof, Kowalski grasped the hose and followed as Baako began climbing.

From three stories above, Maria called down at them. "Hurry! They're coming!"

He didn't bother to look. What good would it do? He hauled with his arms and dug with his toes. He envied Baako, who scampered up and reached Maria well ahead of him.

As Baako ducked through the window, Maria's face appeared. He read the fear etched across her features, saw the urging in her eyes.

Hurry.

12:19 P.M.

As Maria watched, a score of the gorilla hybrids bounded toward them. Even the silverback rolled to its feet, bellowing and looking in their direction. Baako's blow—followed by the chase and the impact against the wall—must have raised the creature's blood pressure enough to shake off the sedative.

It began lumbering toward them, drawing stragglers in its massive wake. With the pack's bloodlust spiked higher, several of the beasts began to attack one another, the larger creatures ripping into the smaller ones, demonstrating again the level of savagery inherited from their engineered genes.

By now Kowalski was halfway up the hose, but it wasn't high enough. Maria glanced to the row of steel boxes positioned below the arch of windows, remembering the nurse's description of the electrical barrier coded to the silver collars around the hybrids' necks. The invisible shield was meant to keep the animals confined below, shocking their collars if they climbed too high.

Kowalski wore no such collar.

"You have to get above the electrical fence," she warned him.

He frowned up at her, not understanding.

"Just keep going!" she urged.

He put his head down and fought faster, struggling to gain ground. Then his grip slipped and he slid a full yard before grabbing hold of the hose again.

He hung there, catching his breath, as the first hybrid reached the wall below him. Luckily it was one of the smaller ones, standing at best seven feet. It jumped and swatted at Kowalski, brushing the man's heels with its fingertips.

That immediate threat was enough to further stoke the fire under Kowalski. He clawed his way up faster, but he was clearly in pain. Sweat beaded and ran down his grimacing face.

The larger beasts reached the wall below and began to climb the hewn rock, digging nails and toes into crevices and pits.

He'd never make it.

Then the hose shifted beside Maria.

She glanced back and saw that Baako had grabbed its length. He tugged, trying to draw Kowalski up faster by hauling on the hose.

Why didn't I think of that?

She braced her feet against the wall and added her strength.

Then the young nurse joined her. Others of the surgical team came to their aid, rallying together, momentarily setting aside their differences. They had all watched the valiant battle below and honored that effort now. Even if it all came to naught once the dust settled, at the moment they refused to lose the man to the beasts below.

Working together, they reeled Kowalski up to the window.

He grabbed the sill with one arm, then the other, but he looked too weak to haul himself over the casement. Maria let go of the hose and pulled him the rest of the way through. He fell heavily to the floor and rolled onto his back.

His lungs wheezed with each breath, but he gasped out, "What . . . what were you saying about some fence?"

A frizzling electrical pop sounded from beyond the window, accompanied by a sharp cry of pain. Maria caught sight of a hybrid tumbling from its perch on the wall. As it fell, a spiral of smoke trailed from the steel collar around its neck. The other beasts either stopped in place or dropped heavily to the floor.

"Doesn't matter now," Maria said and bent down to assist him to his feet.

Baako rushed over and bear-hugged the large man once he was up.

"Thank you for keeping Baako safe," she said.

Kowalski kept a protective hand on the young gorilla's shoulder. "Think it was more the other way around." He turned and glared at the surgical team. "Any of you going to try to stop us from leaving here?"

Small shakes of heads answered him—not that it mattered.

"We're locked in here," Maria explained. "Ever since the sirens blew."

"So we're still trapped."

She touched his elbow. "But at least we're safe for the immediate—"

The lights flickered and went out, sinking the lab into darkness.

No one spoke until Kowalski finally muttered, "You had to say that."

Baako moved to her side and grabbed her arm. He didn't like the dark, but after several tense breaths, crimson emergency lights flared along the top of the walls.

She let out a sigh of relief.

Kowalski offered another thought. "Maybe with the power off, we can get out of here."

He rushed across the length of the room and tugged at the giant steel sliders, but they still refused to budge. He put his fists on his hips, frowning at the doors as if that would open them.

Baako's fingers tightened on Maria's arm. She looked down and saw that his gaze was fixed to the fire hose, which still ran from the wall to the casement window.

Its length twitched and thrummed.

Oh, no.

She turned toward the window as a massive scarred hand reached into view and grabbed the sill.

With the power off, the electrical fence was down.

Backing away in horror, she warned the trapped group. "They're coming!"

22

Gray gasped at the cold as he waded into the dark pool, shattering the perfect reflection of the stars and moon in its mirrored surface. The others followed, splashing after him. Chakikui and Jembe remained on the bank behind him. The elder had honored his pledge to bring them to the lost city.

Apparently that obligation ended at its doorstep.

Left to their own now, Gray led the three others across the pond. He had to swim the last of the distance to reach the mouth of the tunnel that opened in the cliff face on the opposite bank. With the way ahead flooded, there was only a foot of clearance between the waterline and the roof of the tunnel.

As he reached the entrance, he discovered his boots could touch bottom. Ducking his head inside the tunnel, he lifted a waterproof flashlight high.

"Down a ways deeper, it looks like the roof lowers even more," he warned.

"Can we get through?" Lena asked.

"Don't know. We may have to swim and explore for air pockets."

She did not look happy about this prospect.

He wasn't exactly thrilled himself.

Roland waded next to Gray. "From Petronio Jaramillo's account of his journey to the lost library, he claimed he *did* have to swim underwater to reach it."

Seichan waved them onward. "Enough talk. The only way we'll know if anything is actually down there is to just go look."

He heard the clear skepticism in her voice. And she was right. This might all be a wild-goose chase, but the only way they would know was to do what she suggested.

Just go look.

Gray pushed into the tunnel, half swimming along the passageway. The air inside was dank, smelling of wet rock and moss. The beam of his flashlight illuminated some distance down the passageway and shone far into the crystal-clear waters, making it appear as if he floated in glass.

Murmurs rose behind him as they proceeded single file, with Seichan bringing up the rear.

"The walls," Lena whispered to Roland. "They look too smooth to be natural."

Gray ran his fingertips along the roof, realizing she was right. The passageway also ran too straight. They continued in silence, mostly because the water soon rose above their lips. Gray kept his nose high, breathing hard through his nostrils, feeling a panicky edge of claustrophobia set in. From the harsh noises behind him, he wasn't the only one.

Then as he took another step forward, the floor vanished under his boot. Caught by surprise, his head slipped underwater. His flashlight came with him. The beam revealed a set of steps leading down from here.

He twisted and rose back to the surface, careful not to hit his head. He lifted his lips high enough to speak. "Stairs," he gasped out. "Everyone stay here. I'm going to swim down and see if there's any way forward."

"Be careful," Lena managed to sputter out.

Gray intended to do just that. He chided himself for not thinking of renting scuba gear in Cuenca. Then again, who knew if there were any dive shops in that remote mountain village? Either way, if this was as far as they could go unequipped, they could always return tomorrow with proper gear.

Still, a sense of urgency nagged at him. He wanted to blame it on the long plane ride getting here, but he knew it was more than that. Trusting his gut, he took a deep lungful of air and dove underwater.

Kicking hard, he followed the beam of his flashlight down the steep stairs. Silt disturbed by his passage wafted around him, clouding the clear waters. As pressure built in his ears, he finally reached the bottom of the stairs and discovered another dark passageway extending ahead.

He paused, debating whether to continue or turn back.

Clenching his jaws, he pushed off the last step and swam ahead, both drawn forward by the mystery and impelled by the tension behind him. Small chambers opened to either side. The sweep of his lights revealed obscure objects buried in silt and caked with algae. With no breath for sightseeing, he forged on without stopping.

Still, the rooms were clear evidence of prior habitation.

At last the passageway ended at another stair, this one rising in a tight spiral.

He cast his beam up, his lungs aching for air. He knew he was at the point of no return. Literally. He had enough breath to make it back to the others—or he could take his chances and continue forward.

He remembered Roland's account of Jaramillo's story. The man had claimed there was a way through, but that was decades ago, when Jaramillo was a boy. Still, there was no telling if this subterranean system had flooded more thoroughly over the passing years . . . or if these tunnels were even the same ones traversed by the young Jaramillo.

Gray shoved aside these doubts, trusting another's advice instead.

Seichan's words echoed in his head.

Just go look.

12:54 A.M.

Seichan slid past Roland and Lena, scraping along the walls to reach the front of the line. She pointed her flashlight down into the depths. Clouds of silt blocked the beam, hiding even the top step of the flooded stairs.

He's been gone too long.

Over the years, Seichan had been given ample evidence of Gray's competence, of his ability to survive the direst situations. But at this moment she was sure he was dead—not because of any failing of his, but because she didn't deserve the happiness she had found with him. Prior to meeting him, her life had been a solitary one, free of attachments. Though it was rife with bloodshed and terror, it had also made sense to her, requiring no moral ambiguity. Alone, it had been easy to armor herself against the world.

But that was no longer true—and she had conflicted feelings about it.

She sometimes found herself lying next to him in bed, watching him breathe, teetering between holding him tight in her arms to keep him safe and wanting to smother him with a pillow so she could be free.

In this moment, though, she had no moral ambiguity, only certainty and determination. She swept her flashlight through the murk, her heart pounding in her ears, knowing what she wanted.

Get your ass back here, Gray. Don't you leave me.

As if summoned by this thought, the clouds of silt blew thicker toward her. Then a glowing shape dove up. She fell back, giving him room.

Gray surfaced, raising his lips and nose to the tunnel roof. He sucked in great gulps of air. She grabbed him—not caring if he was still out of breath—and pulled those cold lips to hers and kissed him deeply.

He initially stiffened, surprised—then scooped an arm around her and drew her closer. When he pulled back, his eyes glinted with amusement.

"So you were worried?" he teased.

She pushed him away. "Only because I goddamn well know you couldn't have held your breath for that long. You must've found something."

Lena spoke up behind her. "What did you find?"

Gray grinned back at the woman. "I hope you're a strong swimmer."

1:08 A.M.

How much farther?

With her lungs screaming for air, Lena followed at Roland's heels, her gaze fixed to the glow of Gray's flashlight ahead. The man led them up a spiral staircase that seemed to go on forever. She began to dribble bubbles from her lips to ease the strain in her chest, to fool her body into thinking she was about to take a breath.

Then Roland shifted to the side, coming to a stop above her. She shot past him and her head burst out of the water and into open air. She took several desperate breaths.

Thank God . . .

Seichan surfaced next to her. She exhaled one hard breath, looking little bothered by the long swim.

Irritated, Lena turned away and did her best to gain her bearings.

They had risen into a flooded chamber. The stone ceiling stretched a yard above their heads. After the confines of the tunnel, the extra room and breathing space felt cavernous in comparison. A wide set of stairs climbed out of the water ahead of her.

Gray held his flashlight high as he kicked toward the steps.

Lena followed with the others.

Once there, Roland helped her climb out of the pool and onto the stairs. He craned around. "It's warmer in here," he noted.

She realized he was right. Even soaked to the skin, she felt the warmth and humidity of the place, more like what she had expected to find in a jungle rain forest. There was also a distinctly sulfurous scent to the air.

"A sign of geothermal activity," Gray explained, glancing over to Roland. "Didn't you mention this region of the Andes was unusually volcanic?"

"That's right. It's why the soil here is so rich."

Seichan shook excess water from her clothes and limbs. "No wonder whoever built this place chose these tunnels. Comes with built-in heat."

Lena pointed to the steps. "Where do these lead?"

"Come see." Gray set off again. "I explored only as far as the top of this staircase. To make sure it wasn't merely a dead end."

Roland clicked on his flashlight to better illuminate their way up. The stairs ended at a wide landing. As she reached the top, she halted next to Roland, who had frozen in midstep.

The beam of his flashlight blazed across an archway ahead, framing a long hall. The arch was made of gold, sculpted into an elaborate scaffolding of bones and skulls, all appearing to be human. Over time, the humidity and sulfur had left a darker tarnish in the sculpture's deeper crevices, but the bulk of gold remained brilliant.

"Amazing," Roland sighed out.

And macabre, she added. *No wonder the natives who stumbled upon this place deemed it to be dangerous, especially with the stench of brimstone in the air.*

Lena felt a shiver of trepidation as she crossed under the archway.

The others seemed to have no such qualms. Gray led them forward, casting the beam of his flashlight down the long hall. The passageway hewn from the rock was wide and tall enough that a pair of elephants could have marched down its length side by side.

"Look at the walls." Roland washed his light from roof to floor. "They're covered in writing."

Lena drifted closer, studying the rows of script. With only a cursory glance, she recognized Sumerian writing, Egyptian hieroglyphics, Mayan glyphs, and strings of Greek letters. The languages were stacked one upon the other, rising all the way up the wall and down the length of the hall.

"It's like what we saw in the Chapel of Saint Eustace," Roland said.

Lena remembered the writing that Father Kircher had inscribed on its walls and what it represented.

The history of the written word . . .

She crouched and studied the bottommost row of writing—which was clearly the oldest. Here were the same sticklike characters she had seen inscribed on the standing stones in the cloud forest. She ran her fingertips along a few of those lines.

Am I looking at the very first written language?

She stood and stared at the others. "This must be some sort of record of the evolution of language."

"I think you're right." Roland set off down the hall, his gaze continuing to sweep everywhere. "And I wager Father Kircher got his idea about how to decorate his chapel from *this* place . . . which suggests Nicolas Steno must've walked this same hall and returned to tell his friend about it."

Gray searched the walls. "This certainly validates Father Crespi's claims. There's no doubt that these ancient builders had communication with the rest of the world."

Lena stared ahead, trying to picture what might lie beyond the reach of their lights, remembering the stories of a vast cavern system buried under the Andes, spreading far and wide under the continent. She sensed this was only one entrance to this place. According to the natives, Father Crespi's artifacts had come from throughout the surrounding jungle and rain forest, pulled from caverns, tunnels, and vine-covered ruins.

Seichan pointed. "Looks like the tunnel comes to an end up there."

They continued forward and discovered another set of stairs— spiraling down and away. They stopped and gathered at the top.

Roland sighed. "Let's hope this doesn't take us back into another flooded section."

"Only one way to find out." Gray headed down, leading them around and around.

Lena held her breath, expecting with every turn to find a black pool of water reflecting back their light. But as they continued to wind down, the stairs remained dry.

Roland voiced a significant concern. "Surely we must be well under the water table by now."

The thought drew a shiver from her.

Gray touched the walls. "This region of the structure must be sealed off from the surrounding floodwaters."

Lena found little consolation from this observation.

Finally the stairs ended and dumped into a circular room. It was as tall as the previous hall and wide enough that the beams of their lights barely illuminated the far side.

Seichan proved to have sharper eyes than hers. "Looks like another set of stairs lead out of here." She glanced to Gray. "Going even farther down."

Lena barely gave that shadowy side a glance. Neither did Roland, who cast Lena a look with his eyebrows held high. He crossed with her along the curving wall, which was cut and notched into thousands of small niches. The spaces sheltered sculptures of various animals, from as small as her thumb to as large as a full-size horse.

"It's like the gallery we discovered in Croatia," Roland said.

She nodded dully. "Only that was a fraction of this size."

Curiosity and awe drew her forward. She spotted animals representing every facet of life, from every corner of the world. Beetles with iridescent shields of crystal, golden-legged centipedes, crocodiles encrusted with emeralds, monkeys furred with filigrees of copper strands, bison and deer sprouting horns of ivory, scorpions armored in plates of black iron.

The upper levels were dominated by multitudes of birds, all feathered with crystal shards in a kaleidoscope of hues: hawks, sparrows, eagles, pelicans, hummingbirds. Some rested in nests or perched on golden boughs. Others inexplicably hung in midflight within their niches.

On the lowest tiers, life from under the sea or underground was captured in the finest details: porcelain fish, chains of ants, copper-colored lobsters, silver worms burrowing through spheres of quartz, and on and on.

Her gaze whirled at the overwhelming abundance.

"It's a record of life on the planet," Roland said, clearly awestruck. He pointed toward a hippopotamus sculpted of gold with black diamonds for eyes. "Including many that aren't indigenous to this continent."

"I think it's also a record of *art*," Lena added. "The skill to sculpt this garden of life demonstrates hundreds of techniques, encompassing artistic practices from across many cultures. From the smelting of various metals, to the cutting of crystals and gems, to the working of enamels and porcelains."

Lena swept her arm to cover the room. "In many ways, this represents the evolution of *knowledge* as thoroughly as the hall of writing above."

By now, they had circled the room and reached the set of far stairs. These steps led straight down instead of corkscrewing. Even from the

landing, the beam of Roland's flashlight reflected off the surfaces of whatever lay below.

"More gold," Gray noted.

Lena needed no urging to head down, drawn not by the promise of
treasure, but by the curiosity of what would be revealed next. The stairs
were wide enough for them to proceed shoulder to shoulder. Breaths were
held as the view into the next chamber opened up.

As they reached the bottom, Roland made the sign of the cross, then
touched Lena's arm. "We've been here before."

1:33 A.M.

Afraid to enter, Roland kept to the edge and shone his light around the
room. The space was the same size and shape as the gallery above, but here
every surface—floor, walls, ceiling—was covered in beaten gold and decorated with elaborate mosaics of crystalline tiles. It was like stepping into an
illuminated medieval manuscript. Even the motifs were similarly Gothic
with the rendering of people and animals in a stylized, stiff form, all set
amid elaborate whorls of vines, trees, and bushes.

Still, there was a distinctly familiar element to it all.

Lena understood, too. "It's like someone took those cave paintings in
Croatia and replicated them in gold and jewels."

He nodded and followed her as she entered with the others.

The walls showed a riotous display of life cavorting around them:
lions, herds of deer and bison, galloping horses, even a cave bear rearing
up on its hind legs. But here, set among the animals, were smaller figures,
clearly men and women.

Roland stepped closer, examining the features of one, composed of
tiles no larger than the nail of his pinkie. He hovered a finger along a
prominent brow and glanced to Lena for confirmation.

"I think it's supposed to represent one of the Neanderthal hybrids, like
Kircher's Eve," she whispered. "From the way they're depicted here, it's
like these people are trying to protect or preserve the animals. But I think
the art is meant to be more metaphorical."

Gray joined her. "How do you mean?"

"I think it's showing these people defending life in all its forms, perhaps as guardians of the future."

"Like the Watchers described in ancient texts," Roland realized.

"Or Plato's Atlanteans," Lena added.

"And they went by other names, too," he said and continued as the others all looked at him. "When I was reading about Crespi's belief in a lost civilization in Ecuador, I came across references to the Theosophical Society, which was founded in the late nineteenth century. They believed that a small group, what they called the Brotherhood of Saints, were the secret driving force behind mankind's development, by guarding and disseminating knowledge." He nodded to Lena. "Much like your own hypothesis of ancient teachers rising from the hybridization of Neanderthals and early man."

Seichan stood a few yards away, her face lifted high. "Watchers, Atlanteans, Saints, or whatever you want to call them . . . If these are *guardians*, then it's easy enough to tell what they were guarding against."

Roland understood. He craned his neck and stared beyond the animals and their handful of defenders—to the figures that loomed menacingly above. Back in Croatia, these figures had been ominous shadows cast by sculpted stalagmites. But here the enemy was depicted in as much detail as the beasts and their guardians.

He shifted his light to better illuminate those figures. They were shaggy-headed and giant-boned. Under craggy brows, their eyes shone with a fiery bloodlust. They attacked the animals around them with clubs and crude spears. But Seichan had stopped at the most gruesome portrayal: a pair of giants ripping apart a child, tearing the little one limb from limb.

"What are they supposed to be?" Gray asked.

"I don't know." Roland frowned. "Maybe these creatures were meant to be metaphorical, too. Some portrayal of the brutality of ignorance, illustrating what these guardians were defending against."

Lena shook her head. "No. The detail and conformation of these large figures are too accurate. Look at their faces, the rendering of their limbs. I think this was a *real* enemy."

Gray looked aghast. "Who?"

"Perhaps a competing hominin tribe, another branch of mankind's past. We know early man lived alongside more than just Neanderthals. There were small pockets of other tribes."

"But a species this *large*?" Seichan asked.

Lena shrugged. "Some offshoots of *Homo erectus* were considered to be veritable giants. Like a species called *Meganthropus,* or Large Man." She waved a hand to encompass the ring of art. "I think this is a depiction of a real war with this other tribe, a fight for the future of mankind, a battle between brawn and brain, between ignorance and intelligence."

Gray reached toward one of those monstrous figures. "If you're right, this enemy might have been the driving force that eventually united the Neanderthal hybrids. Without this external threat, the tribe of ancient teachers might never have been forged."

Lena nodded. "Perhaps such a danger also explains *why* these teachers needed a home of their own. A place to retreat from the world where they could study and learn in peace, preserving what was important while occasionally venturing forth to share that knowledge."

Roland stared toward yet another staircase on the far side of this room. "But what happened to them? Where did they go?"

As they all headed toward those dark stairs, he feared they might never know the truth—but he was equally scared they would.

1:47 A.M.

Gray led everyone down the wide stairs. The steps seemed to stretch forever ahead of him. He calculated they must be at least fifteen to twenty stories belowground. He pictured their group winding down into a dry well with water surrounding them on all sides.

How far down does this go?

He swiped sweat from his brow. Each level grew perceptibly hotter, the air heavier with sulfur, as if they were descending into hell.

Finally the end of the stairs appeared ahead. A silvery brilliance shone up from the bottom. Initially, he thought there was some light source down there, but once he reached the last few steps, he recognized that the radiance came from their own lights, reflecting off crystal surfaces.

"Incredible," Roland murmured.

Like the golden room above, this chamber was circular, about the same size, only here every surface was covered in crystals. The floor and walls were tiled in what looked to be quartz sheets, set off with gems and other colored crystals. The ceiling featured a moonless starscape created by chunks of quartz set within plates of obsidian. A colonnade of crystal pillars supported it all, appearing Gothic in design with pedestals and capitals adorned with gems and linked one to another by arches.

Under those arches stood a circle of doors encrusted with jewels, their jambs sealed with black wax. Two of the doors—one on each side of the room—had been pried open. Broken bits of their seals littered the floor.

Roland headed to one, Lena to the other.

Gray and Seichan moved together toward the room's center, drawn by what stood in the middle of the space.

Roland called from one side. "It's a library." His light glowed from inside the room. "There are hundreds of bookcases in here, all gold-plated and spreading on and on. And so many books . . ." He knelt down. "There's one on the floor, like someone pulled it off a shelf and left it there. Maybe the handiwork of Jaramillo."

"I found the same over here," Lena reported from the opposite side, using her own flashlight. "Golden shelves. And I can make out more rooms beyond this one."

Roland examined the abandoned book. "No wonder Jaramillo never returned this to the shelf. It's got to weigh twenty kilos. The covers are made of a blackish metal with pages that look like thin sheets of copper. The writing inside is indecipherable, but it appears to be the same linear script we saw on the standing stones aboveground and along the bottom row of that hall of languages."

Lena called out, her voice full of awe. "My books . . . the books over here are composed of fine sheets of a crystalline material, meticulously etched. I can make out geometric shapes and strange designs in them, along with what I swear look like mathematical formulas."

Before the two could wander deeper into those libraries, Gray ordered them both to return. "I need everyone over here."

He and Seichan had stopped at the room's greater mystery.

Standing in the center of the room was a long dais sculpted from a large block of translucent quartz. A human skeleton sculpted of gold rested on top, each bone and joint perfectly rendered. The figure lay on its back, holding a familiar length of golden rod.

"What do you make of this?" Gray asked Roland and Lena as they joined him.

"That must be the Rib of Eve, like we saw carved of ivory at the chapel." Roland ran the beam of his light over its shaft, illuminating the fine striations that marked this ancient yardstick, a length associated with the circumference of the earth. His voice grew hushed with awe. "There's a reference in the Book of Revelation. Chapter 21, verse 15. 'The angel who talked with me held a golden reed to measure the city, its gates, and its wall.' Could this be that same golden unit of measurement?"

No one answered.

Instead, Lena focused her light on the breadth of the skeleton. "That's odd," she mumbled.

"What?" Gray could tell from the skull's conformation that it was a representation of a Neanderthal hybrid, but from Lena's reaction, she must have discerned something else about it.

She gave a small shake of her head. "The physiological detail is amazing . . . but it's also *wrong*."

"Wrong how?" Seichan asked.

"Look at the pelvis." She concentrated her light. "One half is anatomically *female*, but the other half is clearly *male*. There are the similar discrepancies throughout the skeleton, a blending of feminine and masculine conformations."

Gray frowned.

Strange.

Seichan shifted over to the head of the dais, where a waist-high column stood. "And what's this supposed to be?"

Gray joined her. The pillar's top surface was cut at an angle, displaying a symbol they had all seen before. It was a six-pointed star, composed of 73 pieces.

"It's the same as the petroglyph that marked Eve's grave," Lena noted. "Only instead of palm prints, this one is made up of metal and crystal marbles."

"What's it doing here?" Roland asked.

"I don't know," Lena admitted. "But the prominent placement must be significant."

Seichan shrugged. "Or maybe someone really liked playing Chinese checkers."

Gray picked up one of the metallic marbles from its concave socket, wanting to examine it more closely. As soon as he lifted it free, a deep tonal chime sounded, reverberating from all around, as if a gong had struck the crystal room.

Everyone froze.

"Put it back," Lena urged.

Gray obeyed and dropped it back in place. They all held their breaths—but the ringing chime sounded again a moment later.

"Too late." Seichan dropped to a knee and examined the pedestal. "You triggered something, and now there's no putting the cat back in the bag."

Gray pictured the walls of water surrounding this dry well. Was this some sort of booby trap?

Maybe we should've heeded Chakikui's warning about this place.

Another chime sounded.

Seichan squinted at the base of the pillar. "Look at this. I can make out thin threads of copper or gold running from the sockets on top. They disappear into the floor."

Gray dropped to a knee and concentrated his beam into the column. "She's right. It's likely the triggering mechanism." He stood and studied the pattern on top. "And this may be the way to stop it."

"How?" Lena asked. "Are you thinking this is some sort of test?"

"Maybe."

She grew thoughtful. "Like a puzzle, a challenge of one's *knowledge*."

He nodded. "Perhaps to continue from here, the builders required you to prove yourself worthy."

Seichan crossed her arms. "Then I suggest you don't fail."

As if emphasizing that warning, the room rang out again, louder this time.

"I . . . I think that one came faster," Roland noted.

Gray searched around. *If the interval is growing shorter—*

Roland finished his thought. "I think it's acting like a timer."

Gray found *all* their eyes upon him. He took a deep breath, knowing they were depending on him to solve this riddle. He concentrated again on the star pattern, remembering Seichan's reference to a board of Chinese checkers.

But what are the rules of this game?

With the line already crossed, Gray plucked up the metallic ball again, feeling its heft and weight in his palm. He turned to Roland. "You said the covers in your library were made of a dark metal. Would you say this is that same material?"

Roland examined it closer and nodded. "I think so."

Gray removed one of the quartz-like stones from the display and held it toward Lena. "And these are crystal, like the books in the other library."

"Do you think that's significant?" Lena asked.

"Maybe." He held the marbles in his two palms, noting the difference in their weights. "There's a pattern of opposites here. Opaque and translucent. Metal and crystal." He nodded to the golden skeleton. "Male and female."

He sighed heavily, feeling he was close to understanding something but couldn't quite get there. He knew one of the reasons he had been recruited into Sigma was because of his unique ability to see patterns where no one else could, to make connections between disparate elements, to see the whole amidst the parts, the forest from the trees.

Maybe I've lost it. Maybe this time I get lost in those woods.

The chime pealed again, setting his teeth on edge.

"Opposites," he mumbled, knowing that was the answer.

Metal and crystal . . .

Dark and clear . . .

Heavy and light . . .

Male and female . . .

He sensed he was close. He struggled to find other polar properties inherent in the mystery presented here. He picked up another of the metal spheres and rolled it next to the first one. They clicked and stuck together.

His eyes widened. "They're magnetic."

He stared at the marble in his other hand.

And the crystal ones are not.

It was another set of opposites.

He closed his eyes.

But what's the significance?

As another gong sounded, he ran everything he knew about the past two days through his head. His breathing grew more labored. Knowing he was running out of time only added to his tension. What was it about opposites that kept slipping out of his grasp?

Then his eyes snapped open.

Not just opposites . . .

He stared down at the skeleton, at this blend of male and female, the two sides of the same coin.

"They're mirrors of each other." He turned to the others. "I think I know what to do."

Seichan looked dour. "You'd better be right. Something tells me this is a pass-or-fail test."

The room rang again, definitely louder and faster now.

Gray studied the pattern atop the pillar.

What if I'm wrong?

1:58 A.M.

"Where did they go?" Shu Wei asked the boy, looming over his small frame.

His left eye was already beginning to swell from where Major Sergeant Kwan had pistol-whipped the kid. Her second-in-command held the same weapon against the temple of the old tattooed tribesman, who knelt beside a pool of water fed by a cascading stream.

Her strike team had ambushed the pair after sweeping through the forest, following the trail of her four targets. Her group had traveled dark, only using night-vision gear. They had no trouble tracking the others through a forest riddled with mists. The ground was perpetually damp, making it easy to follow their footprints.

Still, once her team had arrived, they had discovered the tracks had vanished at the river's edge. Her team's best hunters—Zhu and Feng—had searched the far banks, attempting to pick up the trail again, but they had returned and reported no sign of the others.

While the two had been gone, she and Kwan had done their best to extract information from the pair of natives. But their captives had proved stubborn. She had quickly come to realize the elder did not speak English, so she had concentrated her attention on the boy.

Tears streamed down his face now, but his eyes shone with defiance. She pulled out a dagger from her boot and drew its dull side along his cheek—then reversed the blade with a flick of her wrist.

"I'll not ask again so politely," she warned.

The old tribesman spoke from the riverbank. The boy glanced over to him and answered, sounding angry. The gaunt man repeated his words in a commanding tone.

The boy sagged, closing his eyes for a moment, then opening them again. He pointed to the far side of the pool, toward the shoulder of a high cliff.

"They went there," he said. "Down into the forbidden place."

Shu searched but saw only sheer rock. She hefted her dagger higher. "Is this a trick?"

The boy sighed in exasperation and waved toward the water's surface. "Cave . . . at the bottom."

She squinted, then spotted the flooded entrance to the mouth of a tunnel. "They went in there?"

He nodded his head, then lowered his chin in shame.

She grabbed him by the shoulder and dragged him to the riverbank. "You'll show us. Take us."

He pulled free, his fear making him strong. "No. Too dangerous."

"Show us or I'll skin the old man while you watch."

She nodded to Kwan, who drew out a filleting knife. She knew from firsthand experience his skill with such a blade. The knife had freed many tongues—both figuratively and literally.

The boy visibly swallowed, looking at his toes.

She dropped to a knee and lifted his chin with the point of her dagger. She softened her voice, turning it silky. "We do not wish to hurt either of you. Once this is over, we'll leave your forests. You can go about your lives as if nothing has happened."

The boy took a deep breath. It didn't look like he was convinced, but he turned his gaze guiltily to the pool. "I will take you."

Good.

She stood and faced Kwan. "Leave Zhu here with the old man. To ensure the boy's continuing cooperation." She nodded across the pool. "We'll dig the others out of that hole ourselves."

He nodded.

She pointed to his filleting knife. "Keep that handy."

Her aunt—Major General Lau—demanded that she learn what the others knew before dispatching them. She intended to do that.

And to allow the Black Crow to collect his trophies.

23

At least Chang Sun did as we asked.

Monk searched the stretch of dark hallway ahead of them as their commandeered truck raced down its length. Only the occasional glow from an emergency beacon illuminated their path.

After learning where the Chinese were holding their captives, Monk had ordered Chang to cut the power to the facility—both to add to the confusion and to help hide their passage through the underground facility. Additionally, as instructed, the lieutenant colonel had diverted any search teams away from their vehicle's path.

Still, not trusting Chang, Monk kept everyone focused. In the open bed behind him, the Shaw brothers guarded their flanks, while the smallest of their team, Kong, crouched with his assault rifle balanced on the tailgate, watching their rear.

"We're almost there," Kimberly reported. She held up her satellite phone, the screen aglow with a schematic of the subterranean lab complex. "Take the next right turn."

Sergeant Chin nodded from behind the wheel and leaned hard as he took the sharp corner into a narrower passageway.

"There should be a ramp ahead that'll take us down to the level where they're holding Dr. Crandall and Baako." Kimberly looked grim. "But we're still a good way off from where Chang said they've caged Kowalski. Some place called the Ark."

Monk pointed ahead. "Maria first, then Kowalski."

Chin pushed their truck faster, as if sensing Monk's fear.

I hope we're not too late.

Gunfire suddenly erupted from up ahead, explosively loud in the confined hallway. Rifle flashes flared out of the darkness. The truck's windshield splintered as Monk grabbed Kimberly and pulled her low. Chin began to slow their vehicle, but now was not the time for caution.

"Floor it!" Monk hollered. "Keep going."

Answering gunfire chattered from the truck bed. Monk leaned out the passenger window with his sidearm clutched in one hand. He aimed toward the enemy. He didn't know if this was a trap set by Chang or if their truck had accidently stumbled upon a search team.

Either way, Monk knew this ambush would cost them valuable time.

That is, if we survive it . . .

As he began firing, he cast out a silent command to those he had come to rescue.

Hold out a little longer, guys.

12:24 P.M.

Kowalski tugged on the handle of the giant steel sliders that trapped them in the vivisection lab. They refused to budge—then a horrendous rip of metal and glass drew his attention back over his shoulder.

A massive dark shape loomed beyond the observation windows. A furry hand gripped the frame of the smaller casement window and tore it completely out, taking most of the surrounding pane along with it. The sudden release caused the gorilla to lose its precarious perch. As it fell, it took more of the window with it.

Through the wide opening, the rank musk of the habitat flowed into the lab.

Maria huddled against the wall next to Kowalski, holding Baako's hand. The rest of the surgical staff cowered on his other side.

A scraping and scrabbling echoed to them as the fire hose twanged and vibrated. More were coming, scaling the rock wall toward the large opening.

Kowalski searched the lab, eyeing the smaller stainless cages, but the bars were too thin to offer any protection. He had witnessed the strength of these monsters. They'd tear into those cages as if they were made of cardboard.

A beast roared, sounding right below the window.

Maria grabbed his arm, her eyes pleading with him to save her and Baako.

He squeezed a fist, knowing he had to do something, even if it only delayed the inevitable. "Stay here," he ordered everyone.

"What are you—?"

Kowalski didn't bother answering Maria, afraid that if he explained it would only make his plan sound even more futile. He pushed away from the doors and back into the lab. He rushed along the row of surgical tables to the abandoned site of Baako's operation and snatched a tool from the instrument table. With weapon in hand, he dashed next to the tautly strung fire hose. Its length continued to jolt and shiver.

Here goes nothing.

He flicked the switch on the battery-powered bone saw, relieved to hear it buzz to life in his hand. He had noted the tool earlier. It wasn't all that different from the cordless reciprocating saw he had in his garage back home.

He raised the oscillating blade and sheered into the rubber and woven fabric of the hose. Once through, the hose snapped, and its end snaked away, vanishing through the shattered window. An aggrieved howl followed, accompanied a moment later by a satisfying heavy thud from inside the habitat.

Kowalski grinned, imagining the beast's surprise at being cut loose. Still, his effort would buy them only a little time. The habitat's rock walls were pitted enough to make them scalable, especially for beasts with such simian strength and agility.

He turned away, hoping it was enough.

A loud huff of aggression drew his attention back around. A monstrous hand rose into view and grabbed the lip of the broken window. Even under the meager light, Kowalski recognized the lighter hair on the back of that clawed mitt.

It was the silverback.

Oh, hell no . . .

12:28 P.M.

With a fist pressed to her throat, Maria watched as Kowalski lunged toward the windows. He lifted the stolen bone saw and slashed the small blade across the large knuckles.

A thunderous yowl exploded. The beast yanked its sliced limb away—but not before grabbing hold with its other hand. Still perched, the silverback reared fully into view, filling the expanse of windows, looking even larger up close. It balled its injured hand and drove its arm like a piston into the window, smashing through the neighboring pane, widening the opening even more.

The blow knocked Kowalski down, sending him skidding on his backside. Still, he kept hold of the bone saw. He waved it defensively at the bloody fingers while scooting away on his rear, pushing with his legs.

Baako let go of her hand and bounded to his aid.

Maria chased after him.

Baako reached Kowalski first. He grabbed the back of the man's collar and dragged him farther away. But the giant paw groped deeper and caught hold of Kowalski's boot. The silverback yanked hard, throwing the man onto his back.

Kowalski swiped with his saw, but its buzzing had died. When he had hit the floor, the battery pack had been knocked free.

Maria snatched it from the floor as she closed the distance. "Kowalski! The saw!"

He understood and slid it toward her. His face looked desperate as he tried to kick his way free. All the while, Baako hung on, trying to keep Kowalski from being dragged through the window.

Maria slapped the battery pack in place, powered it on, and stabbed it down at the fingers. The blade sliced deep, hitting bone with a grinding complaint. As blood spattered, the fingers loosened and batted at her. She dodged the blow, but the saw jolted from her grip and skittered across the floor, sliding under a neighboring set of cages.

Kowalski used the moment to roll to his feet, snatch Baako by the upper arm, and head away from the windows. Maria kept alongside them. All three reached the giant sliders and slammed into it. They rolled around to face the consequences of their action.

It wasn't good.

The silverback gripped both sides of the window and thrust half its body through the shattered opening. The beast howled at them, with jaws stretched wide and fangs bared. As spittle flew, the roar deafened her, the breath reeking of meat and blood.

My God . . .

It began to claw its way inside.

Knowing this was the end, she pressed her back against the steel slider—only to feel it shift behind her. Startled, she fell forward and turned. The giant doors continued to glide along their tracks.

Kowalski pushed her toward the opening. "Go!"

She tried to obey, but the surgical staff had the same idea, crowding forward in a desperate attempt to escape. Then a single shot rang out, and Dr. Han came stumbling backward, breaking out of the group, looking confused and stunned. He fell to his knees, then to his side—exposing a bullet hole through one cheek.

A clutch of Chinese soldiers stormed inside. Maria spotted Jiaying Lau standing with Dr. Arnaud out in the hallway. The major general held a smoking pistol in her hand. She looked stunned, gaping past Maria.

By now, the silverback had dragged its bulk fully into the lab. Shaking with fury, it rose up onto the knuckles of both stiff arms. Behind it, more shadows rose into view.

Jiaying finally shouted, her voice rising on a note of panic. The soldiers opened fire. Another grabbed Maria's arm and hauled her out the door with the rest of the surgical team. She knew her rescue was not out of humanitarian compassion, but merely an attempt to protect an asset.

Kowalski followed in her wake, pushing Baako ahead of him.

The gunfire continued, accompanied by howling. Maria knew the soldiers did not have enough firepower to hold back the beasts for long. Jiaying must have realized the same and barked an order. The men out in the hall snapped to obey their commander and rolled the giant sliders closed, leaving several of their comrades trapped inside.

Without pausing, Jiaying set off down the hall, where a jeep waited at an intersection. "Hurry," she commanded. Though her voice was firm, her face had drained to a pallid hue.

Arnaud strode alongside Maria. "Lau collected me earlier. She was coming down here to deal with you before the power went out."

Deal with me?

"She witnessed your attempt to free your friend," he explained, casting a worried look toward Kowalski—and for good reason.

Once down the hall, Jiaying swung around and leveled her pistol at the man. "Dr. Crandall, get your animal aboard my jeep."

Maria froze in place.

"I'd do as she says," Arnaud warned her.

Kowalski nudged Baako closer to her. "Take him."

Before she could move, something heavy slammed into the steel sliders down the hall, hard enough to make the ground shake from the impact. The upper track of the door bent outward.

Kowalski stepped over and blocked her view. "Go," he urged her.

Both of them knew—whether Maria complied or not—Jiaying would shoot him.

"Go," he repeated, remaining amazingly calm.

Arnaud touched her elbow, trying to get her to obey.

Knowing the paleontologist and Baako would suffer if she refused, Maria took a step away from Kowalski, then another, shadowed by grief and guilt.

Soldiers escorted her away, but Jiaying remained behind.

As Maria left, Kowalski never broke eye contact with her—even when the steel sliders were rammed again, further buckling the tracks. The beasts had almost broken through.

Jiaying raised her pistol higher—when another crash sounded.

This time from *behind* Maria.

She turned in time to see a truck ram into the parked jeep, sending it careening away. The truck braked to a stop, sliding slightly askew. Chinese soldiers rose into view from the back bed, where they had been braced for the impact. They whipped up assault weapons and fired at Maria's group.

She cringed, ducking over Baako to protect him.

To either side, her Chinese escorts toppled to the ground.

Even Jiaying cried out, blood flying from her shoulder as she was knocked to the ground. Still, she managed to fire—but not at the newcomers. Arnaud fell against Maria, his eyes wide with shock. Blood poured from his throat. He tried to speak but only ended up coughing more blood, sinking heavily in her arms.

She carried him down. "Hold on."

But by the time she lowered him to the floor, his body sighed out its last breath, his eyes stared leadenly upward.

No . . .

Kowalski pulled her away.

A voice shouted from the truck. "Everyone over here! Double time!"

The speaker leaned out the passenger window. It took Maria a startled moment to recognize him. The last time she had seen the man was back at the primate center.

It was Kowalski's partner, Monk.

As she struggled to comprehend his sudden presence, a new volley of shots rang out, this time coming from the hallway behind the truck.

More soldiers were coming.

Kowalski pushed her toward the truck. "Move."

Needing no further urging, she ran with Baako. Kowalski trailed, wheezing loudly from his injured ribs.

Before they could reach the safety of the truck, another crunch of steel sounded from down the hall, coming from the direction of the vivisection lab. She glanced back as one of the sliding doors popped out of its track and crashed against the opposite wall. Dark, hulking shapes pushed into the hallway.

Kowalski grabbed Maria's arm. "Time to get out of here."

They crossed the last few steps to the flank of the truck. Kowalski swung her up into the back bed, then leaped in alongside Baako. Once they were aboard, the truck jerked into reverse and sped backward.

One of the disguised soldiers waved them all down as shots pinged off the tailgate. "On your bellies."

They obeyed and the truck gained speed; then the back end suddenly heaved upward, setting her heart to panicking, but the vehicle was only reversing up a ramp. The truck fishtailed at the top, then set off forward.

Spats of gunfire chased after them, but quickly died away.

Still, Maria remained on her belly, an arm over Baako, who hugged Kowalski in turn, all three of them nestled together, a family again.

But for how much longer?

12:34 P.M.

Nearly blind with pain, Jiaying clutched the wheel of the damaged jeep with one hand. She cradled her other arm as agony lanced through her in fiery waves. A bullet had shattered her right shoulder, leaving the limb useless. Blood continued to pour down her side and through her uniform.

But I'm still alive.

And for that she should consider herself lucky.

No, not *luck,* she reminded herself—*perseverance.*

It had taken all her strength to push past the agony of the gunshot and keep moving. Once the truck with the Americans had sped away, she had used the shadows of the dark hall to hobble around the corner and over to the abandoned jeep. She fell behind the wheel, hoping the earlier collision hadn't damaged the batteries or engine. A twist of the key returned a satisfying purr of its electric motor. She righted the front end and raced quickly away.

And not a moment too soon.

As she rounded the first corner, a large shape bulled into the intersection behind her. Even crouched, it filled the hallway, bellowing with rage and bloodlust. The roar chased her far into the complex.

She drove hard, putting as much distance as possible between her and the escaped beasts. Only then did she focus on a new plan. She needed medical attention and a place to regroup. She knew where to go.

Still, by the time she neared her destination, she was faint and nauseated. Her jeep swerved erratically under her weakening control, but the security hub appeared ahead. Its door stood open.

She braked to a hard stop and rolled out, almost crashing to her knees as pain flared. She leaned on the side of the jeep for several breaths, then hobbled the last of the way over to the open door.

She found the hub's commander where she had left him.

With his back to her, Chang Sun stood at the center of the darkened room. The hub's scatter of emergency lights reflected off the glass monitors, giving the space a hellish quality. Anger at the sight of him helped center her.

He had failed her at every level.

As she stumbled inside, she finally noted the hub's technicians. They all lay slumped over their stations; another was sprawled at Chang's feet. Blood pooled across the floor, reflecting the crimson glow of the emergency lights.

"Ah, there you are," Chang said as he turned. "And here I thought I would have to hunt you down."

He lifted a pistol in one hand.

She searched her own holster but found it empty. In her haste to escape earlier, she had lost her sidearm.

He noted her effort and turned his weapon so she could see the pistol's slide had popped, then set it down on a table. He was out of ammunition. He must have emptied the clip while dispatching the technicians. He stepped forward, raising an arm as if to embrace her.

She knew better, but she refused to back away, to show any sign of dishonor by retreating.

His other arm whipped forward and impaled her in the gut with a long dagger. She coughed—less from the pain, more from the impact of his savage thrust. He drove the blade higher, seeking her heart. Something finally popped inside her, causing her lungs to suddenly find it impossible to breathe.

He yanked the blade back out and let her slide to the floor, her back coming to rest against the doorjamb.

He calmly stepped back, cleaned the blade, and returned it to its sheath—then recovered his pistol and polished the gun in the same judicious manner. Once satisfied, he bent down and placed the pistol into her limp fingers. He intended to pin the deaths here on her, to blame her for the escape of the Americans. Her name would forever be associated with failure and betrayal, her worst nightmare.

Her gaze sought his, recognizing in his cold eyes an ambition that far outshone her own.

He crossed to one of the stations and yanked several large levers. The hub flared into brightness as power returned to the facility. The monitors began flickering as the servers rebooted.

Dazed, she failed to comprehend what he was doing.

As if sensing her dismay, he explained. "I've already summoned the army. Now that the Americans have served their purpose, they can be properly dispatched. With their deaths, my triumph will be all the greater, my loyalty undeniable." He glanced to her. "No matter how the Americans might try to slander me afterward."

He read the confusion off her face.

"They threatened to plant false evidence against me if I refused to cooperate. Promised me glory if I should submit to them." He scoffed loudly. "As if I would ever bow to such dogs. Instead, I will use them to forge my own glorious path, so shining that it won't be disputed. Perhaps it may cost my brother his life, but his memory will live on through me, through my children and grandchildren."

Jiaying's eyelids drifted low in defeat as she realized how far she had underestimated the man.

This is my fault.

She also knew this shame must be hers to correct, even if it left her forever dishonored. She used the last of her strength to crawl her hand over to her pocket. As darkness closed around her, she reached inside to her phone and fingered open a compartment built into the back of the case. She did not need to see the glowing button that lay hidden there. She pressed her thumb against the fingerprint sensor atop it.

She had to hold it there for a full ten seconds. It was a precaution against accidentally activating the countermeasures she had covertly engineered into the design of the facility. She had them planted in the event of a foreign incursion into her labs, but also in case she should ever need to exact retribution upon an enemy.

She had never imagined a scenario where *both* situations would arise together.

How shortsighted I've been . . .

Darkness closed around her, dimming the fiery pain. By now she could not tell if her finger was still on the button or if even those ten seconds had fully passed.

Finally she slipped fitfully away, never learning the truth.

The acuteness of that agony followed her into eternity.

12:45 P.M.

As the lights bloomed back to life along the length of the hall, Monk felt a sinking in his gut.

This can't be a good sign.

The turncoat, Chang Sun, must have had a change of heart about cooperating. Monk had already suspected as much after they were ambushed earlier. It was why he had ordered Kimberly to find another exit, fearing that Chang would have bolstered his forces down at the loading bay where his team had first entered the facility.

Kimberly pointed ahead. "There should be an elevator at the far end of this hall, another hundred yards or so. It leads up to a public building located in the zoo. Some nineteenth-century manor house called Chang-guanlou."

"She's right," Maria called out from the truck's bed, speaking through an open window in the rear of the cab. "Major General Lau has an office up there."

Kimberly turned to Monk. "The zoo is likely closed or evacuated. But once aboveground, we'll have to be careful not to draw—"

She was cut off as a series of massive explosions erupted.

Sergeant Chin fought to control their truck, sideswiping through a row of red biohazard buckets. Smoke rolled toward them, coming from the direction of the elevators. Then the lights flickered and died, sinking them into darkness.

Chin drew the truck to a halt and flipped on their vehicle's headlamps.

Through the pall of smoke and rock dust, the twin beams of their lights revealed a roof collapse at the far end. Slabs of broken concrete and twisted support beams blocked the way forward. In the distance, the facility continued to groan and crash. Faint screams echoed to them.

"What the hell?" Monk whispered.

Kimberly shook her head. "Someone must be trying to destroy this facility, to bring it all crashing down."

"Who? Chang?"

She frowned. "I don't know. It makes no sense."

Kowalski offered his own viewpoint, calling from the truck bed. "I don't care who's doing it! Let's get our asses out of here before we become pancakes."

Monk nodded. "What about the way we entered, the loading bay? It's two levels deeper. It might still be open."

Kimberly lifted her satellite phone and examined the station's schematics. "We can try, but . . ." Her voice died away.

"But what?"

"That path is going to take us straight through the area where those gorilla hybrids are loose."

Monk exhaled. "Great . . . but I don't see we have any other choice."

Kimberly agreed and instructed Chin on where to go.

They were soon racing back the way they had come, the beams of their headlights drilling through the smoke. All the while, the facility continued to crumble and crash around them. Kimberly did her best to guide them, but she had to continually recalculate their route, sending them zigzagging around collapsed hallways or skirting fires that had broken out.

More and more people began to appear, some in lab smocks, others in uniforms. All were dazed, bloody, or panicked. A few soldiers took potshots at them, but their efforts were halfhearted. Chin took to beeping his horn, chasing stragglers out of his path, while rifle blasts discouraged the more persistent.

Down one side hall, Monk spotted a pool of sunlight. He called for them to stop, only to discover a collapse that had broken through to the surface. Unfortunately, the way up was too narrow, too treacherous to climb. Even as he examined it, the opening began to crumble in on itself.

Still, for a moment, to see the sky was both heartening and disappointing.

So close, yet so far.

They continued onward—only to come upon an even stranger sight. As they sped toward an intersection, a ghostly row of shapes raced through the smoke and vanished.

"Were those wolves?" Monk asked.

Kimberly stared toward the cab's roof. "While the zoo might be evacuated, the animals are still up there."

Monk pictured the roof collapses creating sinkholes within the various habitats above, allowing the beasts to escape their confinements and flee underground. More and more evidence of such incursions revealed themselves as they headed deeper into the heart of the facility.

As the truck swept along, movement drew Monk's attention into a shattered lab. He caught a glimpse of a pair of lionesses dragging a body behind a table. Down another dark hall, the yip-yipping cackle of a pack of hyena echoed ominously, punctuated by a sharper scream.

Chin hunched further over the wheel and got them moving even faster.

"Take the next ramp," Kimberly ordered, pointing ahead.

Chin obeyed, only to find the lower level raging with fires, the halls choked by an oily smoke. Brighter explosions echoed off in the distance as additional gas lines and propane tanks blew in a fiery chain reaction, spreading ever wider.

"Can we make it through here?" Monk asked.

"It's the only way to reach the exit below," Kimberly explained.

Monk stared out at the hellish landscape, knowing the savage fires here would soon burn through significant support structures, bringing more of the facility crashing down on their heads.

They had to keep moving—and quickly.

As they entered into this subterranean inferno, something large and angry bellowed back at them, the noise echoing all around, making it hard to tell where it originated.

But *what* made that noise was incontestable.

Kowalski moaned from the rear bed. "They're here."

24

Another loud chime reverberated across the crystalline chamber, reminding Gray that he was running out of time. He studied the star-shaped pattern formed of thumb-sized spheres of black metal and white crystal, reviewing all his options.

I have to get this right the first time.

While he concentrated, Roland paced one side of the golden skeleton. On the other, Lena stood with her arms nervously crossed. Seichan merely waited on the far side of the waist-high pillar that supported this mysterious pattern.

"Having second thoughts?" she asked.

"I think I'm on my hundredth," he answered, offering her a tired smile.

"Then hopefully the hundred and first will be the charm."

He hoped so, too, but he knew it would take more than *charm* to solve this.

Over the past few minutes, he had turned the pattern over and over again in his head. He had asked twice to see Father Kircher's old journal, which Roland carried in a waterproof sleeve. He spent time studying the Jesuit priest's calculations, knowing the man's particular fascination with numerology, both the pure mathematics of prime numbers and the cabalistic mysticism of gematria.

Gray ran through the multitudes of opposites inherent in the puzzle.

Bright and dark . . .
Heavy and light . . .
Black and white . . .
Metal and crystal . . .

Fundamentally he kept circling to the same conclusion.

They're all mirrors of each other.

"That has to be it," he mumbled. "Mirrored pairs."

"What are you getting at?" Lena asked. "Maybe if you explained it to us, we could help."

Another loud gong shook the room.

Seichan frowned. "That was only ten seconds apart from the last one. At the rate these intervals are shortening, you have less than a minute to solve this puzzle or forfeit the prize."

Gray pictured the walls of water surrounding this dry well at the heart of the lost city. He swore he could feel the hydraulic pressure of all that dammed water, but he knew it was only his internalized frustration.

"Maybe you *should* talk it out," Seichan offered. "You're not alone here."

He nodded. He had planned on testing his theory with them, but first he had wanted to firm it all in his head. He finally relented and pointed to the star-shaped spread of small spheres.

"From the symmetry here, the answer must be tied to mirrored opposites. You can see it on the board, represented by black metal and white crystal, but the same repeats outward to the libraries on either side of the room." He motioned to the two open doors. "One contains books crafted of metal. The other holds texts carved of crystal. But there's another mirrored pair buried within this design, one tied to mathematics, specifically to prime numbers."

Roland nodded to the board. "The 73 pieces to this puzzle. That's a prime number."

"And we know the *mirror* to that prime number is 37, which as we discussed before apparently has levels of significance from our DNA to the movement of the stars."

"Still, what does 37 have to do with *this* particular puzzle?" Seichan asked.

"Because of that." Gray turned and pointed to the golden skeleton on the glass dais. "This sculpture also hides a mirrored pair, mixing male and female conformations to form a whole. That's the answer."

He read the confused expressions as another chime shook the room, this one loud enough to rattle gems loose from the capitals of the surrounding pillars.

Time was running out.

Lena and Roland looked as anxious as he felt, while Seichan simply appeared impatient, fully trusting him, waiting for him to go on.

Taking strength from her confidence, he continued, "Back at the gravesites in Croatia, Eve's grave was adorned with this same star-shaped pattern of 73."

Lena nodded. "And the bones of male Neanderthal hybrid—*Adam*—were marked with the smaller star pattern of 37."

Gray hovered his palm over the puzzle. "You can plainly see Eve's star depicted here—composed of 73 pieces." He stared hard at the others. "But where's Adam's smaller star?"

No one answered.

He pointed. "It's here, waiting to be revealed, to make this pattern as whole as those golden bones."

The room shook again with a booming chime, cracks skittered up the walls.

"Just show us, Gray," Seichan warned, looking around. "Now or never."

He knew she was right. Setting aside his misgivings, he began shifting the crystal and metal spheres into their proper locations, slowly revealing the smaller star within the larger.

Gasps rose around him as the others began to see the pattern, too.

Lena's voice filled with wonder. "The two stars . . . they *are* both here."

Gray hurried, sensing what was coming. Before he could finish, another clang of metal on crystal echoed forth. But this one didn't stop. It amplified louder and louder, rising up toward a final crescendo.

He rushed to roll the last marble into place, completing the design. As he did so, a bright crystalline note hung in the air, vibrating the room's very molecules, then collapsed into a deathly quiet.

They all held their breaths, but nothing worse transpired.

"You did it," Lena finally exhaled.

The group stared down at the completed design.

Gray had gathered the 37 crystal spheres into the larger star's center, forming Adam's smaller star within Eve's.

"The pattern," Roland said. "One star within the other. Representing the male within the female. I think it's supposed to mirror the act of procreation . . . of life, of the promise of generations to come."

But that was not the only revelation that the pattern heralded.

Beyond the waist-high column that held the completed pattern, the far wall cracked open, parting along two plates of quartz that covered the stone. A new passageway opened before them, exposing another set of dark stairs going down.

No one moved for a full breath.

In the silence, an immense ticking echoed up from that threshold.

Seichan finally spoke, but even she whispered. "Let's hope that's not another timer, some countdown to doom."

Fearing she might be right, Gray got everyone moving. They headed toward the stairs. Gray stopped at the top and shone his light down the long flight, but he could not make out the bottom. He felt a trickle of trepidation at trespassing here, but he remembered Seichan's recommendation upon first exploring this lost city.

Just go look.

That sentiment had been the driving force behind humanity's progress across the ages, a simple imperative fueled by our innate curiosity: to discover what was around the next bend, over the next horizon. It was that same inquisitiveness that impelled us to explore who we are, where we came from, and where we are headed next.

Gray took one step, then another, leading the others downward.

As they descended, the air filled with energy. It tingled his skin and coursed through the static of every hair on his body. He could even smell it, like a summer breeze during a lightning storm.

When he finally reached the last step, he stared into a vast chamber that opened before him. His mind struggled to comprehend the sight before him. In shock, all he could do was get out three simple words.

"Oh, my God."

2:21 A.M.

The sudden silence disturbed Shu Wei.

Since surfacing within this subterranean city, she had been greeted by a distant ringing of bells. She had once hiked the Himalayas and had heard similar chimes echoing faintly off the mountains, often rising from monasteries many kilometers away. She took the bells as a promising sign and followed their periodic tinkling as she led her team up from the flooded antechamber and down a long hallway inscribed with row upon row of ancient languages.

The bells grew ever louder and clearer, ringing with the certainty that she was closing upon her targets at long last. She welcomed that moment, knowing she outnumbered the others nine to four.

Plus I have the element of surprise.

While traversing this buried city, she had continued to keep her team moving silently, using minimal light. Here in perpetual darkness, she could not rely on night vision alone, as some ambient light was necessary for such gear.

Then, a moment ago, when they had been crossing a chamber decorated with animals sculpted of precious metals and gemstones, a loud ringing of chimes cut off abruptly. She had lifted a fist, calling a halt, suspicious at the sudden silence.

Several of her teammates used the moment to gaze at the wealth stored in the chamber. Even her eyes fell upon a gold panther with emeralds for eyes. After she had gained the information she needed from her targets and dispatched them, she would return here.

Maybe the Black Crow will not be the only one returning home with a trophy.

She glanced over to Major Sergeant Kwan, who kept a grip on the native boy's shoulder. Her second-in-command did not even glance once at the treasures here. Then again, his trophies were of a more personal and particular nature.

As the silence stretched, she finally relented and lowered her fist.

Bells or not, it was time to continue their search. She headed for the next set of stairs, ready to flush her targets into the open and put an end to this mission.

Kwan swore, drawing her attention. The boy had broken free of his grip and fled down the steps, moving as swiftly as a gazelle, vanishing into the darkness below. Kwan pointed his pistol, then lowered it, knowing the boy was gone.

Shu Wei stepped beside her second-in-command. She didn't deride the man, nor did she console him, as she knew Kwan's failure was punishment enough.

Ultimately the boy's escape would do little harm to the mission. Even if he reached the others and alerted them, thus removing the advantage of surprise, her team still outnumbered the enemy. And from the information gained by interrogating the boy and old man, her team had arrived with vastly superior firepower.

"Keep moving," she ordered. "But proceed cautiously."

With the enemy alerted, she did not intend to be ambushed.

As she headed down, a moment of petty irritation flared at the boy's small act of betrayal. Once this was over, she would free the Black Crow to collect full payment for this stain upon his honor. From the way Kwan walked stiffly beside her, all but trembling with fury, he would exact his revenge most coldly.

2:23 A.M.

Roland gaped at the impossibility that rose before him. It was as if he had stepped into a clock designed by the Lord himself. A loud ticking echoed off the walls of a cavernous space, a perfect sphere of open air that dwarfed the group gathered at its equator. They were perched halfway up one curve of the wall. The roof arched smoothly above, stretching as high as the first level of the lost city, while the floor delved as deeply below.

The entire vastness was covered in beaten gold.

He was also enthralled by the *energy* trapped within the dark space.

He felt it coursing across his skin, his hair, hanging in the air itself. He watched bluish coruscations skitter softly across the roof and crimson scintillations dance along the mystery below.

But it was what rose before them in the middle of the space that defied reason, that unhinged his senses. Between those plays of energy hung a massive sphere, filling a quarter of the cavern space. One half appeared to be the same blackish magnetic metal that bound the books in the library; the other was quarried of the same white quartz found in the opposite library. The two surfaces were not smooth like the walls, but inscribed with meteoric impacts defining large lakes and low mountains.

"It's supposed to be the moon," Lena said.

He inwardly nodded, afraid to move, lest what he saw vanished.

They had all stopped at a ledge that circled the room's equator. A series of tiered levels continued down from here. But none of them dared venture farther, as if innately sensing that this was beyond all of them, that they were trespassers upon a sight they were not yet ready to view.

He continued to study the giant sculpture of the moon. It hung in the room with no support. He could not fathom what energies suspended it—perhaps some mix of magnetism and charged forces.

Equally inconceivable were the details captured in this rendering. Every lunar mare, crater, mountain, ridge, fault, and channel was carved upon the surface in perfect clarity. And it wasn't just the crystalline surface, which clearly represented the day side of the moon. The hemisphere of dark metal was also similarly inscribed and sculpted, revealing the hidden face of the moon's dark side.

Seichan stared up at that metallic surface, her eyes pinched with disbelief. She kept her voice to a whisper. "How could that be? How could these ancient builders know what was on the other side of the moon?"

Gray noted another mystery. "It's turning. The sphere, it's slowly but definitely turning."

Roland realized the man was correct. The moon wasn't just hanging in space, but it was incrementally rotating. Again the loud ticking struck his ears, making him think of a giant clock, reminding him of something he had read.

"*Sic mundus pendet et in nullo ponit vestigia fundo,*" he whispered.

Lena glanced at him, but only for a moment, before returning her attention forward.

He translated the Latin: " 'Thus the world is suspended, resting its feet on no foundation.' Those words were written by Father Kircher, inscribed on a clock he devised, one driven by magnetism. It was a hollow glass sphere full of mineral oil, which held a copper globe of the earth suspended inside, slowly turning, marking time."

"Do you think he got that idea from here?" Lena whispered.

"I don't know, but Father Kircher believed it was such forces that drove the motion of the planets." Roland pointed beneath the giant moon. "But undoubtedly Nicolas Steno must have been here and reported his discovery."

Filling the bottom of the gold-plated cavern was a labyrinth of raised copper walls, easily as tall as a man, as if inviting one to walk into that maze. However, the entire structure was flooded with a dark fluid, almost to the top of its walls.

"It's similar to the labyrinth gilded on the cover of Kircher's journal," Gray said.

"A pattern found throughout history and around the globe," Roland added, "but this maze is clearly more elaborate, expanded upon, more intricate and convoluted."

He pulled out Kircher's journal and held it up, letting them all compare the maze below to the labyrinth on the cover.

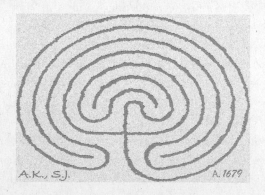

Roland turned to Lena and read the understanding shining on her face. He touched her arm in thanks. "You were right from the very beginning, Lena."

2:26 A.M.

Could it be true?

While Lena struggled to fathom all the mysteries and impossibilities found here, she recalled her first comment upon seeing the labyrinth on the damaged copy of Kircher's journal, the one they had found in the caves of Croatia.

She repeated those words now. "It's like a cross-section of a brain."

Roland nodded.

She studied the more elaborate design below, noting every coppery curve and fold of those walls. They composed a perfect rendering of the gyri and sulci—the hills and valleys—that made up the human cortex and cerebrum.

"It *is* a cross-section of a brain," Roland whispered. "One that is afire with energy."

Lena watched the faint crimson tracery coursing along the copper walls, as if the entire structure were some ancient battery.

And maybe it is.

"But what does it mean?" Gray asked. "A cross-section of the brain supporting a suspended globe of the moon?"

Lena shook her head, remembering Roland's description of the extraordinary, almost impossible to comprehend symmetry and dimension of the earth's only satellite. A globe that produced the tides that supported life, a sphere of such perfect mass that it stabilized the spin and axis of the earth so the planet could become an abiding and secure home for complex organisms to evolve into an intelligence that could look to the skies and wonder.

She stared down at the depiction of the human brain and felt tears rising in her eyes. While she could not answer Gray's question, deep down she knew the wordless truth, sensed the enormity of both what was designed here and what lay beyond these walls.

Roland tried to explain. "Maybe what we're looking at here is these ancient teachers' attempt to comprehend God."

Lena sensed he was close to the truth, but the mysteries here ran even deeper than that, like how the dark side of the moon could be rendered in such detail by these ancients.

Roland sighed, perhaps realizing the same. "Or maybe *all* of this . . ." He waved an arm, encompassing not just this chamber of mysteries, but the greater mysteries beyond. "Maybe it's another ancient intelligence's attempt to communicate to us, to leave behind a message for us to discover, burying it both in our DNA and in the movement of the sun, earth, and moon."

"But what's the message?" Lena asked.

Gray offered one conjecture. "Physicists have always been baffled by how strangely—almost impossibly—the universe seems to be fine-tuned for the creation of life. Take electromagnetic force. It has a specific value that allows stars to produce carbon, the building block of all life. Likewise, the strong nuclear force, which holds atoms together, is also perfectly balanced. If it were a tad stronger, the universe would be made up entirely of hydrogen. A tad weaker, there would be no hydrogen."

Lena understood. "If any of those constants were different, life would not exist." She turned to Gray. "But how does what we're looking at fit into all of that?"

He sighed. "I'm not entirely sure. But I think these ancient teachers built all of this as a model to show us that life too is a fundamental law of nature. Ultimately we were meant to discover these connections—these ratios and symmetries that tie our bodies to the larger universe—and to begin to comprehend a greater truth."

"Which is what?" Roland asked.

"That we're special." He pointed down to the labyrinth of the brain. "That maybe the universe is centered around the creation of intelligent life, in the creation of us. That *we* are a fundamental law of nature."

Silence settled over the group as they contemplated this possibility.

Roland finally mumbled, "No wonder Father Kircher hid this knowledge."

"The world was not ready," Lena added.

And maybe it's still not.

Roland nodded to the labyrinth below. "Nicolas Steno, later in his life, ended his pursuit of paleontology, ceasing his examination of fossils." He turned to them. "Do you know what he devoted the final years of his life to studying?"

Lena shook her head.

Roland turned and stared below. "He studied the human brain."

The ticking of this massive clock suddenly took on a new note, more frantic, less steady. It took Lena a full breath to realize the new cadence was actually footsteps, racing down behind them.

She turned to find a small shape flying at them.

"Jembe?"

2:28 A.M.

From the boy's sudden appearance and breathless descent, Gray immediately knew something was wrong. Seichan stepped over and caught Jembe before he plunged headlong into the mysteries below.

He panted, his eyes wide upon what was suspended in the room, momentarily struck dumb.

Gray took his chin and drew his gaze to his own face. "What're you doing here?"

Jembe pulled his chin free and glanced back. "I run fast . . ." He flitted a hand through the air. "Like a hummingbird. But here is very dark."

Only now did Gray note the dark trickle of blood down the boy's forehead. He must have struck his head while trying to find them.

Jembe clutched Gray's jacket, gasping. "Bad people coming. They have Chakikui."

Gray straightened, staring up.

Was it the Chinese again?

Seichan wondered the same. "They must have followed us."

But how?

Gray pushed that question aside and asked a more important one. "How many, Jembe?"

The boy held up ten fingers. "Another is still with Chakikui."

And all likely armed to the teeth.

He yanked out his SIG Sauer as Seichan did the same. But the odds were not good.

Two pistols against a fully equipped strike team.

"We're too exposed in here," Gray said and started moving everyone up, pulling the boy behind him.

"What about hiding in the libraries?" Lena offered, hurrying alongside him. "Those rooms go on and on, maybe circling all the way around this space."

Roland nodded.

Even Seichan liked the plan. "It's our best chance. We could secure the others while we play a little game of cat and mouse with our guests across the rooms."

As they reached the top step and reentered the crystal chamber, Gray pointed toward the metal library, hoping the gold-plated cases and bulletproof books inside would offer some shelter. He momentarily considered sending everyone into the crystal library, while he and Seichan lured the marauders the other way, but the strike team might send searchers in that direction. If that happened, the others would be defenseless. So he stuck to his original plan.

He passed Seichan his flashlight. "Take them."

"What're you going to—"

"I'll be right behind you."

She nodded and herded everyone toward the open door, taking the light with her.

Rushing through the dark, he crossed back to the gold skeleton and the completed pattern atop the dais. In the past, Nicolas Steno must have successfully closed the doors to the moon room by scrambling the marbles and resetting the mechanism.

Gray didn't need to be that thorough. He reached and merely switched a metallic sphere for a crystal one. With the pattern disrupted, the doors began to close with a soft sighing of hidden gears.

Hurry up . . .

He glanced to the stairs that led down here. Through the darkness, he spotted a faint light flowing from above. The enemy was approaching cautiously, likely edgy, knowing the boy would have alerted them. Still, he needed more time, so he raised his pistol and fired twice in that direction, hoping the threat would give the enemy reason to pause.

Finally the doors sealed shut behind him with a grinding thud.

He waited a full breath in case the mechanism needed time to reset. Then he reached over and plucked one of the metal balls from its socket. As before, a loud chime immediately sounded, a strike of metal on crystal.

With the timer again activated and the countdown restarted, Gray fled low across the floor, hoping to make it through the library door before being spotted.

No such luck.

A spatter of gunfire erupted from the stairwell, cracking and ricocheting off the quartz tiles at his heels. He dove across the library's threshold and rolled farther into the room.

Seichan was there to pull him to his feet. Together they raced behind the nearest bookcase, putting that wall of metal-plated books between them and the door.

"The others?" he asked.

"Two rooms back and to the left. Told them to keep moving if we can't hold them off here."

Another of the chimes echoed.

She grumbled at him. "Like a team of commandos wasn't enough of a threat?"

He showed her the metallic sphere still in his palm. "If need be, I can reset that timer. Maybe even use the marble as a bargaining chip. And in the worst-case scenario, I end up creating the world's biggest distraction."

"You like to live loose and fast, Gray."

"Right now I'll just take *living*."

Furtive movements sounded out in the next room. Something rolled across the threshold, bobbling and spinning across the tiles.

A grenade.

Okay, now that's a better bargaining chip.

Seichan grabbed him, and they both dove away.

2:31 A.M.

Lena involuntarily ducked at the sudden blast. Even from two rooms away, a flare of brilliance reached their hiding place, etching the shelves and the threshold of the door ahead.

She crouched with Roland and Jembe behind a bookcase. Roland shaded a small penlight with his palm, his face lined by worry.

The boy tugged at her sleeve. "Ms. Lena," he said, trying to get her attention.

She realized he was probably scared. He had been clinging to her, trying to get her to listen to him. She put an arm around him.

"We'll be okay," she tried to reassure him, though it felt more like she was trying to convince herself.

"No. I must tell you."

She turned and read the urgency in his eyes. "What?"

He told her.

Roland heard him, too, and grabbed her arm. "We have to warn the others."

2:32 A.M.

Seichan groaned and picked herself up off the floor. The explosive device hadn't been a grenade, but a flashbang meant to stun and soften an enemy.

If not for the shelter of packed shelves, she would have been blinded. But the concussion and noise still felt like a giant had slapped both sides of her head with its palms.

Gray looked no better as he rolled to a low crouch, his pistol raised.

They had retreated to the next room. Gray took one side of the door while she kept to her feet on the other. She spied high while Gray remained low, both of them searching the room they had vacated.

Shadows shifted out there.

Gray fired once—earning a satisfying cry of pain. It wasn't a mortal wound, but it got their attention.

Guessing the enemy came equipped with night-vision gear, Seichan reached to her belt and thumbed loose a small penlight. She flicked it on and whipped it out into the shelves. It wasn't exactly a flashbang, but the sudden flare of brilliance would momentarily blind their sensitive night-vision equipment, stinging any eyes wearing such gear.

"Smart," Gray whispered.

The penlight also revealed a pair of enemies, who fled from that well of brightness. She and Gray both fired. She hit one in the meat of his upper thigh, sending him flying behind a case. Gray clipped the other under his ear, dropping him flat.

One down.

But the enemy was not so easily cowed. Other forces were flanking wide, keeping out of sight. There were too many. She knew it was time to retreat even farther and get the others moving even deeper.

Before she could turn, lights flared brighter, flowing in from the crystal room, a strange crimson flickering.

Then gunfire erupted—at first sporadically, then more fiercely.

Shouts and screams rose, full of blood and pain.

What the hell?

A black uniformed shape came hurtling toward them, straight between two bookcases—then the man's throat exploded, sending him flying forward. A long arrow protruded from his throat. He crashed to the floor, snapping the shaft. The victim crawled toward them, gasping, then his back arched, foam flecking his lips.

She glanced down to the arrowhead on the floor.

Poison.

Footfalls erupted behind her. She swung around with her weapon raised.

"It's Lena and Roland," Gray warned before she fired.

The boy came with them.

Gray waved them all to the side.

Lena exclaimed breathlessly. "It's Jembe's tribe."

Seichan glanced to the boy, who nodded vigorously.

"Chakikui told me to take the bad people in here. So I do, but he also say in secret that my people are in the forest. I try to tell you."

Seichan realized the boy was right. After hearing about the threat, they had all bum-rushed the skinny kid up the stairs and into hiding.

A ringing chime scolded her, sounding much louder now.

As it faded, she noted the fierce firefight had died down to sporadic bursts, echoing from deeper in the library, coming from neighboring rooms as the ambushers drove the Chinese farther back.

"What now?" Roland asked.

"We have to hightail it out of here," Gray said.

"Why?"

"I dropped the ball." He showed Seichan his palms. "In this case, literally. I had the marble in my hand, but when that flashbang blew, I lost it."

Of course, you did. Nothing was ever easy with Gray.

He studied the dark room, his expression grim. They didn't have time to find and replace the lost puzzle piece, especially with an unknown number of enemies still waiting in the shadows.

Another chime sounded, full of dire warning.

"We'll have to make a run for it," Gray announced. "Jembe, you find one of your people. Let them know to clear out, too."

The boy nodded.

Gray clapped him on the shoulder and turned to everyone else. "Ready?"

No one was, but they had no other choice.

2:37 A.M.

"Let's go."

Gray lifted his pistol and swung around the doorjamb. He rushed low in the next room; the others followed his example. He skirted around the dead man and out past the towering bookcases. He paused behind the last one, eyeing the door that opened into the crystal chamber.

It appeared unguarded.

More bodies lay on the floor, both in this room and beyond the threshold; most wore black commando gear, a few only loincloths. Several torches burned out there, abandoned in the crystal chamber.

Deeper in the library, gunshots occasionally rang out.

But that wasn't what worried Gray.

The crystal chamber quaked with another resounding clang.

Time was almost up.

Knowing they could wait no longer, he burst toward the open door. But a dark shape leaped into view at the last moment. Jembe yelled out in his native language. Gray skidded to a stop—with the point of a poisoned arrow poised at his chest.

The tribesman had heard Jembe and shifted aside. The tall man spoke rapidly to the boy as the group fled the library. Jembe pointed up the stairs. The man nodded, cupped his lips, and cast out a loud warbling whistle, recalling his fellow tribesmen.

Gray gripped the warrior's forearm in thanks. Any further demonstration of appreciation would have to wait. "C'mon," he ordered the others.

As he sprinted for the stairs, the final chime sounded, rising again toward the same dire crescendo. Once it reached its peak, the ground bucked under his legs, sending him sprawling. The others fared no better; only Jembe kept his balance.

Around them, plates of obsidian crashed down from the ceiling and shattered into sharp shards. Pillars rocked and cracked.

Gray got everyone up. "Move!"

Behind him, natives dashed out of the library.

Gray led them all up the stairs and across the next chamber, the one covered in elaborate mosaics. As the world continued to shake, tiles rained to the floor, dissolving the images of animals and their caretakers from the walls.

A roaring rush echoed behind him.

Water.

His ears popped as the air pressure spiked higher. He pictured floodwaters filling the mysteries below and rising rapidly toward them, squeezing this only pocket of air.

As he fled, one certainty grew.

Atlantis was sinking for a final time.

2:38 A.M.

"We must go," Major Sergeant Kwan warned Shu Wei.

She stood amid shadowy bookshelves as cold water washed over her boots. The quaking had toppled shelves all around, knocking loose massive volumes bound in black metal. The brown-skinned natives who had ambushed her team had already fled the rising tide.

A part of her wanted to remain here, to accept her defeat with a measure of grace and honor, but a larger fire burned inside her.

For revenge.

Limping on a twisted ankle, she set off. Kwan came forward and helped her, hooking an arm around her waist. Normally she would have shunned such assistance, taking it as a sign of weakness, especially for a woman in the army.

Instead, she leaned more heavily into him, sensing his support was born of more than mere loyalty. His strong arm held her firmly. She would reserve her own strength to deal with her enemy.

She intended to become like the man who held her.

To become a Black Crow, a merciless force who took what was owed.

By the time they reached the exit to the library, the waters had risen to her thighs. Kwan now half carried her, wading swiftly. But a familiar figure blocked the way out.

The old tribesman held a stretched bow, balancing an arrow on his thumb.

It seemed she was not the only one seeking revenge.

Kwan lifted his assault rife with his free arm, but before he could fire, a sharp twang sounded from the right. An arrow pierced his wrist, knocking loose his weapon. Before he could recover it, his body was slammed forward, impaled from behind by a long spear. Blood coughed from his lips.

As Kwan splashed face-first into the water, Shu Wei toppled to the side.

Hands grabbed her from behind, lifted her to her feet, and held her there.

She could have tried to fight, but her waterlogged gear weighed her down and her left leg throbbed in pain.

Instead she stood firm, ready to accept death.

The old tribesman remained at the door, his bowstring tautly drawn.

She stared defiantly back at him as he let his arrow fly.

2:43 A.M.

Gray raced down the long hall inscribed with ancient languages. Huge cracks had split the rows of script. Ahead, an entire section of the floor had broken and shifted askew. As he fled with the others across this shattered landscape, the ground continued to tremor, warning that the worst was yet to come.

I don't want to be here when that happens.

He pictured the city crumbling away into a watery grave.

He slowed to help Lena, noting she had begun to falter. Seichan tried to assist Roland, but he shook her hand loose.

"I can make it," he gasped out.

The only ones who seemed unfazed by the long, desperate sprint were the clutch of warriors behind them. If anything, the natives appeared to be holding back, making sure Gray and the others made it to safety. Especially Jembe, who danced back and forth through them like an excited puppy, but fear shone brightly in his eyes.

Finally the group reached the flight of stairs that led down to the city's flooded entrance. Without slowing, they flew down the spiral stairs. Gray ran a palm along the outer wall to keep his balance.

Suddenly the steps became dangerously slippery, coated with wet moss. His fingertips found the same on the walls. He realized the flooding here must have receded, as the surrounding water table drained into the city's lower levels.

Gray began to slow, wary of the slick and treacherous footing.

Then a huge boom shook the stairs, accompanied by a mighty cracking of rock. Fist-size stones came bouncing and careening down from the upper levels, along with an occasional boulder the size of a pumpkin.

It was all coming down.

Forgoing caution, Gray ran faster, doing his best to avoid being hit from behind by the larger rocks. The group finally piled the rest of the way down and reached where the stairs vanished underwater.

"Everyone stay together!" he hollered. "Help your neighbor if needed!"

He sent Lena ahead, then Roland.

Jembe pushed Seichan from behind, shoving both palms on her rump. "Go!"

Gray didn't argue with the boy and grabbed Seichan's hand. Together they dove into the water and swam down the last turns of the spiral and along a straight tunnel.

Lena and Roland kicked ahead of them, fighting to get free.

Finally they all reached the short flight of stairs that led up to the exit tunnel. They surfaced one after the other, gasping for air. Earlier, the narrow passageway had been flooded almost to the roof. Now the waters splashed around their calves. Exhausted, they marched single file along the final stretch and back to the river pool.

Night breezes, cool and clean, greeted them. The skies shone brightly with a full moon and the wide luminous band of the Milky Way. They crossed the pool and crawled onto the opposite bank.

Gray noted the black boots sticking out from behind a bush, likely the guard who had been left with Chakikui. Seichan removed her pistol and kept it handy, ready in case any of the commandos should make it out.

Gray appreciated her caution, though he doubted they had to worry. He watched the natives file out and join them.

Jembe sat down heavily next to him.

"Where's your elder?" Gray asked. "Where's Chakikui?"

Jembe stared toward the mouth of the tunnel. Gray realized the old man must still be down there. He sat up straighter, but Jembe patted Gray's knee.

"Chakikui is old."

Gray glanced at the boy, believing his words were a callous dismissal. Instead, Jembe added. "He is wise. He knows many ways out."

Roland overheard this. "The natives who brought Father Crespi those myriad artifacts claimed there were many ways into those tunnels full of treasures."

Gray hoped they were both right.

He owed that old man for his life . . . for all their lives.

Lena sat with her arms around her shins, looking little relieved by their narrow escape. Her eyes remained haunted. He could guess her concern.

She was safe—but her sister was not.

25

Maria crouched in the bed of the truck as it raced through the fiery level of the subterranean complex. She clutched a wet handkerchief over her mouth and nose, soaked from a soldier's canteen. It helped filter the smoke, but the heat still seared as the vehicle careened wildly around corners. She slid back and forth across the truck bed, hugging tightly to Baako and holding a cloth over his muzzle.

He whimpered and shivered.

Kowalski dropped on his other side and embraced them both under one large arm. "I've got you, buddy," he assured Baako, bracing his legs to keep them somewhat steady. "It won't be much longer."

She hoped he was telling the truth. Her eyes stung, and her lungs burned with every breath. Still, at least the heat would hold any of the hybrid gorillas at bay. Unfortunately, from the periodic loud bellows, the pack was nearby.

Maybe not on this level, but certainly the next.

As she stared up, she tried to picture bright sunshine, fresh air, cool breezes. Through the smoke overhead, something large wafted past, riding the overheated thermals, a bird from the zoo trying to escape the inferno into which it had been accidentally swept. She never saw exactly what it was before it vanished, but she hoped it made it free.

I hope we all do.

Through the small window in the back of the cab, she heard Kimberly shout to the driver, "We'll never make it to the next ramp!"

Maria clutched harder to Baako, despairing.

"But there's a staircase up ahead," the woman continued. "Stop there. We'll have to go the rest of the way on foot."

The news both relieved and terrified her. She glanced around at the stoic faces of the soldiers. They all looked equally grim.

The truck raced another thirty yards and skidded to a hard stop.

"Off-load!" Monk shouted. "Make for the stairs!"

Kowalski helped her out of the bed, groaning and favoring his left side, but still keeping a firm hold on her. Baako leaped lithely beside them. Once everyone was out, they headed in a tight group to the smoky entrance to the stairwell. A slight breeze blew up from below, chasing some of the smoke away. By the time they reached the bottom step, the air felt almost cool.

Monk flicked on a flashlight, muffling its beam with his other hand.

"Stay behind me," Kowalski ordered her.

Monk led the way, flanked by his team and trailed by Kimberly.

Maria kept hold of Baako's hand, keeping him at her side. At some point his bandage had dislodged, exposing the bleeding laceration atop his scalp. Worry for him remained a constant ache in her chest.

As they headed off, Maria recognized some of the landmarks here. They were not far from the vivisection lab. A booming crash made her jump and turn. Far down a dark hall, a smoldering fire glowed menacingly back at her, revealing that a section of the floor above had burned through and collapsed into this level.

"It's all starting to come down," Kimberly warned.

They set a faster pace, eschewing caution for speed.

After several panicked turns, Baako suddenly clutched her hand and drew her to a stop. Only now, past the pounding of her heart, did she hear a familiar bleating and hooting. Baako tugged her toward a nearby door. She wanted to rush on, but she knew what Baako wanted. With his free hand, he grasped the handle. Already unlocked, the door opened.

"What are you doing?" Kowalski asked, waving for the others to halt.

Baako ducked inside. She had no choice but to follow, drawing everyone with her. Inside was a waist-high row of stainless steel cages. Most were empty, but three of them held young chimpanzees, no more than two years old; a fourth held an older female with gray fur and sagging breasts, likely a breeding female for the lab. The chimp reached an arm through the cage bars toward Maria.

"We have to keep going," Kimberly warned.

Instead, Baako crossed to one of the cages and rattled it. He turned and chained a string of signs together.

[*Open . . . go . . . together*]

"No," Maria said. She pointed to herself, to Kowalski. "*We* must go."

Baako looked forlorn, likely picturing his own confinement in the pens earlier. He continued to clutch the bars. A chimp, no more than a year old, reached up and grasped one of his fingers.

"Oh, fuck it," Kowalski said. He started undoing the complicated latches. "Baako's not going anywhere without them."

Maria joined him.

Kowalski growled at the others. "Help us."

Soon all the cages were open. Kowalski carried one chimp in the crook of his arm. Baako held an older one by the hand. The female hurried to the youngest and clutched the infant to her chest.

Monk stared at them, shook his head, and headed back to the door. One of the soldiers stood guard and waved them to stop. He retreated inside and drew the door closed, holding them all in place. He lifted a finger to his lips.

They all froze.

Something massive thundered down the hall. Maria felt the ground shake, picturing one of the hybrid gorillas. Then it swept past and away. They waited ten full breaths before the soldier risked peeking out. Somewhere in the distance a series of loud screams burst forth, accompanied by fresh gunfire and a roar full of blood and fury.

The soldier glanced back at them. "All clear . . . for now."

They piled out of the kennel room and headed away from the ruckus behind them. The telltale musk of the hybrid's passage still hung in the air.

As the hall turned, the next passageway proved to be a long straight shot, lined by a few sealed labs. Maria realized that if Baako hadn't diverted them into the kennel, the group might have been caught out in the open by the rampaging hybrid.

Kowalski must have realized the same and patted Baako on the shoulder.

They hurried down the length of the hall, slowing only once they neared the far end. Kimberly leaned to Monk, but her words carried back to Maria.

"The loading bay should be around the next corner. It's sure to be guarded by Chang's men."

Monk turned and signaled his team. They secured the butts of their rifles more solidly to their shoulders.

Kowalski tried to pass her his small chimp, grimacing at those small arms tightened around his throat. She helped him, freeing the frightened creature and nestling it against her chest. She also reached out and took the older female's hand, drawing her close.

Kowalski signed to Baako.

[*Fast*]

Baako grunted and drew his young chimp up onto his back, where it balanced with its thin arms hugging the gorilla's neck. Baako modified Kowalski's last sign.

[*Very fast*]

"You got it." Kowalski lifted a shotgun that Monk had handed him earlier.

Monk glanced back to Baako with a small grin. "That son of yours is a chip off the old block."

The words were meant to be good-natured jibe, but Kowalski seemed to take them at face value.

"Yeah, he's a good kid." Kowalski pointed his shotgun forward. "Let's do this."

1:22 P.M.

Monk headed around the corner, leading the others. A short hallway dumped into the larger, cavernous loading bay area. He kept everyone close to one wall, trying to stay out of sight for as long as possible. His ears strained for any sign of the enemy, but all he heard were the echoing groans, sharper explosions, and sonorous crashes of the imploding complex behind him.

Ahead, all was quiet, but his nose picked out the traces of a fetid musk through the persistent reek of smoke.

It set his teeth on edge.

He finally reached the threshold of the loading bay and studied the rows of towering racks. Several had toppled over, spreading outward like a cascade of dominoes before coming to a stop, dumping their contents into heaps of broken crates, scattered barrels, and crushed boxes.

Monk had a filtered view of the exit on the far side, where light shone into the space. The giant doors of the dock—which had been closed before—now stood halfway open, likely cranked up enough to facilitate a fast evacuation. Lamps from the Underground City's roadways glowed outside.

Still not spotting any activity, Monk took a deep breath and moved out into the loading area, skirting between the dark rows, sticking to the shadows as best he could. As he edged past a pile of tumbled cardboard boxes, the view fully opened.

Oh, crap . . .

Uniformed bodies lay everywhere, torn, ripped, and trampled. Blood slicked the floor and sprayed the walls. Weapons lay spent, a few still smoking and steaming in the pools. Some had limbs gripping them, but no bodies.

In the center of the carnage, a large furry mound lay sprawled face-down. Half its skull had been blown away, likely from the impact of a rocket-propelled grenade. Monk searched and spotted the long black tube of a launcher, abandoned near the crank for the loading doors.

"So much for Chang's reinforcements," Kimberly whispered at his side.

Monk hoped the lieutenant colonel was among the dead, but he had a more immediate concern. Beyond the door, the parking lot had emptied out. The frantic evacuees must have commandeered anything with wheels and fled. The only remaining vehicle was a large blue dump truck.

He turned to Kimberly, who also was staring at the massive loader. "We need the keys."

Likely the only reason the truck was still here was that the keys were with the driver. Monk recalled Sergeant Chin pistol-whipping the man shortly after their team entered. They had rolled his unconscious body behind a pile of wooden pallets.

But was he still here?

Monk squinted and spotted a pair of boots.

He sighed with relief. "On my mark, I'll go for the keys. You get everyone aboard that truck."

She nodded.

He glanced to the others to make sure they all understood, then hissed a recommendation. "Haul ass."

He turned and sprinted out into the open. He aimed for the stack of pallets as the rest of the team rushed headlong toward the open bay doors. Monk came close to falling several times, his boots slipping on the blood-slick concrete.

A splintering crash drew his attention back around.

Sliding on his boots, he looked over his shoulder.

A massive shape bulldozed through a mountain of crates and boxes, scattering them and toppling more of the towering racks as it burst out of its hiding place. It leaped the last of the obstructions and landed heavily on its back legs and one forearm. It hunched for a breath, exposing the saddle of silver fur across its back. Then it heaved high and let loose an ear-shattering roar. One fist pounded its chest, sounding like thunder.

Holy sh—

Monk scrabbled away from it. "Keep going for the truck!"

He twisted around and ran for the driver's body. He heard the beast crash back down to all fours. He felt the ground shaking underfoot as it pursued him, drawn by his shout. The pools of blood trembled all around.

Monk dove at the last moment, flying through the air. As he landed, a massive fist slammed down atop the stack of pallets, smashing through them with an explosion of broken wood.

Monk reached out, snatched the ankle of the driver, and rolled away from that savage blow. He crouched over the body as splinters peppered him, expecting to feel the beast's other fist flatten him to the floor.

Instead, a booming shout rose from near the loading bay doors. "Hey, asshole! We're not finished yet!"

1:26 P.M.

Kowalski watched the giant silverback wheel toward him, likely recognizing his voice, remembering its former adversary—or *meal*, as the case may be.

He hauled the length of the rocket launcher to his shoulder.

Now I feel properly dressed.

A moment ago, as the beast thundered toward Monk, Kowalski had split from the others and sprinted to the RPG launcher abandoned near the exit, snatching up two grenade rounds from the floor nearby.

He had quickly loaded one and now pointed the weapon's muzzle at the silverback as it swung to face him. Still, he waited until Monk finished pawing at the body under him. Finally his partner leaped to his feet and dashed toward the smaller side door.

The silverback dropped to one arm, glaring over at Kowalski, its breath heaving from the bellows of its lungs. From the shine of those dark eyes, the beast definitely knew him.

Kowalski centered his aim.

Hard to miss this shot.

With Monk clear, Kowalski fired, the explosion deafening. A trail of smoke spiraled away from the tube and sailed toward the silverback.

But the beast rolled to the side at the last second, clearly recognizing the weapon's threat from the demise of the dead beast on the floor. This one clearly learned from past mistakes.

Missing its target, the grenade struck the far wall and detonated with a flash of fire, blowing away a chunk of concrete.

The silverback continued its defensive roll and ended back on all fours, ignoring the spray of concrete shards pelting its back.

Kowalski didn't have time to reload, so he turned tail and did what Monk had instructed them to do.

Haul ass.

His partner had already reached the truck's cab and climbed into the driver's seat. The truck's engine growled to life, spewing out gouts of black smoke from its diesel engine.

Kowalski raced toward the back loader of the truck. He caught sight of Monk's worried face in the large side mirror. He knew the source of his partner's concern. In that same reflection, the silverback came bounding into view. Its hind legs slid in the slippery blood; then it charged toward him.

"Go!" Kowalski hollered, swinging the launcher to get the truck moving.

He sprinted faster, his gaze fixed to the side mirror. The silverback filled that reflection, roaring at him, throwing off ropes of drool as it bared its fangs.

Kowalski knew he wouldn't make it, especially as the truck finally got a head of steam and started speeding up. With every step, his cracked ribs tore more deeply into his side.

He stumbled, his strength giving out.

Then gunfire spattered from the dump truck's bed. Rounds whined above his head, aiming for the silverback. Monk's teammates must have climbed out of the cab and into the back bed, trying to help Kowalski.

The effort spurred him to keep going.

Finally he reached the bumper and grabbed the rungs of a ladder welded along one side. His fingers slipped loose. Unbalanced, he used the last of his strength to fling himself headlong toward the ladder. One hand caught and snatched hold.

The toes of his boots dragged as the truck kicked up faster.

He glanced back.

The silverback thundered toward him. Its tough hide and thick bones were impervious to the rifle fire. One arm reached toward him, but he cracked the beast across the knuckles with the tube of the rocket launcher.

The arm dropped, but the beast continued its pursuit.

Kowalski tossed the launcher up into the bed, needing both hands to climb the rungs. Once secure, he pulled his dragging boots up onto the bumper and scrambled quickly, but the truck still accelerated too slowly. The silverback narrowed the distance, reaching again for him as he clung to the rungs.

Then the rocket launcher protruded above the back tailgate and pointed toward the silverback. Kowalski craned up, confused, especially seeing who wielded the weapon. It was Maria. But the only grenade round left was still tucked in the back of his belt.

Still, the silverback noted the implied threat.

A loud boom startled Kowalski, almost making him lose his grip.

The silverback had a similar reaction, dodging and rolling to the side like it had before, believing it was being fired upon. But it was only Maria kicking the tailgate with her boot, mimicking a grenade launch.

Kowalski hung from the ladder, staring at the silverback. It had come to a stop and bellowed at them, possibly realizing it had been tricked.

Kowalski lifted an arm and gave it a one-fingered salute.

Better luck next time, chump.

"Hold on!" Monk called from behind the wheel.

Kowalski turned the other way.

Ahead, trundling toward them was a convoy of military vehicles, running side by side, filling the tunnel ahead.

It was the Chinese army.

Kowalski sighed.

Now who's the chump?

1:31 P.M.

With Kowalski safely aboard, Monk slowed the truck. He tried to ignore the convoy closing down on them as he turned to Kimberly.

She frowned deeply. Ever since the truck had started moving, she had been studying the sketchy map of the Underground City supplied to them by Kat.

"The army is coming from the direction where we first entered the Underground City."

Monk drew the truck to a stop. "So we aren't leaving the way we entered."

"No." She glanced over her shoulder. "But there's an intersection we passed about a hundred yards back."

Monk remembered. The cross tunnel had been larger than this one. "Where does it lead?"

"No idea. It's not on Kat's map."

"Okay, let's go see."

Eyeing the rearview mirror, he set the vehicle into reverse. The silverback had come to a halt fifty yards past the cross tunnel. By now its angry bellowing had drawn more of its kind into the tunnels. Hulking dark forms lumbered along the passage to join their leader.

"You'll have to make that turn fast," Kimberly warned.

No kidding.

Still, Monk kept his speed moderate. He wanted to make it look to the convoy as if he was only a lowly truck driver trying to escape the mayhem, maneuvering to get out of the army's way.

Then gunfire chattered from the front vehicles. Rounds splintered the cab's thick windshield and pinged off the front grill.

Okay, that's not going to work.

As he picked up speed, Kimberly ducked lower and removed a set of binoculars from her jacket. She studied the convoy, taking stock of the threat, then swore under her breath.

"What?"

"In the front jeep. Lieutenant Chang Sun."

You've got to be kidding me.

Kimberly scowled. "He must have taken off during the chaos and met the incoming convoy. He's likely the one who summoned them."

And now he's coming with the cavalry to play hero.

Monk raced their vehicle faster in reverse, chased by the convoy. Gunfire erupted over the top of the cab as Sergeant Chin and his men returned fire from the truck bed.

Everyone else, including Baako and the group of rescued chimps, were also back there. The thick steel walls surrounding the bed should keep them as shielded as possible.

Monk kept his focus on the side mirror as he raced backward. In the reflection, he saw the other massive hybrids had reached their alpha leader and gathered at the silverback's side. The gunfire, along with the approach of lights and vehicles, kept the group wary—but not likely for long.

The silverback fixed his dark gaze upon their truck. It hunched on all four limbs, shoulders thrust forward, waiting for them to return, perhaps believing they intended to go on the offensive.

Sorry to disappoint you, dude.

Monk reached the intersection and braked hard. He cranked on the wheel, fishtailing the back end slightly to come to a stop with his front end pointed toward the side tunnel.

Turned askew now, Monk had a clear view toward the approach of the convoy. Lights blazed toward him.

"What are you waiting for?" Kimberly asked.

Monk held the brake and gunned the engine, revving it to a throaty growl, choking the space with exhaust. He held his ground until he could make eye contact with Chang Sun, who sat in a passenger seat of an open jeep.

Kowalski called from the back. "They're coming!"

He wasn't talking about the Chinese.

Monk watched Chang Sun sneer with satisfaction.

Good enough.

Monk let loose the brake and hauled on the wheel. Tires screamed, rubber smoked—and the truck shot off down the other tunnel.

As he had hoped, the convoy had been so focused on the large dump truck, which mostly filled the road, that they had failed to note the hulking army lurking in the shadows beyond their vehicle.

In his mirrors, Monk watched those two forces collide.

The massive gorillas pounded into the jeeps and trucks, leaping over trunks to rip soldiers from their seats, tearing through the canvas of troop carriers.

The tunnel made a sharp turn ahead, and he lost sight of the battle.

He finally turned his full attention forward.

Now where do we go?

1:58 P.M.

After twenty minutes of traveling through ever-darkening tunnels, Maria allowed herself to breathe. She sat in the bed of the dump truck, surrounded by warm, furry bodies.

Baako leaned against her with a dozing chimp nestled in his lap. On her other side, the older female nursed her infant. In her arms, Maria cradled the small one-year-old, his tiny head resting trustingly on her shoulder. His soft breath brushed the hollow of her throat.

She remembered when Baako was this young.

Kowalski sat cross-legged against the side of the dump truck, staring at her.

"What?" she whispered.

He shrugged. "You look good."

She stared down at her disheveled condition, then frowned at him.

Right.

He wiped a palm over the stubble of his scalp. "I mean, you look . . . I don't know, *content*. Like you know where you fit in the world."

Her frown softened into a smile. "Maybe."

At least better than a few days ago.

"You look good," he repeated, leaning back, letting his eyes close, but not before a slight grin played about the corner of his lips.

She knew this time he wasn't talking about contentment. But she didn't press the matter and accepted the compliment, more flattered than she had a right to be.

The truck's engine suddenly coughed once, jolting the bed—then twice more. Finally it gasped out a last gout of exhaust smoke and died.

She straightened, twisting around.

Monk called back through the back window of the cab. "Out of gas. Think the fuel tank got punctured by a stray round at some point. But Kimberly knows where we are. There's an exit a half mile ahead. We'll have to hoof it from here."

With Kowalski's help, Maria got everyone moving and off-loaded.

Once on the ground, they set off down the shadowy tunnel. Monk led with a flashlight. Its single beam was enough to illuminate their way.

After several minutes of hiking, Kimberly pocketed her phone and stared ahead. "The exit is near the Forbidden City. Once there, I'll head up with Sergeant Chin. We'll fetch a vehicle." She glanced over to Maria's charges. "Perhaps a paneled van to help ferry our unusual cargo. With attention likely to be focused back at the zoo, we should be able to slip out to the countryside and arrange an evacuation. Still, we should—"

"Quiet." Monk cut her off and covered his flashlight with his palm. He motioned for them to retreat to the side.

"Now what?" Kowalski groused.

Then Maria heard it, too.

The growl of an engine. Lights appeared behind them, rounding past the far bend. The vehicle surely had spotted the abandoned dump truck.

Monk clicked off his flashlight and turned to Kimberly. "Is there any place nearby to hide?"

"Not that we could reach in time."

Monk swore and waved everyone down. His men dropped to a knee, leveling their weapons, guarding Maria and the others.

The vehicle drifted toward them, then stopped ten yards away. The glare of the headlamps blinded them, but it was clearly a Chinese military vehicle. The open-air jeep had a shielded machine gun mounted on the back, which swiveled toward them.

A soldier called over. "There is nowhere else you dogs can run."

Maria recognized that superior tone.

From Kowalski's groan, he knew the man, too.

2:16 P.M.

That bastard has more lives than a friggin' cat.

As the jeep's engine continued to rumble loudly, Chang Sun remained hidden behind the machine gun's shield, plainly intending to keep whatever lives he still had left. The coward must have fled the altercation at that crossroads and come after them, intending to claim the glory of their capture.

Sergeant Chin test-fired a few rounds at the driver, but even the windshield proved to be bulletproof. More firepower was needed.

Kowalski began to lift his RPG launcher, but Chang strafed a line of fire in front of Monk's men.

"Remain where you are," Chang warned. "And I might let some of you live. To be paraded and prosecuted as American spies."

Kowalski lowered his weapon.

"But I have no need for the animals," Chang said. "Send them forward so I can dispatch them quickly."

Maria stepped in front of Baako, her stance easy to read.

The muzzle of the machine gun shifted toward her chest.

"You'd better do as he says," Kowalski growled. "It's better that Baako die here than be brought back to some lab."

Maria breathed heavily, remaining stiff. Finally she sagged, knowing he was right. She turned to Baako and signed to him.

[*I love you*]

He whimpered and hugged tightly to her.

"Now!" Chang barked.

Kowalski yelled back at him. "Let them say good-bye, you jackass!"

Maria dropped to her knees and embraced Baako, as if trying to envelop him completely. She held him for a long breath, but she must know Chang had only so much patience. She finally let him go and encouraged him to take the chimpanzees around to the front.

Baako carried the two little ones, while holding the hand of the mother who nestled her infant to her chest. They moved out between the beams of the jeep's headlamps, becoming shadowy silhouettes against that glare, as if already ghosts.

The gun barrel lowered toward the group.

Maria leaned into Kowalski's chest, hiding her face, bracing herself against the coming gunfire.

"It's going to be okay," Kowalski told her.

This was no lie.

With everyone focused toward the front of the jeep, no one paid any attention behind it. A patch of shadows grew darker back there, bunching to form a massive hulking shape.

Chang wasn't the only survivor of that earlier altercation.

The silverback crept silently upon its escaped prey. The beast was clearly injured, dripping runnels of black blood. One arm hung at its side, a dead weight. It drew up behind the jeep. The occupants, deafened by the rumbling engine, remained unaware.

Monk encouraged their group to retreat.

Chang must have believed they were clearing away from the slaughter of Baako and the chimps. "It will be over soon," the bastard promised.

It certainly will be.

A massive hand grabbed Chang from behind and plucked him out of the machine gun mount. The shock of the sudden assault strangled the man for a breath. Then he twisted around and caught sight of what held him.

He finally screamed.

Panicked, the driver leaped out of the jeep, only to take two well-placed rounds through the forehead from Chin.

The silverback ignored the blasts and lifted Chang's struggling body to its mouth. It planted the man's skull between its molars—then slowly clamped down with a sickening crunch of bone.

After Chang went limp, the silverback tossed the body into the shadows and lowered to a fist. It glared over the top of the jeep at their group.

Kowalski already had his rocket launcher loaded and positioned atop his shoulder, the sights fixed on that massive bulk. There was no escape this time. The silverback glowered at him, huffing, building up steam for a fight.

Bring it.

Then a shadow blocked Kowalski's view. A furry hand rose and pulled the muzzle of his launcher down. Baako stood with his back to Kowalski, facing the giant.

The young gorilla rose as tall as he could. He signed to the other, pointing both fingers up, then toward the silverback.

[*Go*]

The silverback hunched lower on its one good arm. Blood pooled beneath its half-ton bulk. That dark gaze swept from the defiant stance of Baako to the lowered weapon.

Baako repeated his sign.

[*Go*]

The silverback grunted, sagging in exhaustion, then lumbered heavily around. It slowly limped back into the darkness.

No one moved, fearing it might return.

Finally Maria dashed forward and hugged Baako.

Kowalski remained wary. He didn't know if the silverback had backed down because of its injuries, or from Baako's sign of defiance, or because of the peaceful act of lowering the weapon.

Likely all of the above.

No matter the reason, it appeared to be truly gone, disappearing into the shadows, perhaps to become some future urban legend, a monstrous yeti of Beijing's underworld.

Kowalski passed Monk his launcher and crossed to Baako. He clapped the gorilla on the shoulder. "Look who's the new alpha around these parts now."

Baako swung an arm in good-natured play, but he ended up smacking Kowalski hard in the side.

"Ow! Watch those ribs."

Baako lifted his brows high, worried he had truly done him harm.

Kowalski reassured him. "It's okay. Remember we're—" He formed the F sign with fingers and traced a circle.

[*Family*]

Baako nodded vigorously, chuffing his understanding. He looked from Maria, back to Kowalski—then tapped his thumb against his forehead, looking earnestly up at him.

[*Papa*]

"Hey, whoa there, buddy." Kowalski backed a step. "Let's not get ahead of ourselves."

26

"That's the official story out of China?" Gray sat across the desk from Painter Crowe, the director of Sigma. "A gas leak?"

Painter tilted back in his chair, using both hands to comb his fingers through his hair. "That's what you'll hear on CNN and Fox News about the devastation at the Beijing Zoo. But no one's fooled in the back channels. China is being allowed to save face in return for their cooperation in exposing any other operatives within the U.S. academic fields."

"And you trust they'll be thorough?"

"Of course not, but it's a start at cleaning house. In addition, China has agreed to sign the moratorium against any further research into the engineering of the human genome."

Gray raised a skeptical eyebrow.

Like signing a paper will stop them.

Painter shrugged. "The genie is out of the bottle. All we can try to do is rein in such research as much as possible. Even the two Crandall sisters have discontinued their research using animal hybrid models."

"What about the other asset that came out of China?" Gray asked.

"Gao Sun? Our current guest at a black-site detention center?"

Gray nodded. Monk's team had returned with the soldier, to answer for his murder of an Emory University student at the primate center. With the chaos surrounding events at the zoo, no one was bothering to look for the soldier. The prisoner had been transferred to a covert facility, to serve out a life sentence.

"He's fully cooperating," Painter said. "Though he's still not talking."

Gray frowned, not understanding.

"I should say he's still not *able* to talk. Kowalski clocked him good before they left China. Broke the man's jaw and knocked out four front teeth. And that was only *one* punch. Monk pulled Kowalski off the guy before he could do any real damage. Still, Gao's jaw was wired shut. He'll be taking all of his meals through a straw for several weeks."

The bastard deserved far worse.

"And what's the word from Ecuador?" Gray asked.

"Father Novak gained permission from the Vatican to take up residence at the Church of María Auxiliadora in Cuenca. He'll be overseeing the archaeological excavation of the lost city. The boy Jembe is helping him coordinate with the local Shuar tribes. He remains optimistic that they'll be able to recover significant artifacts."

Gray nodded. It sounded like Roland was on his way to assuming the role of Father Crespi, while continuing to follow the footsteps of Athanasius Kircher.

"It's a shame we lost both sets of Neanderthal hybrids' remains," Painter added. "We could have learned much from the DNA of those bones."

Gray wasn't so sure.

Maybe it was for the best.

He pictured the massive sculpture of the moon suspended in the golden cavern. For the thousandth time, he wondered what had become of those ancient builders. Had they died off or had they found a new place to hide? Then again, maybe they had simply ventured forth and assimilated into the world at large, joining the rest of humanity on its journey into the future.

He considered the graves found in Croatia, the last remnant of those ancient Watchers on the European continent. Sigma may have failed to preserve those hybrid bones, but if Roland was successful, the discoveries out of Ecuador held the potential to alter our understanding of man's place on this planet—and possibly beyond.

Gray ran through a handful of additional inquiries and questions with

Painter, then headed home. He took the Metro, where he picked up his bicycle and sailed through the dark streets.

Overhead, the moon was no longer full, but the mysteries locked in its symmetries and dimensions still hung in the night sky, welcoming anyone to explore, to question, to look beyond the next horizon.

Gray reached his apartment complex and locked up his bike. He crossed the moonlit greensward to his front door, ready to set aside such mysteries for the night.

He opened the door and found the apartment empty and dark. For a panicked moment, he believed Seichan was gone. Lately he had sensed her unease in the quiet moments of their shared life, as if she wasn't quite ready to accept it—or maybe believed she didn't deserve it. She tried to hide such misgivings, thought perhaps she had fooled him, and he let her believe it.

Over time, he had grown to know her nature, respecting her hard up-bringing, accepting her suspicions. In many ways, she was a feral creature, barely tamed, one that would not respond well to force or demand. So he simply let her have the space to work through the demons of her past, being there when she needed him and backing off when she didn't.

He crossed the dark apartment, recognizing from the faint hint of warm candles that he was not alone after all.

He opened the master bath door to find Seichan draped in a steaming tub, her naked body barely hidden under a layer of bubbles. An iced bottle of champagne rested on the floor nearby, along with two crystal flutes. The only illumination came from a ring of tall candles.

He smiled, recognizing this scenario, remembering their time ensconced in a hotel room overlooking the Champs-Élysées.

Seichan lifted an eyebrow, as if reading his thoughts. "I believe we were rudely interrupted before."

He began shedding his clothes, more than ready to be here for her now.

Who the hell needs Paris?

Kowalski slapped a fat fly off his forearm, certain it was carrying some exotic disease.

What's taking so long?

He glared up at the morning sun as it beat down like a hammer into the jungle glade. On the other side of the green meadow spread a row of raised platform tents, their accommodations for the past three days as the group acclimated to the weather and the challenges ahead. They had arrived in this rift valley, nestled between volcanic peaks, for a particular introduction.

"How much longer?" Kowalski groused to the girls.

Lena and Maria knelt on either side of Baako, preparing him for his first day. The twin sisters doted on the young gorilla, as if about to send their child off to kindergarten. Then again, Baako wore the same exasperated, frightened, and excited face of a typical kindergartner.

Tango sat in the grass nearby, panting, tongue lolling. Maria had brought the Queensland pup to help ease Baako's transition.

After events in China a month ago, Maria had decided to begin the process of releasing Baako into the wild, choosing the protected gorilla reserve of the Virunga National Park for his home. She and her sister planned on spending the next six months in the Congo, helping with his transition. They were supported by a team of local zoologists who were familiar with such matters and who were also doing the same for the group of chimpanzees rescued from the lab. Most of them were still too young, but they were being cared for until they were old enough to make that leap into the wild.

Kowalski had come along, too, using up two weeks of vacation. He also planned on visiting a few times while Maria remained here. He remembered last night, sitting on his tent's veranda, watching the night skies glow from the lava pooled in the cone of Mount Nyiragongo to the north. They had shared cold beers and remained together until dawn—but not always on the veranda. The beds were surprisingly nice.

Yeah, I'll be coming back.

"Okay, I think we're ready," Maria said, straightening up with her hands on her hips. "Are you, Baako?"

The gorilla lifted both arms and clenched a pair of fists at his shoulder.

[*Brave*]

"I know you are," Maria said.

She took him by the hand and guided him toward the forest's edge, trailed by Tango. One of the local zoologists, Dr. Joseph Kyenge, waited in the shadows. Beyond him, the hulking forms of a small band of gorillas, maybe five or six, watched curiously from the fringes of the forest as their group approached.

A few hooted at them.

The plan was for the zoologist to help make some introductions. It was better that this was done by a stranger than either sister. It was the first step in breaking that bond so Baako could live free.

Kyenge dropped to a knee and offered encouragement. "Come, Baako, come."

Maria let go of the young gorilla's hand. Baako stood there a moment, then glanced back to Tango, chuffing toward his friend.

Maria spoke softly, while signing. "Baako, Tango can't go with you. This isn't his home."

Baako looked to the forest, then retreated over to Kowalski, lifting both arms for a hug.

He dropped to his knees for a proper good-bye.

Baako nestled into his chest, making a soft, plaintive sound.

"Hey, bud, it's going to be okay." He ran a palm over the gorilla's head, feeling the new growth of stubble from where he had been shaved, noting the healed scar there. "What's wrong?"

Baako leaned back but continued to look down. He gave a sad shake of his head while thumbing his chin once, then repeated a one-handed version of his earlier sign.

[*Not brave*]

Kowalski felt his heart break a little. He took Baako by the shoulders and made him look at him. "You are the bravest kid I know," he said, not bothering to sign, trusting Baako to understand well enough. He pointed to the gorillas in the jungle. "Any of them give you trouble, they'll have to answer to me."

Baako hugged him, pressing the top of his head into Kowalski's chest. Though he trembled less, Baako remained unsure.

Kowalski dropped to his rear in the wet grass, keeping the next conversation private. He patted his chest and lifted his thumb to his forehead, fingers high.

[*I'm your papa*]

Baako's brows lifted hopefully.

Kowalski placed a palm on Baako's chest, then saluted the same hand down to an arm cradled at his belly, resting it there and staring hard at Baako.

[*You are my son*]

Baako's eyes widened. Then he lunged hard into Kowalski, knocking him back, rolling with him in the grass, and aggravating the taped section of ribs.

Wincing, Kowalski finally managed to sit up. "Okay, now that's settled." He waved brusquely toward the forest. "Go make some new friends."

Baako bounded up and raced happily toward his new life.

Shu Wei woke out of a fever dream—and into a nightmare.

Her senses returned in bits and pieces. She smelled forest, her own blood. Mucus dripped down to her lips, stinging. The world swirled in hues of green leaf and blue sky. Her stomach ached, rising bile in her throat. She had no sense of time, remembering the past days fitfully.

Where am I?

She recalled Kwan falling, of her body being lifted and held. She remembered the arrow striking her in the stomach. She tried to stare down, but she could not move her head. She felt a stiff board under her back and tried to shift her limbs, but failed in this effort, too.

Why am I tied down?

She remembered being dragged through water, then passing out. When last she had woken, her body had been racked with fever, her body burning brightly. She vaguely recalled a bare-breasted woman applying a mud-colored salve across her stomach. It hurt so much she had passed out again.

Now I'm awake . . . still alive.

She took deep breaths through her nose, unable to speak as her mouth was bound. Still, a moan escaped her.

Then a familiar face rose into view.

It was the old tribesman again. He spoke to someone out of view. Shadows fell over her body as more gathered around.

She struggled, thrashing.

Let me go.

The natives ignored her. The old man lifted a curved bone needle that trailed a length of sinew. She kept hearing one word over and over again.

Tsantsa.

She struggled to understand. If the tribe had healed her, what did they want now?

Another familiar face leaned over her and seemed to recognize her confusion. It was the boy. He lifted an object into view. At first she thought it was a wizened and leathery piece of native fruit, but then she spotted the sewn lips and eyelids, the fall of dark hair. It was a shrunken head.

But not *any* head.

The face bore a unique pattern of scars.

Kwan.

The savages had turned the Black Crow into a trophy.

The boy lifted the shrunken head higher and named the object in his hand, smiling brightly. "*Tsantsa.*"

Understanding dawned on her. She tried to scream, feeling the sting across her lips. She stared at Kwan's sewn mouth and knew the same had been done to her.

But the natives were not finished.

The old man leaned over her, lifting his thick needle—and reached for her eyelids.

EPILOGUE

TEN YEARS LATER

"Dr. Crandall, the sun will soon set," Kyenge warned in his musical Congolese accent. "You must not be out here alone, and I must return to my missus."

Maria patted the dog at her side as she sat in the meadow. "I'm not alone. I have Tango."

"Of course you do. And I don't mean to disparage such a glorious companion, but he is very old and sick."

She sighed sadly at this truth.

Hepatocellular carcinoma.

It was inoperable and malignant.

Tango had only a few weeks left.

It was one of the reasons she had come to the gorilla preserve at the Virunga National Park, hoping to glimpse Baako, hoping the presence of Tango might lure him from the forest.

If only so he could say good-bye.

Maria owed them both that much. But she had not seen Baako for over five years, which was actually a good sign. He had acclimated and seemed happy. She knew he was still alive, as the rangers occasionally caught sight of him and his troop.

She listened to the forest as it settled from the day and woke for the night. Bats swooped through the trees and out into the open, casting out ultrasonic nets. Insects buzzed, burred, and whined. Birds sang to the setting sun or rising moon. Monkeys hollered their constant complaints.

"Dr. Crandall, perhaps you can try again tomorrow."

She sighed and creaked her way to her feet, stretching kinks. She had been here since the early morning. And this was her third day. She had to accept the truth and get Tango back home.

"I think it's time for me to return to the States," she admitted.

Kyenge looked sadly upon her. "I'm sorry."

Then she heard a heavy chuff, the note deeper than she remembered, but familiar.

Smiling, Kyenge stepped back, allowing Maria to move closer to the forest.

"Baako?"

The thick wall of leaves parted, and a large shape bulled into view, leaning on the knuckles of one arm. Dark eyes stared at her. The wide rump was saddled with silver fur, marking his maturity.

A hand rose and thumbed that wide chin.

[*Mama*]

She cried and ran forward, trailed by Tango, who came more slowly.

Baako eyed the dog and let out a soft wheeze, his version of laughter. Tango sniffed toward him, then began wriggling his backside as if he were a pup again, recognizing the scent of his big friend.

Maria reached Baako and did her best to hug her arms around his beefy neck, but her limbs barely reached. He hugged his free arm around her, leaning on her, almost crushing her under his weight.

Tango joined them, letting out an impatient bark.

Baako let go of Maria and settled to his rump, legs out. Tango leaped up and climbed into that furry lap. Baako let out a long sigh of contentment.

His gaze searched the meadow, then touched a thumb to his forehead.

[*Papa*]

Maria pushed closer, not sure what to say. She signed to him hoping he would understand.

[*Let me tell you a story . . .*]

Over the next hour, she told him the truth—but not all of it. Some parts were too painful for her to speak, even with her hands. When she was done, Baako had sagged his head, crouched over Tango, rocking very gently.

Giving him a moment, she stared down at the diamond glinting on her ring finger. She knew she should remove it, set it aside along with the mix of pain and joy it represented.

But not yet . . .

She wasn't ready. Instead, she rose and crossed over to Baako. She came over and nestled with him in the dark, under a full moon. They remained together that way for a long time, until finally a soft hoot rose from the forest. Baako grunted back and motioned with one arm.

From the edge of the forest, a smaller shape revealed herself, a female gorilla with a child cradled to her breast. The female pointed toward Baako, then motioned to her chest. She followed this by cupping her palm and sliding it along the arm that held the infant ape.

Maria's eyes widened with amazement, recognizing the gesture and what it implied

He taught his mate to sign . . .

The female repeated the same combination, only more imperatively this time.

[*Come . . . night*]

Maria grinned, realizing Baako was being scolded for staying so late. Maria's gaze dropped to the child, whose small eyes shone back at her.

She turned and signed to Baako.

[*You are a papa now*]

He grunted his acknowledgment, then reached over and brushed his knuckles along Maria's cheek, clearly saying good-bye. He rose to his feet, making plain that it was time for him to return to the forest, to his troop, to his family.

Maria backed away, having to let him go.

Tango followed after his friend, still wagging his short tail.

Baako looked from the dog back to Maria.

She signed to him, though she suspected Baako's sharper senses had already discerned the sad truth.

[*He is old. He is sick*]

Baako shook his head and pinched fingers to his cheek, drew it to his ear, then back again. He corrected her one last time.

[*He is home*]

Baako turned away and shambled into the forest with Tango, the two friends determined to be there together at the end.

She watched them go, knowing she would never see the two again.

Neither glanced back.

This broke her heart—and made her immensely happy.

Deep into the night, Baako sits with his troop gathered in the forest. All are asleep. Even Tango lies curled against his side. He balances his boy between his folded legs, then gently takes those tiny fingers and molds them through a series of letters. The little one is too young to understand, but he will as he grows older.

It is the name he has given the child.

In honor of another.

He repeats those letters again.

[J-O-E]

Finally, small eyes drift closed, and Baako takes the child to his chest. As he rocks gently, he stares up through the crowd of dark leaves to the shining face of the moon, at the beauty of the stars . . . and wonders about everything.

AUTHOR'S NOTE TO READERS: TRUTH OR FICTION

Once again we are at that moment when I will do my best to extract the truth buried within the story. I thought I'd also use the following pages to answer the one harrowing question that all authors fear: *Where do your ideas come from?* To that end, I'll attempt to explain the genesis of this story, along with sharing how I stumbled upon the basic ideas.

Here we go.

First, this novel started out as an exploration into the origins of human intelligence, basically seeking to discover where we came from and where we are headed next. This line of inquiry led to the discovery of an intriguing anthropological mystery. For the past 200,000 years, human brains have been roughly the same size and shape, but for some inexplicable reason, roughly 50,000 years ago, there was an explosion in art, ingenuity, and civilization. Why? No one knows. This conundrum has been given the name the Great Leap Forward and has baffled both anthropologists and philosophers.

Why *did* human intelligence suddenly surge ahead?

Various theories have been proposed, but no true consensus has ever been reached. The most common thought is that the Great Leap Forward coincided with early man's migration out of Africa, when we were exposed to foreign lands and unique challenges, which stimulated new innovations and ways of looking at life.

But what if it was something *more*? What if during this migration, early man encountered something more powerful than simply new lands, something that changed our DNA? Geneticists know that it was around this same time that man first encountered Neanderthal tribes and began to interbreed.

One accepted fact of biology is a condition called hybrid vigor, where the mating of two different species results in an offspring of a stronger constitution than either parent—and this applies to their intelligence levels, too. Here's one example: mules are the result of the crossing of a female horse with a male donkey, and spatial intelligence tests confirm that mules are in fact smarter than either parent.

But could hybrid vigor also apply to us? Could the union of Neanderthals and early man have created children with some enhanced intelligence? We can never say for sure as there is no current way to produce that pure hybrid, an individual truly 50 percent *Homo neanderthalensis* and 50 percent *Homo sapiens* (though we're not far from achieving that goal, which raises a whole slew of ethical questions). Still, we do know that our interbreeding with Neanderthals was beneficial enough that we still carry their DNA in our genome.

So exploring this possibility became the seed from which this novel grew. But let's look more closely at some of the facts and tease out what's true and what's not.

Neanderthals and Other Hominins

Our understanding of the history of early man and our relationship with other tribes has changed rapidly over the past couple of years. Even over the course of writing this novel, I had to keep tweaking the story line to address the latest revelations. We do know it wasn't just Neanderthals that left traces in our genomes, but also an extinct species called the Denisovans, who contributed an important and unique gene that allows Tibetans to live at high altitudes. Likewise, over the past year, another fingerprint in our DNA suggests there was a *third* extinct species that also added to our genome, but anthropologists have yet to identify those individuals—though they do believe they lived somewhere in the Far East and were likely an offshoot of our earlier relative *Homo erectus*.

This brings us to another important hominin species, *Meganthropus*, which was a *Homo erectus* offshoot who lived in the Far East and was a contemporary of early man. Could this be that mysterious long-lost contributor to our DNA? What we do know from the fossil record is that this species was indeed large, by some estimates well over nine feet tall.

Likewise, *other* hominin species shared the planet with us, including the hobbit-like *Homo floresiensis* from Indonesia and the mysterious Red Deer Cave people of China. So ultimately the true history of early man continues to grow and expand.

Lastly, while this final beast isn't a hominin, it's worth mentioning that the extinct species of giant gorilla, *Gigantopithecus blacki*, truly existed in the Far East, surviving long enough to share the planet with early man. The beasts towered ten feet tall and weighed half a ton each. Some believe such creatures may still exist today, thriving in remote areas of the Himalayas; they may possibly even be the basis behind the legends of yetis and abominable snowmen.

For this novel, I based the creation of the hybrids on a savage combination of *Meganthropus* and *Gigantopithecus*.

But for more information on Neanderthals, I recommend:

Neanderthal Man: In Search of Lost Genomes by Svante Pääbo

Nonhuman Primates

This novel contains volumes of information about gorillas, their intelligence, and their comprehension of self, including the fact that sign-language-capable gorillas will teach other gorillas to sign and are fond of naming objects, people, and other gorillas. Much of this intelligence and consciousness applies to other great apes (chimpanzees, orangutans, and bonobos) and is exemplified by the character of Baako. There's been a growing movement to recognize primates as worthy of equal protections. The European Union, Australia, Japan, and New Zealand already ban or tightly restrict the use of great apes as research animals. The United States has no such restrictions and continues to use gorillas and chimpanzees in projects with limited oversight or supervision. Maybe it's high time we revisit this policy.

China

I spent time in China researching this story and learned how wonderful the people are there, but there remain serious issues, mostly centering on the government's level of secrecy and espionage. I did visit the Beijing Zoo and found the state of that zoological park to be appalling. The government continues to hint at changes and plans to move the place into a larger facility outside the city with more modern accommodations. So hopefully now that I've blown it up, they'll get on with those plans.

This story also centers on the Chinese government's ongoing and pervasive system of hacking, espionage, and infiltration. It seems a month doesn't go by without some new report of such an attack. Likewise, the placement of foreign nationals in U.S. colleges and institutions—much of it sponsored by the American taxpayers through grants and financial aid—is growing into an ever-larger threat to our national security, not to mention shipping much of our intellectual capital abroad.

Also, as I was writing this story about the cavalier nature of China's willingness to explore the manipulation of human embryos, my newsfeed began to fill with reports of a group of Chinese researchers who were dabbling with altering the human genome at the level of germ cells, which is the first step toward wresting control of human evolution. And according to an article in *New Scientist*, at least one U.S. group and several more in China are continuing this work with human embryos. So how far from the truth is this story line? How far into the future might this come true?

Apparently it's yesterday's news.

Father Athanasius Kircher

I mentioned this Catholic priest at the beginning of the novel, a man known as the Leonardo da Vinci of the Jesuit Order. Almost every detail of his life found in this story is accurate: from his volumes of work, both practical and fanciful, to his own adventuring, which included being lowered into Mount Vesuvius before an eruption. I found his mix of science and faith fascinating. I'd certainly love to have him over for dinner sometime—along with his paleontologist friend, Nicolas Steno.

The history of Kircher's connection to the Sanctuary of Mentorella is also true, including the fact that his heart is buried there. And while I *did* add the "history of languages" inscribed on the chapel walls and the secret chamber below it, it's worth mentioning that Kircher was a clever engineer, crafting all manner of mechanical gadgets and automatons. Stanford University has reconstructed a handful of his devices, including his magnetic clock, and there's an entire museum dedicated to his work in Los Angeles called the Museum of Jurassic Technology.

Lastly, I was not the first one to notice that Kircher's map of Atlantis that appears in *Mundus Subterraneus* (a map he claims came from ancient Egyptian sources) bears a striking resemblance to South America.

So let's move on to that distinct possibility.

Atlantis and Father Carlos Crespi

The description of Crespi's collection of artifacts (numbering more than 70,000 items) is accurate but the collection continues to be shrouded in mystery. What is known for sure is that Father Crespi firmly *believed* the artifacts represented solid evidence of a lost civilization hidden in Ecuador, one that had communication with the rest of the globe. Most archaeologists contest this claim and believe the natives' gifts were forgeries and fakes. But with the dispersal of his collection into various museums—

both government and private—no one has truly done a proper accounting. To me, it defies common sense that natives would craft such forgeries from gold and precious gems. Likewise, Crespi was no fool. He held multiple doctoral degrees, lived in the area for over five decades, and knew the area and its natives far more intimately than any archaeologist.

For more details about this collection, check out:

Atlantis in the Amazon: Lost Technologies and the Secrets of the Crespi Treasure by Richard Wingate

As to how the story of Petronio Jaramillo and Neil Armstrong ties into Crespi's discoveries, a comprehensive and thoroughly fascinating firsthand account of this history was written by Stan Hall, a man who was there. It's an exciting and thought-provoking read. In that same book, I discovered Jaramillo's account of his journey to the lost library. I loosely based our heroes' trip to that drowned city on that account, from the sculpture garden to the golden skeleton atop a crystal dais. Of course I took generous liberties from there. Check it out:

Tayos Gold: The Archives of Atlantis by Stan Hall

Ancient Civilizations

In this novel, there was much discussion about the possibility of a lost civilization of ancient teachers—whether you call them Watchers, Atlanteans, the Brotherhood of Saints, or simply an unknown group of megalithic builders. The details concerning the mysteries of the megalithic yard and its connection to the circumference of the planet are as described in this book. But I've barely scratched the surface on the true history of this discovery. For a more faithful and comprehensive account, I recommend you read:

Civilization One: The World Is Not As You Thought It Was by Christopher Knight and Alan Butler

These same authors also expanded upon the importance of the number 366 in relation to the earth, sun, and moon. So let's move a little farther out.

Mysteries of the Moon

Okay, I have to admit that I never questioned the strange coincidence that during a total solar eclipse the shadow of the moon perfectly covers the face of the sun. But it is *strange*. It occurs only because the moon is 400 times smaller than the sun, while also sitting 1/400th distance between the earth and the sun. Isaac Asimov described this odd alignment as "the most unlikely coincidence imaginable."

The other ratios and dynamics described in this book are also accurate and come from the following shocking book:

Who Built the Moon? by Christopher Knight and Alan Butler

Here's one of those "coincidences" described mathematically, revealing the magic of the number 366.

$$\frac{\text{Polar circumference of the earth}}{\text{Circumference of the moon}} \quad \frac{40{,}008 \text{ km}}{10{,}917 \text{ km}} \times 100 = 366\%$$

What else can we do with numbers?

The Number 37

Despite Doug Adams's assertion in *The Hitchhiker's Guide to the Galaxy*, the ultimate answer to life, the universe, and everything is *not* 42.

It's 37.

In Knight and Butler's book, they derived the number 366 by dividing the arc-minute circumference of the planet into 6 seconds. I scratched my head at this decision, looked at my watch, and decided to divide that arc-minute into the usual 60 seconds. Doing this, I came up with the number 36.6—which still demonstrates the magic of that fundamental planetary code, but if you round that decimal up, you get 37.

I did this arbitrarily, but afterward I realized I had just read an article in *New Scientist* titled "Is the Answer to Life, the Universe, and Everything 37?" It presented evidence that buried in our genetic code is the prime number 37. That number repeats over and over again, both in our code and in the amino acids produced by that code.

Likewise, through the cabalistic numerology known as gematria, one finds that same prime number buried within the first line of the Bible (along with the number pi). And paired with its mirrored prime (73), you do indeed discover strange patterns of six-pointed stars.

Lastly, yes, the average temperature of the human body is also 37 degrees Celsius.

What does this all mean? Is it evidence of some cryptic communication, a sign of God's hand, or simply a coincidence? Just food for thought: the possibility of this number appearing by random chance in our genetic code alone was calculated to be:

1 out of 300,000,000,000,000,000,000,000,000,000,000

So I'll let you make your own judgment, but I certainly wouldn't buy a ticket if those were the odds of the lottery.

In the meantime, for those seeking to learn more about how the universe is uniquely—almost impossibly—tuned to support life, check out this book written by an Arizona State University cosmologist:

The Goldilocks Enigma: Why Is the Universe Just Right for Life? by Paul Davies

Final Thoughts

I don't know if there is any message buried within this synchronicity of ratios found both imprinted in our genetic code and out among the symphony of the stars. Maybe it's nothing more than a mystery to make us wonder and respect what lies around us, no matter our beliefs. Maybe it's a call to preserve this planet, its species, this garden of life; to respect that empathy and intelligence around us in all its myriad forms; to remember that love might not be solely a human trait.

Or maybe it's as simple as looking at the moon and wondering who we are and where we're heading next. That's the very question that started this novel—and perhaps a good place to stop.